THE DEER KING
~SURVIVORS~

Nahoko Uehashi

Translation by Cathy Hirano
Cover art by Masaaki Yamamoto
Map art by Yui Ohara

This book is a work of fiction. Names, characters, places, and incidents are the product of the author's imagination or are used fictitiously. Any resemblance to actual events, locales, or persons, living or dead, is coincidental.

SHIKA NO OU Vol.1
©Nahoko Uehashi 2014, 2017
First published in Japan in 2014 by KADOKAWA CORPORATION, Tokyo.
English translation rights arranged with KADOKAWA CORPORATION, Tokyo through TUTTLE-MORI AGENCY, INC., Tokyo.

English translation © 2023 by Yen Press, LLC

Yen Press, LLC supports the right to free expression and the value of copyright. The purpose of copyright is to encourage writers and artists to produce the creative works that enrich our culture.

The scanning, uploading, and distribution of this book without permission is a theft of the author's intellectual property. If you would like permission to use material from the book (other than for review purposes), please contact the publisher. Thank you for your support of the author's rights.

Yen On
150 West 30th Street, 19th Floor
New York, NY 10001

Visit us at yenpress.com ✦ facebook.com/yenpress ✦ twitter.com/yenpress
yenpress.tumblr.com ✦ instagram.com/yenpress

First Yen On Edition: October 2023
Edited by Yen On Editorial: Jordan Blanco
Designed by Yen Press Design: Andy Swist

Yen On is an imprint of Yen Press, LLC.
The Yen On name and logo are trademarks of Yen Press, LLC.

The publisher is not responsible for websites (or their content) that are not owned by the publisher.

Library of Congress Cataloging-in-Publication Data
Names: Uehashi, Nahoko, author. | Yamamoto, Masaaki (Illustrator), illustrator. | Hirano, Cathy, translator.
Title: The deer king / Nahoko Uehashi ; illustration by Masaaki Yamamoto ; translated by Cathy Hirano.
Other titles: Shika no ou. English
Description: First Yen On edition. | New York : Yen On, 2023.
Identifiers: LCCN 2023022304 | ISBN 9781975352332 (v. 1 ; hardcover) | ISBN 9781975352356 (v. 2 ; hardcover)
Subjects: CYAC: Plague—Fiction. | Survival—Fiction. | LCGFT: Light novels.
Classification: LCC PZ7.U277 De 2023 | DDC [Fic]—dc23
LC record available at https://lccn.loc.gov/2023022304

ISBNs: 978-1-9753-5233-2
       978-1-9753-5234-9

10 9 8 7 6 5 4 3 2 1

LSC-C

Printed in the United States of America

~SURVIVORS~

Nahoko Uehashi

Contents

Pika Palu Eggs   1

Chapter 1: Survivors
1 Bitten   5
2 First Encounter   15
3 Light in the Ashes   23
4 Out of the Mine   29
5 Pyuika in the Mist   37
6 Rite of Love   43

Chapter 2: A Plague from the Past
1 Devil's Spawn   51
2 Into the Mine   67
3 History of the Disease   77
4 Subterranean Streams   89
5 The Village of the Molfah   95
6 Following the Trail   103
7 Vanished into Snow   111

Chapter 3: In the Land of the Reindeer
1 Preparing for Winter   121
2 Mohoki   129
3 Yuna   137
4 In the Summer Forest   143
5 Summer Light   149
6 Golden Sunbeams   155

Chapter 4: Black Wolf Fever
1 The Royal Hunt   161

2	Attack of the Black Dogs	169
3	Two Different Approaches	179
4	In the Hall of the King of Aquafa	187
5	Outbreak	193
6	Battling the Disease	201
7	The New Remedy	209
8	Allergic Reaction	213
9	The Curse of Aquafa	223

Chapter 5: Inside Out

1	Rumors	233
2	Change	239
3	The Raven	249
4	A Messenger Bearing Wet Feathers	255
5	The Woman in the Bath	265
6	The Echo Master	273
7	Behind Me, My Child	281
8	A Burning Arrow Piercing the Darkness	287

Chapter 6: In Pursuit of Black Wolf Fever

1	Stepmother, Stepsister	295
2	Tomasolle	301
3	The Head of the Inner Circle	307
4	A Bleak Winter Village	321
5	Toxic Grain	329
6	Makokan's Home	337

List of Main Characters

Van
Leader and sole survivor of the Lone Antlers, a band of warriors who resisted the Zolian invasion. He was captured and enslaved in the salt mine of Aquafa.

Yuna
A little girl Van rescued from the salt mine.

Tohma
A young man from Oki who was saved by Van after being injured.

Ohma
Tohma's father.

Kiya
Tohma's mother, a Zolian who emigrated to Oki.

Hohsalle
A gifted physician and descendant of the Ancient Kingdom of Otawalle, which fell to ruin two hundred and fifty years ago.

Makokan
Hohsalle's servant.

Milalle
Hohsalle's assistant.

Limuelle
Hohsalle's grandfather. A renowned physician who cured the Zolian emperor's wife of a fatal illness.

Tomasolle
Hohsalle's brother-in-law and head of the School of Living Creatures at the Otawalle Academy of Deeper Learning.

Shikan
Tomasolle's assistant who belongs to the Ahfal Oma, the People of the Fire Horse, on the Yukata Plains.

King of Aquafa
Ruler of Aquafa, a kingdom subjugated by Zol. He has pledged allegiance to the Zolian Empire.

Sulumina
Niece of the King of Aquafa. Wife of Yotalu, an influential Zolian.

Tohlim
The king's confidant. Known as the living encyclopedia of Aquafa.

Malji
Leader of the Aquafa Slave Trackers.

Sae
Malji's daughter and one of the best trackers.

Suohl
Also known as the Echo Master. An old shaman who lives in Yomida Forest and who can transfer his spirit to a raven.

Natalu
The Emperor of Zol. He has placed great trust in Limuelle ever since Limuelle saved his wife from a fatal illness.

Governor Ohan
A Zolian governor who rules over the former Kingdom of Aquafa, now the province of Ohan. Hohsalle saved his life.

Utalu
The governor's arrogant and overbearing eldest son.

Yotalu
The governor's second son. Possesses an intellectual disposition.

Lona
The chief priest-doctor of the provincial governor.

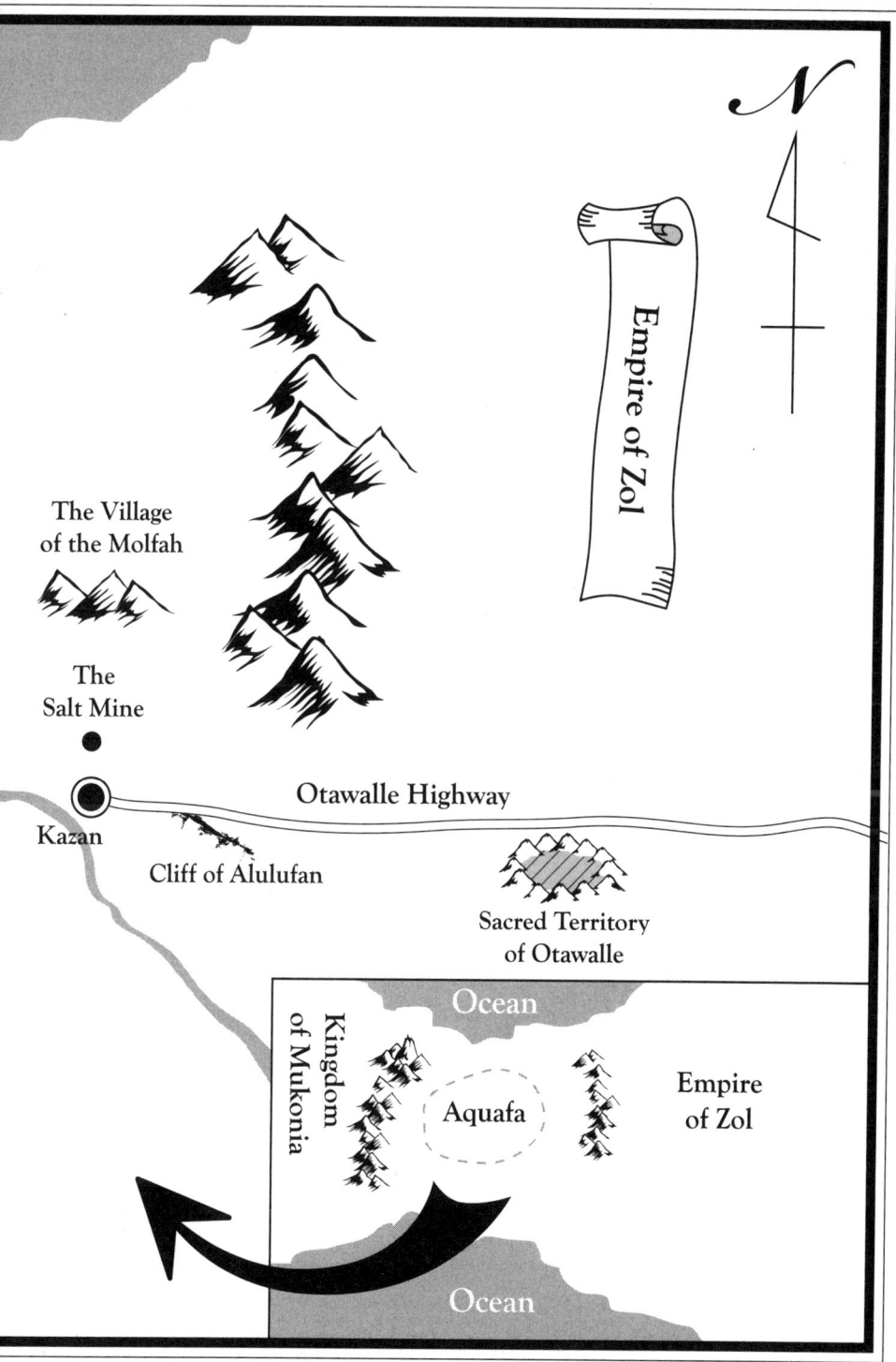

*My spear, these shining antlers,
Fearless, unfettered.*

*Behind me, my fawn.
Bend low, Antlers, to shield this young life.*

The Deer King
— Pika Palu Eggs —

The boy burst into the room with an anguished cry. "Grandfather!"

A man in his prime looked up and placed the book he was reading on the table. "What's wrong?" he asked.

The boy scrunched up his face. "The pika palu are dead!"

The man pushed back his chair and stood. He and the boy strode off toward the room where the pika palu, the shining leaves, were kept.

Sunlight poured through a large bay window that looked out onto a courtyard. A huge aquarium stood in the room. Green fronds swayed in the clear water, and beneath them floated dead gray leaves. The boy peered at the tank and then gazed up at his grandfather. His lips trembled.

"I looked after them properly, just like you told me. I changed the water and—"

The boy's grandfather laid a hand on his shoulder. "It's all right. It's not your fault."

"But!"

"Relax. Look closer. Do you see something on the weeds?"

The boy frowned and stared at them, pressing his forehead against the glass. His eyes grew round. "Oh!" he breathed. Countless tiny beads clung to the leaves. He looked up at his grandfather. "Eggs?"

The man nodded. "That's right. Eggs." He looked into the tank. "Every pika palu dies as soon as it has laid its eggs."

The boy's face clouded over. "They die without raising their children?"

The man nodded. "Pika palu aren't the only living things that must fend for themselves from birth. It's the case for a surprising number of creatures."

The boy gazed into the aquarium as though lost in thought. "But why? Why do they die as soon as they lay their eggs? Do the eggs kill them?"

His grandfather shook his head. "No." He fixed his eyes on the leaf-like objects floating silently in the tank. "They already have the seeds of disease inside them."

"They what?"

"Pika palu carry the seeds of disease within them." His grip on the boy's shoulder tightened slightly. "All living things do. They live for as long as they endure but perish once they give in." He sighed. "Just like everything else in this world."

Chapter 1: Survivors

1
Bitten

Once again, he dreamed of dappled sunlight.

If he looked up, he would see snow-covered mountains far in the distance.

He sat on a sun-heated rock, his fishing line trailing in a mountain stream in his homeland.

Why?

Why did he have the same dream every night here in the slime-smeared bowels of the earth?

The stream—it was so beautiful. Tree branches lazily stretched over the water. Come autumn, their leaves would weave a tapestry of red and gold across the stream.

A withered leaf, its life force spent, fluttered onto the water's surface, casting a small shadow on the streambed while it was swept away.

Someday, that will happen to all of us.

Resignation pierced his youthful heart like some divine revelation as he watched the leaf yield to the torrent.

Was that what drew him repeatedly to this same swift-flowing stream?

Van grimaced. *If that's the case...then I'm a fool.*

Strangely, he never dreamed of the battle along the banks of the

Kashuna River, where Zolian forces had crushed him and his men like twigs in a vise. Van had loved his comrades like brothers and, during his waking hours, graphically recalled how they were cut down before him. Yet he never saw them in his sleep. He never dreamed of the foul, greasy net that had snared him as he stood, alone and spent like a worn-out rag, in the corpse-strewn field. Nor of the events that had led to his incarceration in this horrible place, a salt mine of Aquafa.

However, there was one face that surfaced in his dreams at times. That of the first man he ever killed—an officer astride a magnificent steed bellowing instructions from behind his troops. The desperate fight in the mountains of Van's native land had only just begun. From afar, the man had seemed the epitome of an arrogant Zolian commander. When Van had skillfully cut him off from his forces and charged his flank to put an arrow through his breast, the man's head jerked backward. As the Zolian's helmet toppled off, the face revealed had been far younger than Van envisioned. The Zolian's youthful countenance as he stared in fascination at the arrow protruding from the links in his armor. The surprise in his eyes—*Am I really dying?*—followed by the certainty—*Yes, I'm dying.* The man's grimace of fear and agony. All these images remained seared in Van's memory.

Van had gone on to kill countless men in the ensuing conflict. Eventually, death became commonplace.

And here he was, confronting death once again.

Two months had passed since Van's imprisonment in this hellhole, where the survival rate was at most three months. Mine slaves toiled like ants, descending deep into the earth to fill their baskets with rock salt. Then they trudged back to the surface with the load biting into their shoulders, continuing the process all day. At night, they slept shackled to iron pegs buried deep in the rock wall. Come morning, the routine began again.

When he arrived, Van had thought that if he kept kicking the base of the iron pegs he was shackled to, they would loosen eventually. Yet they were embedded so deeply into the rock that no matter how many times he kicked, they never budged, and his body, pushed to its limit on the barest of rations, soon had no energy to spare.

Was his mind now preparing to give up, dragged down by his weakened physical state?

Fool...

How could a tree mercilessly felled in its prime possibly resign itself to the fate of a withered leaf? Van wasn't young, but he was still only forty. He should have possessed the guts to keep fighting this yoke until he expended the last drop of life, and his body was worn to the bone.

But within the emptiness lurking at the bottom of his heart, he found only the barest thread of attachment to living. Perhaps that void would provide some comfort when he slipped at last to the bottom of the mortar of death, a reminder that this was all his life had come to in the end. Futility screeched and twisted in his gut at the thought, making him want to laugh, or weep. Yet he did not wish to choose death.

If ever Van did elect to die, he could surely find many ways to do so, but he did not want to give in to the pain and take his own life. He knew he must persist until the last spark within him faded.

He heard the quiet, rhythmic knocking of the ventilation fan that sent a meager flow of air to the dark recesses of the mine. Stirred by a groundwater-propelled wheel, it pushed the air down a long series of wind boxes. That feeble breath was the slaves' link to life. Sooner or later, the day would come when Van would hear it no longer.

Behind his closed lids, he saw a thin stream of clear water. A small voice whispered, "Clickety-clack, clickety-clack." A toy waterwheel turned—the waterwheel he'd made for his son. Van recalled how his own father made one for him ages ago. It made only a faint splashing noise, but his son provided the sound effects, mimicking a real waterwheel. The boy's breath, faint and soft, brushed against his upper arm.

Light filtering through the trees danced on the dry alabaster rocks on the far bank of the summer river. Birch bark dazzled white. Delicate green leaves fluttered, whispering in the wind.

His son looked up, then touched him on the elbow and pointed into the woods.

Ah...

A deer. A flying deer. A pyuika.

A buck stood in the dark green shadows among the trees. It was past its prime but surprisingly large. Its antlers climbed up to pierce the sky like leaping flames.

Van rose, took his son by the hand, and approached the great animal. Its form wavered like a heat haze, threatening to vanish at any moment. Gripping his son's hand, he whispered, "Could it be...?"

Van's eyes flew open. A scream sounded from somewhere. The beautiful light fled, and Van was yanked back to the foul stench and darkness of reality.

There it is again... Quite far off.

The ground beneath the mine's surface was like a beehive, riddled with chambers left by salt extraction. The sound Van heard did not come from any of the slaves shackled on his level. He heard their voices continually. Morning, noon, and night, the chamber was filled with groaning, weeping, and bestial howls that could hardly be called human. The sounds were so constant that they had faded into mere background noise. The noise Van just heard was different, however. Perhaps that was why it had penetrated his consciousness.

Urgent cries echoed hollowly, piling to create layers of sound. Voices screamed in terror.

At first, the sounds had come from the upper tunnel that led outside, but the commotion rapidly descended farther down.

What is that?

Frowning, Van sat up just as the slave shackled nearest to the entrance of the shaft rose, dragging his chains. He saw the man's figure, silhouetted against the torchlight from the main shaft, jerk back, and he heard him shout. A shadow slid like dark water into the chamber.

A dog...?

Van thought he saw a flash of fur in the wavering light, but it was too dim to discern the thing's shape clearly. It resembled a wolf but appeared smaller.

An ossam?

Ossam were fierce and vicious mountain dogs native to Van's homeland. The creature's movements seemed similar. But what would an ossam be doing here?

The shadows of the slave and the beast merged in the doorway, and a scream rented the air.

The man sleeping beside Van bolted awake and peered into the darkness. Turning to Van, he called, "Uriya ki? Ono, logi?" but Van couldn't understand a word. Almost all those working in the salt mine were either Zolians sentenced to death or slaves from conquered lands to the south. Van doubted that anyone else here came from Aquafa.

He shrugged at the man beside him, then looked for anything he could use to defend himself. If the chains that held him to the rock were fastened to his wrist, they might have served as a weapon, but they were fastened to his right ankle, which made them useless.

A pack of the black beasts rushed toward Van and his fellow slaves, attacking anyone they passed.

"Oja! Oja! Oja!" the man beside Van shouted while waving his arms to fend one of the creatures off, but it didn't yield. When it leaped on the man, Van kicked its flank as hard as he could with his free foot. The beast gave a short yelp but twisted aside just before it struck the wall, kicking the rock with its feet and landing on all fours. Van marveled at the beast's uncanny reflexes.

Golden eyes shone eerily in the dark, glaring at him as though in contemplation. Then a dark mass filled Van's vision, and warm wind enveloped his face. The beast's breath smelled curiously of green wood, like a split sapling. Fangs sank into the arm he instinctively raised to protect his throat. Viselike pressure was followed immediately by the pain of rent flesh. Groaning, Van grabbed the animal's snout with his free hand and slid his fingers along its muzzle, jabbing them into its eye.

The beast released his arm with a squeal and staggered back a pace or two, its gouged eye closed. Instead of fleeing, it bit the leg of the next slave in the line and bounded deeper into the chamber, biting everyone it passed before vanishing into the darkness.

Van pressed his hand against the gash on his arm while gasping for breath. Although the wound throbbed painfully, it hardly bled at all. The other slaves chattered excitedly while clutching their wounds. Unable to escape, chained to the rock as they were, the terror had been intense, yet no one appeared grievously injured.

The man beside Van gripped his leg and cursed, "Ottaku ehzeh! Lagi logi, ged maieh!"

Van frowned at him.

Why?

Why had the beasts attacked?

Ossam or wolves would only attack people if they were starving or to protect territory or their young. Had they come charging into the mine because they were being chased? It was possible that they might bite instinctively if they were overcome with fear. But…

That creature wasn't afraid.

The golden eyes that had met his for an instant had shown no trace of fear or confusion. Rather, they had been cold and calculating.

The eyes of a warrior. A warrior dispassionately obeying orders.

Van shook his head. There was no use thinking about it. He squeezed the gash on his arm and let the blood drip onto the floor.

It's going to be pretty swollen by morning, he thought in disgust. But there was no use worrying about that, either. Van was suddenly overcome with exhaustion, as though his body were filled with lead. Perhaps it was a reaction to the sudden terror. Moving his chains aside, Van lay down and, with a deep sigh, closed his eyes.

The next morning, the slave girl who brought their breakfast moved clumsily, as if she, too, had been hurt. When she passed Van a bowl of thin gruel, he glimpsed what looked like a makeshift bandage made of rags wrapped around her forearm.

The slave foreman's footsteps, which usually echoed through the chamber as he marched down issuing orders, sounded tired and listless.

* * *

On the third morning after the incident, the slave girl's hands trembled violently, and she spilled the gruel. Even in the dim light, Van spied the rash on her face and hands. He wondered if she had rubella. Recalling the medicine his mother had given him as a child, he said, "Try drinking some tsukki, cocklebur powder, if you can find any." Although he doubted she understood, his concern must have been evident, because she raised her eyes and smiled faintly. However, even smiling seemed to be an effort.

Seven days after the attack, the man beside Van failed to rise in the morning. He lay curled up in a ball, as though in pain. Van called to him but got no response. Reaching out to give him a shake, he found the man's body was already cold. Van vaguely remembered hearing the man coughing violently in the night. He might have groaned later, but Van had been so exhausted that he only lay and listened. Now he wished that he had gotten up and rubbed the man's back. Van's body felt oddly feverish and heavy at the idea, pushing the thought to a distant point in his mind. Here and there, he could hear people coughing, a dry, rasping sound like withered branches rubbing against one another.

The next morning, four more of those who lay chained to the rock wall in Van's chamber failed to wake. When Van left for work, he saw corpses scattered about the other chambers as well. The slaves who could still move and the slave drivers with their whips who supervised them all had racking coughs that grated in their chests.

Somewhere in his mind, Van knew a disease was spreading, but this didn't trouble him. *They won't be forced anymore to carry these loads that bite the shoulders, shred the flesh, and scrape the bones. Soon, I won't have to, either.*

On the night of the eighth day after Van was bitten, he was seized by a splitting headache, and his body was racked by chills that made his teeth rattle in their gums. Fierce shudders rippled through him in successive waves, then gradually lessened, replaced by a soaring fever. His temperature was so high that he thought he must be breathing fire. Instead of visions of dappled light, he was assaulted by a horrendous nightmare that caught him in the throes of the fever.

A tree root stretched toward Van, reaching for the wound on his forearm. He screamed and tried to cover the gaping sore but found he couldn't move. The root burrowed through the hole in his motionless limb, drilling its way up to his shoulder. There it forked. One prong headed toward his neck, while the other moved from his collarbone down toward his chest. Inching along, they separated into multiple tendrils that tunneled through his veins, spreading slowly through his body.

The pain was excruciating.

Van screamed soundlessly. Again and again, he prayed for oblivion, sure that he could no longer bear the pain. But in dreams, such prayers were futile. Van experienced the moment the root reached his brain in vivid detail. He had braced himself for stabbing pain, but instead, when it shot through a point deep inside his head, a hot rush of pleasure numbed his body. Van's abdomen hardened from stomach to groin, and he arched back, trembling.

The ecstasy lasted a long time. His heart beat so fast that he felt it would burst. He couldn't breathe.

When death felt near, myriad lights burst behind his eyes, then were sucked together by some unknown force, whirling and expanding. Luminous granules scraped against the inner walls of his body, which in turn slowly crumbled.

I'm falling apart...

Van's body was dissolving into fine glowing particles. Even the solid rock that should have been beneath him shattered. Everything connected to him dissolved into light, tumbled into chaos, merged and mingled.

He saw himself reflected in each drop of light emanating from his disintegrating body.

Van hurtled back through time with dazzling speed. There was his wife with her playful smile. His son's laughing face. His mother, father, and older brother. The door to his house. Wazu, his dog, trotting out from the door's shadow. The smell of smoke from the hearth. The clear light of the sun dappling the ground through red leaves.

Don't go.

Van desperately strove to stop the tide, to pull his disintegrating body back and bind the fragments together. The strength of that thought must have imparted some power, because, with agonizing slowness, the infinite grains of light that had burst forth in a shower now began to gather and weave themselves into the shape of his body.

2
First Encounter

Van awoke to a searing thirst. Groaning hoarsely, he forced his eyes open, audibly cracking the rheum that glued his lashes shut. The back of his hand brushed the cool rock wall. Everything appeared strangely bright. Van could even discern the downy hairs on his forearm. A scab had formed over the wound where the beast's fangs penetrated his skin.

He vaguely remembered being delirious with fever and having a nightmare.

Last night...

Had it really been just the night before? Van had lost all sense of time. How long did he sleep? The dream had seemed to go on forever, yet even that memory felt nebulous, as if his mind had slipped into some blank space.

I'm hungry...

No. This was not mere hunger. The inside of his stomach felt like it was being roasted on a spit, and the sensation worsened by the second. Van's hands shook. If he didn't eat something soon, he might faint. But chained as he was to the wall, he could not go looking for food. He broke out in a fine sweat at the thought of how long he might have to wait for the morning gruel to arrive. He was thirsty, too. And dizzy... Yet those things aside, Van felt more clearheaded than he had in a long time—the clarity that came after sweating out a high fever.

Everything seemed so quiet. The only sounds to be heard were scurrying rats, insects, and the turning of the ventilation fan. No echoes of human voices, no traces of human presence.

Is it still the middle of the night?

An uneasy Van turned away from the wall and staggered to his feet. A shock ran through him at the sight that greeted his eyes.

Corpses lay sprawled across the chamber as far as he could see.

Both the man diagonally across from him and the man chained to the wall beyond had been alive last night. Now they, and every other on this level, were dead. Van knew at a glance that they weren't merely sleeping. The torch had long since burned to ash, leaving only the faint glow from the shaft for light, yet he could see their faces clearly, still twisted in the agony of death.

Van began to shake in the stillness. His heart pounded, and his throat constricted.

What happened here? What's going on?

Nothing made any sense. The only thing Van knew for certain was that he had to get out of here. Something inside him implored him to flee. That, and the gnawing hunger in his belly.

Leave. Now. Before it's too late.

He broke into a dash, only to have his feet whipped from under him as the chain around his right ankle pulled taut with a *clang*. Van managed to catch himself with both hands before colliding with the rock floor.

Damn!

Anger erupted inside him. Van was filled with revulsion for this thing that held him and wouldn't let him go. He grabbed the chain and pulled, letting rage fuel his muscles. The metal plate and bolts that attached the chain to stakes driven into the stone screeched in protest. Van knew he could never yank it off, yet he didn't care. Spurred by a burning rage and bellowing with the effort, Van ground his teeth and pulled. The muscles in his arms and shoulders bulged and trembled.

Suddenly, Van felt one of the thick metal rings of the chain twist like toffee. Before his eyes, the loop widened, then popped, sending him tumbling over backward. He fell on his bottom in a heap of disheveled straw and gazed in amazement at the chain hanging from his hand. Then, coming to his senses, he leaped to his feet and broke into a run, dragging behind the severed length of chain still fastened to his ankle.

The rasping of his breath filled his ears as he raced up the gently sloping tunnel toward the vertical shaft that led to the outside world. He saw light far above. A thick rope swayed in the shaft, suspended from a pulley frame silhouetted against the glow. Grasping the salt-encrusted crossbars of a sturdy wooden ladder, Van hauled himself up rung by rung.

As he approached the upper levels, the shaft grew steadily lighter. When he reached the second level, he heard the tramp of horse hooves.

So it survived...

The horse must have heard him. It snorted and turned its head languidly to gaze at him from its wooden pen erected against the rock wall. Nothing else moved. Squinting, Van surveyed the chamber, but all he could see were dead slaves. He gritted his teeth and continued to climb.

Those beasts... Van pictured the creatures that had attacked the slaves a few days ago.

How had they managed to get down this ladder? No dog or wolf could have done that, let alone climb back up.

Then again...

Van recalled how nimbly the beast had twisted in midair before hitting the wall, turning the rock into a springboard to land on its feet. If its kind could move like that, Van wouldn't put it past them to scale this narrowly hewn shaft by leaping back and forth from wall to ladder.

What were they?

The slaves died only after they were bitten. They were exhausted from heavy labor, but that alone shouldn't have wiped out the entire lot. Occasionally, a chamber would fill with poisonous gas expelled from some underground pocket, but if that were the cause, the men sleeping near this shaft should have been spared. Van couldn't imagine gas killing so many people on different levels.

Everyone had come down with colds and chest-splitting coughs, which Van was pretty sure began after the attack. He chewed his lip as he thought on the way the beasts had bitten each slave with methodical detachment, as if carrying out orders. *But... If that was the cause of death, then why am I still alive?*

His hand grasped the last rung of the ladder, and he heaved himself over the lip of the shaft and rolled into the chamber that led to the mouth of the mine. He squinted at the entrance. The westering sun dyed the rock wall a pale orange.

Late afternoon already? Not morning? How long did I sleep? Half a day? Even longer?

Van pursed his lips and stepped outside.

Golden light bathed his body. A cool autumn breeze touched his cheeks, and soft sunlight falling through rustling leaves gilded the world around him.

There was no trace of anyone else. The guards who manned the turrets to prevent escape and protect the mine, the slave drivers, and the foremen were nowhere to be seen. The faint drone of flies announced what had become of them.

Van shivered, chilled by the breeze. He had to eat. It didn't matter what, as long as it was edible. Looking around, he spotted several buildings. When he was first brought here, Van had been blindfolded, and when he and the other slaves had carried salt out of the mine, they were jammed together and closely watched, affording him no chance to look around.

A lookout tower was the first thing to catch his eye. The row of houses beside it had to be the quarters for the overseers. To the east of those stood two other buildings, one large and the other small. Both sported several chimneys. Van believed them to be the kitchens where the slaves' meals were prepared. The storage sheds beside them seemed to confirm this guess.

Van tried all the doors but found they were firmly shut. His hunger was so acute now that he abandoned all caution. He kicked the closest door, then threw himself against it repeatedly. It was likely bolted from within, for it refused to give way, even though it opened a crack. Van persisted until he heard a *snap* from inside, and the door flew open at last. He staggered inside and struck his shin on something hard. Swearing, Van rubbed his leg. Three chairs lay sprawled across the floor.

They must've barricaded the entrance with these.

Silence filled the room. A shaft of light came through a window, and dust motes danced slowly in the air. Women lay on the floor, caught in the dim light. One of them had died with her hand outstretched toward the water jug. They seemed to have collapsed in the middle of a meal. Slices of a bread called fahmu lay on the table, and soup had been spilled. Van remembered the ragged bandage on the arm of the slave girl who had brought the food.

If they barricaded the doors with those chairs… They must have been afraid of something. The beasts? That meant they had attacked here as well.

Shards of broken dishes had been swept into a pile in one corner of the room. Van could almost see the women, their faces pale with fear, sweeping the floor and discussing what had happened. They must have decided to bar the door at night so they wouldn't be attacked in their sleep. A day had passed, then two, then three… Perhaps they wondered if they caught colds when the coughs began. Ultimately, they were forced to work despite their fevers and collapsed.

Van gazed at the dead women, recalling how his body had suddenly felt like a lead weight. Here and there, dark red spots colored the bloodless skin of the women's cheeks and necks—possibly marks of the fever that overtook them.

Van's head felt as if it were splitting in two, his breath came in painful gasps, and his body trembled. However, he could not bring himself to ignore the corpses of these women. Placing his shaking palms together, Van closed his eyes and prayed that their souls would be welcomed in the Land of Eternal Spring. Then, opening his eyes, he looked around.

The rich aroma of food had filled his nostrils for some time. Looking up, Van saw bundles of dried red peppers and garlic hanging from the ceiling, along with ropes of sausages. On top of a large cooking counter in the center of the room was a huge, round loaf of unsliced fahmu, obviously left there just after it had been removed from the oven.

This was clearly not where slaves' meals were prepared. They were only given a sloppy barley gruel. Van had not seen sausages or fahmu for ages. He first strode over to the water urn, scooped out a ladleful, and gulped it down. The cold liquid tasted like sweet nectar. He drank until his thirst was slaked, then grabbed the fahmu from the counter, ripped off a chunk, and sank his teeth into it. The loaf was enough to feed a family of four, but he polished it off in no time, swallowing the first bite without bothering to chew, then tearing off another mouthful, then another.

Somewhere in the back of Van's mind, a voice cautioned him not to eat too much. His stomach had grown accustomed to too little. "If you gorge yourself now, you'll die," the sober voice advised. But Van couldn't stop. It was as though a bottomless pit had opened inside him, and no matter how much he ate, it would never be filled.

Van reached up and yanked on a string suspending a sausage rope, pulling it down. He bit into the salty meat. The cold congealed fat tasted unbearably good. Heat flamed through him like a dying candle springing back to life, sparked by the scent of meat after such a lengthy deprivation.

Finally, Van paused and wiped the back of his hand across his mouth. As he did so, he thought he heard something. He raised his head and listened intently. Yes, there it was again. It sounded like crying.

Did someone else survive?

Where was it coming from? By listening carefully, Van located the direction of the sound and stepped outside. The crying was clearer now.

Next door?

The adjacent building was quite large but cruder than the first. Its doors appeared similarly barricaded. Although Van was in better shape than before, he could not summon the strength to break one down this time. Perhaps he wasn't desperate enough.

Looking around, Van saw a window set high on the east wall. He went back and retrieved the chair he had struck his shin on and, using it as a step, climbed through the opening.

The dimly lit interior was far plainer than that of the neighboring structure. Numerous earthen ovens stood in the sprawling kitchen, and large, blackened pots rested upon them. Doubtless, this was where the slaves' food was prepared.

Here, too, the bodies of dead women, some quite young, lay motionless. Van gritted his teeth upon catching sight of the shackles around their ankles. These girls were slaves, too. When the war ended, they must have been rounded up from their homelands and brought here.

The ashes from the ovens had all been removed and piled in a bin, and the blackened pots had been washed and dried. Only two ovens had yet to be cleaned out, and the dark pots on top still contained gruel. After cooking for the men who labored in the mine, the women must have cleaned up and set to making their own meals when they succumbed.

Although still muffled, the crying was much louder than before, yet none of those sprawled on the floor appeared to be alive. One body toward the back of the room was propped against an oven, as if to block the firebox. The scarf covering the woman's head was askew, and strands of hair clung to her cheeks. She looked to be only twenty-two or twenty-three. She likely perished while struggling to stay upright and keep her back pressed against the oven. The woman had fought through fever and hallucinations to guard whatever was in that oven from the beasts.

Van gently picked her up in his arms and moved her away from the opening. The crying became sharp and clear. Van peered into the oven and saw two dark round eyes, presently wide with surprise. A little child with tearstained cheeks gazed up at him, a crust of fahmu clutched in one round fist.

3
Light in the Ashes

Van woke with a start at the soft *thud* of a log shifting in the fire. How long had he been asleep? The sky visible through the smoke vent above was still dark. This was no time to be sleeping, but after Van had filled his stomach and tended to other tasks that demanded attention, he was overtaken by weariness.

Van spent the night in the slaves' kitchen. After discovering the girl, he had left her where she was for the time being and went to look around while the light lasted. Unfortunately, he failed to find superior shelter. He'd already kicked in the door of the neighboring building, which meant it wouldn't do. The slaves' kitchen was a sturdy structure, and it was equipped for a fire. Van could also hide the little one in a firebox if those things attacked again. Plus, it was near the shaft to the salt mine. The kitchen was likely built here for transporting the slaves' meals, meager as they were, into the mine. At this distance, it would be easy for Van to flee with the child into that labyrinth, if need be, and they would stand a better chance of escape in the tunnels, which crisscrossed underground.

Salt was akin to gold, and the Aquafa mine was a precious source of revenue. Once news of what had happened here got out, the place would be swarmed. Van needed to get away before officials and their soldiers arrived. But he had dared not venture into the darkness last night for fear the beasts still roamed about.

Men came to haul away the salt at regular intervals. Van didn't know when they last visited, but judging by the stockpile in the storehouse, he doubted that they would return tomorrow. Still, he didn't know how things worked and could not accurately guess when someone might come or why. There had to be merchants who delivered food and officials who regularly checked on work progress. Van had no choice but to stay here last night, but he judged it best to leave before dawn tomorrow.

His first task had been to search through the foreman's house to find the key and remove the manacle around his ankle. When it cracked open and he felt the weight fall from his leg, Van was filled with a profound sense of release. Now he knew what a dog felt like when it shook its body after having its collar removed.

Van threw the shackle and broken chain down a vertical shaft, then returned to the foreman's house and took just enough money to survive short-term. He was careful not to take more than needed, and he further concealed his theft by removing money from several places. Upon capture, a runaway slave would be whipped but not executed. No one was foolish enough to kill a horse or cow that could still be used. However, a slave who stole from or murdered his overseers would be drawn and quartered as an example to others. It was galling enough to have been made a slave, but the mere thought of being condemned by such biased reasoning made Van sick to his stomach. While he felt no twinge of guilt about taking the money, he didn't want to provide anyone with an excuse to accuse him so unjustly.

Before sunset, Van had been able to gather clothes that would disguise the fact he was a slave. He also took a tinderbox, a dagger, and a sword in addition to the money. The sword's blade was the slightly curved style favored by the Zolians rather than the straight ones Van was used to, but he couldn't complain. His best find was a well-kept bow that fit his hand perfectly, along with a quiver of arrows.

Van returned to the kitchen with these items to find the little one still curled up in the oven, sucking her thumb. Her dark round eyes watched him. He crouched down, wondering what to do. Fleeing with a child was madness, yet Van couldn't convince himself to leave her. She was a funny-looking little thing. The girl's mother had been dark-skinned, like the people of the Yukata Plains in southern Aquafa, but the girl was fair, and the shape of her eyes reminded him of the Zolians. Although Van had no way of knowing the identity of her father, he could think of only one reason for her existence under these circumstances, and it made him sick. If he left the child here, even if she survived, the fate that awaited her would be the same as her mother's, perhaps even crueler. Slaves were treated no better than livestock. If they were too much trouble, they would be slaughtered. Even if it were considered more profitable to let them live, they would never be treated as human beings.

"Hey," Van said softly. The girl blinked. He stretched out his arm. She looked at it for a few moments, then reached out with her own small hands. Perhaps she wasn't the type to fear strangers. He took her in his arms, pulled her from the oven, and set her down on the ground. She wobbled a bit but didn't fall. "Mauma." She reached for the body of the woman Van had laid to one side, and he held her steady so that she could bury her face in her mother's breast.

She sobbed inconsolably. Perhaps she wondered why her mother didn't wake and hold her. Van let her cry for a long time before pulling her away. She squirmed and flailed at him with her pudgy hands, but he picked her up and held her firmly in the crook of one arm while he set some water on to boil. Then he removed her clothes and sponged her clean.

Strangely, the girl's crying didn't bother him. He felt calm and detached as he washed her, as if he were watching himself from a distance. While wiping the filth from her skin, he noticed a long thin scratch that had scabbed over under her left ankle.

So she was grazed by fangs, too.

Van glanced at the scab on his own arm. "Another survivor, are you?" he muttered. Dozens of people had occupied the mine, yet only two had lived. He was struck once again by how odd this was.

The bath must have soothed the girl, because as soon as he wrapped her in a soft cloth, she fell fast asleep, still sucking her thumb. The weight of the sleeping child cradled in Van's arms filled him with peace, as though the spot where he stood in this room full of corpses was lit by a warm glow. The body of the girl's mother, which lay beside them, had already sunk into darkness such that only a gray lump was visible. In the dim light, the living and the dead, the floor and the ovens, melded into shadow. Only the damp heat of the child in his arms confirmed that there was life here.

The girl opened her eyes groggily a few times and whimpered a little as though in remembrance, but when Van laid her in the makeshift bed he'd assembled, she passed out again. The temperature had dropped drastically with the sun. Although it was preferable to the mine, which sucked the warmth from one's body, Van still felt cold.

She must have felt it last night, too... Van was amazed that the girl had managed to survive. He lit a fire in one of the ovens to keep them warm and gazed absently at the sleeping child beside him. As he did so, sleep overtook him.

A bird cawed in the distance. Dawn was near. Van shook himself and rose, then stirred the embers in the oven. He added a stick, and the flames crackled to life. After filling a large empty pot with water, he put it on the stove and brought it to a boil. He then transferred the water to a wooden basin that had been standing against a wall to dry. That done, he removed his clothes—a patchwork of blankets and rags—soaked them in the hot water, and used them to wipe his body.

Van hadn't washed in so long that his skin was covered in a thick scum, and the water turned filthy in no time at all. He dumped it out and added more, repeating the process several times. Once cleansed, he donned the clothes he'd stolen and threw the rags and dirty water on the garbage heap outside. By the time the first rays of sunlight appeared, he'd prepared and eaten his fill of hot porridge. He woke the little one and began spooning her slightly cooled porridge. She was still half-asleep and, at first, just rolled the food around her mouth with her tongue and spat it out. As she woke, however, she seemed to realize she was hungry. Her eyes grew bright, and she practically devoured the spoon and Van's fingers along with it.

He laughed deep in his throat. "Hey, don't eat my fingers. They'll give you a stomachache."

The girl peered up at him, eyes round. "Manma, onyage?" Van didn't understand, but she was grinning at him happily, glad, it seemed, to have some food inside her. He gave her the spoon, and she began scooping up the porridge and eating it quite competently. The soft white light of the morning sun caressed her porridge-speckled cheeks. Mesmerized, Van gazed at the downy hairs glistening on her skin.

4
Out of the Mine

An imposing iron fence surrounded the salt mine. On the south side stood a gate that opened onto the broad road used to transport rock salt out of the compound and bring supplies in. The guards surely opened it each morning, but now, with no one to do so, it remained closed. Van could probably have located the keys if he searched the guardhouse, but he elected to climb the fence instead. He knew the top was covered with spikes to deter escapees and invaders, but he didn't want anyone to guess from the open gate that someone had escaped. He took a discarded wooden tub and placed it at the bottom of the fence near the garbage heap. Climbing on top of this, he laid a frayed and thickly folded horse rug over the spikes. He threw his bag over first, then scaled the fence with the child on his back. Once on the other side, he stretched up and tipped the blanket back on the mine side of the fence. With any luck, people would assume that both bucket and blanket had merely blown off the garbage heap.

If they use the dogs, there's no chance of escaping anyway.

Van realized he'd not heard a single dog barking. Several accompanied the slave foreman wherever he went, yet Van detected no sign of them anywhere.

Were they attacked, too?

If the dogs were tied up in the kennel when the beasts came, they could have been mauled to death. *I should have checked yesterday.* Unfortunately, it didn't occur to him until now. *I'm losing my touch.* Before, Van would have noticed such details immediately. The endless days of hopeless slavery must have whittled away at his once well-trained mind.

Van stared at the forest that lay before him and sighed. The little one clung to his neck without a whimper. He'd strapped her to his back with the baby sling he found beside her mother. Perhaps that had reassured her. It had certainly made it easier to climb over the fence.

"Good girl," Van whispered, jiggling her a few times.

"Nyaga, tonton!" she exclaimed. While Van gathered his luggage, she chattered away contentedly, probably quite used to being carried piggyback while her mother worked. Van slung the bow across his back, buckled the sword around his waist, and grasped the quiver in one hand and the bag in the other. Despite the load, Van's body felt light and easy. Perhaps it was thanks to finally having enough to eat.

He set off into the forest thick with evergreens that stretched toward the heavens, obstructing the sun even in late autumn. It was quiet and gloomy under the trees, but the stunted underbrush made walking much easier where there was no path.

Van had no clear idea of what he would do next. His homeland, the mountainous Toga region, had already fallen into the hands of the conquerors. Toga was located on the westernmost edge of Aquafa, the last part of the kingdom to have been swallowed by the slowly advancing wave of Zolian troops. Against the mighty Empire of Zol, the mountain clans on the frontier had stood no chance. Even the smallest child had understood that. However, Van's people had also known their existence would be little better than that of slaves should they give in without a fight. Fleeing hadn't been an option, for the Kingdom of Mukonia was to the west, and it ruled its subjects with a cruelty that exceeded the Empire of Zol.

Aquafa had shrewdly allied itself with the invaders and became a province of the empire, thus ensuring its people the status of ordinary citizens. But the various clans scattered throughout the mountains of the Toga region were not regarded as Aquafaese, even though they spoke the language and had fought to protect its borders from Mukonian incursions. Under the King of Aquafa, the clans had been considered independent and allowed a loose autonomy in their own affairs in return for their allegiance. Thus, Zol refused to recognize the mountain peoples as citizens under its regime.

Only after devoting many years to securing a stable government in central Aquafa did the Zolians finally turn their full attention to the last stage of annexation: the subjugation of the Toga region. The King of Aquafa had sent messengers to each clan offering to negotiate with Zol for a guarantee of safety in return for allegiance to the empire. As the former ruler of a land that was now merely a province, however, the king could only parley to spare their lives. He had no say in determining the status of their clans. The involvement of a former ruler simply presented too many problems when treatment of clans in subjugated territory was tied to imperial management of the frontier.

It was Zolian policy to relocate lower castes to other parts of its conquered territory. Failing to receive ordinary citizen status like the Aquafaese meant the clans would be forced to leave their homelands and eke out a miserable existence in an unfamiliar place. After long deliberation, the leaders of the Gansa saw no alternative but to feign resistance. They decided to greet the invading forces with a band of daring warriors ready to fight to the death and demonstrate that they were not easily beaten and would make useful allies. This, they hoped, might allow them to negotiate for more acceptable terms should they offer to submit to Zolian rule and form a vanguard to protect the empire's new western flank. If the Zolians recognized that the clans were well versed in the mountainous terrain and could serve as a buffer against Mukonia, the Gansa might be permitted to stay.

It was a band of death warriors known as the Lone Antlers that arose to challenge the Zolian forces and fight this hopeless battle. Its members were all men who, for one reason or another, had been robbed of normal lives. Ancient in origin, the band was said to have emerged when the gods first appeared in the form of pyuika, flying deer, and its members were exempt from the rules that bound the Gansa clan as long as they vowed to serve as its shield, giving their lives to protect it should the need arise. Even outsiders fleeing some calamity in their own land were welcomed as clansmen if they chose to join these warriors. It was the existence of the Lone Antlers that allowed the elders to even consider a strategy of quasi-resistance.

There was one other factor that made the elders' strategy feasible. The Toga Mountains ran along the western border of Aquafa, which was constantly plagued by incursions. The would-be invaders brought disease in addition to war. Over the last few decades, successive epidemics had swept through the mountain clans, decimating the greater part of the population in some areas. As a result, many men who had lost their families to war or disease sought out the Gansa and joined the Lone Antlers, and its ranks swelled to unprecedented numbers.

When the elders had approached Van, leader of the Lone Antlers, with their proposal, he and his men accepted this mission eagerly, for each of them carried a burden of sorrow and despair.

At last, I have a legitimate reason to make that final journey to my wife and son, Van had thought. His parents, grandparents, and elder brother had all passed away, and life without his wife and child had long seemed empty and meaningless. While the Land of Eternal Spring warmly embraced those who died of illness, accident, or old age, anyone in their prime who gave in to sorrow and took their own life would find no welcome there. Pyuika Riders, in particular, were sworn to expend their lives for the glory of their comrades. Should Van break that vow, he would be condemned to walk the Road of Constant Day.

Van had occasionally thought that would suit him, wandering that white, never-ending road while dragging his long shadow behind him. However, if there really was a Land of Eternal Spring where his wife and son awaited him, he didn't want to inflict the pain of disappointment upon them. The living had no way of knowing if such a realm existed, but since Van was going to die anyway, he would do so with his eyes set toward his loved ones.

From the day they had received the elders' command, Van and his men plunged headlong into battle. They lured the enemy into the steep and rugged mountains and forests of Toga, then emerged without warning from the shadows of the trees or hurtled down sheer cliffs, outmaneuvering horse and rider with the lightning speed and agility of their pyuika. For almost two years, they resisted, and their tactics bore fruit. The Pyuika Riders struck terror into the hearts of Zolian troops, forcing the enemy commanders to consider retreat and to offer the tribal elders favorable terms for a truce. As the negotiations proceeded, the Lone Antlers continued to play the part of fanatics defying the elders and fighting to the death. Then, having fulfilled their mission, they fell.

The elders and the clansmen are wise, Van thought. *They would not let the lives of the Lone Antlers go to waste. Surely they must have wrung whatever advantage they could from our efforts.* While Van worried about what had become of his homeland, he knew the success of his guerrilla campaign had also won him many enemies among the Zolians. To return home would be to risk capture and further suffering for his people, something he wished to avoid at all costs.

The dark green branches shook in the breeze, scattering splinters of sunlight across the forest floor. *I was already a dead man*, Van mused. How ironic that he had managed to survive even the battle at Kashuna River and the attack on the salt mine.

"Ocha, tonton?"

Van laughed as a pudgy little hand tugged on his ear. "Hungry, are you?" The girl was toying with his earlobe instead of responding, pulling and twisting as though it was very entertaining. It didn't hurt, and he let her play, but the sensation awoke old memories, and sorrow pierced his heart. Van suppressed the feelings that threatened to rear their heads and dragged his mind back to the question of where to go from here.

So what shall I do?

Van knew the surrounding terrain quite well and what towns were located where. After the deaths of his wife and son, he'd wandered aimlessly for a long time. When rumors of the impending Zolian invasion had reached him, he and his comrades disguised themselves as merchants and explored Aquafa and other lands.

I guess we should head to Kazan first.

Kazan was a large trading center. Once the capital of Aquafa, it was now the seat of the Zolian governor who ruled the province. Van had been there twice. It was a confluence for traders from all parts of the empire, and he should be able to learn the latest news and maybe even find some sort of work there.

I'll also need to locate a foster parent for the little one. There was a shrine in Kazan dedicated to the gods of all the peoples that converged on the city. Surely a priest would take pity on an orphan. There was no guarantee this plan would work, however. Van would just have to go and see.

The sky darkened, and it began to drizzle a little before noon. The dense canopy blocked the rain, keeping them relatively dry. Still, Van slipped the child from his back, took off his moku, a hooded cape, and then, after hoisting her onto his back once more, threw it over the two of them. She immediately began to fuss, seemingly annoyed by the hood over her head. Van was jiggling her on his back to quiet her when he smelled smoke. He paused in wonder. That one faint whiff told him the smoke came from a fire cooking wild boar. Van knew exactly where it was coming from, too. In his mind's eye, he saw a young man, alone, tending a fire in a hollow shadowed by moss-covered rocks. The image flashed through his brain and was gone. He decided to steer clear of that direction and began searching for a trail. That's when the child began to cry.

"Oncha, nyaga! Nyagaaa!" Pushing her hands against his neck, she arched backward, bawling at the top of her lungs. No matter how he rocked her or whispered urgently for her to hush, she simply would not stop. The commotion she made was so loud that it startled the birds from the trees and flushed the mice from the underbrush.

Van gave up any attempt at stealth. "Hey now!" he demanded. "What's all the fuss about?" At that moment, he heard a faint voice from beyond the trees.

"Is someone there?"

The person spoke not Zolian but Aquafaese. And the accent was that of the clans along the border. Van started, thinking it must be one of his comrades, but the lilt at the end of the question informed him that it was someone from the north, so he decided to hurry on, ignoring the call. The tone, however, changed abruptly from a query to a desperate plea.

"If there's someone there, don't leave me. Please! Help me! I've twisted my leg and can't walk!"

Van still would normally have ignored the entreaty. Woods like these were full of thugs who didn't hesitate to feign an injury and then leap upon unsuspecting do-gooders to kill them for their valuables. But a vague sense of doubt stayed Van's feet. He didn't know why, but he knew with absolute certainty that the man was not only alone but merely a youth. The image that had passed through his mind at the smell of smoke seemed as real as if he had witnessed it with his own eyes. He wanted to find out why. He wished to see if there really was a hollow among some mossy rocks beyond those trees...

I must be crazy to go looking for trouble like this.

Van loosened his hunting knife in its sheath. Then, with the child still screeching on his back, he plowed through the underbrush toward the smoke.

5
Pyuika in the Mist

Three rocks stood in the shade of an enormous spruce tree. A young man sat in the hollow, leaning his back against one of those rocks, his leg stretched out in front. His face was ghastly pale, and he looked as if he was about to faint from exhaustion. A reindeer cart like those used by the nomads of northern Aquafa stood beside him, but the reindeer that ought to have been hitched to it was nowhere in sight.

The youth was roasting a hunk of meat on a stick over a campfire. Although garbed in the reindeer hides nomads wore, his face illumined by the light of the flames was a strange mixture of features that Van could not place. His narrow eyes and flat nose appeared Zolian.

Is he a hybrid?

It had been many years since Aquafa came under Zolian rule. While some Zolian settlements excluded other peoples in an effort to protect the purity of their lineages, many intermarried with Aquafaese. This was particularly common in the north, where the first interracial generation was already growing up. This youth had to be one of them.

When Van stepped out from behind a tree and into the hollow, astonishment spread across the youth's pale face. Clearly, he had not been expecting a man with a child strapped to his back. His gaze flicked to Van's hand resting on the hilt of a dagger, and his eyes filled with fear.

"P-please d-don't kill me!" The youth's lips trembled, and he tried to back away. Judging by the tattooed lines across his cheeks, he'd already gone through the rite of passage and been recognized as an adult. While Van found it odd to see the marks used by the northern Aquafaese on one who looked so Zolian, he felt only a slight twinge of pity for the incongruity rather than any aversion. He looked around cautiously, then removed his hand from his weapon.

"How did you twist your leg?" he asked quietly.

The young man blinked. Color gradually returned to his face. "Ossam," he whispered. Moistening his lips, he hesitantly related his story.

"I was on my way to sell hides in Kazan, y'see… That was three days ago now… Fallen trees blocked my usual way, so I tried a new route… But it turned out to be a heck of a long way 'round. When it got dark, I had to camp here. It must've been past midnight when this pack of ossam came out of nowhere, like a black wave… I jumped in the cart to hide, and they just flowed around it and disappeared. But my pyuika was scared silly and wound herself 'round that tree, practically strangling herself on the tether. I tried to untangle her, but she wouldn't stay still. When I finally set her free, she yanked the rope and knocked me over. Then she ran off into the forest…"

Having twisted his ankle so badly that he could not walk, he had settled down to wait for someone to pass by. "I figured someone'd come through here on their way to or from the salt mine, but it's been three whole days, and I was sure I was done for. I was scared out of my wits…"

He appeared so forlorn and helpless that Van found it hard to believe he was old enough to have been through the rite of passage. He stood silently gazing down at the youth. Then he turned and walked over to the tree where the pyuika had been tethered. The little one's howling had ceased abruptly as soon as Van had reached the hollow, either because she was distracted by this new development or simply no longer bored. She was now entertaining herself by making clucking noises with her tongue. After stroking the bark where the rope had cut into the tree trunk, Van turned to the young man.

"You said you had a pyuika, right? I thought the northern clans only used reindeer."

The young man looked suspicious. "You mean you don't know?" When Van didn't respond, the youth sighed. "Maybe it's different where you're from, but around the end of the year before last, we were told, official-like, that if we raised pyuika instead of reindeer, they'd cut our taxes. So everyone rushed to get pyuika from Toga. How were we supposed to know they're so high-strung and hard to handle? Now everyone's saying it's not worth the measly cut in taxes. We thought it'd be easy. I mean, they're just another kind of deer, right? What a mistake!"

Van smiled. Raising pyuika required certain skills. People who knew nothing but reindeer would have a hard time of it.

Now I remember...

Some time ago, Van had heard a rumor that the people of the Okuba clan, who lived near the Gansa, were rounding up pyuika and sending them to Aquafa. The Okuba had once been pyuika herders and nomads like the Gansa, but they surrendered to Zol much earlier, becoming serfs, and were now scattered across the province.

When they had heard that the Zolians ordered the Okuba remaining in the Toga region to supply them with pyuika, the Lone Antlers had had a good laugh. *"We've given them so much trouble, they've decided to try riding pyuika themselves,"* they had joked. It had not occurred to them to fret. Pyuika were nothing like horses or reindeer. Confident that it would be impossible to raise up pyuika riders in just a few years, they had expected the Zolians to abandon this attempt in frustration. However, the Zolians were evidently more determined than Van had expected.

I suppose my people might even be helping them.

As he mulled that over, the sound of the rain intensified.

"Oh great, now it's gonna pour," the youth grumbled. He shoved the firewood under the cart to keep it dry and then looked up at Van with pleading eyes. "There's a tarp in the cart, but I can't get up."

Van slipped the toddler from his back and held her out. "Hold her for me." The young man cradled the girl with a surprisingly well-practiced touch.

Van pulled a rainproof canvas sheet from the cart and made a roof over their heads by fastening it to the cart and a rock. It barely sheltered the three of them. Van sat down beside the others and pulled some fahmu and cheese from his bag. "Want some?" he asked, and the youth nodded.

"Thanks. There's food in the cart, but my dang leg hurts so bad I haven't been able to stand since yesterday. All I had was the meat I'd removed from the cart before this happened. Help yourself. It's boar. Pretty tasty, too, thanks to the big acorn crop this year."

Van smiled. "Looks good." He cut off a hunk of fahmu and laid a slice of cheese on top. He skewered this with his knife and toasted it over the flames until the cheese melted into a glossy coating. He passed this piece to the youth, who nodded in thanks and reached out to take it. But just as his fingers grasped it, a little hand tried to snatch it away.

"Whoa there! Not so fast." Laughing, the youth moved it out of reach. "Yours is coming. Hang on a minute."

Van laughed, too, and handed the little girl a piece of untoasted fahmu for the moment. She must have been hungry, because she began munching on it diligently. "You're just full of energy, aren't you?" he said.

The youth raised his brows. "And she sure can yell."

Van grinned. He was right. No one would have guessed she was a girl from how she cried. Her bawling had been so loud that it rumbled in his belly.

The three huddled together as the rain pelted down. Van toasted more bread and cheese, sprinkled the succulent boar with salt, and ate. The cheese was made from cow's milk, and although it was not unpleasant, he felt it lacked flavor.

"You told me pyuika are hard to raise," Van said. "Have you ever milked them?"

The youth eyed him with surprise. "You can drink pyuika milk?"

"Sure." Van gazed into the flames. "Reindeer milk is sweeter and creamier than that from a cow, but pyuika milk is even creamier. It has a richer flavor, too. Cheese made from pyuika milk is the best."

Through the incessant drumming of the rain on the tarpaulin, a strange sound came from the forest. *Pwohhh.*

The youth glanced toward the rain-drenched trees. "What's that? Didn't sound like an elk." The forests of Aquafa were inhabited by huge elk that towered over men. In the fall, bulls in their prime sported magnificent racks of antlers, and cow elk would call them in high, strained voices like a muted horn.

The sound was so familiar that Van smiled without realizing it. "What's your pyuika's name?" he asked softly.

The youth looked at him questioningly. "What? Oh, Tsupi. In our dialect, it means 'rebel.' My father named her that. She's pretty stubborn for a female."

"I see." Van stroked his chin. "Has Tsupi ever butted you in the back?"

The youth looked even more puzzled. "In the back? Yeah. All the time. She'll butt me from behind when I'm least expecting it. Almost knocks me over. Didn't used to. She only picks up bad habits, never any good ones."

Van laughed. After a brief silence, he replied, "If I bring your pyuika back, will you introduce me to a fur trader in Kazan?"

"Eh?" The youth looked taken aback. "To a fur trader? You're a hunter?"

Van gestured with his eyes to the bow he'd shoved under the cart to keep dry. "I'm a good enough shot that I can live off hunting, but circumstances prevent me from returning to my homeland. I was on my way to Kazan to find work. A fur trader would know the hunting rights in this area and the regulations. But they tend to be protective of their territory, so I doubt they'd give me or any other stranger the time of day."

"Well, yeah, guess that's true…" The youth's eyes slid away as though he was thinking.

He'd probably recalled that he knew nothing about this man he shared shelter with. Fur traders were important customers to reindeer herders. The youth was surely considering what would happen if he introduced someone who ended up causing problems later.

Van smiled. This youth was a good man. One capable of thinking ahead. After finishing a chunk of boar, Van thrust the stick that was his makeshift roasting spit into the ground, brushed off his knees, and stood. Then he drew the lead line from under the cart. The youth looked up quickly, a question in his eyes.

"I'll go look for her. Take care of the little one for me, will you?"

"Yeah, sure, but…"

Van pulled the rope taut in his hands and cheerfully replied, "You can think about whether you want to introduce me to a fur trader in Kazan on the way there. I was planning to go anyway. You won't get there alone with that leg, so we may as well travel together, at least to the town gate."

6
Rite of Love

Raindrops shook the foliage, and Van was drenched almost as soon as he stepped out from under the tarp. It was a cold rain, yet it did not bother him.

Pyuika were far more affectionate than the youth realized. Once they had bonded, they never forgot a friend and quickly succumbed to loneliness when separated. Butting was a sign of affection, and the fact that Tsupi had often nudged the young man in the back showed that she had become attached to him. She was far from home, and no other pyuika lived in these woods. Even if they had, a doe would not be accepted into a different herd. During any other season, there would have been no need to search for her. She would have returned to the youth as soon as the scent of ossam faded.

But this was fall, the mating season. Pyuika and elk were similar. Although pyuika bucks were smaller than bull elk, mature female pyuika were similar in size to cow elk, which made interbreeding possible. Van's clansmen sometimes mated pyuika with elk deliberately to breed larger stock. Van guessed from Tsupi's call that the scent of a bull elk had put her in heat, and she was wandering the forest in search of him. Still, she hadn't gone far. If he could get close enough to see her, he'd be able to bring her back.

Van approached the tree where Tsupi had been tethered and

squatted down to gaze at the wet leaves on the ground. As his eyes grew accustomed to the sight, he could vaguely discern the shape of hoofmarks. He could also smell pyuika urine, something he'd noticed when standing here earlier. When frightened, pyuika leaked urine as they ran. Van's clansmen gave dogs this scent when tracking them.

Van felt a sudden quiver of doubt. Even when in estrus, the scent of urine did not linger this long. Three days had passed since the pyuika fled. Why was the scent so clear? Van could even tell that it was old. Not only that, but he could see the trail of urine speckling the ground in a dotted line like the silvery slime left by a snail.

He felt as though there was a sluice gate deep within his nose, perhaps right between his eyes. When it shifted, scents flooded his brain and were instantly transposed into images. But something inside him hesitated to open it all the way. What would happen if he did?

Van stood motionless in the gray, rain-drenched forest, struggling to control his pounding heart. What was happening to him?

Something had changed, and he sensed that it was rooted in the night of the attack. He was afraid to consider what that might mean. Deeply afraid. Yet a strange pleasure also pulsed deep within him. A feverish heat crawled across his skin. He felt as if a thin membrane was just ready to peel away. And when it did, he would come face-to-face with a new and lustrous self like a butterfly breaking through a chrysalis to spread wide its damp wings...

A sharp voice rang through his mind. "Don't let go."

Van closed his eyes and gripped the lead line in his hands.

"Don't let go of yourself."

Something warned him not to surrender to this strange sensation. Yet at the same time, he heard a voice inside his heart protesting quietly, "But it's already part of me..."

Van drew a deep breath, then slowly opened his eyes. The smell of wet trees and earth soaked into his brain, gently easing the tightness in his mind. He sighed.

Time to bring back that pyuika.

He would follow the trail, visible to his mind's eye, and bring back the doe. He would do whatever needed doing. And as he did, he was bound to see more clearly just what form this new self would take, even if he might not like it.

Perhaps because Van had mastered his feelings, the scent trail was much more distinct. When he followed it to the point where he could no longer see the flicker of the campfire between the trees, he noticed a small pool of pinkish liquid glimmering on the ground. A bull elk had marked its territory. The surrounding mud was trampled with pyuika prints.

So you've fallen in love, have you?

Van sensed the presence of deer beyond the distant timbers. He heard rough snorting and stamping hooves. The sounds mingled with the smells in his brain, and a vivid image sprang forward. Van closed his eyes and stared. Two stately bull elk stood facing each other, their impressive antlers lowered. Each snorted in warning, nostrils flared to smell its opponent.

Van opened his eyes and walked stealthily toward where he knew they would be. He peered out from the shadow of the trees. The scene before him was exactly as he'd imagined.

Massive bodies collided. The ground shook, and the air rang with the clash of antlers. Again and again, the two bulls locked heads and pushed, straining against each other with every ounce of strength for one simple reason: to proclaim their virility. One forced the other's head to the ground, twisting its neck and pressing its face into the dirt. The weaker bull struggled, unwilling to capitulate, but the difference in strength was obvious, and it finally backed away, limping. The victor did not pursue but merely watched the loser disappear into the woods. The rain had stopped, and the late-afternoon sun gilded the grass. In this golden light, the victor and the pyuika enacted the rite of love with Van as their silent witness.

When Van returned to the campfire leading the pyuika, the youth's mouth dropped open, and his eyes widened. "Tsupi!! How the heck did you do it?"

Tsupi kept nuzzling Van's armpit. He stroked her nose and made a clucking sound as he tethered her in the shadow of the trees. Tsupi clucked back at him, shaking her head. After ensuring she was settled, Van walked over and sat by the fire. "Did you know that pyuika will come to you if you make that clucking noise?" he asked.

The youth shook his head. "No. The Okuba we bought her from said she'd come if we called her name. So that's what I did."

"I see. That works, too, but you should learn how to cluck with your tongue as well." Van smiled as he warmed his cold fingers at the fire. "Your Tsupi will bear the young of an elk next spring."

"She'll what?" The youth's eyes grew even rounder. "You mean pyuika can mate with elk?"

"Yeah. The calving is hard, but when successful, the young are very strong."

The youth fell silent and gazed into the flames for some time. The child slept contentedly in his arms. The only sounds were the pyuika munching grass and the wood crackling in the fire. After a long silence, the youth looked at Van as though he'd awoken from a dream. "You're from Toga, aren't you? I can tell by your accent."

Van nodded, then told him the story he'd prepared in advance. "I'm from the Maso clan. We live by herding pyuika and hunting, but my wife divorced me when I fell for an immigrant from the south. Not a very noble reason, I'm afraid, but that's how I became a wanderer."

The Maso consisted of just a few families that lived deep in the rugged mountains. The Zolians had not deemed it worthwhile to send in soldiers to subjugate them and left them to themselves. There was little chance that his lie would be exposed, for the Maso never came down from the mountains, preferring to ask neighboring clans to serve as middlemen in trading furs and meat.

"Maso? First I ever heard of them. Never knew such a clan existed."

"It's just a few families, so it's not surprising no one around here knows of us. If you're in doubt, ask the Okuba. They'll know."

The youth nodded but did not seem totally convinced. "What about the kid?" he inquired.

"The woman's," Van answered brusquely. "She got sick and died pretty quick."

The youth blinked but asked no more questions. He shifted his gaze to the fire. After some consideration, he raised his head and looked at Van. "Thanks for finding Tsupi. I owe you."

Van nodded. The youth licked his lips and continued. "If you're set on it, I'll introduce you to a fur trader, but if you're looking for work, I think I can find you a job."

Van cocked an eyebrow. The youth hesitated a moment, then said in a rush, "I mean, I can't promise nothing because it's up to my father to decide, so even if you come with me, if he says no, you're outta luck. But as far as I'm concerned, it'd be great if you did." He broke into a grin, and his face flushed. "Sorry. I run my mouth when I get worked up. What I meant was, come back with me. We're a small clan and not well off, but we'll find a way to feed you and the kid.

"See, a sickness took my elder brother. And my father's got a bad back. That's why I had to take the furs and meat to market on my own." As the youth spoke, he seemed to make up his mind, and a strong light shone in his eyes. "If we're going to have enough left over from taxes to survive, we've got to breed more pyuika, but for some reason, they don't mate and they don't bear young."

The young man glanced at Tsupi. "If you're right about her bearing young, we've got to make sure she delivers safely. But none of us has ever seen a pyuika calve, and you just said it's harder when they've mated with an elk, right?"

Van nodded. "Yes, that's true."

"Well then, if you'd come live with us, you'd be a huge help." He implored Van with his eyes. "I'm begging you. We can't afford to lose Tsupi. I'll convince my father and the others, so please come." He offered a hand. "I'm Tohma yu Oki, Tohma of the Oki clan."

Van accepted Tohma's hand and gave his name in return.

Shafts of late-afternoon sunshine cut through the rain-drenched trees. Gazing at this luminous tapestry, Van recalled the stream in his homeland and the leaf swept away by the rushing water.

Chapter 2:
A Plague from the Past

1
Devil's Spawn

As they crested the gently sloping hill, the salt mine finally came into view through a gray curtain of drizzling rain. Figures scurried about like ants below. The dirt road, which was wide and well packed for transporting rock salt down the gradual incline, was slick with rainwater. Yotalu, the second son of the Zolian governor, rode ahead, the hooves of his fawn-colored horse slipping on the mud.

"They don't have enough sense to use lime on these roads?" Hohsalle grumbled.

Makokan rode beside him. A towering, broad-shouldered man, he handled his high-strung black steed with ease. After overhearing this remark, he smiled wryly. "Why don't you suggest that to Governor Ohan on your return?"

Makokan glanced at Hohsalle, who only shrugged. Hohsalle's lips were blue with cold under his black hood. Makokan frowned. The mountains were chilly enough already, and the rain only made it worse. The long ride from the crack of dawn must have taken its toll on the mohalu, the young master. Makokan wondered if he should have tried harder to dissuade him.

Hohsalle raised an eyebrow, as if reading Makokan's thoughts. "Stop worrying," he snapped. "I'm fine." Turning in his saddle, he dug in his heels and urged his horse to a trot. Makokan followed suit, still frowning.

* * *

Hohsalle was an exceptional young man in every respect. He was one of the Sacred, a descendent of the great ruler who founded the Ancient Kingdom of Otawalle. That alone set him apart, but he'd also trained under his grandfather, the renowned physician Limuelle. His talent had blossomed at an early age, and he began teaching at the Otawalle Academy of Deeper Learning when he was just fifteen. Although only twenty-six, he was now the director of the research wing of the academy's Institute of Medicine, and all of the ruling class of the Zolian Empire knew his name. He had been catapulted to fame for assisting his grandfather in curing the emperor's wife. But even before that, Hohsalle had saved many others from mortal injury and disease.

One of them was Makokan. After being rolled away into a corner of the stadium, Makokan had lain in agony on the flagstones, waiting for death. When Hohsalle's slender form had drifted into his darkening vision, he felt certain he was about to die. Like all stake-fighters, he knew the youth was one of the Sacred, and that the emperor had given him permission to gather the corpses of those felled at the stadium.

Makokan's wound should have killed him, but it didn't. Hohsalle's miracle-working hands had hauled him back from the brink of death. Makokan remembered waking in the mohalu's hall to see him nodding in a chair by the window, the pale bluish light of dawn illuminating his profile.

He stayed up all night for me, a lowly fighter?

Hohsalle had opened his eyes, smiling upon discovering that Makokan was awake. "So you survived. A true man of the Ofal Oma, the People of the Yukata Mountains. You're as tough as your horses." His sophisticated tone was at odds with his youthful countenance. "I hear you're from a family that serves the Inner Circle. One day, you'll have to tell me how someone from such a straitlaced upbringing came to be a stake-fighter."

Makokan had felt no surprise that Hohsalle knew him, just bitter resignation. No matter how low he might fall nor how far he might flee, he could never sever his bond with the Sacred. For those born into their service, there was no escape from their masters, save death.

What Hohsalle had seen in his expression at that moment, Makokan could not guess, but a cold glint had flashed in his eyes. "Don't get me wrong," he'd said. "If you were still a servant of the Inner Circle, I wouldn't have spared you a glance. Though you were on the verge of death, I would still have passed you by. I despise those who hide in the gloom." Hohsalle brought his face closer, quietly adding, "You battled so carelessly, yet you always won. I enjoyed watching you fight. I collect the living as well as the dead, you know. What would you say to serving me—as my attendant?"

What an odd man, Makokan had thought. Frightening, yet with a strange charisma.

The Zolians called him the Devil's Spawn behind his back. Makokan guessed their uneasiness had more to do with the strange presence he exuded than their ingrained aversion to the Otawalle. It was rumored that he'd slept with the Lord of Hell in exchange for a way to save the lives of those doomed to die. At times, Hohsalle's behavior seemed so eccentric that Makokan couldn't blame people for thinking as much, but he suspected it was the Zolian priest-doctors who'd spread this tale, for they feared and despised Hohsalle and his grandfather, Limuelle.

Zolians revered physicians as "the fingers of the god" and believed that medicine, which determined who lived or died, must adhere to the divine teachings. Doctors served as priests of the Zolian religion, the Pure Heart Creed. If the priest-doctors pronounced a patient's condition incurable, the accepted practice was to leave them in the hands of the god and administer only those medicines that would allow them to die in peace.

However, Emperor Natalu was a decisive man open to new ideas. When his beloved wife was stricken with a mortal illness, he'd refused to give up hope. Hearing that Limuelle and Hohsalle had miraculously saved others from the same disease, he'd summoned them to treat his wife despite strong opposition from his advisers, who considered

Otawalle curatives heretical. The two men had cured her completely. Impressed by their skill and knowledge, the emperor had begged them to remain as palace physicians and teach the priest-doctors the superior medical science of Otawalle. The palace doctors were appalled and rose up in fury, resulting in a clash between the association of priest-doctors and the emperor. The situation only settled when Limuelle and Hohsalle announced their intention to decline the offer, but the incident had already sown the seeds of trouble. The news spread through the empire, alerting the Zolian aristocracy to the wonders of Otawalle medicine.

To choose possible healing over certain death was only human. One by one, nobles who'd been diagnosed as incurable by the priest-doctors covertly sought Otawalle physicians. The association of priest-doctors was incensed. Its members warned the nobility that if they strayed from the true path, the empire would surely fall into ruin. The Pure Heart Creed was the fabric that bound the sprawling empire together, and neither the emperor nor the aristocracy could openly oppose what the priest-doctors said. Even now, a decade after the emperor's wife's recovery, Otawalle's medical science was still officially branded as heresy.

The fact that the Zolians already viewed the Otawalle with fear and aversion further complicated things. The harmonious rule of the Ancient Kingdom of Otawalle, which had flourished for thousands of years, contained the salt mine, the Yukata Plains in the south, the Oki District in the north, and the Toga Mountains in the west. The Otawalle had excelled at medicine, engineering, and the arts. Its citizens had penned odes to the affluent lives they led. The roots of its political structure, however, had been shaken by the spread of a strange disease that wiped out most able statesmen before sweeping through the kingdom as a full-blown epidemic. That occurred about two and a half centuries ago, precipitating the kingdom's rapid decline.

Some claimed that the skills wielded by the Otawalle had overstepped the bounds of human knowledge and infringed upon the realm of the gods, incurring their wrath, but the truth was now veiled in darkness. Upon realizing that their kingdom was failing, the members of the ruling class had calmly prepared for the inevitable, just as an elder statesman might have stepped down to make way for the next generation.

The last ruler, King Takaluhalu, moved the capital to the trading center of Kazan in Aquafa, which had remained untouched by the epidemic, and transferred his authority to its young Aquafaese ruler in exchange for his pledge to grant local autonomy to the diverse peoples of the realm. Thus began the Kingdom of Aquafa. The surviving Otawalle established the Sacred Territory in a valley ringed by rugged mountains and dedicated themselves to honing their knowledge and skills in medicine and other fields.

The Academy of Deeper Learning was the focal point of Otawalle knowledge, and even children of lower birth studied there to prepare for professions suited to their capacities. However, few students remained in the Sacred Territory once they reached adulthood, for the Otawalle had chosen to have no country of their own, a fact reflected in the motto carved above the academy's main entrance: *Live By Helping Other Nations Live*. They scattered and settled in other regions, using their expertise to make their livings. The technology and craftsmanship produced by the academy and its graduates were highly coveted by other countries and had become pivotal to Aquafa's prosperity.

Long ago, the Otawalle also founded the organization known as the Inner Circle, which extended its information-gathering network to every corner of the kingdom, like a spider spinning its web. Even after relinquishing the reins of government, the Otawalle retained the Inner Circle and continued to exert a clandestine influence over political affairs by supplying successive Aquafa rulers with information. If the Kingdom of Aquafa were likened to a human body, then the Sacred Territory of Otawalle would be its head. The current king had capitulated to the Zolian Empire after only a few skirmishes, and many suspected that the Otawalle warned him of the empire's crushing military strength and convinced him of the merits of negotiation over conflict.

The Otawalle were among the first to express allegiance to the Empire of Zol, capitalizing on their outstanding technology to earn a spot in the conquering nation's good graces. Although Otawalle medical practices faced rigid opposition from the orthodox priest-doctors, their construction skills, such as bridge building and tunnel boring, were highly valued, and their engineers were entrusted with key projects. Otawalle's superior technology also drove Zolian development in the fields of mining and metallurgy. Thanks to these achievements, the Otawalle were now in the odd position of being highly respected despite having been subjugated, and of being appointed to responsible positions despite being feared and shunned.

Many Aquafaese were uneasy with the Otawalle's apparent lack of scruples, but they were also acutely conscious that it was Otawalle's shrewd negotiating that saved Aquafa from the ravages of war and ensured it some degree of autonomy. While the Aquafaese were a little disillusioned with the Sacred Ones, they certainly didn't despise them. The Zolians, however, came from lands far to the east and had expanded their territory across the land like an advancing thundercloud. To these invaders, the Otawalle inspired fear precisely because they were unknown.

Merchants who traveled the highways joining the east and west referred to the secluded mountain valley that concealed the Sacred Territory as a "demon-infested place" and made wild claims that those who lived there drank human blood and lived for a thousand years. By the time the Zolians began negotiating Aquafa's annexation, they undoubtedly had realized such rumors were unfounded, yet their distrust of the inscrutable Otawalle was deeply rooted. At the same time, they knew that the Otawalle possessed technology so advanced that it could only be called magic. While this, too, inspired loathing, the Zolians now depended on it.

Emperor Natalu and Governor Ohan knew full well who would save them should they fall ill. That's why the former treated Limuelle as a respected friend and the latter appointed Hohsalle to positions of trust, despite protests from priest-doctors. Hohsalle had already rescued the governor once. As Ohan lay recovering, he'd exclaimed, "Surely the fact that you were here in my time of need could only have been divine intervention." His ministers would have been shocked by the remark had they been present. Governor Ohan was well-known for his arrogance and greed, yet the look on his face had been one of abject adulation.

The direction of the wind must have changed. The smell of smoke thickened as the entrance to the mine came into view. Hohsalle's face tensed. Spurring his horse forward, he rode up to the gate where Yotalu was speaking with an officer who'd come to greet the party.

"My lord," Hohsalle called, pushing a stray lock of hair from his forehead. Yotalu turned. "I advise you to don your mask. And could you please ask the workers to halt the burning for a while?"

As if suddenly aware of the ashes dancing on the wind, Yotalu hastily drew out a mask and tied the strings behind his head. "Why stop them?" he asked in a muffled voice. "If the bodies aren't burned immediately, the disease could spread."

Hohsalle nodded as he donned his own mask. "Yes, of course, you're right. The bodies must be cremated to contain the illness. However, I should like to examine some of them first. That's why I came, after all."

The officer's nose wrinkled in evident disgust. Catching sight of his expression, Yotalu scowled. "How dare you!" he thundered, and the officer jumped. "My father owes his life to Sir Hohsalle!" The officer, his face rigid, bowed deeply and apologized, then spun on his heel and hurried off toward a large brick building that belched smoke.

"You there!" he shouted. "Stop the burning!" At this, a group of serfs hauling a cart piled high with corpses came to a slow halt. As Hohsalle rode up, the eyes of the soldiers supervising the work widened in recognition, then slid away fearfully. One of them bent his middle finger in the sign to ward off evil. A cynical gleam entered Hohsalle's eyes. He touched a finger to his lips, then flicked it in the soldier's direction, as if throwing something. The man paled and began to tremble.

"Mohalu," Makokan said in reproach, but Hohsalle merely made a sound like a contented cat, his lips twitching at the corners. Then, wiping the smile from his face, he dismounted and, passing the reins to Makokan, walked over to the corpse-laden cart.

Makokan dismounted as well, leading the two horses as he followed Hohsalle. The soldiers gathered a little distance away, watching and muttering in low voices. Although he could not hear the words, Makokan could guess that they were talking about the "Devil's Spawn." He paused to tie a cloth over his mouth and nose and, while he did so, looked around.

Convicts had been brought in to do the dirty work, and Makokan could see them piling the corpses onto carts here and there. Iron rings were clasped around their necks, and fear showed on their faces. The soldiers watching over them from afar appeared just as frightened. Hohsalle had walked over to a heap of bodies piled haphazardly beside the cart and inspected them intently. Not feeling inclined to examine the corpses himself, Makokan continued to survey their surroundings.

The salt mine was located in a bowl-shaped valley surrounded on all sides by steep hills and mountains; the north and west slopes were densely wooded all the way up to their peaks. An impressive iron fence followed the edge of the forest and encircled the compound, compensating for any lookout tower blind spots. There was only a scattering of trees on the south and east sides, and the line of vision was relatively clear. Excluding the road, the terrain there was steep and rocky, making it virtually impossible for armed attackers to move swiftly.

That's likely why they left the road muddy, too, Makokan thought. He doubted it was the result of ignorance. It was far more likely a deliberate strategy to protect the mine from attack. The more he looked, the more impressed he was by the defenses. *After all, they're digging white gold here.* If they were at all careless, the governor would face severe consequences. *Yet...*

Despite all the measures taken to protect the mine, the guards had failed to avert this disaster.

Makokan shifted his gaze back to his mohalu. He was staring at the bodies. The stench and miserable state of the corpses did not seem to offend him. Makokan shuddered involuntarily at the stillness of Hohsalle's face. "Sir?" he called.

Hohsalle started as if waking from a trance. "Look here." He pointed to the calf of one body. The flesh had already turned the color of ash, and the marks of a dog bite stood out quite clearly. "Every corpse bears marks like these. There are also traces of a rash from head to toe." Hohsalle sighed and wiped a hand across his forehead. Sweat had gathered on his pale face, despite the cold.

Makokan's scalp prickled with fear. While he'd been shocked to learn that all the workers in the mine died, it did little to frighten him. He'd assumed the cooks had mistakenly mixed poisonous mushrooms or herbs into the food. However, these corpses bore scars made by fangs. Food poisoning wasn't the cause of death. These people had perished after being bitten.

What kind of illness could possibly unnerve the mohalu like this?

Makokan's heart began to race. Something very strange was going on, and here he was, stuck right in the middle of it.

Hohsalle drew on a pair of gloves and urged Makokan to do the same. Then he ordered him to get the mikimu, an insecticide of powdered minerals, from his bag and spray it on the five corpses laid out in front of him. Once the white cloud had settled over the bodies and vanished, Hohsalle nodded. "Let's undress them. It's been cold, and they've been thoroughly sprayed, so there shouldn't be any problems. Still, be careful. Keep an eye out for fleas or ticks hiding in their clothes."

The bodies weren't stiff, merely cold and heavy. "I would guess more than three days have passed," Makokan remarked, trying to take his mind off his fear.

Hohsalle nodded. "Rigor mortis sets in quicker when someone has been doing heavy labor, yet there's no trace of it now, so I'd say it's probably been about four."

The bodies were clothed in little more than rags. When they were stripped, Hohsalle closed his eyes briefly, then began examining each one closely as if caressing it with his gaze. He inspected all five from head to toe, muttering to himself the whole time. Once finished, he stood and stretched with a great sigh. Yotalu stood behind Hohsalle with an anxious expression, watching intently. "Do you know the cause?" he asked.

Hohsalle turned to face him but did not immediately respond. After another sigh, he said, "I cannot accurately identify the disease without examining the bodies more thoroughly."

Yotalu's gaze didn't waver. "But you have an idea, don't you?" When Hohsalle did not answer, he took a step closer and whispered, "Please tell me. What is it?"

Hohsalle peered down at the bodies. "I can only guess based on what I have seen and the situation…but I believe that it may have been mittsual."

Makokan leaped away from the bodies, afraid to so much as breathe in case something invisible might detach itself from one of them and latch on to him.

A faint smile colored Hohsalle's eyes, and he shook his head. "Don't panic. It doesn't suit a great lout like you. There's nothing to worry about. If it is mittsual, you're not going to catch it from these corpses."

Yotalu had been listening to this exchange in silence, but now he frowned and looked at Hohsalle. "Excuse my ignorance, but I have never heard of this 'mittsual,' as you call it. Is it dangerous? Some kind of plague, for example?"

Hohsalle's smile vanished, and he nodded. "Yes. It means 'black wolf fever.' I was teasing Makokan, but in reality, it's a pestilence he has every right to fear. You were wise to have the bodies burned so quickly. In addition…" His eyes flicked to the cart, which was drenched in the freezing rain. "We're very fortunate that it's been so cold. Cold enough for frost to fall for the last three days. And no fires have been lit here since they died, right?"

Yotalu nodded, but he still looked puzzled. "Yes, that's true. I heard there was even a thin film of ice on some of their clothes."

"Then we should be fine. The disease will not spread from any of the bodies here."

"…Why?"

"Because there are no insects swarming. Black wolf fever can be transmitted by wolves and the wild mountain dogs called ossam, but it's even more dangerous when carried by fleas or ticks that have bitten infected beasts or humans."

Yotalu paled and brushed his sleeves.

"There's no cause for alarm. Fleas are mostly dormant when it is cold enough for frost, although they can survive all winter long if they are in a warm place, such as a dog's body or where there's a hearth."

Hohsalle stared at the colorless scenery through the mist of the icy rain. "You've no idea how fortunate it is that this place was isolated for over four days in the freezing cold." He gave a short sigh. "Even so, you should make sure that those who have touched or come near the bodies do not leave until they have washed thoroughly, including their hair, and changed. The clothes they are wearing should be burned."

Yotalu's eyes widened. "Really? Are you sure that's necessary?"

Hohsalle nodded. "Absolutely."

Makokan stared at his mohalu wordlessly, noting the strange quality in his eyes. He could guess what the man was going to say next.

"Once, long ago, this sickness wiped out six thousand people. Black wolf fever pushed my people's kingdom to the brink of extinction."

Yotalu turned pale as wax. "What of a remedy?" he whispered.

Hohsalle shook his head. "An effective cure has yet to be found."

Yotalu swayed slightly, the strength leeched from his knees. "Do all those who suffer from it perish?"

Hohsalle shifted his gaze once more to the bodies. "Not always. Some who were bitten apparently survived. But the ancient records show that of those who contracted the disease, eight out of ten died. It is a dreadful scourge." Hohsalle's face was paler than usual, but his voice had regained its calm since speaking of Otawalle's demise.

Yotalu took a deep breath, as if to steady his nerves. "This black wolf fever, is it different from mad-dog disease?"

"Yes. While both can spread through dog bites and are fatal and without cures, rabies does not kill so quickly. Symptoms of rabies only appear after fourteen days, even if the bite is near the head. Until then, the victims have no clue that they are infected. With black wolf fever, however, historical records indicate that symptoms manifest within days, and the disease rapidly progresses, leading to death. That's one reason I suspect it may have been the cause here."

"...I see."

"There has been no increase in incidents of rabies, correct?"

Yotalu shook his head. "Nothing was mentioned in the regular reports."

Hohsalle stared at the bodies being loaded onto carts. "Rabies is not transmitted from human to human," he explained. "Even if it were spread in that way, it would be very odd if it killed so many so quickly. It is possible that diseased rats might have proliferated some kind of plague, but the bites on these five corpses clearly did not come from rats. And as I've explained, ticks and fleas aren't active when it's this cold. Considering the temperature and the harsh conditions in the mine, a flu epidemic is a conceivable cause, but it's challenging to imagine it leaving no survivors. The logical conclusion in this case would be poisoning, either deliberately or from accidentally tainted food. However, there's no evidence of diarrhea, nor do the corpses exhibit any other symptoms characteristic of the various poisons that might have killed them. Of course, I cannot be absolutely sure of that because several days have passed, and there are some poisons that disguise their work as that of a disease.

"Because the bodies bear bite marks and traces of a rash, we must accept that black wolf fever may be the cause. Therefore, both possibilities—poisoning and black wolf fever—should be considered when examining this case."

Yotalu frowned. "What about the black plague? I've heard it's transmitted by rats."

Hohsalle shook his head. "No, we can rule that out. The black plague typically causes swelling in the glands under the armpit, behind the ears, or in the groin, as well as ulcers and gangrene. None of the corpses show any evidence of those symptoms. Additionally, I noted several other qualities not associated with the black plague, and the shape and color of the rash on all the bodies closely resembles the historical descriptions of the rash that accompanied black wolf fever."

Yotalu's face looked pinched and cold. He wrinkled his nose. "You said fleas can spread it, but what about decomposing bodies? Are you sure we can't get it from these corpses?"

Hohsalle laughed. "Yes, I'm certain. We should be fine. Of course, if we have caught it, we're doomed. But even if we haven't, we're all doomed to die someday anyway, aren't we?"

Yotalu blinked, clearly uncertain as to whether he should feel reassured or not. Makokan coughed pointedly, and Hohsalle assumed a more sober expression. "My lord, I have a rather urgent favor to ask of you."

"What is it?"

"I want thirty bodies, including those you said had a thin film of ice on them, packed into coffins and delivered to my clinic in Kazan. Do you think that would be possible?"

Although this request meant obtaining permission from Lona, the priest-doctor who served as the governor's chief physician, Yotalu nodded immediately. "Of course," he replied. Lowering his voice to ensure no one would overhear, he added, "I appreciate your consideration, but there is no need to worry. I am sure Sir Lona would never interfere with anything you wish to do."

The governor once took critically ill because Lona misdiagnosed his condition. Hohsalle saved the governor's life, but he never mentioned Lona's error, thus protecting the priest-doctor's position. As soon as Lona had realized his error, he requested an audience with the governor. Despite knowing that a confession could mean his death, Lona apologized for endangering the governor's life through his ignorance. That was the sort of man he was. Though taciturn and hard to read, Lona was driven not by the desire to protect his authority but by the desire to follow the divine teachings—unlike most priest-doctors.

As it turned out, the governor valued Lona's imperviousness to pressure from the imperial court's priest-doctors so highly that he'd requested the man remain in his service. After much consideration, Lona had stayed on. He never complained about the governor's dependence on Hohsalle or his tendency to award him special privileges, nor did he report these details to the association of imperial priest-doctors, thus protecting Hohsalle in his own way. It was thanks to Lona that Hohsalle was able to practice medicine so freely in this province.

"Considering how serious this is," Hohsalle said quietly, "he will have no choice but to report what has happened to his superiors."

Yotalu nodded. "Yes, but you know that Sir Lona can be trusted, and we are used to dealing with the court. Please do what you judge to be best without worrying over the consequences."

Hohsalle's expression relaxed. "Thank you... Oh, and please be sure to have the corpses thoroughly sprayed with pesticide."

"Certainly." Yotalu turned and called out to an officer, ordering him to prepare carts and coffins and giving him instructions for delivery.

The officer saluted and was about to return to his troops when Hohsalle stopped him. "If at all possible, I want them delivered while they are still cold and before they start to decompose. It's much harder to determine the cause of a disease once rot begins. It's also harder to make medicines. Several days have passed already. It may be too late, but I want to give it my best effort."

The officer saluted again and hurried off. Hohsalle turned to Makokan. "Fetch me a pen and paper, will you? And lend me your back."

Makokan sighed but did as he was told. He took paper, a pen, and an inkwell from his pack, then bent down so that Hohsalle could use his back as a desk. "Excellent," Hohsalle said. "Nice and wide, but a bit too soft, perhaps." Makokan could tell from his young master's lighthearted tone that he was in high spirits. While Hohsalle often adopted a flippant attitude, Makokan knew he rarely became truly excited. Now, however, it was as though a fire were burning brightly inside him.

By the time Hohsalle finished scribing a letter to his assistant at the research wing of his clinic, the soldiers had returned with the carts and coffins. Hohsalle gave the letter to Yotalu. "Please have this delivered to my assistant along with the corpses." Then he faced the officer. "Were you the first one to discover the tragedy here?"

The officer tensed and shook his head. "No. It was the guards who came to replace those on duty. They came back and reported it."

"I see. May I talk with them?"

The officer bowed. "I will fetch them immediately."

The soldiers stood at attention before Hohsalle, their expressions rigid. One of them was the same man who had made the sign to ward off evil. Hohsalle was no longer in the mood to tease him, though. He looked at the group, his face still. "There are a few things I wish to ask you. Tell me whatever comes to mind, no matter how insignificant it may seem." He began with easy questions, such as how often they changed the guard and how the mine kept in communication with the outside. Once their tongues had loosened, Hohsalle inquired about the morning they discovered the disaster. From their responses, he learned that the last report from the mine, which had been fourteen days ago, mentioned nothing unusual, yet when the soldiers reached the site early yesterday, they found no survivors and saw no beasts.

"So every single person died, is that right? Including all the slaves chained below?" The eyes of one young soldier wavered slightly, a fact the keen-sighted Hohsalle didn't miss. He fixed his gaze on him. "Did someone survive?"

The soldier licked his lips and glanced at his commanding officer, who cleared his throat. "There is a possibility that one slave may have escaped."

Yotalu paled. "What?"

The officer went on hurriedly. "It is just a possibility. We haven't checked the numbers yet. I intended to confirm them first before informing you, sir."

Yotalu groaned. "What do you mean by 'possibility'?"

"The slaves are shackled inside the mine at night, but there is one spot on the third level where a chain has been broken. It's not clear whether a slave was actually shackled there or not, though. The chains are such that not even several men pulling in tandem could break them. However, they have been in place for a long time. Perhaps the links in that particular spot were no longer useable, in which case no slave would have been kept there."

The officer gained confidence as he spoke, and his tone strengthened.

"The men responsible for supervising the slaves have all died, thus the only way to find out is to check the number of slaves we found against the total in the records. I was just about to have my men do that."

Yotalu gazed at the officer intently. "But there must be numbers carved into each chain, right?"

The officer's red-rimmed eyes shifted. The place was in total chaos, and he had probably decided it wasn't worth the time to go all the way down into the mine and check the number for the sake of one slave. "Yes, that is true, but the records are not very well kept, and some of the numbers are missing…" Undoubtedly, even the officer thought his words sounded like an excuse. He swallowed the rest of his explanation and bowed deeply. "I beg your forgiveness. I will take the records down into the mine and compare them immediately."

Hohsalle had been listening to this exchange contemplatively, but when the officer finished, he perked up and looked at Yotalu. "I'd like to see that broken chain. Would you take me there?"

2
Into the Mine

It was not until after lunch that Hohsalle and Makokan were led into the mine. As everyone responsible for the mining operations had died, a capable guide had to be located first. Hohsalle had suggested to Yotalu that they eat and discuss measures to be taken while they waited.

The gray-haired guide the soldiers found appeared to be over sixty, yet looked robust, and his gait was sturdy. However, Makokan was startled by his face.

An Aquafaese?

He wondered why Yotalu would ask such a man to lead them through the mine. Makokan glanced quickly at Hohsalle, but his mohalu betrayed no emotion as he gazed at the aged guide.

The old man bent his knee and bowed to Yotalu.

"I remember you," Yotalu said. "My grandfather used to call you the walking encyclopedia of Aquafa. Your name is Tohlim, right?"

The man raised his head and said in a deep voice, "Yes, I am Tohlim. You were only twelve or thirteen when I met you, sir, and I did not think you would remember. I am honored."

Yotalu smiled. "That's right. It was before I reached manhood. That was long ago, but it seems to me that the mine was kept in much better shape while you were the supervisor."

A complex medley of emotions flitted across Tohlim's face, but

Yotalu's expression remained unchanged. It was the Aquafaese who discovered and developed this mine that produced the salt that had provided much of the kingdom's wealth for centuries. And it was Yotalu's father, Governor Ohan, who had ordered them to abandon their traditional methods of operation and adopt the Zolian style of using war slaves as expendable labor. This had left a bitter taste in the mouths of the local people. Yotalu must have known all this, yet there he stood, quietly ignoring the feelings betrayed by the old man's face.

He's more capable than I realized, Makokan thought. Aquafa formed the westernmost frontier of the expanding Zolian Empire, and he'd judged Yotalu too soft and delicate for the responsibilities of a governor's son. But perhaps he was one of those who ruled not through force but through kindness. Or maybe his gentle demeanor masked a bold decisiveness.

I wonder if it's true that he went alone to the King of Aquafa to ask for his niece's hand in marriage.

Makokan had assumed the tale was fabricated to dispel images of Yotalu's father as a cruel conqueror and portray him instead as a magnanimous ruler who paid proper respect to the King of Aquafa. Now, however, he wasn't sure. He and Hohsalle had stayed at Yotalu's hall last night. Not only had his wife and son seemed cheerful and content, but the hall itself, while Zolian in structure, incorporated certain features of Aquafaese design. It was far airier and more inviting than the residences of other Zolians, including the governor's.

Yotalu was not one to vaunt his authority as the second son of a prince elector. He always addressed Hohsalle with the courtesy befitting those of high rank. *He's a man to be valued*, Makokan thought as he gazed at Yotalu's aquiline profile. He just might be able to curb his elder brother, Utalu, who'd inherited his father's arrogant and overbearing nature. If so, he would be a key link in bridging the gap between Zol and Aquafa. *He's not just practical; he's bold and flexible, too. It was wise to bring Hohsalle to the mine before reporting this crisis to the priest-doctors.*

Their Aquafaese guide evidently realized this as well, for there was no trace of sarcasm in his voice as he responded to Yotalu. "You are too kind, sir. My management of the mine was never adequate, but I am truly honored that you remember it."

Yotalu smiled and turned to Hohsalle. "Are you acquainted with Tohlim?" he asked.

"Of course. I may be an Otawalle outlander who only cares about medicine, but I visited Aquafa frequently as a child."

Yotalu nodded, his expression impenetrable. "I suppose you would have."

Makokan frowned. *So I'm the only one who doesn't know him?*

Hohsalle caught sight of Makokan's face and grinned. "It's your first time meeting Tohlim, I take it? He was once the supervisor of the salt mine and knows everything about it. A real living encyclopedia. We couldn't have a better guide."

Tohlim smiled and bowed. "It has been a while, sir. Your praise is undeserved, but I thank you. It will be my great pleasure to guide you through the Gem of Aquafa."

Hohsalle smiled. "Thank you."

※

Makokan found the dark shaft's size surprising. A ceiling of glistening black rock towered above, and a wide road ran deep into the darkness ahead.

Water dripped slowly into a cask from the end of what appeared to be a gutter that extended along the tunnel wall. After glancing at the salt-encrusted barrel, Tohlim turned to Yotalu. "Forgive my impertinence, but would you like me to supervise the brine until you have things more under control?"

Yotalu nodded. "I was about to ask you if you would do just that. While it will be hard to replace the slaves, the worst blow was the loss of everyone who knew how to process salt. If you could find some men for us, I'll convince my father and brother to hire them and make sure they're adequately paid."

Tohlim bowed his head. "Of course. It would be my pleasure."

Hohsalle gazed about the tunnel, apparently oblivious to this exchange. Although wood frames supported the tunnel at strategic points, the majority of it was bare rock. In the torchlight, ribbons of glittering white streaked the black surface like a crystalline glaze.

"Salt is a strange thing." Tohlim's voice echoed hollowly. "In some places, it emerges in stripes like this, while in others it appears as crystal droplets that bloom like flowers. And far below, it forms great quartz-like pillars. Salt dwells within the depths of the earth in a surprising variety of forms." In his hand, he held not a torch but a large glass-paned lantern that cast a steady light on their surroundings.

"That's a nice lantern. Was it made for the salt mine?" Hohsalle asked.

Tohlim smiled. "Yes," he replied. After giving Hohsalle a quick glance, he added, "The oil in this lamp lasts exactly six malu. That's about six hours. In the past, that was how long the mine workers stayed underground. Even when cut off from the sun, they could tell from the amount of oil consumed how much time they had left before they needed to quit." Tohlim didn't look back at Yotalu. Makokan believed his words would have ceased to be a simple explanation and become a criticism if he had. Anger emanated from the elderly man like a soundless vibration.

After some time, the group arrived at a yawning hole encircled by a railing. "This is the shaft to the lower levels," Tohlim stated. "Rock salt and brine are hoisted up from below with a pulley."

Makokan peered down, resting his hand on the railing. Gooseflesh rose on his cheeks. He couldn't see the bottom, only the ladder extending endlessly into the blackness. A thick rope suspended from a pulley on the ceiling swayed faintly in some barely perceptible draft of air. The end of it wasn't visible.

"We're not going to climb down that ladder, are we?" he whispered.

Hohsalle laughed. "What? Are you scared?"

Makokan stared at him. "Who wouldn't be?"

Hohsalle raised an eyebrow. "I'm not." He sounded so unperturbed that the others regarded him with surprise.

"I'm not particularly looking forward to climbing down there myself," Yotalu admitted. He turned to the officer. "There ought to be lifelines."

"Yes, sir, right here." The officer took some leather belts that were hanging over the fence and handed one to each of them.

"Down to the third level, right?" Tohlim asked, and the officer nodded. Tohlim checked the length of the lifelines, then fixed the belt around his waist with practiced movements and clipped the metal hook on it to a ring attached to the end of a lifeline. "Allow me to go first. Climb down after me and be careful not to slip. The rungs are covered in salt." He looked at Makokan. "Metal corrodes quite swiftly in the salt mine, but wood lasts a very long time."

Tohlim climbed down the ladder with the nimbleness of a younger man. Makokan sighed and followed after him cautiously. Hohsalle, who came next, must have been telling the truth, for he showed not the slightest hesitation.

A cold draft blew up from the hole, smelling of the tide. Makokan wondered if this was what it smelled like at the bottom of the ocean. The faint scent of offal stung his nostrils. There was another smell intermingling with it that he couldn't place. *Horse? But why?*

Just then, Tohlim's voice rose from below. "You left the horse down here, did you?"

The officer's voice floated down from above. "Yes."

As he passed the second level, Makokan saw a horse craning its neck anxiously to look at them.

"It turns the pulley," Tohlim explained. "Poor creature. It will never see the light of day again."

Something white flashed at the edge of the hole. "A cat." There was a smile in Tohlim's voice. "When you keep a horse in the mine, you'll get rats coming after its fodder. The cats come and go as they please. They helped make the harsh conditions easier to bear when I worked here."

Hearing that there were rats, Makokan glanced up at Hohsalle. "It shouldn't be a problem," Hohsalle remarked calmly. "We're a long way from any towns or settlements. Still, we'd better make sure all the luggage is examined to prevent any stowaways from leaving the mine." Tohlim and Yotalu made no comment on this and merely continued down the ladder.

Finally, Makokan heard Tohlim announce, "We're almost there." Then he disappeared.

Makokan reached one foot gingerly off the end of the ladder. His foot touched solid ground, and he relaxed as he stepped off the last rung. Beads of cold sweat trickled down his nape and ran along his spine.

That's better. It's good to have the hard earth under my feet.

He tried to forget that he would have to climb up that same ladder to get out again. Behind him, he heard the hard footsteps of Hohsalle and the others walking on the stone floor. The echoes suggested that this chamber, too, was huge, but there was only thick shadow beyond the light cast by Tohlim's lantern.

"Are there any torches?" Makokan asked.

"Yes, in the wall brackets," Tohlim replied. "Just a moment, please." Instead of lighting the torches, however, he took a long slender pole off a hook on the wall. Something flapped loosely at the tip, which was long enough to reach the ceiling.

For wiping away soot? Makokan wondered. Tohlim lit the end and, raising the pole up high, brushed the flames along the rock ceiling, as if stroking it. The burning tip occasionally flared brighter. He continued until he had brushed it across the entire expanse. "It looks all right," he said finally, then lowered the pole and extinguished the flames.

"Were you burning off flammable gases?" Hohsalle asked.

Tohlim looked back at him. "Yes. It must be done meticulously on this level to prevent disaster. In my father's day, the chambers once burned for months."

Hohsalle looked up at the dark ceiling. "It didn't seem like much gas pooled there."

"No. I'd say they must have burned it off about four or five days ago."

Makokan's eyes narrowed. *The last report was fourteen days ago, and the officer said that it indicated nothing out of the ordinary. Whatever happened here must have occurred in the last five days.*

Tohlim lit the torches, and a glow spread through the chamber. Yotalu drew in his breath audibly at the sight revealed before them. Bodies lay sprawled across the floor, stretching as far as they could see.

"It doesn't smell as bad as I would have expected, considering the number of bodies," Hohsalle remarked as though to himself. "Perhaps the saline content of the air is denser in the lower levels." He stared for a moment at the chamber, perhaps contemplating something, then turned to Tohlim. "Would you lend me your lantern?"

Tohlim handed it to him. Hohsalle walked with it over to the closest body and knelt to examine it closely.

"Is it black wolf fever?" Yotalu asked.

Hohsalle nodded. "Probably. Of course, I cannot say for sure yet, but the signs are very similar to those on the corpses we saw above." He stood and addressed the officer. "Will you take us to the place?"

The man nodded and moved deeper into the chamber, carefully stepping around the corpses. All were shackled at the ankle and chained to the wall by iron stakes driven deep into the rock. The slaves had no chance to escape when the beasts attacked. The thought of their hopeless terror made Makokan feel sick, and he clenched his fists tight.

"Here it is…" The officer pointed to an empty spot between two corpses, a gap like the sort left after a tooth was knocked out. The chain attached to the stake in the wall was broken.

"No ordinary man could have done that," Tohlim said.

Hohsalle looked up at Makokan and smiled. "Go on. Pull it and see. You're strong enough to snap a horse's neck. You just might be able to do it."

Makokan took the lantern from his mohalu and knelt to inspect the chain. One of the iron links had stretched and broke. Although the chain was rusty from the brine, when he gave it a tug, it felt solid and heavy in his hand. He braced his knees and wrapped the chain around his wrist, then leaned his body weight against it and pulled as hard as he could, but it didn't budge.

"So not even you can do it?"

Makokan shook his head. "No, not even me. It might break if a horse pulled it, I suppose." He crouched on one knee and shone the light carefully across the floor. One glance at the dirty straw scattered across the space was enough to tell him that someone had been sleeping here. He looked at the officer, who stared back at him sullenly. Although it was now obvious that the officer had known this all along and had been making excuses, Yotalu didn't reprimand him. Instead, he gazed grimly at the chain.

"If he couldn't manage it alone, perhaps someone came to his aid."

Makokan grunted. "That's true." He couldn't tell what had happened here, but he did spy a drop of blood on the floor. The slave must have been injured. Makokan raised his head to tell Yotalu, when his eyes met Hohsalle's. They bid him to stay quiet. Only an experienced tracker could discern that single bit of blood on the black rock floor, yet Hohsalle had apparently noticed it some time ago.

If the slave here was bitten, too, he must have squeezed that blood out himself, Makokan thought. The bites he'd seen so far were all too shallow to bleed much.

But if he was bitten, then why didn't he die?

Makokan looked at Hohsalle again. His eyes seemed empty, like his soul had left his body. Doubtless, he was concentrating on something. Makokan wished he could see what was spinning round on the other side of that smooth forehead.

The officer removed a sheaf of paper from his robe and began searching for the number on the chain in the list of slaves and their homelands. The dim light made it difficult to read, for he ran his finger from the top of the list and checked the chains of the other slaves nearby. Then his finger stopped. "It appears to have been Van of the Gansa clan."

Makokan felt Yotalu jerk beside him.

"Did you say Van of the Gansa?"

The officer looked up, evidently surprised by Yotalu's tone. "Yes, sir."

Yotalu pointed at the papers. "There are remarks written on the back. Does it say where he was captured?"

The officer hurriedly brought the light back on the records. Squinting, he read out the words. "He was seized during a battle on the banks of the Kashuna River."

Yotalu took the list from him to confirm it, then clicked his tongue as he gazed down at the mangled chain. "Of all the..." Noticing the officer's questioning look, he said with a groan, "You were just transferred from the southern forces, so I suppose you wouldn't know much about the war here in the west. Still, you must have heard of the Lone Antlers."

The officer's eyes widened. "Yes... Oh, I see. Were those crazed warriors of the Gansa?"

Yotalu nodded. "If he was captured at Kashuna River, then there's no mistake. The man who was shackled here was none other than Broken Antler Van, the leader of the Lone Antlers." Hohsalle and Makokan clearly had trouble following this exchange, so Yotalu explained. "The Gansa is a clan from the Toga Mountains. Their Pyuika Riders caused us no end of trouble. It's just a small clan, but it took us a long time to subdue them. Have you never heard of the Lone Antlers?"

"I have," Hohsalle replied. "They attacked out of nowhere, riding their fleet-footed pyuika."

Yotalu smiled ruefully. "Had they only fought like that in the mountains of their homeland, which they know like the back of their hand, it wouldn't have been so surprising. But the Lone Antlers never shied away from assaulting our fortresses in the forests or out on the plains. They were complete madmen and as cunning as foxes."

His eyes flicked to the broken chain. "Van was their leader. He stood out from the rest because the left branch of the antlers that crowned his helmet had been snapped off. Our soldiers grumbled that arrows never seemed to touch him, even though he always rode at the head of his men."

Hohsalle, who'd been listening intently, remarked, "You seem to know a lot about this man, even though he was only the leader of a small group from an obscure mountain clan. He should have been no more than a thorn in your little finger."

Bitterness surfaced in Yotalu's eyes, then faded again. "He killed two of my best commanders. And he seems to possess a devil's luck. The Lone Antlers were wiped out at the battle of Kashuna River, yet he alone survived. They told me he just stood there like a dead tree amid a mound of bodies." The echoes of Yotalu's voice sounded through the cavern, and silence descended over the group as they stared at the empty spot on the floor.

The corners of Hohsalle's mouth twitched. "And here, once again," he murmured, "he alone survived in a heap of corpses." His tone changed. "Was he a big man? Someone who looked strong enough to break this chain?"

Yotalu shook his head. "No. From what I hear, he wasn't large, but he was lean and as fierce and daring as a wolf."

Hohsalle grunted. No one spoke for a while, each lost in their own thoughts in the cadaver-strewn mine chamber. A slow smile spread across Hohsalle's face. He raised his head and looked at Makokan. "Could you trail him?"

Makokan frowned. "No. That's impossible."

"But I thought you learned how to track."

Makokan sighed. "It's true that my father taught me the skill, but I haven't tried it for over twenty years. I don't have enough experience. Besides…" He looked around the cavern before continuing. "It's too late. My father used to say that tracks are living things. Traces fade with time. You can't follow the trail of a slave who escaped days ago. The fastest way to catch him would be to send out a search party." Makokan found the need for an explanation puzzling. His young master knew all this. So why had he bothered to ask?

Yotalu smiled. "You need not worry. We can handle this without your help. In such cases, we take a two-pronged approach."

"Two-pronged?" Hohsalle inquired.

Yotalu nodded. "Yes. We'll send out an official notice and a search party, and we'll also call in experts to follow the trail from where he escaped." He maintained a faint smile as he faced Hohsalle and Tohlim. "The Aquafa Slave Trackers have often aided us with their superior hunting skills."

Tohlim kept his mouth firmly shut, but his expression was grim.

3
History of the Disease

Yotalu's hall was situated in the suburbs of Kazan. The architecture was of Zolian design with black roof tiles and white walls, but the inner garden sported Aquafaese landscaping. A floral fragrance wafted through the open windows. Water drawn from the great Mahalu River that flowed through the plains gurgled in the channel, keeping the plants well hydrated.

Makokan sat by the window overlooking the garden and gazed absently at the soft purple shadows cast by the late-afternoon light. He could hear the gentle sound of Hohsalle's breathing. The young master had managed to keep his eyes open until a few moments ago. Now he was slumped in his chair, fast asleep.

And no wonder.

They had left at dawn yesterday for the salt mine, and after returning to Yotalu's hall, Hohsalle had gone straight back to his clinic in Kazan, refusing Yotalu's invitation to stay and rest. The corpses were already there, and Milalle, Hohsalle's assistant and bedmate for many years, had begun working on them with the help of several other aides.

Hohsalle's clinic sported the unlikely name of Chimya Tolosse, Nest of Little People. It was built through the kind offices of the governor and contained three research wings and a residence where Hohsalle lived with his assistants. When in Kazan, he usually secluded himself there for days.

As soon as the group had arrived, Hohsalle tried to make for the building where the corpses were delivered. However, Milalle had seized him by the elbow and steered him toward the dining hall instead, ignoring his protests. The other aides had long since finished their evening meal, and the room was quiet, but Milalle had lit a fire in the hearth and placed a pot of meat-and-onion stew in the coals to keep it warm.

Watching the color slowly return to his mohalu's face as he savored honey-sweetened tea and tender chunks of meat, Makokan had been reminded that Hohsalle could not do without Milalle. Three years Hohsalle's senior, Milalle was plump, short, and not especially beautiful, but she handled the temperamental Hohsalle with the cheerfulness and patience of an older sister. She was Otawalle, but of common birth. Meanwhile, Hohsalle was one of the Sacred. The disparity in their social ranks was a difference akin to that between heaven and earth. Yet when Milalle believed deference a hindrance, she scolded Hohsalle without reservation and spoke her mind. Perhaps that's why he always seemed so at ease with her, like sloughing off a layer of torn skin.

Last night, however, they were anything but relaxed. Hohsalle had seemed to be in a tremendous rush, and Milalle, too, was unusually agitated, talking between every mouthful. The content of their conversation had left Makokan far behind. Still, it was clear that the reappearance of mittsual had filled them with excitement. It was almost as if they'd been waiting for this to happen. Makokan found this so puzzling that he had to ask them why, even though he knew they'd make fun of him.

As he'd expected, Hohsalle had quipped that he wouldn't understand even after an explanation, but Milalle said, "On the contrary. I think you would understand very well, Makokan." She poured him more tea as she continued. "People fear ghosts because they are difficult to pin down. If they had bodies and could be captured, no one would be afraid of them. Diseases are similar. Once we can identify a particular illness, we can search for ways to treat it." Her eyes glowed. "So of course we're excited! After two hundred and fifty years, we've acquired bodies infected with mittsual! I can't wait to tell everyone in the apothecary section at the academy. We need to draw up a plan and get to work!"

"You mean you can make medicine from dead bodies?"

Milalle opened her mouth to answer and then frowned. "Hmm, now that *will* be hard to explain. To put it very simply, those bodies are like treasure chests. There may be as many as three types of medicine locked away inside them."

"Really? Three?"

"Yes. Firstly, those corpses house the disease agents that cause mittsual. If we can identify them, we may be able to weaken or kill the agents to make a less potent version of the infection. That alone would be wonderful. Administering it to people would build their resistance to mittsual. Additionally, once we've isolated the agents, we can search for substances that suppress or eliminate the illness. In other words, we could develop an anti-mittsual drug. It's also possible that the victims of black wolf fever might have developed unique substances in their body to combat the disease agents. We call these antibodies. If we identify these, they could be used to develop a serum to help those infected with mittsual fight it off."

Makokan frowned. "But the corpses you brought back are people who lost their battles with the disease. It killed them. Doesn't that mean their 'antibodies' or whatever you call them didn't work?"

Milalle's eyes widened. "Oh, Makokan! What a smart question!" Then she laughed. "Oh dear. I'm sorry. I didn't mean it that way."

"It's all right. I'm used to it."

"It was just such a good inquiry, you see. When developing medicines, the issue isn't really whether the antibodies worked or not, but rather that they were made by someone else. You're right, though, that the effectiveness of any medicine built from antibodies obtained from these corpses would be very limited. Even if it helped suppress the occurrence of the disease or mitigated some of the symptoms, there would still be no guarantee that a person who survived wouldn't catch it again if they were bitten a second time."

Milalle's eyes gleamed. "A serum formulated from the blood of someone who actually survived mittsual would be far better than anything made from those who died of it. Of course, it would still be limited in strength and duration."

So that's why Hohsalle asked me if I could track that Lone Antler. Makokan stared at Milalle. She had a distant look, like a little girl daydreaming. "But aren't you afraid?" he questioned. "This is work to develop medicine, but you're still dealing with mittsual."

Milalle grinned. "Sure, I'm afraid. But think of it this way: I'm about to meet a legendary enemy, and one that's returned from the dead. I can't wait."

At this, Hohsalle raised his brows and grimaced. "You hear that, Makokan? Now, that's a true hero. Sometimes I think she's more a man than I am."

Milalle snorted. "If you're done eating, let's get started," she said. Grabbing Hohsalle's elbow again, she steered him in the direction of the research wing.

Makokan couldn't guess how those two had spent the rest of the night, but it was clear that Hohsalle didn't sleep a wink. When Makokan had visited a little after noon to convey Yotalu's request that Hohsalle come to his hall, the young master looked annoyed and told Makokan to go instead. Makokan had finally convinced him to come but wondered if he should have told Yotalu that Hohsalle wasn't well and let him sleep instead.

Thick slices of cake and cups of aromatic tea were laid out on the large round table by his side. Makokan had devoured his down to the last crumb, but Hohsalle only sipped his tea, never touching the cake.

The high-pitched warble of a songbird reached Makokan's ears, gradually drawing closer until it was right by the window.

Hohsalle jerked, then blinked. After rubbing his eyes, he gave a sheepish smile when he realized what roused him. The two men leaned out of the window. A boy of about ten was walking by with a large birdcage swinging from his hand. It was Yotalu's younger son.

"Sir Olimu?" Hohsalle called out, and the boy glanced up. He blushed when he saw who it was. Olimu was half Zolian and half Aquafaese. Last night, Makokan had thought that he looked more Zolian, perhaps because of his black hair. Now, however, his eyes and high-bridged nose made his resemblance to his mother, and thus his royal Aquafa lineage, quite clear.

Hohsalle smiled. "What manner of bird is that?" he asked.

"A minalu," the boy responded, cheeks still flushed.

Makokan leaned out farther to get a better look. Minalu could be trained to sing beautifully, and in Aquafa, people regularly held contests to see which performed the best. Recalling how his father had taught his minalu to sing, Makokan smiled. "That's a beauty. But they're hard to train, aren't they?"

The boy nodded. His nervousness before his father's guests was so obvious that Makokan took pity on him. "Forgive us for interrupting you. Please continue on to the aviary." Olimu bowed his head with evident relief and hurried off.

"It's strange," Makokan said quietly. "He looks just like Lord Yotalu, yet there's a clear resemblance to his mother around his eyes and nose."

Hohsalle's mouth curved upward. "And I suppose that brings up some complex feelings for you."

Vexed by his mohalu's tone of voice, Makokan retorted, "And what about you, sir?"

Hohsalle yawned. "Were I to tell you what I thought, it would take all night."

Makokan was about to reply when there was a knock on the door.

"Come in," Hohsalle said. The door opened and Yotalu entered, followed by a servant bearing a tray with a flask of wine and cups. The servant poured the wine, then bowed and exited.

Yotalu lowered himself into a chair across from Hohsalle. After picking up a glass of wine, he invited the two men to do the same. He took a sip, then looked intently at Hohsalle. "Are you all right?" he asked. "You look very pale."

Hohsalle smiled faintly. "I'm fine. I just haven't slept. You need not worry that I've contracted black wolf fever from poking around in those cadavers."

Yotalu gave a quick, involuntary smile, then immediately turned sober. "How is it progressing? Have you found anything?"

Hohsalle shook his head. "No. I'm afraid that it's still too soon. Yesterday, I spoke as though we had already diagnosed the illness, but the records are all ancient, and we must rule out the possibility of any other disease first."

"I see... I apologize for interrupting by summoning you here, but I just received a response from my father and brother to the message I sent last night." Yotalu explained that Governor Ohan and his eldest son, Utalu, had set out for a conference with the emperor in the capital. Fortunately, however, they had not yet traveled far from Kazan. "They both take this matter very seriously. I knew nothing about black wolf fever, but they seem to be well informed of its dangers. They cautioned me that any mistake in the way we handle this could spell disaster and urged me to consult you about what to do."

Hohsalle nodded. "I will do everything in my power. My plan was to inform the Sacred Territory about the outbreak and request advice, but I didn't wish to do so until I'd received your father's permission. For that reason, I have not sent any missive yet."

It was not information that could be shared lightly. If news of the disease spread, it could throw the populace into a panic and make the realm vulnerable to invasion. But when he heard Hohsalle's plan, Yotalu smiled. "We would wholeheartedly welcome the support of the Otawalle. After all, we know nothing of this disease. Sir Lona is of the same opinion. He told me to consult you first."

Hohsalle blinked. "Is that so? I am very grateful."

"I asked my father for his opinion as well. Considering the urgency of this situation, he cannot avoid telling the court priest-doctors, but he and my brother will know how to handle them diplomatically while listening to the emperor. In the meantime, my father told me to follow your instructions and requested that you share the wisdom of the Academy of Deeper Learning. We hope that you will guide us in this matter."

A grin slowly spread across Hohsalle's face. "His Excellency, Governor Ohan, is indeed a decisive man."

Yotalu smiled wryly. "Yes. That is one area where my father never shows his age. I have much to learn from him." His face turned grave. "Do you have any idea why the disease revived at this time? My father and brother were very perplexed by this. According to my father's letter, there have been no reported incidences of black wolf fever in over two centuries."

Hohsalle nodded. "It is just as your father said. In fact, the last recorded epidemic occurred two hundred and forty-seven years ago, and no other has been reported since. It's possible that some individuals have contracted it since then, but no records indicate scores of people dying from it."

Yotalu frowned. "Then why now?"

Hohsalle stroked his chin slowly with his slender fingers. "I don't know. If we investigate, we may find the reason. But many things about plagues elude us. They appear out of nowhere and kill hundreds of people, then fizzle out and vanish just as abruptly." His mouth curved in a bitter expression. "It caused the downfall of my people's kingdom, so you can be sure that my ancestors have studied it thoroughly. Yet there are still many unanswered questions."

Yotalu gazed at him. "Please share with me what you know. In as much detail as you can."

Hohsalle leaned back in his chair. "Actually, there isn't that much to tell, but I will try. Where should I start? Have you ever heard the *Ballad of the Fall of Otawalle*?"

"No."

"Well, it's an epic tale that begins with the line, 'Bringing black shadows from the white mountain peaks.' *Black shadows* refers to wolves with glistening black fur unlike that of any wolves around the Otawalle capital. The decline of Otawalle supposedly began when noblemen went hunting in the Toga Mountains for sport and brought back such wolves. The first ones probably didn't carry the disease. Enchanted by their magnificent pelts and clever faces, the noblemen vied with one another to collect them. Beast merchants and hunters took to capturing and selling the wolves to the noblemen. According to historical records, some bred them with dogs. Black wolves were in such demand that there were merchants who specialized in them."

Hohsalle raised his glass and took a sip of wine. "One spring, a rumor began to spread. Black wolf merchants who'd been bitten by the animals fell victim to a strange and fearsome disease. They came down with high fevers and went into convulsions that made their limbs as hard and stiff as boards. After they developed rashes, they died within a night and a day.

"When he heard of this, the Divine King of Otawalle banned all black wolf trade. Soon after, the illness appeared to mysteriously vanish, but when summer approached, it emerged again. And this time, the victims perished in droves, even though they had not been bitten by wolves."

Yotalu listened without moving a muscle.

"It was a hot and muggy summer. The disease started in the poorest districts, where people lived crammed together, spreading throughout the capital from there. The Academy of Deeper Learning physicians guessed that the disease had transferred from wolves to the fleas and ticks that sucked their blood, then to rats. The result was a rapid increase in carriers. By the time the capital took to exterminating rodents and pests, thousands of people had already perished."

"And then?" Yotalu asked, voice a whisper. "How did they get rid of it?"

Hohsalle held his gaze steady. "They abandoned the capital."

"They what? Oh. So that's when the Grand Edict of the Exodus was issued?"

"Yes. That tale dates from this period. The last king of Otawalle, Takaluhalu, deserted the capital, which had prospered for a thousand years. As I'm sure you know, the kingdom's main cities were located on three islands in a large inland sea. This afforded excellent defense against invasions, but the enclosed environment is also thought to be one reason the plague became so lethal. At the same time, it turned out to be a very effective means for sealing it off. The king left behind the sick and those who refused to leave, destroyed the long bridge between the capital and the mainland, and abandoned his own people—all to save those not infected."

Yotalu, his face taut, stared at Hohsalle as he carried on dispassionately. "The scene described in the ancient records reads like a farce. The pale-skinned Otawalle took off their clothes, shaved the hair from their bodies, and walked in single file across the bridge, naked and weeping. Those left behind met a cruel end with nothing funny about it.

"Takaluhalu turned his back on his people. Perhaps he concluded that he was not fit to rule. He moved the capital here, to the trading city of Kazan, which had miraculously escaped the plague, and relinquished his crown to Kazan's young ruler. In that way, the Kingdom of Aquafa was born of our flight from black wolf fever."

When Hohsalle finished, the only sound was the rustle of the curtains brushing the wall in the breeze.

"If there is any salvation to be found in this tale," Hohsalle finally concluded, "it's the knowledge that the disease does not spread from person to person and that the symptoms manifest very quickly after the victim, whether man or beast, is bitten by an animal."

Yotalu nodded. "That's true. Otherwise, people who have contracted the disease might move about and spread it unknowingly." He cocked his head. "But if the wolves carried such a virulent illness, why didn't they all die on their way to Otawalle?"

Hohsalle's eyes lit up. "Excellent point!" he said before laughing. "Forgive me, but that is a very perceptive question. As you've noted, some beasts that carry a sickness do not experience symptoms. The same appears to be true for humans. Some people fall prey to a certain disease, while others do not. And of those who succumb, some die very quickly, while others survive. I believe that within this incongruity lies a clue to the nature of disease."

"I see," Yotalu replied. He looked as though he'd recalled something and said, "Speaking of surviving, what about that slave who escaped? Are you sure there's no chance he will spread the sickness?"

Hohsalle raised his brows. "I don't think so, but we can't be certain of anything. We haven't even determined if this is black wolf fever. However, judging from what we saw here, I do not think it will spread from person to person." He rubbed his cheek. "From the state of the bodies, it appears that all the victims were exposed, developed symptoms, and died almost simultaneously. If one person had been infected first followed by a gradual spread, someone would have had time to inform us of the outbreak."

Yotalu nodded slowly. "Yes, that makes sense."

"Plus, this disease is virulent. Based on what we saw in the salt mine, the symptoms manifested very quickly after infection, and almost everyone died. Now, the slaves undoubtedly possessed low resistance because of their weakened constitutions, but the disease also felled the slave keepers. Despite this, no one working at the mine since the incident has exhibited signs of the illness. It would therefore appear that the infection was not caused by fleas or ticks. Nor does it seem likely that it was wind-borne."

"In other words," Yotalu said, "at this stage, the disease only propagates through bites from a beast. It sounds as though the best preventative measure may be to hunt down the animals carrying the disease. What do you think?"

"Yes, that is the logical conclusion. Exterminating rats and mice would be prudent, too."

"Ah, now that will pose more of a challenge." Yotalu stroked his chin. "By the way, we've recently received complaints about sheep being attacked by wolves or ossam. We're not sure which. If there's a possibility they carry the sickness, we'll need to act immediately."

Hohsalle shook his head. "Hunting down wild dogs or wolves might have some effect, but I think it will be hard to prevent this disease with such a random approach."

Yotalu frowned. "Why?"

"If the wolves or ossam that set upon the sheep were carriers, the shepherds would have been bitten and died, yet you've received no reports of such developments, correct?"

Yotalu's eyes widened. "You mean that rather than hunting ossam indiscriminately, we need to determine which ones are the carriers and exterminate them?"

"Yes."

Yotalu's face clouded over, and he muttered half to himself, "In that case, I'll have to order Malji to find and cull the beasts while also tracking Broken Antler Van."

"Malji?" Hohsalle repeated.

Yotalu raised his face and looked at him. "An Aquafa Slave Tracker. Do you know him? There are several good ones, but he's their chief and one of the best."

"Yes, I know him," Hohsalle replied with a smile. "Malji. It's been a long time. If you send Tohlim, please allow me to go with him."

"What?" Makokan interjected, surprised by this sudden comment. "But I thought you needed to examine the bodies?"

"The results of our present efforts on that front won't be clear for several days, and the corpses still in the mine won't decompose terribly quickly. Besides, it will take at least one or two days to bring them out of the mine."

"But you haven't slept."

"I'll get some proper rest tonight."

"But it's getting colder, and the trackers live in the mountains."

Hohsalle clapped Makokan on the shoulder. "You're my servant, not my mother. Stop worrying."

He shifted his gaze to Yotalu and said solemnly, "I told you that some people who are infected succumb while others survive, but we cannot predict who will fall into which category. Kingdoms and nations are irrelevant when it comes to disease. I am a physician, and as such, I have sworn to devote my life to saving people's lives."

To Makokan, this statement had come out of nowhere, but Yotalu appeared to comprehend Hohsalle's intention, because he nodded gravely. "Feel free to accompany Tohlim. If there is anyone who can save this land from black wolf fever, it is you. Please let nothing else distract you. Focus on eradicating it."

4
Subterranean Streams

Aquafa was located northwest of what was previously the Ancient Kingdom of Otawalle. Long, cold winters and short summers made much of it a hard land for growing crops, but salt produced from the mine, the Gem of Aquafa, and the high-quality furs taken from the beasts that lived in its densely forested mountains attracted merchants and traders.

Although the cold could be severe, southern Aquafa was blessed with the broad Yukata Plains, renowned for the horses bred there. Known as ahfal, or fire horses, the creatures possessed coats as red as flame, as well as fierce temperaments and tremendous stamina despite their small statures. Once, they had borne the feared Aquafaese cavalry, but when the kingdom was subjugated, the Zolians requisitioned the ahfal stud horses. The empire had also turned Aquafa's grassy plains into pastures for sheep brought by Zolian immigrants. It was these shepherds who had recently been plagued by the ossam attacks Yotalu mentioned.

The Ahfal Oma, the People of the Fire Horse who once populated the Yukata Plains, had been scattered. Some now lived in the highlands with Makokan's people, the Ofal Oma, the People of the Yukata Mountains, while others made their livings by raising horses for caravans. Many had moved northwest and struggled to eke out a living in unfamiliar lands, unwilling to settle in towns or cities. Hardly any had moved to Oki in the north. The Oki region had ever been a point of convergence for nomadic reindeer herders from different areas. However, those who lived in forested mountain areas were only semi-nomadic and supplemented reindeer herding with hunting. These people were more accepting of the Zolian immigrants, many of whom were also reindeer herders, and they had begun to intermarry extensively. For the Ahfal Oma, who continued to nurse a bitter hatred for the Zolians, this fact made the Oki region a place to be shunned.

Oki was not the only place populated by people who supplemented reindeer herding with hunting and gathering. One such group lived southeast of Oki. Its people were the slave trackers Yotalu referred to, and to reach their settlement, the three men had to follow a narrow trail that cut through a deep forest. Tohlim rode in silence through the trees, but when they emerged onto a rolling grassland, he glanced at Hohsalle. "Does Malji still visit the Sacred Territory?" he asked.

Makokan looked from Tohlim to his young master in surprise. *What? The chief tracker we're to meet frequents the Sacred Territory? Really?*

"I believe he's left that up to his son," Hohsalle said, ignoring Makokan's evident confusion. "At least, that's what I heard. I doubt he comes much anymore. The last time I met him was about three years ago."

Hohsalle glanced at Makokan, his eyebrows cocked. "Honestly. You were born into a family that served the Inner Circle. Didn't you follow any of our conversation yesterday? Who else would the Aquafa Slave Trackers be but the Molfah?"

Makokan started. "Oh… You mean these slave trackers we're going to see are the King's Net?"

He knew there was a clan entrusted with capturing thieves and spies when the king ruled Aquafa. People still regarded their tracking skills with awe. They seemed to have thrown an inescapable net over the entire kingdom and came and went so swiftly, it was as if they were invisible.

Tohlim sighed. "The King's Net," he muttered. "I haven't heard that moniker in a long time." He peered up at Makokan. "But it would not do to use it in front of them."

Makokan was about to ask why, when Hohsalle spoke from beside him. "They've been forced to hunt escaped slaves since Otawalle and Aquafa came under Zolian rule. It would only annoy them to hear us use their old name." There was a glint of irony in his eyes. "While on the one hand, they were the king's trusted trackers, they also employed their skills at the service of the Otawalle. Many Molfah worked for that stuffy old Inner Circle of the Sacred Territory, which you declined to serve. Yotalu's a clever man. He's fully aware of that connection, but still let us come."

Makokan scowled. *So that's what that exchange yesterday was all about.* He felt ashamed for only realizing it now. "Do you still have links with them?" he inquired.

Hohsalle laughed. "Of course. Malji in particular. His eldest son has been seriously ill since childhood. My grandfather treats him personally, keeping him alive. In that sense, we've maintained an intimate relationship."

A chill spread through Makokan's chest. The Sacred Ones of Otawalle still covertly used the trackers of Aquafa whom they had once governed. *In other words...* The old relationships of control continued unbroken. Even after Aquafa's subjugation to the Zolian Empire, those bonds had survived like a network of underground streams. If the thin crust of the earth were peeled back, a web of relationships entirely different from those visible above would be exposed—the bonds of the old kingdoms.

And Yotalu knew. He knew, yet prudently suspicious and trusting, he used both the Molfah and the Otawalle for the Empire of Zol. Makokan shuddered. *Like one spider weaving its web over another's.*

Hohsalle and Tohlim carried on their conversation, seemingly oblivious to Makokan's turmoil.

"Malji is still the chief," Tohlim said. "He's healthy and vigorous and remains a strong leader, but he seemed to age quite suddenly after he lost his wife."

"Is that so? He must be over seventy by now. Are there any other trackers with skills to rival his?"

"As you said, his eldest son has a chronic illness. His second son would have been an excellent heir had he lived, but he died young. His third son is certainly adept, and there are many others who are good trackers." Tohlim paused, gazing off into the distance. Then he quietly added, "But I think Sae is the best of the lot."

Hohsalle blinked. "Sae? A woman?"

"Yes. Malji's eldest daughter. She must be thirty-two or three by now. She married once but came back." Tohlim grinned. "She's a quiet woman, so you wouldn't guess it at first sight, but I think she surpasses even Malji when he was in his prime."

"Really?" A gleam of interest shone in Hohsalle's eyes. "I had no idea such a woman existed."

Tohlim's smile broadened. "The men of the Molfah have to protect their reputation. Even when the credit belongs to Sae, they aren't likely to let on. However…" He scratched his nose. "I once asked her to do some tracking for me and witnessed her abilities firsthand. Quite astonishing." He paused to look directly at Hohsalle. "You wish to keep that slave for yourself rather than give him to the Zolians, don't you, sir?"

Hohsalle raised an eyebrow. "What makes you say that?"

"You noticed the blood where that slave was chained, yet you didn't tell Yotalu."

Hohsalle's face sobered, but then he smiled. "No wonder they call you the king's right-hand man."

Tohlim watched him without responding.

So that's how things are, Makokan thought. *Tohlim has far more influence than he lets on, like someone who controls events from behind the scenes.*

Hohsalle breathed a long sigh. "That slave must have been bitten just like the others. He was bitten, and he survived… You're quite right. To me, he's more valuable than any precious gem."

Tohlim gazed at Hohsalle intently. "He would not be a gem to just anyone. Only in your hands would that diamond in the rough shine."

He took a deep breath and faced the mountains, hazy in the distance. "Sometimes the gods play cruel tricks. To think that death should scorn Broken Antler Van even though he was a Lone Antler."

"Ah, I'd forgotten that," Hohsalle said with a grim look. "The Lone Antlers, a tragic band of men seeking a reason to die."

Tohlim shrugged. "I suppose even the savage mountain people are not immune to despair. The Lone Antlers sought death, not life." He looked at Hohsalle with a faint smile. "Did you know that Van also had another name?"

"No."

Tohlim's smile deepened. "He was called Head Snatcher."

Hohsalle's brows shot up. "Did he behead his victims?"

"No. The name comes from a term used in falcon hunting."

"Ah…"

"Experienced falcons grasp the heads of their prey instead of the back or tail so that it can't escape or fight back. When Broken Antler Van attacked, he always went straight for the leader. The commander could hide behind hundreds of men, but Van always found his way through. He took out the army's head first. That was how he fought."

Hohsalle's eyes shone. "He sounds like quite a character!"

Tohlim nodded. "I've heard he didn't go in for flashy displays of strength. He fought methodically, yet something about him captured people's hearts. I often heard the clansmen around here discussing him. They cheered every time he bested his enemies. The Zolians despised him for the same reason, of course. So when he alone survived the battle of Kashuna River, instead of executing him, they made him a slave and chained him in the depths of the salt mine." Tohlim's eyes narrowed, and he shook his head. "If he's the one who escaped, he won't be easy to catch."

"I see what you mean." Hohsalle grimaced. "I was hoping to avoid making him wary or hostile. If he's as smart as you say, that's going to be a problem. I don't want to complicate things by sending in an inexperienced tracker."

"Yes, that's wise. If so, I recommend that you send Sae. She's an intelligent woman and will know how to handle it."

Hohsalle raised his brows and looked at Tohlim with a hint of a smile in his eyes, as if amused to see this elderly man so taken with a woman. "Well, if you recommend her that highly, I'll take your word for it. Can you arrange it for me?"

5
The Village of the Molfah

The sun, which had never set all summer but instead crawled across the horizon as if reluctant to dip below it, now sank quickly. The mountain slopes had deepened in hue from pale red to purple, and as the three men pushed on, they spied reindeer dotting the landscape. Herds were moving down from the lush summer meadows to the lowlands before the cruel winter snows made passage impossible. The northlands were harsh on plants and trees. The lichens the reindeer preferred took a long time to grow back once eaten, and the herders had no choice but to move slowly along with their flocks.

Being a hard place to grow crops made it a challenging place to eke out a living. Rather than dedicating themselves to a single occupation, the people who resided here mastered several so that they had another to fall back on when one lifeline failed.

From the time they could walk, those born into the Molfah clan were taken into the mountains by the Kuleh, elderly trackers in their twilight years who taught them the skills they would need to survive in the wild. During this training, the Kuleh identified which of their charges were best suited to hunting and which to herding. Hunters would join the Molfah of the Mountains, while herders would join the Molfah of the Plains. This process of selection was the same for girls and boys, but some girls chosen for the mountains moved to the plains when they came of age to marry herders.

The Molfah of the Plains had already come down from the summer highlands to the winter pastures. Tohlim walked inside the stone windbreak that sheltered their settlement, and they bowed their heads respectfully and spoke a few words in greeting. At the sight of his companions, however, the children's eyes grew round, and they stared open-mouthed. A mixture of curiosity and wariness flickered in the faces of the adults. They must have been wondering what prey the Molfah of the Mountains would be asked to hunt this time.

Beyond this settlement, the trail led into the mountains, where the landscape changed dramatically. Autumn had dyed the tree leaves a delicate gold, and the forest glowed in the pale light of the late-afternoon sun. Deer calls echoed occasionally from deep in the woods—*pwoh, pwoh*. The horses plodded along a narrow, almost invisible path, their hooves crunching the fallen leaves. As Tohlim rode along, he kept his eyes on the trees, as though searching for something. Suddenly, he brought his horse to a halt and leaned forward to peer at the slender branch of a larch. Then he turned to his companions and told them to dismount. "It looks like they've camped here this year."

As Makokan alighted from his horse, he asked, "Was there some kind of mark?"

Tohlim looked back at him and nodded. "Yes. You can tell where they've decided to settle by the way they break the branches. But you need to keep in mind countless possible locations. Otherwise, the signs are meaningless." He held his horse firmly by the bit. "From here on, the path will get even narrower. Please be careful not to disturb the underbrush. The Molfah won't like it if we leave tracks."

Makokan frowned. "Then wouldn't it be better to keep riding instead of walking? It would be easier to control our horses that way."

Tohlim's eyes twinkled. "The mark on the branch indicated that there's a trap up ahead. Probably a fine string stretched across the path somewhere at the height of a rider's chest. One touch, and you'll be killed instantly, so be careful."

Makokan closed his mouth and led his horse meekly along the path. After following what appeared to be no more than an animal trail for a while, he caught a whiff of smoke. Dogs barked a moment later; the sound echoed sharply in the air.

Tohlim pulled a small whistle from his robe and blew. The barking dwindled and then ceased.

"Amazing," Makokan murmured.

Tohlim smiled. "Molfah hounds are well trained."

The bushes were likely planted deliberately as a skillful camouflage. Although there seemed to be no end to them, the three men emerged into a broad clearing after only a few more steps. Following close on the heels of Tohlim and Hohsalle, Makokan stopped involuntarily to stare at the scene before him. There were rows of tents pitched in the clearing, yet they blended so smoothly into the surrounding woods that there didn't seem to be anything out of place, either due to their green hue or their deft placement. Even though Makokan spied dogs and people and smoke rising from the tents, it didn't look as if a settlement was there.

Tohlim walked forward, and an elderly woman approached him slowly. She greeted him with a cheerful smile and inclined her head, bending her slightly stooped back. "It is fine weather, Master Tohlim," she said.

Makokan stared at her in surprise. She spoke perfect Otawalle. The old woman turned to smile at him, perhaps amused by his reaction, before bowing low to Hohsalle. "Welcome, Young Master of the Sacred Land."

Hohsalle nodded, returning her smile. "It's been a long time, hasn't it, Mulyo? I'm glad to see you looking so well."

"Thank you. I am fortunate to have most of my teeth still." Then her expression grew serious, and she returned her attention to Tohlim. "I assume you have business with my elder brother."

"Yes. I have an urgent request. May I see him?"

Mulyo's face clouded slightly. "Your timing is a bit unfortunate. He has gone out with the men to hunt autumn bear."

"Ah, I see. When did he leave?"

"Three days ago. If they are quick, he might return tonight, but I'm afraid I cannot predict when he will return."

"Yes, I suppose it will depend on how the hunting goes. Well, it can't be helped. We'll just have to wait."

Mulyo watched Tohlim as he stroked his chin, then asked, "Some of the Kuleh are still here. Would they be of any help?"

Tohlim blinked. "Hmm. It's really something I need to speak to Malji about directly... By the way, did Sae go, too?"

"Sae?" Mulyo raised her brows and laughed. "Sae is here, of course. She may not always behave like one, but she is a woman, you know."

Tohlim grinned as if embarrassed. "That's right. You said that Malji went bear hunting. I really have grown old."

Obviously, she wouldn't be out with the men, Makokan thought. *No matter how skilled, no woman can hunt bear.*

Perhaps Mulyo read Makokan's thoughts, for she smiled at him. "Molfah women do not hunt bear. Not *cannot*—*do* not."

"Because bear belong to the earth," Hohsalle said, and Mulyo nodded. Seeing Makokan's puzzled expression, Hohsalle added, "The Molfah classify all things into those of the earth and those of the wind. Bears and women both belong to the earth, so women don't hunt bear. Men belong to the wind, as do deer and rabbits, so men don't hunt them. Right, Mulyo?"

"Yes, that is correct."

Well, that's a troublesome way to do things, Makokan thought. He understood that every land had its own approach, but in a harsh region like this, such a system would surely make things more complicated and cut down on efficiency.

Mulyo looked up at him. "Does it seem strange to you?"

"Um, well..." Makokan scratched his beard. "If that's your way, then I have no business commenting on it. Still, I can't help thinking that you must miss a lot of game that way."

Mulyo grinned deeply. "We often go hunting together with our husbands or brothers, so it does not matter as long as someone catches something."

"Oh..." Makokan smiled sheepishly. "I never thought of that. It didn't even occur to me that the women hunted. Still, restricting types of game to men or women must mean letting some get away. You'd catch more prey if both could hunt the same animals."

Mulyo nodded. "You're right. That is very likely why the gods taught us to follow this way. When I was young, the Kuleh often told us that the forest survives because we let some game get away."

A silenced Makokan cast an indignant glance at Hohsalle, who was laughing. The young master said nothing to Makokan, turning to the old woman instead.

"Mulyo, we have something we want to ask your niece as well. Would it be all right to talk with her without going through Malji first?"

Mulyo thought for a moment and ultimately nodded. "You said it was urgent, so it should be fine, but will you tell my brother what orders you give her when he returns?"

"Of course."

"In that case, please feel free to meet with her. She's behind that tent over there. I will send someone to fetch her. Allow me to invite you into my tent while you wait and serve you some tea. You can talk together there when she comes."

"Thank you, but there's no need to send anyone to fetch her. We'll bring her to your tent."

Mulyo nodded, then made a brief gesture with her hand to some young men who were watching from a distance. They glided over the ground toward the group and took the horses without Mulyo uttering a word. They appeared to be as well trained as hunting dogs. A single gesture was enough to launch them smoothly into action.

As the group made for Mulyo's tent, they heard children chattering excitedly. Although Hohsalle had not asked them to, Tohlim and Makokan let him lead the way and stopped beside him when he halted in the tent's shadow.

There was a grassy area behind the tent. A stream ran between it and the edge of the forest, as though stitching the two together. A group of children was gathered around a great tree on the bank. Its branches had been skillfully employed to hang a large deer carcass. The head and rack of antlers remained intact, but the body had been neatly skinned from the neck down, exposing white fat and red flesh. The innards were likely removed as soon as the beast was killed. Its hollow cavity shone crimson.

"All right, Auntie! I've got it!" a boy of about ten shouted in a high-pitched voice while grasping one of the deer's haunches. His voice was confident, but his feet were far from steady. A girl who appeared to be his sister told him to hang on tightly, while an older boy asked him if he needed help and offered to take over.

Amid the clamoring children, the slight woman the boy had called Auntie continued to butcher the deer calmly. She inserted her hunting knife and drew it around the pelvic bone while speaking to a tall girl who watched with intense interest. Then, with a word to the boy gripping the haunch, she sliced the tendon that attached it. The haunch severed neatly at the joint, and the boy, his face flushed with effort, staggered under the weight, doing his best not to drop the leg. The other children ran up to assist, and together they laid the haunch gently on an old hide spread across the grass.

Incredible. Makokan had seen deer butchered countless times. He knew how to detach the hind leg by inserting the knife at the pelvic bone and cutting the tendon, but he'd never seen it accomplished so swiftly and effortlessly. Even from this distance, he recognized that the woman's hands moved with extraordinary dexterity, cutting through the carcass as though it were a lump of soft lard.

The woman evidently sensed that she was being watched, for she glanced toward the visiting group. Upon realizing the three were merely observing, she smiled and inclined her head, then returned her attention to her work. The children were another matter, however. They kept looking over their shoulders and whispering to one another. The woman merely carried on with her task, occasionally calling out instructions to one of the kids.

Only when the carcass was completely dissected and all its parts lay on the hide did Hohsalle finally move. Tohlim followed. "Sae," he called out as he approached.

The woman handed her hunting knife to the tall girl beside her. "It's a fine day, Master Tohlim," she said quietly, placing her hands on her knees and bowing in greeting.

She looks like a nice person, Makokan thought. He felt flustered when she raised her head and gazed straight at him. Although she was certainly over thirty, she possessed bright brown eyes and looked much younger than her years. A modest ornament adorned the thong that bound her hair at the nape of her neck, and she sported no trace of makeup. No matter how he looked at her, she didn't seem like an accomplished hunter.

Hohsalle came to a halt in front of the woman. "So you're Sae. I'm Hohsalle Yuguraul. I have come to ask for your help."

Sae's eyes wavered ever so slightly. "Young Master of the House of Yuguraul, I am honored to meet you. What do you wish of me?"

Hohsalle's face brightened at her words. "You waste no time in getting to the point. Wonderful. I can see why Tohlim has so much faith in you."

Although she smiled at this praise, a wariness remained in her eyes. To Makokan, the tiny dimples in her cheeks appeared somehow sad. He stared at the little huntress, pressing his lips together.

6
Following the Trail

Sae arrived at the salt mine of Aquafa with almost no luggage. There was no knowing how long a journey they might have ahead as they pursued the fugitive's trail, yet she had brought with her only a small leather satchel slung across one shoulder and a hound. Looking at her, Makokan remembered the Aquafa maxim: "Travel light like the trackers."

Sae had ridden pillion on Tohlim's horse, and now she slipped off from behind him and bowed low to Yotalu, who'd come out to greet her. Yotalu gazed at the woman with keen interest. "The messenger told me about you. You're Malji's daughter, are you?"

Sae nodded. "Yes. My father is in your debt."

Yotalu smiled. "No, I'm indebted to him. I hear that Malji has already left to hunt the ossam."

"Yes. He and his men are searching the forests around the mine."

Makokan recalled the gruff-looking chief. He'd listened silently while Hohsalle explained what he wanted. Maybe Malji had been tired from the strenuous hunt, but an air of gloom hung over him that seemed to stem from more than fatigue. When Hohsalle had finished, Malji merely nodded and summoned the other men. He'd calmly told them they would embark on a long journey at daybreak, and the trackers, weariness still etched on their faces, waited motionless, without a word or a nod, until he gestured for them to leave the tent.

And now they're in these forests, Makokan thought. He pictured their hound-like figures flowing soundlessly through the shadowy underbrush.

"He said he would present himself in three days and report on progress," Sae said.

Yotalu nodded and then glanced at Sae's hound. "That's a good-looking animal. Is he yours?"

Sae grinned and looked down at the dog sitting erect, ears pricked, at her feet. He seemed to know the discussion concerned him, for he gazed up at his mistress. He was large and fierce looking, perhaps part wolf. "Yes. He's aided me for a long time now."

"I see. But it will be hard to follow the scent now, no matter how keen his sense of smell. Seven days have passed since the slave escaped."

"That is true. And I was told it has rained in the meantime… While I can't guarantee success, there are a few things I could try. Would you be willing to permit me, sir?"

Yotalu looked slightly taken aback, as though realizing that this small and seemingly demure woman possessed an unexpectedly strong core. "I leave it to you. If there's anything you need, just say so."

"Thank you." She bowed her head and turned her attention to the mouth of the mine. "If anyone here is well acquainted with the lives of the slaves, I would like to speak with them."

"I've already asked one of the patrolmen who seems quite knowledgeable to guide you."

Hohsalle stood to one side, listening to the conversation between Yotalu and Sae. He glanced at Makokan. "You should give her a hand, too."

"Huh?" Makokan blurted out, surprised.

"Stay with her until she finds that slave," Hohsalle said casually. "And report back to me everything you see and hear."

Makokan blinked. "But I am your servant. I can't leave your side."

Hohsalle smiled. "I don't need a babysitter, so shut up and do as I say. And don't get in her way."

Makokan scowled but didn't think it sounded like such a bad assignment. He was, after all, very curious to see what this woman could do.

"And...," Hohsalle added as if it was an afterthought, "keep your hands off her." He sounded as flippant as usual, but his face was serious. "She's a lonely woman. For someone like you, she'd be a bottomless pit."

Without responding, Makokan stared glumly at Sae as she talked to the middle-aged man Yotalu had summoned.

Sae listened carefully to everything the soldier had to say, down to the most minute and irrelevant-sounding details, before she finally headed into the salt mine, leaving her hound at the entrance.

She and the soldier climbed down the shaft to the escaped slave's former level. Corpses still lay in the dark tunnel. Sae's expression clouded at the sight, and she put her hands together in quiet prayer. Makokan noticed her fingers trembling, and he frowned. After raising her head, Sae made her way to where the escaped slave had slept. She stood there staring motionlessly for so long that the soldier took to shifting his feet out of boredom. Sae got down on her hands and knees and, with her cheek nearly touching the rock floor, stared at the bedding. After a while, she stood and carefully approached the rock wall to examine the broken chain. She touched it, then looked at the floor and frowned.

"What's wrong?" Makokan asked.

Sae looked up and seemed about to speak but ultimately shook her head. "Nothing," she said quietly. Next, she stood with her back to the wall, and although she stared at Makokan and their guide, her eyes appeared unfocused.

She doesn't even see us, Makokan thought. *What on earth can she see that isn't here?* He looked at her eyes and saw that they were moving rapidly, as though tracing the movements of the escapee. Although he knew this was impossible, he could not help but think it.

Sae took a deep breath and bent to carefully select some pieces of straw from the bedding and tuck them into her belt.

"I am sorry to have kept you waiting. Let us leave now."

When Sae emerged from the tunnel, her hound, which had waited faithfully where she had told him to, stood and wagged his tail joyfully. Sae removed the bit of straw from her belt and held it under his nose. His demeanor changed instantly. His muscles grew taut from the tip of his nose right through his neck, and his tail pointed straight out behind him. He put his nose to the ground, then raised it high and sniffed the air repeatedly. He must have been unable to find a clear trace, however, because after a while he lowered his head and whimpered as if puzzled.

"Using a hound to track him won't work," Makokan said. "It rained, and the ground has already been trampled by so many people."

Sae looked at him. "Yes. But I am hoping that some traces may remain in places that weren't touched by the rain." She made a sign to her hound to follow her and headed toward the buildings near the entrance to the shaft.

Ah. Of course. The scent inside those buildings wouldn't have been washed away. Still, so many days had passed, and other people had surely entered and exited repeatedly to remove bodies. Makokan doubted there was much left to find.

Sae paused and turned to the soldier. "Did one of you break down that door?"

The soldier shook his head. "No. It was like that when we arrived. We did prop it open with a pole, though."

"I see." After asking him about the building and its use, Sae bowed her head and thanked him, then let him return to his work.

Makokan watched him leave before approaching Sae. "What did you find when you looked at the chains in the mine?" he asked quietly.

Her eyes flickered, as if she was trying to decide whether to tell him, but finally, she sighed and said, "You will probably think that I have lost my mind, but I believe that Broken Antler Van snapped those chains himself."

Makokan stared at her, speechless.

Sae laughed. "That seems to be the only possible interpretation for the signs left there, at least."

Makokan frowned. "What signs?"

"I believe," Sae began quietly, "that he forgot he was chained to the wall and tried to run. His right leg was pulled out from under him, and he fell forward. Like this." She thrust her right leg out behind her and gestured with her hands. "He must have pitched forward, because there are signs that he caught himself with both hands. Also…" Sae turned around. Bracing her legs, she lowered her hips and pretended to pull on a chain with both hands. "The straw where he slept showed the marks of his feet, as if he'd dug in his heels and strained against the chain like this. If someone had helped him…" She moved back a few paces and pointed. "…The straw would also have been disturbed here. But I found nothing like that. Instead…" Sae sat down suddenly, mimicking the movement of someone who'd lost their balance and landed on their butt, then rolled onto her knees and hands and pushed herself up quickly. "I only saw evidence of someone who'd fallen, then jumped up and set off at a run."

Makokan stared at Sae, his mouth open. Where in that straw had she glimpsed such things? He'd examined it himself. It had certainly been disturbed, but did she really discern all that just from the way it was scattered?

Sae looked down and gently stroked her dog's ear. "That is how I read the signs, but I may be wrong. If we find him, please ask him yourself." She turned away and walked toward the entrance to one of the kitchens, the roof of which was crowned by a row of chimneys. Her hound's disposition changed as she drew near, and he began eagerly sniffing the broken door.

"It looks like Van's scent's still here," Makokan said.

Sae nodded, her eyes fixed on the door. "He must have thrown himself against it repeatedly. Look here." She gently nudged the dog's head aside and pulled something from the splintered wood. "His clothes were frayed, and one of the threads got caught." She passed it to Makokan and stepped inside the building.

There were no corpses within. The long counter had been pushed aside, probably by serfs or soldiers to make room to carry out the corpses. Just as she had done in the mine, Sae initially stood motionless, gazing at the scene, then she crouched, bringing her face almost to the floor, and stared at the room from that low vantage. She repeated this process over and over, pausing by the counter and looking up at the strings of sausages hanging from the ceiling. Sae moved slowly toward the rear and finally out the back door.

Following her, Makokan found himself confronted by a separate building that appeared to be another kitchen. "This must be the slaves' kitchen. The door on this one isn't broken."

"Yes." Sae nodded. She walked around to the side of the building, which was gently bathed in the afternoon sun. Something evidently caught her attention, because she bent down and peered closely at the ground. After rising, she approached a spot underneath a window set high in the wall and once again crouched to stare at the ground. She stood and briskly returned to the first kitchen. Makokan had no idea what Sae was thinking, but she soon came back carrying a small chair in one hand. With her other, she pointed at the ground.

"Someone has brushed the dirt across this place with their palm. He must have put this chair on the ground here and stood on it so that he could climb in through the window." She turned the chair upside down to show Makokan, and he saw that there was indeed dirt on the bottom of the legs. "He erased the marks left by the chair and then put it back inside."

Makokan frowned. No matter how hard he looked, he couldn't see any sign that a hand had brushed over the dirt.

"Stand here and examine the ground like this," Sae said.

Makokan did as instructed. Once he bent his knees to get down to her level, he thought he spied a slight difference in the pattern of dirt in that one spot compared to the earth around it. It was so insignificant that Makokan was sure he would never have recognized it had Sae not told him it was there.

Sae looked up at the window. "If it hadn't rained, it likely wouldn't have been visible, but the rain made the ground moist, leaving a faint trace of his palm."

She raised her hand to the level of Makokan's forehead. "Judging from the tracks left in the mine, I would say he's about this tall. He appears to be strong and nimble."

Sae drew a strand of hair from the bundle of straw in her belt and showed it to Makokan. "This hair is brown, almost black. Although it shows some damage, it is still thick and strong compared to that of the body that was beside him. He was probably brought here not long ago." Her eyes darkened. "The hair of slaves subjected to ill treatment for a long time is thinner and more brittle, and the color is lighter, too."

Makokan listened to her low voice in silence. He now understood why even a man of such high status as Tohlim held her ability in great esteem. Her tracking skills were superhuman.

But...she's not cut out for this. The thought spread through Makokan's mind.

Sae gave a short sigh and, after handing Makokan the hair, turned on her heel and entered the slaves' kitchen. It was large and empty. Dust motes danced slowly in the sunlight that flooded through the doorway. Footprints covered the floor, undoubtedly left by the men who'd cleared away the corpses, but Sae examined each of them carefully. Her hound, too, sniffed eagerly. Evidently, Van had been here. As the autumn sun descended and the first hint of twilight pervaded the room, Sae bent down and peered into one of the clay ovens. She remained motionless before it for some time.

"Did you find something?" Makokan asked. Sae started and then stood without a word. Her eyes and nose were barely visible in the blue dusk, and she resembled a phantom.

"He seems to have spent the night here," she whispered at last, and she looked down at the space in front of the oven. "He also washed.

There are marks of a tub here on the floor. It might have been one of the female slaves, but there are no other such marks in front of any other oven, so I believe the slaves bathed elsewhere. Which means that before he left, he washed—"

The rest of her sentence was cut off by the sound of someone calling.

"I think they're looking for us," Makokan said. Sae nodded and exited.

A faint glow remained at the edge of the sky, a reminder of the sun, but the vault above them had already turned the color of night. A soldier bearing a torch approached, lighting the way for a tall man behind him—one of the Molfah. He glided up to Sae and, without any preamble, said, "The chief calls. We found something in the forest."

7
Vanished into Snow

The whispers of a wandering river crawled up the bluff on the wind. To the right rose a sheer rock wall; to the left lay a sudden drop into the broad valley far below. The trail hugging the cliff was barely wide enough for a single cart to pass. Makokan sighed from atop a reindeer mount.

"Who would've thought I'd end up in a place like this?" he grumbled. Winter came early here. Although the first snow had not yet fallen, it would bury this mountain trail, making it impassable once it did. Already, the surface was slippery with mud from the frost-melt. Now he knew why Sae suggested they go by reindeer rather than horse.

The reindeer of Aquafa were large and sturdy. Not even Makokan's hefty frame seemed to tax his mount. And unlike those of horses, their hooves splayed under a load, making them ideal for walking on soft snow, and the sharp edges kept them from slipping on ice. Without reindeer, they could never have crossed the pass at this time of year. Still, no matter how well suited they were to poor footing, they were bound to slip and tumble into the valley below if they were made to carry on much longer in these freezing winds.

Sae must have heard Makokan grumbling, because she looked back at him and smiled. "We're almost there. We should be down in the valley before dusk. There we can seek shelter in a village."

"I sure hope so. I've got a feeling it's going to snow tonight."

Sae looked up at the sky and nodded. On the other side of the valley, a low range of mountains stretched as far as the eye could see. Their snowcapped peaks shone faintly against a band of yellow sky, above which hung ash-colored clouds. The gray expanse seemed dull and swollen, as though concealing the light of the sun behind it.

"I wonder if we made the wrong decision. Had I known it would take this long, I would've waited until spring." Makokan had agreed to this plan because he'd believed they could make the trip and return before the snow fell, but at this rate, even if they found the fugitive, their road home would be cut off.

Looking at the grand vista before them, Sae remarked, "Even if it snows, we can always set up camp."

Makokan grimaced. "You must be joking. There's no way I'm going to do that. Let's go back."

Sae looked at him and laughed. "You know very well that even if we turn back now, we'll still have to camp in the snow. There's no need to worry. Everything will be fine. Once we find a village, they'll let us stay until spring."

Makokan was tempted to retort that he had no intention of being shut up for the winter in a backwater, but he held his tongue. He knew he was partly responsible for his predicament. He'd agreed to Sae's proposal, after all. "Tracking is a gamble," she had said. "If we wait until spring, things might change. We should leave immediately and search the valleys of Oki."

How could Makokan have known that Sae had intended to spend the winter here from the start? *This is why I don't like dealing with trackers.* He sighed internally. For them, life on the move was normal, and they didn't care where they spent the night. *Damn! I wish I could sink into a nice hot bath.* A long soak in a hot tub, good food, and a soft bed protected by thick walls and a sturdy roof. That was the way to live. He exhaled deeply, then breathed in the scent of snow on the wind.

It was Tohlim who'd determined that the slave likely fled to the Oki region, but it was the clues that Sae found that had led him to that conclusion. Sae's father and his band of trackers had located a doused campfire in the forest. From the tracks around it, Sae had gleaned that the fugitive met someone traveling by cart. Her hound, too, had done a good job. Though days had passed, he caught the slave's scent on the ground near the firepit and let Sae know without a doubt that their quarry had been there.

After carefully examining the site, Sae had announced that the man the slave had met appeared to have been too injured to walk. The footprints left in the rain-wet soil indicated that someone had braced themself to lift another person into a wagon. She had also determined from the hoofmarks that the cart was pulled not by a horse or reindeer but by a pyuika.

The first thought that occurred to everyone was the pyuika herders of the Toga Mountains. Then they remembered that these days, pyuika were raised even in this part of Aquafa under Zolian policies for the western region. But pyuika were hard to handle. Farmers and merchants wouldn't typically hitch one to their cart in place of a horse or reindeer. The logical assumption was that a nomad from the north had stopped to light a fire here on his way to sell furs and other goods in the city.

Sae followed the cart's ruts and realized they were indeed headed for Kazan. Not even she, however, could follow their tracks once they entered the streets of that huge trading center—not when there were hundreds of other carts. The rest of the search was left up to Tohlim.

It took him less than three days to find out what had happened to the slave, a fact that made Makokan shiver. Tohlim had contacted the street merchant union of Kazan and ordered them to inquire if someone selling furs and traveling by a pyuika-drawn cart had been injured. This command had spread rapidly among the diverse peoples living in that sprawling city, and information had poured in with a speed that demonstrated the firm grip exercised by the Aquafaese aristocracy.

Many men had arrived with pyuika-drawn carts to sell furs, but only one had been so badly injured that he couldn't walk—a young man named Tohma. A fur trader reported that Tohma had been supported by a sturdy-looking man. Guessing that he must be the escaped slave, Tohlim had passed the information on to Sae.

"The man was around forty years of age with dark brown, almost black hair, and he fits your description perfectly. He told the fur trader that he expected to be working for Tohma's people and would likely return." Here Tohlim had paused, his face clouding over. "But we don't know exactly where Tohma's clan lives. It's a common name, and although we know he's from Oki, it's a big region that spans a wide plain and a low range of mountains and valleys. There are many nomadic settlements scattered throughout that area."

Tohlim had suggested it would be better to wait for spring, but Sae shook her head, claiming that if they were to search for him, then the earlier they went, the better.

The sun, which was a small white dot burning dully through the gray clouds, now slipped down to show itself beneath them. Rays of golden light poured across the wide basin below. The sun was still fairly high, but once it began its descent, it would disappear quickly behind the rim of the mountains to be followed by the shroud of night. Fortunately, the cliff trail had already begun to slope downward, and the pair was slowly nearing the valley's bottom. Makokan spied the shapes of men here and there in the distance following their herds, a sight that cheered his spirits somewhat.

It's still a gamble whether we'll find a settlement before the sun sets, Makokan thought. Just then, Sae brought her reindeer to a halt, cocking her head, listening for something.

"What's up?" Makokan knew as soon as the words left his mouth. Something was there. He felt it. Goose bumps crawled along the right side of his body—the side facing the rock wall. He looked up and glimpsed movement at the top. A black face poked through the underbrush.

Ossam?

No, it was too big for a mountain dog. A wolf, perhaps? Once he caught sight of the first, he saw what seemed like countless others here and there in the bushes, staring down at them. Their yellow eyes gazed at him intently. Cold fear stabbed through the pit of Makokan's stomach. He placed his hand on his sword hilt, loosened his blade, and drew it from the sheath. As if on cue, the black shadows launched themselves into the air and raced down the vertical cliff directly at him with astonishing agility.

Suddenly, one of them flipped and fell with a squeal. Makokan realized with surprise that Sae had leaped from her mount, bow in hand, and was loosing a fierce volley. Makokan could barely follow the movement from quiver to bowstring before another arrow shot with a *thud* through a black shadow. With each arrow, another beast writhed in the air, smashed against the trail, and fell to the valley below. However, Makokan had no time to watch.

The raw, bloody smell of beast breath hit him in the face, and he swung his sword upward and away. He felt the weight leave his sword as one creature's body arced through the air and plunged over the cliff, but the next beast was already upon him.

As there was no time to pause and disengage, Makokan swung his blade from side to side as if striking down stones flying through the air instead of stabbing. Sweat stung his eyes. The reindeer beneath him pranced about in fear, making it hard to keep his balance. For one second, he lost his focus...and a beast lunged straight for his throat. He raised his arm to guard his neck and braced himself for the fangs, but the animal shrieked and wheeled aside.

Sae stood with her bow aimed in Makokan's direction.

She saved me.

But in doing so, she had left herself exposed, and a moment later, a beast pounced upon her. She staggered under its weight, and Makokan saw her foot slip off the edge of the trail.

"Sae!" He leaped from his mount and flung out his hand, but there was no way he could reach her in time. She fell down the steep incline, her body bouncing against the dry brush in a cloud of dust. From far above, he saw the two, beast and woman, flung apart, and then, finally, a spray of water. A white speck floated to the surface and was swept away by the rushing torrent.

"Sae!" Makokan leaned over the edge of the cliff and shouted until he was hoarse. His voice was carried off by the wind, leaving a blanket of overwhelming silence.

There was not a living beast left in sight. Had the one that attacked Sae been the last?

Makokan looked around, drenched with sweat, his chest heaving, then stared once again at the bottom of the cliff. Something soft and cotton-like brushed his eyelids.

Snow.

Snow. Falling soundlessly, like a sigh from the gray heavens.

Makokan gazed stunned at the valley below, then rose and shook his numbed head to get a grip on himself.

Come on, hold it together.

The arrow-pierced bodies of the beasts lay scattered along the trail. Some still twitched in agony. He gazed at their forms—larger than dogs but slightly smaller than wolves—then at his reindeer, which stood trembling with fear, its reins tangled in a bush, preventing its escape.

Sae's reindeer had evidently fled long ago, for he couldn't find it anywhere. Speaking soothingly, Makokan approached his mount slowly and picked up its reins. The familiar feel of the leather in his hands helped him regain a little composure. After wiping his sword on his sleeve, he returned it to its sheath and then loosened his sword belt and slung it diagonally across one shoulder. He swung himself up onto the skittish reindeer's back, braced his thighs, and urged the reluctant animal down the cliff. Makokan knew the risk. Without his reindeer, he would be as good as dead. But he was confident of his skill as a rider. He'd control it better by riding than leading.

Once over the edge, the reindeer picked its way steadily down the incline. It was still a long and terrifying descent, but at least it had started partway down the road where the slope was gentler, and Makokan managed to reach the riverbank without injury.

Snow was now falling thick and fast.

"Sae!" Makokan called her name until his voice began to fail, overcome with anxiety as he rode along the bank searching for any indication of her. Unfortunately, the snow blinded him, and he could not find her. He thought he heard a dog barking downriver, yet when he peered ahead, all he spied was flying snow.

The sun had not set, but a white shroud covered the world in a sullen glow, and howling wind buffeted the desolate land.

Chapter 3:
In the Land of the Reindeer

1
Preparing for Winter

The weather stayed fine until late afternoon, but as the sun traveled across the sky, the wind picked up, driving the snow before it. Atop a steep hill, Van gazed down upon a broad valley, velvety blue in the twilight. Sparks of light glowed like fallen stars in the indigo darkness. With a deep sigh, Van slipped the sled harness off his shoulder. Although small, his reindeer-hide cloak, which had belonged to Tohma's elder brother, wrapped his body in warmth, and the well-sewn seams of his gloves and boots kept his hands and feet dry even when damp with snow. Despite this, just being outside in this icy land was enough to freeze him to the core.

With his eyes fixed on the lights of home, he clapped his hands to get the blood flowing. His thoughts wandered to the child he had named Yuna, meaning "little fish." *I wonder what she's up to*, he thought. Tohma's grandmother, Manya, always hummed while she worked, and Yuna had picked up the habit. Whenever she was happy, she hummed slightly off-key, sounding exactly like Manya. Thanks to Yuna, that tune was now seared into Van's brain.

He pictured how she would greet him when he walked into that tent. Her face would light up, and she'd totter over and jump into his arms, crying, "Ochan!" She was soaking up words like a desert soaked up rain, but for some reason, she still called him Ochan instead of Onchan, the word most children here used for tohchaku, or "father." Yuna sounded so adorable when she said it that he had deliberately refrained from correcting her.

The boar meat lashed to the sled Van pulled was frozen solid. It was good that he'd gutted, skinned, and butchered the animal at the site. The snare was far off, and he'd only arrived at it early in the afternoon. Van could have carried the carcass back after removing the innards and cleaning the cavity, but the scent of snow had wafted on the air. Thus, he'd decided to carve the boar up on the spot. Although this had delayed his return, the meat would thaw quickly on the hearthstone, making it easy to separate. Tonight, they would eat their fill of boar stew.

Almost two months had passed since Van and Tohma had arrived in Oki. It had been late autumn when he chanced upon Tohma in the forest near the salt mine and accompanied him to Kazan to sell his load of furs and purchase provisions. Van had used the money he'd stolen from the salt mine to buy a reindeer and cart. They reached Tohma's home before the first snowfall. Tohma had led him to a valley in the Oki region on the northernmost edge of Aquafa. This, he explained, was their winter home. In summer, they would cross the mountains and camp in the grasslands and hills closer to the sea.

The gently sloping dale along the river where they wintered was slightly warmer than the bottom of the broad basin through which the river drained. Mountains blocked the winter clouds, protecting the camp from heavy snowfall so that even in the coldest months, the reindeer could scratch through the snow with their hooves to reach the lichens they preferred. "That's why we drive our herd to this valley every year before the snow falls," Tohma had explained during their journey.

Lichens were slow growing, though. Once consumed, it took them several years to return. Each winter, the reindeer herders stayed in a different spot. "We won't camp here for another few years," Tohma had said. From his description of their life, Van had realized that reindeer herders dealt with unique problems. Pyuika left too long in one spot would also devour all their favorite buds, leaves, and grasses, and Van's people migrated to a new grazing ground each season. But the plants pyuika ate grew back quickly, which meant the herders could return to the same place each year.

To the Zolians, whose only experience was with cattle and horses, pyuika and reindeer probably seemed alike, but they were quite different. A reindeer herder ignorant of pyuika would find it very difficult to raise them. Van understood what must have driven Tohma to beg him for help, but he also knew that Tohma's family would be sensitive to what the rest of their clan would think. If, as Van suspected, Tohma's father was married to a Zolian immigrant, he would be particularly reluctant to welcome anyone who might bring trouble. Tohma was clearly anxious about how his father and uncle would react when he brought home a stranger, and he repeatedly warned Van during their journey that it would be up to his father whether he could stay with them.

However, Van had been resigned to that from the start. If Tohma's father denied him, he'd deal with it. Even if they refused to shelter him for long, he figured no one would be so merciless as to shut him out in the cold with a little child. If they permitted him to stay for the winter, that would at least afford him time to plan his next move.

The settlement was tiny, just three tents inside a windbreak made of stone. Tohma's family emerged to welcome him home, only to stand and gawk speechlessly at the burly stranger he'd brought. As Van had suspected, Tohma's mother was Zolian, but she seemed so at home with these northern people that he assumed she'd lived here for a long time.

Tohma's father, Ohma, looked older than Van expected, and he guessed that he must have been married before and then remarried much later after losing his first family. His face was tense, but he listened intently to Tohma's explanation, digesting each word. When Tohma finished, he nodded slowly and extended his hand, thanking Van gravely for helping his son. Ohma explained that the decision of whether Van would be accepted as a mikucha, an adopted clan member, was ultimately up to the clan chief. But for the time being, he was welcome to stay. So long as Van lived and worked with them, they'd share their food and tent. Ohma spoke plainly, but Van was touched by the strength in the man's gnarled hand as it gripped his own.

Van soon learned why they had welcomed a stranger into their midst without probing further. The two families that made up this tiny settlement were extremely poor. Ohma explained matter-of-factly that it took at least twenty reindeer to support a single family. To make things worse, the only man in his prime was Ohma's younger brother, Yoki, and the only youth was Tohma. Once, there were more men and children, but a devastating avalanche struck their camp four years ago, and the year before last, Yoki's son and Tohma's older brother both died of a contagious disease.

Yoki's daughter was married and had children of her own, but they were also poor, and as they lived in the forests far to the northwest, they rarely met with the rest of the family. If worst came to worst, Ohma could explain their situation to the greater clan at the gathering and ask to be accepted into another family. Members of the clan always came to one another's aid in times of need, and other families that were fairly close would not deny requests for aid, but to be a burden was shameful. Also, the women would be uncomfortable living with people they didn't know well, and they'd be expected to care for the elderly. Tohma's family preferred to carry on as it was, if possible. Although Ohma never said as much, Van surmised that the fact that his wife, Kiya, was Zolian was another reason he was reluctant to move in with others.

Kiya and her family were reindeer herders from the northern outskirts of Zol, and many Zolians had been forced to abandon the region and resettle. Kiya's family emigrated when she was a young girl. One by one, her kin were struck down by disease or accidents, leaving the survivors struggling to survive. Ohma's family had come to their rescue. As mutual assistance was a common practice in both cultures, the two families soon became close, and it was just a natural progression for Kiya to develop an attachment to Ohma. Her relatives lived nearby, and the two families continued to aid each other, but neither was well off.

Although they barely made enough to scrape by, Tohma's family still had to pay a head tax on every reindeer. Taxes were lighter for those with Zolian blood, but as this only applied to Kiya and Tohma, it didn't help that much. Desperation had spurred Ohma to sell some of the reindeer and start raising pyuika, which were subject to less tax. But due to lack of knowledge, any attempt to raise and breed them had failed, and now Ohma and his family teetered on the brink of disaster.

Tears had rolled down their cheeks as they ran their trembling fingers over the load of grain, dried fruit, potatoes, and beans that Tohma purchased with the money from peddling furs. These were indeed the staples of life. However, it was the arrival of another mature male, one who knew of pyuika, that truly kindled the flame of hope in their hearts—the hope they might manage to survive without asking the clan for help. The way Ohma's and his family's eyes had shone as they gazed at Van, a complete stranger, struck him to the core.

The knowledge that Van was needed naturally moved him to respond. Winter was fast approaching. There was no time to lose if they were to ensure that both the young and the old could survive until spring. Tohma's injury prevented him from doing heavy outdoor labor, so Van put him to work sharpening the hunting knives and preparing traps. Meanwhile, he set about making enough firewood to last the winter. This meant cutting and hauling logs from the forest, splitting them, and piling the wood to dry. Yoki had already started before Tohma and Van arrived, yet the supply was far from adequate.

Once he was sure they had enough, Van helped Ohma and Yoki fix the winter corral that would shelter the reindeer and pyuika. For much of the year, people in this region didn't bother to fence in their herds. There was no fear that any of the animals would wander away. As long as the fawns were kept tethered, the does would never roam far, and as reindeer moved in herds, the rest would remain close to the settlement, too. Winter, however, was another matter. When game was scarce, reindeer were the perfect prey for hungry wolves, or the Black Brothers as they were commonly called. Herders required a strong fence high enough to keep predators out.

The hunting dogs, each with a length of wood hung from its neck and a slightly anxious expression, watched the men as they worked. Big-eared and quick-footed, they were the best companions for chasing down game, but they had been trained to hunt, and there was no guarantee that they wouldn't attack a reindeer calf. Ohma explained that was why they hung wood around the dogs' necks when they were near the settlement. The wood caught on the frames of corral gates, preventing the dogs from passing through if one happened to be left ajar.

Whenever he tired of sharpening the ends of the wooden fence posts, Ohma would pause, wipe the sweat from his face and bellow, "Hey! Why don't one of you take yourself into that forest and tie some wood to the necks of our Black Brothers?" This was apparently such an old joke that even his wife merely smiled tolerantly.

To prepare for winter, they had to build the corral, set aside a stock of food, hunt boar, deer, fowl, and fish, smoke the meat, and make sausages. While the herders were skilled hunters, Van had practically been born to this life. Even in this unfamiliar forest, he always returned with some kind of quarry. The first time he had brought back a kill, Ohma's expression softened into a smile. "You hunt well," he'd said. He'd recognized at a glance that Van possessed both the heart and the skill to avoid making an animal suffer needlessly. Everyone had looked noticeably more cheerful as it became clear that they would soon have sufficient food with the supplies Tohma brought back and the extra game Van caught.

Unfortunately, while they might survive the winter, spring would bring its own problems. The reindeer were their livelihood. Despite the family's small herd and meager funds, the tax collector would still visit next season. Unless Ohma and the others showed him that they'd successfully bred pyuika, there would be no decrease in their taxes. Van guessed that this knowledge weighed heavily on the women's minds, because they sighed often. They worked ceaselessly from dawn until dusk, handling the daily chores that kept the household going and sun drying seasonal fruit they'd collected and smoking meat for the winter.

Living and working beside them, Van rapidly grew to know Tohma's people well. He could tell that they sensed he was a man with a past, yet they never inquired. Perhaps they feared he would leave if they pried. Van was just thankful that they'd welcomed him into their midst so warmly. He doubted anyone would waste time and money searching for one escaped slave, but he was still a fugitive. There was no telling when he might have to leave, or in what way, so he worked hard to pay back the debt he owed the family in whatever small ways he could.

And the best thing I can do is to help them raise pyuika.

At this thought, a warmth rushed through his chest, and Van smiled involuntarily. Just to be with pyuika again lifted his heart, regardless of the reason—a reminder that he was still a Pyuika Rider deep down.

2
Mohoki

As soon as winter preparations became less demanding, Van turned his attention to the pyuika. When he'd first seen how they were treated, he was appalled. Several stakes were driven into the ground inside the corral, and each pyuika was tethered to one. Even Tsupi, who'd pulled the cart here quite willingly, reared and snorted when Yoki grasped her reins, and she threw herself repeatedly against the stake once hitched to it. Seeing Van's expression, Yoki spat the juice from his chewing tobacco on the ground. "You wouldn't believe how high these critters can jump. They'll leap any fence, no matter how tall. We gotta tie 'em up to keep 'em in, and then we gotta feed 'em, too. And believe me, they eat a lot. They're nothin' but trouble."

Frowning, Van asked him, "Didn't the people who sold them to you tell you about mohoki?"

Yoki looked puzzled. "Mohoki? Never heard of it. What's that?"

At this, a sadness spread through Van. The men from Okuba who'd come selling pyuika must have known about mohoki. It was a type of lichen that grew on old trees, but for some reason, pyuika loathed it and dared not venture anywhere near it. They were easily penned in by braiding dried mohoki into ropes and tying some on all four sides of a fence. Mohoki made it possible for herders to corral the high-spirited pyuika. Without it, they would leap over the fence or, if it was too high for them to escape, fall into a decline.

Like reindeer, pyuika were grazers by nature, so raising them in enclosures wasn't ideal. Even if they had to be penned at night when wolves were on the prowl, they were better left to roam freely during the day. Still, many of their habits differed significantly from those of other deer species. Although they were herd animals, the extent of a herd was broad and vague, the only clear unit being a doe and her fawns. Despite this independent streak, pyuika were also very loyal and prone to loneliness. A pyuika that bonded with a man while still a fawn would never forget and would come at the sound of his whistle. The creatures migrated with the seasons but habitually traveled the same well-worn paths, which meant their movements could be controlled simply by planting mohoki in strategic places along these routes.

The children of Van's clan spent their days in the forest with the adults, learning the habits of the pyuika, observing how fawns were singled out for training and how they bonded with men. In this way, they naturally developed the ability to pick out and train pyuika. So it had been since ancient times.

If the Okuba traders had deliberately refrained from telling Tohma's people about mohoki, which was essential for raising pyuika, it could only mean they'd feigned obedience to Zol while secretly hoping their breeding efforts would fail. Van understood how they must have felt. Yet it wasn't the Zolian soldiers who would suffer from this little deceit but the Oki. Not only had they gone into debt to purchase the pyuika, but they'd be heavily taxed if the pyuika didn't reproduce. Whereas successful breeding meant a little windfall for the soldiers, for the Oki, who'd sold off reindeer and gambled their future on the pyuika, failure spelled destitution.

But if they succeed... The thought of Zolian soldiers mounted on pyuika made Van's gorge rise, and he grimaced. That was something he just couldn't accept.

So I'm stuck...

Van took a deep breath. No matter which choice he made, it was going to hurt. Knowing this, he opted for the less painful one. That was probably what the Okuba traders had thought when they decided to turn a blind eye to the hardship they'd cause the Oki. But the Okuba, like Van's people, were once renowned Pyuika Riders. Surely the pitiful state of the pyuika moved them. If so, then their decision hurt them as well as the Oki.

Van closed his eyes. An image of a pyuika surfaced in his mind. Unrestrained, antlers high, racing like the wind...

He opened his eyes and gazed at the drooping heads of the pyuika. *I can't abandon them.*

He recalled something his father had told him long ago. *"No matter how much we may try to convince ourselves otherwise, we use the pyuika for our own ends. Never forget that. Pyuika Riders are a sorry lot. We spur ourselves onward with soul-stirring songs, all the while begging our mounts for forgiveness."*

Although a heavy drinker, Van's father had been a good man, someone who understood what it meant to lie to oneself. Watching the pyuika, Van thought, *He's right. We've used you for our selfish designs. It's my turn to yield, not yours. I may hate the thought of Zolian warriors astride your backs, but that pain belongs to me. I left my homeland of my own free will, but you were dragged here without a choice.*

War, subjugation, oppressive taxation, people suffering under a regime that squeezed them dry—these were the problems of men, not pyuika. And they were so complex that the impact of sacrificing these flying deer would prove infinitesimal. After acknowledging this, Van felt the turmoil in his mind recede. *In the end, all I can do is try and relieve the suffering of those before me—the pyuika and the people living here.*

On the day the winter preparations were finally completed, Van fastened a blade to a pole to make a long-handled scythe, slung a basket across his back, and went into the forest to gather mohoki. The south side of the wood received plenty of sunshine, and the trees, which were mostly deciduous, had already relinquished their leaves, leaving the forest bright and airy.

As he walked through the dry brightness, leaves crunching underfoot, he felt forlorn. For some reason, feelings from his childhood came flooding back. He recalled the cold sensation that used to steal through his chest as a boy when he'd been separated from his friends in the forest while looking for mohoki. He had only to call out, and his friends would answer, yet the shame of his own fear kept him silent.

Must be because this forest is unfamiliar. It felt different from the woods in Van's homeland, which he knew like the back of his hand. Still, the dappled light that fell through the fluttering leaves onto his face, the faint dusty scent rising from the fallen leaves, permeated his skin and made him feel alive. A bird warbled, the reedy autumn song of the red-tailed kohttoli. Van halted, his ears attuned to the lonely refrain, a vision rising before him of his young wife, one hand resting on the white bark of a tree trunk. Her face was laced with shimmering threads of golden light as she listened to the birdsong. A delicate flush colored her smooth cheeks; her heart was filled with a simple joy. Unaware she carried his child. Blissfully ignorant of the fate that awaited her.

Van closed his eyes and stood motionless in the sunshine. People and time passed by—there was no way of stopping them. The clear light of autumn seemed to bleach his body and all else white.

A rustling sound issued from the bushes, and Van's eyes flew open. For a second, his gaze met that of a deer, a young one. Filled with curiosity, it had probably been sneaking a peek at this intruder. Now that it had been discovered, it turned in panic and bounded off into the forest. Van smiled as it crashed through the underbrush. Young deer were boisterous. He envied their unconcern.

Van shifted the basket on his back and began walking again. This was no time to stand about daydreaming. Mohoki would be harder to spot once the sun began its westward tilt.

As Van grew accustomed to the angle of the sun and the way the trees grew, he found that he could guess fairly accurately what kind of plants would grow where, even in this unfamiliar forest. Mohoki clung to the bark of old trees and could live for a thousand years just breathing mist, or so it was said. He would have to forge deep into the north side of the forest to find some. Following his intuition, he made his way through the trees.

After some time, a familiar scent registered in his nostrils, and he raised his head. Beyond a curtain of lacy branches in a dip between damp trees hung with fog, he glimpsed the top of an ancient timber that reared its head above the surrounding wood—just the kind where mohoki thrived. However, it was still a considerable distance away.

How did Van pick up the scent from here? He frowned. *It's happening again...*

The tingling sensation that he'd almost forgotten prickled in his nose. This uncanny sense of smell seemed to awaken when stimulated, though why, he could not tell. The familiar raw odor of mohoki assaulted his senses unpleasantly. It had never bothered him before, but now, even the faint whiff of it from this distance stirred a strange clamor in his breast. It repelled and yet drew him at the same time, as if two creatures with opposing dispositions were warring over the sensations within him, unsettling him. The very thought of drawing closer, of gathering the lichen and carrying it back in his basket, made him shudder, but he had to do it.

Covering his mouth and nose with his right hand and rubbing the goose bumps on his arm with his left, he advanced toward the towering tree. Yellow, hairlike tendrils of mohoki hung in profusion from its branches, like strands of silk trailing from the tattered sleeves on the bony arms of an aged nobleman. The familiar sight now appeared totally bizarre. Van was torn by a longing to touch it and horror at the very thought of doing so. A powerful urge to turn and run rose inside him, clutching his stomach and making his legs quake.

Disturbed by the sensations taking hold of his body, Van squeezed his eyes shut and fought to control his breathing. His mind struggled to regain composure and rein in the turmoil that assailed his senses.

As the impulses rolling through him abated slightly, a thought streaked through his mind. *Ah, so that's why the pyuika stay away from it. This is what they feel.* But Van wasn't a pyuika. Where was this feeling coming from? *My body's becoming something I don't recognize.*

Fear crawled up through Van's breast, and he clenched his jaw. Sucking air through clamped teeth, he strove to master his fear and, through sheer force of will, managed to subdue this body that no longer seemed his own. He opened his eyes and glared at the mohoki in defiance. *You are you, Van,* he told himself. *And this stuff hanging here in front of you is mohoki. As a Pyuika Rider, you need it. You must cut it down and take it back to those who are waiting. So stand tall.*

With this thought, he swallowed the large, hard lump of fear. He could almost feel it forcing its way down his throat, and then, abruptly, it was gone. His body relaxed with sudden relief, and he broke into a cold sweat. Taking a deep breath, he readjusted his grip on the scythe and tackled the task of harvesting.

Van had done this countless times since he was a boy, and his hands moved automatically. As he worked, he felt himself gradually being restored to normal. But the feeling never left him that somewhere deep inside lurked another self, waiting for a chance to awaken.

It was almost dusk when Van returned to the settlement, but he immediately set to work on the pyuika fence. Normally, he would have dried the mohoki and woven it into rope, but he was too impatient to wait. The sight of the pyuika bound to stakes upset him so much that he could not be still until they were set free.

Ohma and the others stood off to one side and watched Van work without interfering. However, their expressions changed to apprehension when, after winding mohoki around strategic points in the fence, Van walked inside the enclosure with a stick of firewood in his left hand and an ax in his right and approached a large buck that brandished its antlers. While making short clicking noises with his tongue, Van severed the rope that attached it to the stake with a single stroke of his ax.

The buck reared, waving its forelegs in the air, and then brought its antlers crashing down toward Van's head. The spectating men gasped, but at that moment, Van poked the buck under the jaw with the stick of firewood. The great animal collapsed and fell to the ground with a *thud*, as though its strings had been cut.

As the men murmured in consternation, the buck shuddered, waved its legs in the air, and then rose and shook its head. Perhaps noticing it was free for the first time, it broke into a trot and ran around the enclosure, staying clear of the fence. Van watched silently, waiting for the buck to calm down. When it finally slowed and began to graze, he approached another stake and repeated the same process with each of the pyuika. When all the others were free, Van finally approached Tsupi, who now carried young. He calmed the excited doe with clicking sounds and quietly severed the rope. She bounded up and down like a fawn and then butted Van in the back and nuzzled him under the armpit before strolling away to munch on the grass.

By this time, the long shadows that had lain across the meadow had deepened into dusk. Van stepped outside the fence and wiped the sweat beading his brow.

Ohma walked up to him. "You all right?" he asked.

Van nodded, still wiping his face. He was so exhausted that his very bones seemed to groan, yet the fatigue came not from the work but from having sustained the full brunt of the pyuika's anger and the odor of mohoki. When Van had stepped outside the enclosure, beyond the range of those sensations, something inside him went slack, and he broke into a sweat.

It was so dark that Van could barely make out Ohma's facial features, yet he clearly saw the emotion burning in his eyes. "...Osumari anamanoh," Ohma murmured. Although the accent differed slightly, Van recognized the ancient words of gratitude used by his own people.

Thank the gods.

These men were glad that Van had come. A quiet relief enveloped him, like a warm blanket draped over his shoulders.

3
Yuna

The little girl Van had rescued quickly made herself part of Ohma's family. After many years without a child in their midst, the women were delighted to have a little one to care for. Thankfully, she wasn't the type to make strange, and soon, she was playing on Kiya's lap as if she'd always done so. When Tohma's grandmother Manya had asked Van for the child's name, he told her "Yuna" because that was the first thing that came into his head. He'd been a little nervous when Yuna stared blankly the first time Manya called her by name, but now, she happily referred to herself in her childish lisp as Yunacha.

A strange twist of fate had brought them together, but the way Yuna's face lit up at the sight of Van filled him with deep and quiet joy. Every evening as he sat by the hearth and placed her on his lap, he thought how fortunate he was to have found her in that oven.

Returning in the blue twilight from the long day's hunt, Van felt a pleasant fatigue seep through his body. Just coming home each day to the camp at the foot of the gentle slope brought him peace. He stopped the sled in front of the tent, unloaded a chunk of boar meat onto his shoulder, and called out a greeting as he raised the tent flap. Yuna, who'd been playing by the hearth, jumped up, her face aglow.

"Ochan! Ochan home!" She started to run toward him only to trip on the edge of a hide that Kiya was tanning. She fell flat on her face before Kiya could catch her and burst into deafening wails.

"Oh dear! Honestly, Yuna!" Kiya swept her up and rocked her, but she wouldn't stop crying.

Grinning, Van slid the meat off his shoulder and laid it in the coldest part of the tent, then he took Yuna from Kiya and raised her high into the air. Her eyes opened wide, and she gurgled with laughter each time he swung her up again.

"One moment, she's crying, and the next, she's laughing. What a busy girl." Manya laughed as she sewed by the hearth. Beside her, Tohma looked up from braiding rope and smiled.

Ohma, who'd gone out with his hatchet to chop up the carcass, came back with two more lumps of meat. As he sat down by the hearth, he said, "You snared a big one. Must've been heavy."

Van put Yuna down. "There are lots of tracks made by large, mature boar, but I haven't seen many younger ones."

Ohma nodded. "Me neither. It's been like that for a while now."

Tohma, who'd begun sharpening a hunting knife, raised his head. "Uncle Yoki says maybe it's because there're more Black Brothers."

"I guess he's right. But I wonder why. Good thing our herd's small this year. We can keep them all corralled for the winter. But when they calve in spring, we're going to have to stay up all night to guard them."

Van took the sharpened knife from Tohma, warmed it in the flames of the hearth, and set to cutting the meat into smaller chunks. While keeping his hands moving, he asked, "Don't you have a rite to ward off the Black Brothers?"

Ohma regarded Van with surprise. "You mean the people of the Toga Mountains do that, too?"

Van nodded. Wolves were not like other creatures. Born from the same god as men, they'd been created to hunt and live with their fellows. However, they were closer kin to the god that brought them into being than men were, and so were considered sacred beasts worthy of awe. They ran along the border of the Land of the Dead and slipped into the depths of that darkness at will. As such, they were to be revered and never spoken of familiarly as "wolves" in the way of the blasphemous farmers.

The Toga Mountains had once been home to handsome wolves with glossy black fur, but they were rarely seen anymore. Most had been eradicated long ago as bearers of some dreaded disease. In their place, ossam, the wild mountain dogs, ran rampant, as if they owned the place. However, there were still some gray wolves in Toga, and the elders claimed they helped keep the ossam population in check.

Naturally, wolves attacked pyuika, but although this was a problem, wolves could not be killed as if they were prey. Instead, they had to be warded off with fire or shouting to let them know they were causing people suffering and to dissuade them from attacking. The sendoff rite could only be used when the wolves' numbers proliferated to the point that they no longer listened, even when treated with respect.

Ohma stared into the fire, rubbing his chin. "If they keep on increasin', I suppose we'll have to consider that. It'll probably come up at the clan gatherin' next month if everyone's havin' the same problem."

From there, the conversation naturally shifted to the subject of families living nearby. Just as the talk began to peter out, a delicious smell wafted from the hearth. Fat dripped from hunks of meat that had been skewered on sticks and stuck in the ashes around the fire, and it sizzled as it hit the flames, emitting a mouthwatering aroma. Each time a drop hit the hearth and flared, Yuna clapped her hands and laughed.

Kiya smiled. "The hearth god must be happy. Those sparks are his breath."

"'Cause it's yummy?"

"That's right. The hearth god loves boar fat." Kiya lifted the lid from a bubbling pot. A cloud of steam rose, and with it the aroma of tenderly stewed boar cooked with vegetables. "That's just about the end of the greens, so enjoy them while you can," she said as she ladled out the contents. The farmers living along the river raised these particular greens under the snow. This made them very sweet, and Kiya bought some whenever the farmers came to peddle their wares. Soon, however, the snow would deepen, preventing their passage. For the rest of the winter, the family would have to depend on carefully rationed portions of the nuts and fruits stored during the fall and root vegetables, which lasted long when buried under the snow.

The stewed meat was so tender that it melted in Van's mouth, and the rich flavor spread across his tongue. Although delicious, it tasted different from his wife's. *Probably because Kiya doesn't use oki*, Van thought. His wife had always cooked boar with oki, a plant that had a nice fiery bite to it when raw, but that turned soft and sweet when stewed, soaking up meat fat. He missed its sweet flavor and aroma, and the touch of heat. That and pau, a fragrant bread made with wheat flour that was perfect for sopping up what was left. Kiya baked only a dark, sour bread made of rye. Van guessed that it was too cold to grow wheat here. Even so, Ohma and the others ate it happily.

"Never had this 'til Kiya came," Ohma told Van. "Were we ever surprised the first time she made it! Never tasted anythin' so good." Kiya blushed at this praise. "We've the Zolian immigrants to thank for bringin' things that'll actually grow in this frigid land. Like rye and ogi beans. It's a miracle that anythin' grows here at all. But we heard the plains people were furious. They accused the Zolians of plantin' things that drove their horses crazy. They even attacked the immigrants."

Van remembered that incident. It happened some time ago. The Yukata Plains in the south were originally home to the Ahfal Oma, the People of the Fire Horse, but the Zolian invaders took it over to pasture their sheep and cultivate beans and rye. Many fire horses died from eating rye, and the enraged Ahfal Oma set fire to a village of immigrant farmers. Zolian soldiers had to be called in to quell the uprising, and it ended with the execution of the instigators. As punishment, the Ahfal Oma were driven from the Yukata Plains, becoming a people without a homeland.

"Perhaps they didn't know about rye," Kiya said, breaking the abrupt quiet. "That the grain can turn toxic."

That's possible, Van thought. But Aquafa wheat was cultivated on the plains where the Ahfal Oma had lived. Surely horses ate of it, too. *Perhaps the Aquafa wheat doesn't turn poisonous.* That was probably it.

While the People of the Fire Horse curse the Zolians for planting a poisonous grain, the people of Oki thank them for bringing a delicious food.

Each time Van ate the dark pau, he wondered what the people of his homeland in the Toga Mountains thought.

"Guess it all depends on where you live," Ohma said as he sipped his stew. "Plants're different, and animals, too. Just like Zolians don't drink milk. You told us that, Kiya. Remember?"

Kiya smiled gently. "You didn't believe me at first, either, did you?"

Ohma's eyes opened wide. "'Course not! Who'd have thought anyone would refuse to drink milk? It's just common sense. They raise horses and cows. Why wouldn't they drink their milk?"

"Because true Zolians are followers of the Pure Heart Creed," Kiya said. "They're not allowed to let anything defiled pass their lips. They believe that humans were made to drink their mother's milk, and that consuming that of an animal will make them bestial. People who live in the cities and the farmers in the south, they're all believers. But while we're called Zolians, my people were just absorbed within the empire as it spread. We're not followers of the Pure Heart Creed, and we've been raised on reindeer milk since who knows when. And I bet we're not the only ones."

As Van listened, his thoughts turned to Yuna. She'd been taken from her mother before she had a chance to remember her cooking. For her, the taste of home would be Kiya's cooking. She sat there now, concentrating on her stew, clutching the bowl in one hand, lips glistening. It seemed only a short time ago that she burned her mouth after taking a big gulp of something hot and made a huge fuss. Yet she'd already learned to blow on her food to cool it down and to take smaller bites. Van couldn't help smiling as she pursed her lips and blew repeatedly on a spoonful of stew.

"No need to keep blowing," he said. "It must be cool by now."

But Yuna shook her head emphatically. "No. Hot."

Recently, she'd begun to talk back, and Van supposed she must be entering a new phase in her life. He often wondered how old she was. He would try to guess based on memories of his son and his nieces and nephews, but there was no way of knowing for sure. Eventually, he reasoned she must be between one and a half to two. On their way here, she'd remembered her mother and cried, especially at bedtime. But she'd stopped that and now slept soundly, snuggled up against Van's chest.

She probably doesn't even remember her mother's face. The thought made Van pity the young woman who'd placed Yuna in the oven and propped herself in front of it to protect her. He needed to tell Yuna when she grew a little bigger and was old enough to understand. There wasn't much he could say. *Still, I will tell you how much your mother loved you,* Van thought as he watched Yuna gobble her stew.

4
In the Summer Forest

The long dark winter seemed as if it would continue forever, but as the sunlight that caressed their faces changed its hue, the blizzards receded, the snow melted, and tightly furled buds swelled on the dew-laden branches.

Spring in the north was like a child. Freed from restrictions, it burst forth bright-eyed and high-spirited. Verdant grasses sprouted, multi-hued flowers bloomed across the moist, dark earth, and the forest donned a mantle of unfurling leaves and blossoms.

If spring was a child, then summer was a young maiden, exuding a perfume of young leaves that set hearts aflutter. With early summer came the birthing season, and everywhere in the forest, creatures bore and reared their young.

*

"…Are you sure you can find her?" Tohma whispered.

"Yes." Van smiled. "The calving place is almost always the same."

*

When spring came, Van had told the men to let the pyuika roam free. They'd worried that the animals might never return, but Van convinced them it was the best thing to do. Pyuika were wilder than reindeer and rebelled against any kind of restraint, which made it impossible to domesticate and raise them like livestock. The secret was to acclimate them to the presence of people and form a personal bond. Both pyuika and deer roamed the hills and forests, but whereas deer traveled astounding distances in areas where the snow fell deep, the range traveled by pyuika was much narrower, perhaps because they could eat a greater range of foods.

In the Toga Mountains, where Van was born, boys stayed close to the men, watching over the pyuika herd as it roamed through the forest. By doing so, they came to know their habits so well that they could guess quite accurately where a pyuika might be at any given time. Wild pyuika would never become accustomed to people after they reached maturity, but if they were exposed to their scent from birth and bonds were carefully nurtured, then the connection endured for life.

Pyuika were unusual among deer species in that they always bore twins. The one chosen to be separated from its mother and accustomed to humans was always the larger one that drank more milk. Van still remembered his father's singsong voice as they had watched over a young doe calving, surrounded by the thick fragrance of green leaves. "...The weak one to the mother, the strong one to me."

Although both bucks and does could be trained for riding, bucks were impossible to control during mating season, so those singled out as mounts were gelded. To take all the strongest males would weaken the next generation, though. Thus, the clan meticulously considered the condition of the herd when deciding how many fawns to train. Bucks shed their antlers in the spring, but for some reason, geldings did not. Gelded pyuika also possessed slightly less muscular strength, but this was offset by greater stamina because they wasted no energy mating. They were more obedient, too.

When Van explained to Ohma and the other men how pyuika mounts were raised, they shook their heads incredulously. Ohma sighed. "Really? What a lot of trouble! It's much easier to raise reindeer, and they're a lot more useful, too."

Van conceded that was probably true. The milk, hides, meat, and bones of reindeer were all usable, and the animals could be ridden or harnessed to pull loads. While pyuika milk was delicious, and the meat was occasionally eaten if an excess number of bucks had to be culled, to the people of the Toga Mountains, pyuika were not a source of livelihood. Rather, they were precious comrades raised specifically for riding. The Toga Mountains were located farther south, where the earth was rich and wheat and potatoes were cultivated in the valleys. Forests offered plentiful sources of game and herbs, and the Toga Mountain clans maintained a flourishing trade with people passing through on their way between the peaks. The meaning of pyuika in the lives of the people of the Toga Mountains was thus completely different from that of reindeer in the lives of the Oki.

As Ohma and the others came to realize this, they began to see the pyuika in a different light.

"In other words," Ohma said with a crooked smile, his eyes on the pyuika bounding out of the corral and into the forest, "the Zolians haven't got a clue." Van laughed and nodded.

Ohma was right. Those in command had assumed that pyuika could be bred like horses, but they were gravely mistaken. The two creatures were quite different. To raise pyuika bucks as mounts, they had to be selected at birth and gelded before they matured so that they wouldn't come into rut. It took considerable time to raise pyuika suitable for riding while breeding and increasing the herd at the same time.

"Thanks to you, looks like we can breed them after all," Ohma continued, "but even if we do, they'll be useless to the Zolians." Worry showed in his eyes.

Once they realized this, the Zolians would almost certainly abolish the tax reduction for pyuika breeders. Ohma's family had a year or maybe two... Van wondered if it was better for the family to use the money saved from raising pyuika to buy back reindeer. It was likely a wise choice, but what would become of the pyuika when they were no longer needed?

That wasn't Van's only concern. Once the Zolians learned that pyuika bonded solely with those who raised them, they might conscript the young men of Oki into the army as Pyuika Riders. It would be just like the empire to create a guard of men from the borderlands to protect the frontier. Van hadn't shared these thoughts with Ohma yet. It would only compound his worries, and having to choose between poverty or conscription would break his heart. There was no point in burdening him with the possibility of future suffering when they hadn't even successfully bred pyuika yet.

There must be a way to manage by balancing the number of reindeer and pyuika. But I'll worry about that when the time comes. For now, I need to make sure that Tsupi calves successfully. Only if she delivered her young safely in this foreign land, and if she and the other pyuika mated this fall and bore young next year, would Ohma and the others be able to raise enough money for the future.

As summer neared, another obstacle to raising reindeer and pyuika together became apparent: The reindeer's migration to their summer pastures coincided with the pyuika calving period.

"Last year, the pyuika bore no young, you see, so we just hitched 'em to a rope and led 'em along after us," Ohma explained. Van believed the stress of being forced to follow such an unnatural rhythm was probably another reason why they'd failed to breed. Still, the reindeer couldn't be left in their winter pasturing grounds over the summer when the horseflies and mosquitoes swarmed, and the grasses were thin. Reindeer were omnivorous and would even eat mice and insects. However, they needed to move to pastures where the sea winds blew horseflies and other pests away in summer.

For several days, Van and the family discussed what to do, until finally, Tohma suggested that they ask neighboring families for help. Ohma slapped his thigh in assent. They decided to approach Zolian immigrant families like Kiya's to see if they'd consider it. They sought Kiya's immediate kin and her distant relatives, and all responded with enthusiasm. They'd been struggling to breed pyuika, too, and had been eager to meet Van ever since they had heard that someone well-versed in handling the creatures had moved in with Kiya's family.

Everyone gathered to consult, and it was finally decided that three young men—Mino, Chida, and Moki, all nephews of Kiya—would stay with Van and Tohma to learn about raising pyuika. The others were to take the reindeer to their regular summer pasture. Kiya offered to stay behind to care for Yuna, for which Van was grateful. He simply couldn't suppress the loathing that rose inside him at the sight of Kiya's nephews, who understandably looked completely Zolian. Their flat, inscrutable faces conjured vivid images of enemies Van had faced on blood-soaked battlefields, and he felt as if something were caught in his chest. The three youths, in turn, seemed intimidated by this stranger and followed him through the forest every day in grim-faced silence.

In the end, it was Yuna who broke through the awkwardness.

One morning, Van and the young men were preparing to leave when Yuna ran into the tent, and Kiya's nephews burst out laughing. Wondering what was going on, Van turned to look and cracked up himself. Yuna was clutching a large basket, one nearly half her size, filled with glistening red raspberries and mocho that she and Kiya had picked. There was nothing particularly amusing about that. However, in her eagerness to carry, and probably eat, as many as possible, Yuna had also filled her mouth with berries. Her face was stuffed so full that her lips were stretched open, and her cheeks bulged like a chipmunk's. To top it off, she had carefully placed a mocho berry in one nostril as well.

She could not even close her mouth to chew and swallow, and stood there grunting, her eyes darting back and forth desperately. Laughing so hard he could hardly breathe, Van staggered over to her and, holding her face with one hand, dug the berries out of her mouth with the other. She heaved a sigh of relief, and the berry popped from her nostril and flew across the floor, making Van and the others collapse once again into laughter.

"Not funny!" Yuna insisted, shedding angry tears, but everyone was howling so hard that they were crying, too. Kiya returned at that moment and smiled quietly at the scene. She picked up Yuna, wiped the girl's tears, and said, "Now, now, don't be angry," but Yuna was in a huff for some time after.

Later, Tohma told Van, "Mino and the others couldn't believe you'd crack up like that."

Van looked at him in surprise. "Why?"

Tohma grinned. "Don't you know? You look so tough. The first time I saw you, I thought you were gonna kill me."

So that's why, Van thought. *They were afraid of me. Guess I am pretty dense.*

Their silence and poker faces were just a front to cover up their fear. This thought brought to mind the faces of the young warriors Van trained long ago. They, too, had clammed up and looked inscrutable, as if declaring, "I'm not afraid of anything." The fact that the Zolian youths reminded him of the young men of his homeland seemed strange. *Time changes everything*, Van mused. If he kept at it, one day it would no longer seem incongruous at all to train these foreign men and lead them through the forest in this unfamiliar land.

By the time Tsupi's belly had expanded and her calving drew near, Kiya's nephews had become as talkative as Tohma and peppered Van with questions.

5

Summer Light

"Stop," Van whispered. Tohma froze, and Kiya's nephews followed suit. They watched Van with tense faces. He stooped slightly and pointed at a thicket beyond a tall spruce tree in the shade of a large mossy rock. A cloud of insects hovered in a beam of white sunlight that shone through the canopy. Two brown ears twitched in the shadows, brushing away the mosquitoes.

"See her?" Van whispered.

Tohma peered toward the bushes and then paused, eyes widening. "Oh... Is that Tsupi?"

"Yes. She's about to give birth."

Tsupi paced round and round the same spot, sniffing at the earth, then lay down only to stand up again.

Van stepped aside quietly to let the others take his place. "Watch carefully," he said. What looked like two black sticks protruded from between the doe's hind legs.

"Hooves?" Tohma asked quietly.

"Forelegs. The head will come soon."

The head popped out, pressed between the two spindly forelegs, and then the whole body slid out onto the grass.

One of the youths laughed in excitement. "She did it!" Tsupi's head swiveled toward them, perhaps sensing that they were there, and the young men froze. As they waited with bated breath, Tsupi rose and began pacing in circles again. Then she stopped and gave birth to a second fawn. She bent over them and began licking vigorously. Once their slippery, wet bodies were licked clean, they struggled unsteadily to their feet, standing on wobbly legs that looked so thin they might break. Although newborn, they were already trying to reach their mother's teats. Trembling, they nuzzled her belly, searching for milk.

"You can do it," Tohma muttered.

His cousins joined in, their fists clenched. "Come on. You can do it. A little lower."

Finally, the firstborn found a nipple and began to suck. Moments later, the secondborn also began to drink thirstily. Tsupi licked the ears of her newborns as they tasted their first milk.

"Well done," Van said with a smile. "You calved those elk fawns all by yourself."

The doe was strong and would probably bear many healthy young. Despite her major feat, she cared for her newborns as if it was the most natural thing in the world. Watching her, Van felt something quietly fill his heart. To give birth, and one day, to die—the ordinariness of this extraordinary process spread through him like a translucent wave.

Somewhere, a bird sang. A breeze rustled the treetops, and the sunlight filtering through the leaves danced on the doe and her fawns.

The sun's light changed to the bright heat of summer, and flocks of birds traversed the heavens, their high voices echoing. They were migratory birds, returning from their winter grounds in the warm south to spend summer in these northern lands. While following the tracks of a boar along the lakeside, Van heard a honking that rang through the air like a gong. Birds glided down one by one, as if sliding out of the sky, and landed on the water. Flame-red streaks on the undersides of their feathers flashed with each wingbeat.

Matsukala, spark ducks. Van had seen them often in his homeland during the fall. His people said that the ashimi lichens favored by pyuika grew thicker in years when large flocks of matsukala migrated to Toga.

Just the sight of them made Van happy. *They come here this early in the year, do they?* This must have been where they spent the summer, leaving for their journey south when they felt autumn coming on and stopping to rest in the Toga Mountains. As he watched the birds that would soon make for his home, he thought, *Tell the mountains and streams of my homeland that I'm here and somehow surviving.*

The fawns grew rapidly as summer pressed on. Van took the youths into the forest with him daily, and while they hunted, he taught them all he knew about the lives of pyuika. One day, he was setting a trap in the woods when Tohma, who'd been checking on the doe and her young, came rushing back and announced that the fawns had vanished. "Maybe they were attacked by a fox!" His cousins returned shortly after, their faces anxious. They reported that Tsupi was grazing with the other does, but the fawns were nowhere to be seen.

Van continued with his work and only stood when he'd finished setting the trap. "Come with me," he said.

He strode off, and the others hurried after. When he reached the grassy clearing in the forest where the herd was grazing, Van saw it was as Tohma had said. Tsupi was there without her fawns. After examining how the herd was scattered, Van moved downwind so as not to startle them and crouched down in the shade of a tree. "Sit," he said. "It's going to be a long wait."

The young men looked at him with puzzled expressions but did as they were told. Van took some leaves from inside his shirt and divided them up among the group. Wordlessly, the young men squeezed them to extract the juice and spread the grassy-smelling liquid on their faces and necks to repel mosquitoes. Hunting and herding both involved long waits, and they were used to it.

For a long time, the pyuika ambled here and there, munching on the grass or rearing up on their hind legs to nibble on tender new leaves. Finally, however, Tsupi moved away from the herd. As soon as he saw that, Van stood. He signaled to the others and followed Tsupi at a good distance. She walked through the trees until she reached a fallen log covered in moss.

Tohma breathed in sharply. A small figure appeared from the log's shadow and tottered toward Tsupi on unsteady legs. Then a second figure sprang out from the shadow of a rock. Eagerly, they shoved their noses beneath her belly and began to suck her milk.

The young men stared with stunned expressions. "The fawns are too young to eat grass yet," Van explained. "But their mother has to consume a lot to produce milk, so she hides her young in the shadows of logs or rocks." Van looked around and smiled. "During this season, you'll find many little ones hiding quietly in the bushes." Then his face grew serious. "If you could choose, which one of those fawns would you pick to raise?"

The young men exchanged looks. After a pause, Mino finally said, "…If it were me, I'd choose the firstborn."

Van looked at the others. "You too?"

Tohma and Moki nodded, but Chida stammered, "I think the secondborn is going to grow quite big."

"Why?"

Chida blushed. As the youngest, he was shy and usually just went along with what his elders said. It took him a long time to answer, perhaps because he was flustered over expressing a differing opinion. Van waited silently. Finally, Chida said huskily, "…Because it walks faster."

At that, Van smiled. "You've got good eyes," he said. He pointed to the fawns. "Look at their legs. Do you see how the limbs of the secondborn are just a little closer together? It can stand strong without splaying its legs for balance." The young men gazed closely at the fawns for a moment and then nodded one by one. "The fact that its legs and hips no longer sway when it walks shows it's drinking enough milk to build a sturdy body. If a fawn suckles frequently but doesn't grow very fast, it means it's not good at suckling."

The others listened intently. "Both of those fawns are developing well. If it isn't taken by foxes or wolves, the firstborn will also become a strong and healthy adult. But it's the second one that will be hardy enough to bear a man on its back and run without flinching. That one's going to be a good pyuika."

Van smiled. "This is the most important time for bonding. We'll approach the fawns while their mother's away and let them gradually get used to our scent." The young men nodded, eyes shining with excitement. Chida, in particular, beamed from ear to ear.

Each night around the hearth, Van shared folktales of pyuika or things he'd learned through experience about pyuika riding. Occasionally, while watching the faces of his audience, illumined by the slow-burning fire, he wondered if his son would have listened to him with a similar expression had he lived. As he felt the warmth of Yuna nestled against him asleep in his lap and listened to her breathing, he recalled his son, who'd been taken from him so abruptly. Yuna had already grown quite heavy, and her cheeks were rosy. Once, Van's son had been alive like this, too. Some lives were so short. Others were long. What was it that made the difference? Why had an innocent little boy who'd done no wrong died so easily? Why had the sickness chosen his child and wife?

Van felt suffocated with rage over life's unfairness when he reflected on that. The chest-rending anger and grief that came roaring back to life each time he remembered his son, the futility that felt like a hole in his gut, these would surely never heal until he died.

Van loved Yuna from the bottom of his heart. But raising her would never mend the grief of losing his son. Nor would training these young men to ride pyuika bring back what he once lived for. Still, there was a kind of peace here, like the ease that came when immersed in the clear autumn sunlight. Before Van knew it, the feeling that he was living on borrowed time had faded. He sensed that, somehow, he was putting down roots.

But behind him lay a shadow. Like the shade beneath a tree bathed in light, that cold and deepening darkness stretched even longer when he stood in the sun's warm rays.

6
Golden Sunbeams

In the northern woods, the seasons passed swiftly from summer to fall. When flocks of migrating birds began their journeys across the skies and the leaves turned a shining gold, bucks sharpened the tips of their antlers and bellowed like broken flutes in their efforts to attract a mate. By the time the first frost fell across the land and Ohma and the others returned with the reindeer, the young men had come to admire Van like a father. Van, too, found it hard to part with them. But the return of the reindeer marked the beginning of winter preparations, and Kiya's nephews bade him a reluctant farewell and returned with their families to their settlement.

That fall, four of Ohma's pyuika had been impregnated. Later, word reached them from Kiya's nephews that three does from their herd would also bear young, news which they all celebrated. Van slipped into the forest with Yuna when the tax officer arrived, and the man, his spirits buoyed by the knowledge that the pyuika were finally breeding, left without noticing the addition of two new people. With a tax reduction secured, Ohma and his family decided to spend the surplus on winter supplies. Van's hunting had also produced more furs to sell this year. Kiya's nephews offered to go to Kazan, and Ohma gladly gave them his furs and dried meat to peddle. They returned with their carts heaped with provisions and clothes, and the two settlements gathered to celebrate with a great feast.

When it was over, and Kiya's family left for their own settlement, Ohma grinned at Van. "It's all thanks to you," he said, clapping Van on the shoulder.

Yuna, who stood at Kiya's feet, announced, "All tanks to Ochan!" and clapped Van on the leg, which made everyone laugh.

Last year, everyone had been worried while preparing for winter, but now, thoughts of the coming spring brought smiles to their faces as they worked and shared stories of their experiences that summer.

Later, Van often recalled this year in his life—the early summer morning when Yuna had gone into the forest with Kiya and returned with her mouth full of mocho berries, the warm summer days spent with Tohma and Kiya's nephews, the fall when they'd watched the pyuika perform the Rite of Love, that long night in late fall when they had gathered for the feast and roared with laughter at the tales they shared. The memory of that year continued to burn like a warm light deep in his heart.

The following spring brought plenty of rain and endless days of dreary weather, but by early summer, the skies had cleared, and the pyuika all bore healthy young. Tohma had become quite skilled at handling pyuika and rode through the forest on the back of one of the fawns Tsupi had borne the previous year.

Kiya's nephews sent word that their pyuika had also given birth and asked if Van would come and help, so Van set off for their settlement, where he stayed for some time to aid them in bonding with the young. All the fawns that year were sturdy little creatures. At first, they became more attached to Van than to Kiya's nephews, and the three young men looked anxious. But they persevered, and the fawns gradually began to show affection toward them as well. After telling them to send for him if they needed any help, Van left the youths engrossed in bonding and returned to Tohma's settlement. He knew that when people were forced to learn on their own through trial and error, they often came to understand more than when they relied on others to teach them. And Van was quite confident that these three would grow and develop fine without him.

As in the previous year, Ohma's family collaborated with Kiya's relatives to take the reindeer to their summer pastures, but when the autumn winds began to blow, they came home quickly. "The writing spiders are buildin' their webs high this year," Ohma said. "It's gonna be a harsh winter." And he set about preparing for the autumn sacrifice. Last year, they had had too few reindeer to offer any, but this year, the herd had produced many calves, some of which were weaker than others. Ohma was planning to sacrifice calves for both years.

To offer sick calves would be disrespectful to the gods, but if they culled those that were healthy yet did not look strong enough to last through a harsh winter, they could decrease the burden on the herd and increase the family's store of winter provisions.

Although the Gansa had also performed this rite each year, when Ohma began preparing for the ceremony, Van left and wandered into the forest. He found it too painful to watch the young being slaughtered. Bereft of any desire to hunt, he sat in a hollow near the camp and simply basked in the bright light that fell through the golden larch trees. This spot reminded him of the woods behind his family home. Perhaps that was why he felt at peace whenever he came here.

Closing his eyes while awash in that golden radiance, Van felt as though he were at the bottom of a body of water linked to some distant place. If he swam gently, he would reach the place where his wife and son were.

Like blood from the prick of a needle, a bead of sorrow rose and spread slowly through Van's chest. As he drew in a deep breath, he heard a voice.

"Ochan!"

Van opened his eyes in surprise and saw a little figure dashing at full speed through the trees toward him. Although her steps were still a little unsteady, Yuna plowed ahead without tripping over any roots.

Struck by how she'd grown so quickly from a toddler into a child, Van watched her silently as she trampled the fallen leaves. When she caught sight of him, she beamed. "Ochan! Found you!"

She leaped into his arms and pressed her nose against his as he swung her up. The tip was cold like that of a puppy.

"How did you know I was here?" he asked.

She giggled. "Yunacha jus' know. Yunacha sees you. Gwam and Gwamp say, 'No! Don't touch weindeer!' So Yunacha come find you."

Van smiled. With everyone too busy to pay her any attention, she must have gotten lonely and come in search of him. She was canny, and she sometimes came running to him like this when he was out of sight of the camp. This seemed rather odd now that Van thought about it, but he supposed such things happened. Pyuika fawns found their mothers even when they were distant, so perhaps some invisible bond connected him and this child.

The warmth of Yuna's body in his arms and the scent of sunshine filled him. A deep affection welled up inside, and he hugged her close. Yuna's small hands squeezed him back.

I want to watch over her until she grows up. I want to see her become a young woman and a mother. I want to see everything...

This desire rose unbidden, confusing Van. He felt as though he'd thought the unthinkable, and it scared him.

Even after the sacrifice, they were still more than enough reindeer. Auctioning a few would provide money to purchase plenty of food. Ohma was in high spirits. "It's been a while since I was there, but we're bound to meet up with old friends and hear what's going on in the world," he said as they packed for the journey. This time, Tohma was going, too. He was grinning with unsuppressed joy at having reindeer to sell.

Yuna waved vigorously as the young men, each astride a reindeer, rode off into the clear autumn sunshine. When she could no longer see them from her height, she pestered Van to hoist her onto his shoulders and continued to wave long after they were out of sight.

Chapter 4:
Black Wolf Fever

1
The Royal Hunt

Clouds swept like brush strokes across the pale blue sky. The clear autumn sunlight illuminated a large white pavilion on the edge of the grassy plain. The blue dragon banner of Zol and the flying horse banner of Aquafa were raised high, fluttering in the breeze.

The royal falcon hunt at which the King of Aquafa entertained the governor required careful preparation. The tradition had begun over ten years ago as a venue for the king's falconers to demonstrate their prowess. Later, Zolian falconers had joined in, and it was now a contest of skills between the two.

The front of the long pavilion had been flung open, and the guests inside relaxed in field chairs while waiting for the hunt to commence in the meadow before them.

"You mustn't fall asleep, sir," Makokan hissed.

A drowsy-looking Hohsalle snorted. "But we have to wait so long before it starts," he complained. Sunlight caressed his chin.

Men dotted the field, each standing motionless with a falcon perched on his fist. Aquafaese falconers wore red headbands, while the Zolians wore blue. Occasionally, one or two birds tensed when the wind carried the faint baying of the hounds, but for the most part, they waited in quiet contemplation for the beaters and hounds to drive their prey to them.

"People who can't wait make lousy hunters," Makokan said, just as the king's steward approached. The man dropped to one knee behind Hohsalle.

"Sir Hohsalle Yuguraul, I beg your pardon, but if you would kindly come with me, you have been invited to partake in a light meal." It was Aquafaese etiquette not to announce the source of the invitation, an indication of the king's respect for his guest.

Hohsalle nodded and stood. While he privately considered protocol bothersome, he always behaved with calm composure toward those of high rank, rarely showing his mischievous streak the way he did with people like Makokan. A chair had been set aside for Hohsalle in the area reserved for the king's guests of honor, but he'd excused himself until the meal, claiming that he preferred to observe from another vantage point. Most likely, he'd wished to avoid the strain of spending the whole event with the king and his guests.

When Hohsalle approached, Yotalu smiled and inclined his head. Hohsalle bowed in return and sat where the steward indicated. As his attendant, Makokan sat in the seat behind him.

The priest-doctor Lona, his expression as still as water, bowed his head slightly when his eyes met Hohsalle's. To Makokan, the man looked far more like a spiritual seeker than a doctor. His young apprentices kept glancing surreptitiously at Hohsalle, obviously unable to suppress their curiosity. Makokan remembered Hohsalle saying that he wished for a chance to talk with some of the younger priest-doctors because they seemed interested in Otawalle medicine.

Looks like he was right, Makokan thought, but then he smiled inwardly. *Or maybe they're just curious about the Devil's Spawn.*

Refreshments had already been laid out on the long table, but the king and the governor spared them no attention. Heads together, expressions solemn, they were absorbed in a whispered consultation and didn't notice when Hohsalle joined them.

The autumn breeze wafted through the tent, filling the space with the sweet aroma of scented wine from the carafes on the table. On the west side, where the king and his family sat, the board was spread with such dishes as lapateh, a cheese mixed with chopped dried fruit, and lachu, yogurt with candied fruit, while the dishes placed before the governor and his family consisted of such delicacies as deep-fried golden rice cakes dusted with sugar, none of which contained milk.

As Hohsalle sat down, the woman beside him smiled and offered him some lapateh. Her hair was swept up in Aquafa style and held in place with an ornamental Zolian hairpin. It was Sulumina, the king's niece and Yotalu's wife.

Hohsalle bowed his head and thanked her, taking the small plate of lapateh she offered him and popping a piece in his mouth. His expression changed to one of surprise. "What an unusual flavor. It's so rich and creamy."

Sulumina's face lit up. "Yes, this is Oki laputa, made from reindeer milk. I love it, so I always ask our nurse to get some when the season comes around."

Makokan frowned. The mention of Oki brought to mind Sae, who'd slipped to the bottom of the valley and vanished into a blizzard. The following spring, Makokan had searched everywhere for her, but he failed to find either her or the escaped slave.

So this cheese comes from that valley. That northern land where the herders who followed the reindeer lived.

"Is this what cheese made from reindeer milk tastes like?" Hohsalle asked.

"Yes. It's a little different, don't you think? Don't the Otawalle eat cheese made with reindeer milk?"

"No, we don't. The Sacred Territory is farther south than Aquafa, and the merchants from Oki rarely make it that far," Hohsalle replied. Lowering his voice, he added, "You know, I would have thought Lord Yotalu would dislike food made with milk."

Sulumina smiled wryly. "Oh, he'd never touch it himself. And I expect that he doesn't wish to see me eating anything made from the milk of beasts, either, so I never do so in front of him. But..." Her eyes twinkled impishly. "I treat myself and the boys when he's not looking. In front of their father, the boys behave as though they would never dream of eating anything made with milk, but they both love such things, especially soft lachu made from reindeer milk. They seem to have taken after me."

Hohsalle chuckled. "An excellent habit. Yogurt is very good for your health, you know. Please continue eating it—when Lord Yotalu isn't looking, of course."

Sulumina raised her brows, then smiled and nodded. "We Aquafaese prefer lapateh and lachu made from reindeer milk. But recently, it has been tough to come by. Almost everything is made with sheep's or cow's milk. Our nurse has kin who have connections with the reindeer market, and they always set some aside for us. But without that, it would be impossible to get." She sighed. "My sons prefer products made of reindeer milk, too, but my brother's children insist that lapateh made from cow's milk is better and refuse to eat reindeer lapateh."

As he listened, Makokan realized he'd not eaten Oki laputa for some time. Unlike Sulumina, he didn't miss it, because he'd been raised on cheese and yogurt made with mare's milk. Still, it was true that Oki laputa seemed to have recently vanished altogether from Aquafa taverns. In the past, cheeses and yogurts in Aquafa were all made from reindeer's or mare's milk, but since the settlers from Zol arrived, the markets had been flooded with cow and sheep products. And as these were cheaper and easier to obtain, they'd quickly become popular. Makokan guessed that the number of reindeer might also be declining due to the Zolian army's recent push to breed pyuika. The Zolians, who saw the Kingdom of Mukonia to the west as a threat, probably hoped to use pyuika to strengthen their defenses on the mountainous border region.

The king and the governor were still lost in conversation. Aquafaese and Zolians had distinctly different facial features, yet the two elderly men were eerily similar in stature—large and solidly built without any traces of flabbiness.

They're both hounds in active service, Makokan thought. *They've no intention of relinquishing their thrones to their sons yet.*

Recently, the governor seemed obsessed with building up his

military. Rumor had it that the Zolian emperor was not particularly interested in expanding farther westward, but Governor Ohan, concerned by movements along the Mukonian border, believed that Zol should demonstrate its ability to protect this border and to push beyond it.

The emperor's reluctance to beef up the army in the western territory probably stemmed from a lack of resources due to the intensifying conflict along Zol's southern frontier. It was only natural to prioritize a battle already underway over one yet to come. However, it was surely frustrating for the governor.

Once, when the topic of strengthening the army came up, Makokan had asked Hohsalle, "Do the Mukonians really want to invade Aquafa?"

"Most likely," Hohsalle had responded, looking bored. "To the Mukonians, the Toga Mountains are all that stops them from pushing east. They're not too high to cross, but the climb to the pass would exhaust their troops. More importantly, it would be hard to keep soldiers supplied with provisions. If Mukonia conquered Aquafa, however, it would have a base from which to attack Zol."

"But the Toga Mountains keep Zol back as well. Wouldn't it be easier for both sides if neither of them tried to seize the Toga region?"

Hohsalle had laughed. "You're truly a man of no ambition." Then, turning serious, he added, "In a relationship between two nations, complacency is dangerous. The country that assumes it's safe because there are mountains will lose. The governor and the king of Mukonia are both well aware of that, which is why Aquafa will continue to be strategically important as long as those two powers exist."

Pouring them some tea, Milalle had interjected, "Creatures that consume other creatures are stronger, you see... Yet those that are consumed don't cease to exist."

"Oh, your Otawalle nature is showing," Hohsalle had said with a grin.

Makokan had frowned, unable to follow their conversation. Passing him a cup of tea, Milalle had explained. "The people of Otawalle don't believe that anyone wins or loses. If we're going to be eaten, then we'll focus on being eaten well. Because the one who is eaten becomes the body of the one who eats." She smiled, looking a bit embarrassed. "We have a saying: 'Live by helping other nations live.' And we've followed that motto for centuries."

Makokan had nodded to himself as he watched the faint ripples on the surface of his tea. Milalle's explanation had captured the nature of the Otawalle people perfectly. The body that was their own kingdom had been destroyed, but they'd survived by being absorbed into a different kingdom. Makokan was confident that it was a difficult way of life. One that required considerable talent and resolve, but that was how the shrewd Otawalle had survived.

After pouring herself a cup of tea, Milalle had muttered, "By helping others live, we can also live. By making others happy, we become happy." To Makokan, her words had sounded like a prayer.

Distant barks grew closer as the dogs skillfully drove the game toward the waiting hunters. A falconer with a red headband glanced toward the tent and bowed, signaling that the hunt was about to begin and that the audience should keep their eyes on the field.

The air within the pavilion tensed with excitement, and a look of quiet anticipation rose on the spectators' faces. The king and the governor finally ceased talking and gazed out at the field.

"Lord Mazai is looking very calm," Hohsalle remarked. "Which, as a prizewinner, I suppose is only to be expected. He can probably read the location of the prey just from the baying of the hounds and the behavior of his falcon."

Falconry was considered an accomplishment of the nobility, and the men of the royal family were taught how to raise and train falcons from childhood. Mazai, the man who'd just signaled, was the king's nephew, and his skill was such that he always vied for first place.

Beside him stood two boys: his eldest son, Izam, and Yotalu's son, Olimu. Makokan's eyes narrowed as he peered at the two slender figures, their faces obviously pale and tense even from this distance.

Ah, that's right. Olimu is Mazai's nephew.

Yotalu's wife, Sulumina, was Mazai's younger sister, which made the two boys cousins. Although Makokan understood this relationship, something still squirmed uneasily in his gut as he watched the pair standing so close together. One was the royal offspring of a conquered country, and the other was the son of the conquerors. Not yet a man, Olimu would not participate in the hunt. He'd probably been positioned with his uncle, a superb falconer, to learn from him. Yet Makokan still found it provoking that Yotalu would stand his own son with the Aquafaese right in front of his grandfather—the Zolian governor—and his men.

In contrast to Yotalu, who chatted pleasantly with the royal family of Aquafa, his older brother, Utalu, stood on the grassy field, proudly sporting the blue headband of the Zolian team. The falcon on his arm was a species with blue-tinged feathers, a rarity in this area. Utalu must have been quite annoyed at losing to Mazai last year. Even from the pavilion, Makokan felt the pride that emanated from him.

The baying of the hounds grew louder still. The falconers shifted, facing where they judged the prey would emerge. At that moment, the shrubs behind them rustled, and black shapes leaped out, one after the other.

For an instant, Makokan thought the hounds were returning from that direction. The king and his guests also appeared to think so, for they merely frowned and watched silently as the black figures sped across the field. Only when the beasts hurled themselves, speed unchecked, at the falconers did the onlookers' niggling sense of doubt turn to alarm.

End of Part I

2
Attack of the Black Dogs

Someone screamed.

As the falconers turned, shielding their hawks, black wolflike beasts leaped upon them. Their bared fangs gleamed, and strings of saliva streamed from their jaws. The falcon on the fist of the closest Zolian rose with a screech of fear. As the man flung up his arm to guard his throat, he was bowled over.

Another beast rushed straight for Utalu, but he was a veteran soldier. Without the least sign of confusion, he launched his falcon into the air, drew his hunting knife, and confronted his attacker.

Mazai shoved the boys behind him, but the three were surrounded by the pack and disappeared from view.

The meadow, previously bathed in gentle autumn light, became a melee of shouting men and snarling beasts. The king's calls for his nephew collided with those of Yotalu for his son. Sulumina shrieked, "Olimu! Olimu!"

The king and his guests leaped to their feet, but the guards held them back, preventing them from rushing out of the pavilion. Aquafaese and Zolian soldiers ran to the aid of the boys and falconers, only to falter mid-step as more beasts burst from the underbrush and raced toward the pavilion.

Waving his arm, Yotalu shouted, "Go! Go! Help Olimu! We'll hold the pavilion!"

"Quick! To Mazai!" bellowed the red-faced king.

Amid this chaos, Makokan drew his dagger and placed himself before Hohsalle. The creatures sped into the pavilion, toppling the tables and chairs. The sound of shattering dishes mingled with shouts and screams. Women trying to flee within the narrow confines of the tent became entangled with the men who aimed to protect them, making it impossible for the guards to wield their swords.

The animals slipped among the crowd and attacked. One leaped at Sulumina. Makokan lunged forward and tried to strike it away with his dagger, missing by a hair's breadth, his reach impeded by a chair. Sulumina threw up an arm to protect her face, and the creature bit her hand. Hohsalle grabbed her from behind and dragged her away just as Makokan flung aside the chair and brought his dagger down on the beast's muzzle. The animal evaded with surprising agility, avoiding the point. Still, Makokan felt the blade graze its face, and it cringed and jumped away.

He was about to chase after it when Hohsalle shouted, "Watch your back!" Makokan felt rather than saw another beast attack from behind. Flicking his knife to his other hand, he swung his arm sideways behind him and slashed. Although the blade failed to connect, the beast still retreated.

Suddenly, the animals went still. Their ears pricked up, like they were listening intently. With feverish eyes still locked on the men, they drew back reluctantly, as if pulled by an invisible string, and ran from the pavilion.

The floor was strewn with broken crockery and spilled food, and women crouched on the ground, trembling and crying with terror. Those men who were bitten clutched their wounds, staring vacantly as though bereft of their souls.

Hohsalle grabbed a flask of wine from the floor, shook it to check that there was still some left, then seized Sulumina's trembling hand.

Squeezing the mouth of her wound, he washed it thoroughly with the wine while, at the same time, speaking to Makokan. "Were you bitten?"

His chest heaving, Makokan turned to look at him. "What?"

"I said, were you bitten?"

"Oh," Makokan whispered, then looked at his hands. There was blood on his dagger and on the fist that held it, but he felt no pain. "No, I wasn't."

"Are you sure?"

"Yes."

Hohsalle sighed. "Don't move and don't touch anything," he said. Turning to the rest who still stood in stunned silence, he called out, "If you've been bitten, please raise your hand."

A scattering of hands rose. Some men lifted theirs on behalf of Zolian women huddled on the floor. The king, the governor, and Yotalu appeared to have been spared, but many were not so fortunate.

Lona looked at Hohsalle and said, "I think we should wash their wounds."

"I agree," he replied. "Be sure to squeeze the blood from the mouth of the injury first."

Lona nodded and began calmly instructing his apprentices. Hohsalle addressed the rest. "Those of you who weren't bitten, please help by gathering whatever wine you can." He called out to the servants standing at the side of the tent. "Split up and bring me all the water you have! Water or wine, bring it by the bucketful! If there's soap, get that, too. And hurry!"

The servants ran off, and everyone jumped into action, suddenly filled with life again. Lona and his apprentices approached the injured and started treating their wounds.

Yotalu, his face pale, hurried over to his wife. "Were you bitten?"

Sulumina nodded while Hohsalle continued to wash the laceration. She was trembling. "I'm all right. What about Olimu?"

Yotalu cast a worried gaze toward the field, then gave his wife's shoulder a reassuring squeeze. "I'll go see. You stay here." He rushed outside.

"I'd like to help," Makokan said from behind Hohsalle.

His mohalu didn't even bother to look up. "Stay put!" he snapped. "Your hand is covered in that beast's blood, right? Make sure none of it gets in anyone's mouth or cuts!" He instructed the servants to wash the bites of the other victims with wine. They rinsed each injury for a long time, then repeated the whole process with water when it arrived. The bites weren't deep, but some of the women were so overcome with panic that they sobbed and screamed. It seemed like the commotion would never end.

The king and the governor recovered their composure swiftly and issued commands to their soldiers to check on the damage.

"Sir Hohsalle!" the king called. "If the wounds only need washing, please leave that to the others and go check on those outside." Hohsalle nodded and hurried out of the pavilion.

Mazai, his son Izam, Utalu, and Olimu were among those bitten that day.

*

The morning after the disturbance, Hohsalle visited the governor's palace to check on Utalu. As he had to visit all the victims, he had only snatched a quick breakfast before setting off from the clinic. Governor Ohan was evidently expecting him. As soon as Hohsalle explained the purpose of his visit to the guards, he was immediately led to a chamber deep inside the palace. Its weighty door was twice a man's height. Sliding it open, the servants announced his arrival, and the people within all turned to look.

"Ah, there you are! We've been waiting for you. Come here." The governor gestured with his hand, and as Hohsalle approached the chair where Utalu sat, Lona, who was taking his pulse, moved to one side to make room.

"May I?" Hohsalle inquired.

"Yes," Lona answered, his expression detached.

Hohsalle bowed, then he dropped to one knee, took Utalu's arm in his hands, and removed the bandage. The bite wasn't deep, and there was hardly any swelling.

"It's nothing. Not even worth looking at," Utalu said testily, pulling the sleeve back down over his wounded limb. "It doesn't even qualify as a wound."

A servant brought a cup of hot tea on a tray and placed it in front of Hohsalle.

"Have some tea," the governor said. "We had no time to talk properly yesterday, but I believe you mentioned something about a medicine to prevent mad-dog disease."

Hohsalle nodded and glanced quickly at Lona. "Yes, to protect those who were bitten. Just in case. It's made from a weakened version of the disease agent that causes the illness in animals and helps the body to fight against it."

"And if he drinks it, he won't get the sickness?" the governor asked, but Hohsalle shook his head.

"It is not administered orally. Rather, it must be injected with a needle, several times, leaving a few days between each injection."

The governor frowned at this. Rubbing his arm, Utalu growled, "I won't let you do that to me." Suspicion flickered in his eyes as he glared at Hohsalle. "It may have been weakened, but it's still the same disease, right?"

Hohsalle opened his mouth to speak, then seemed to think better of it. Finally, he said slowly, "Very simply put, yes. It is a new method of treatment, and there are, as yet, few cases in which it has been used, so we cannot say that it is without any risks. However, as you know, once rabies manifests itself, there is nothing that can be done. Death is inevitable. With the method I developed, twelve people have survived so far without exhibiting any symptoms."

Utalu snorted and started to say something, but phlegm caught in his throat, and he began to cough. Picking up the tea in front of him, he took a sip and then said hoarsely, "They didn't show any symptoms, you say, but maybe that was because they weren't infected in the first place."

"I am afraid not. The dog that bit them died of rabies."

Utalu's lips twisted in a sneer, and he shook his head. "As a heathen, you wouldn't know, but those who follow the divine teachings faithfully would not succumb to mad-dog disease, even if a rabid animal bit them. It's a disease that afflicts those defiled by beast spirits. I'm sure that many who let the milk of beasts pass their lips perish, but it's well-known that in Zol only those who live near animals, such as the border peoples and the lower classes, ever contract that sickness. Is that not so, Lona?"

Lona raised his eyes. "So it is said, my lord. However, to faithfully obey the Teachings is no easy task, and therefore, it is possible that not all nobility escape infection."

Utalu frowned in apparent annoyance. "And just what is that supposed to mean? We drink no milk from beasts and eschew all vices. How, then, could we become defiled?"

Lona, his face expressionless, answered matter-of-factly, "Defilement can transfer itself to one's body regardless of one's intentions. There are times when one only realizes they have been defiled after becoming ill."

Irritation rose in Utalu's eyes. "What're you trying to say? Are you suggesting that I should let this heathen inject me with poison?"

Lona shook his head. "No, my lord." A strong light gleamed in his eyes. "Clearly, to defile one's body by introducing the blood of an animal out of fear for one's life is to stray from the Heavenly Path."

Hohsalle stared at him, taken aback. He'd never heard Lona speak this sternly before.

"There is no medical cure for rabies," Lona stated with his eyes fixed steadily on Utalu. "Therefore, if one contracts it, the true response would be to accept it as the will of heaven."

Utalu pursed his lips, looking embarrassed. Hohsalle had listened silently to this exchange, but now he looked at Utalu and spoke. "I was merely informing you of the possibilities. What you decide, what action you choose, is entirely up to you."

The governor looked back and forth from his eldest son to Hohsalle, as if unable to decide, but when Utalu softly touched the Pure Heart charm that hung at his breast, he nodded. Hohsalle frowned slightly but inclined his head. "As you wish," he said.

After raising his head, he gazed at the governor. "There is one other possibility that concerns me. May I have your permission to speak?"

The governor's expression turned grim in apparent anticipation of what Hohsalle was about to say. "You mean black wolf fever?" he asked in a low voice.

"Yes. There has already been an outbreak at the salt mine. While my fear may prove groundless, if those were ossam that attacked us, it would be best to take precautions."

Utalu's expression did not waver, but his jaw tightened. A stern light gleamed in the governor's narrow eyes as he fixed them on Hohsalle. "What kind of precautions? What do you think we should do?"

"Two things come to mind," Hohsalle responded calmly. "The first is to deal with the ossam that harbor the disease. The second is to take care of the people who may have been infected. As I mentioned before, it will not be enough to simply seek out and exterminate the beasts. If it is black wolf fever, the ticks or fleas on infected beasts could switch to human hosts. We must therefore develop a thorough plan and proceed with caution."

The governor nodded. "I understand. That's what the Sacred Territory advised after that incident at the salt mine. We should do the same thing again, right?"

"Yes. Please."

"One other thing. I've been speaking with Lona. Since black wolf fever is native to this land, we know very little about it. We'll need your help, as you know far more than we do. If those beasts were indeed infected, do you have a cure?" The governor's face was pale, and his eyes betrayed his anxiety.

"Unfortunately, we have not found one yet," Hohsalle answered.

"However, thanks to what happened at the salt mine, we were able to obtain samples of the agent that causes the disease. We have many experienced medicine makers focusing their efforts on developing a cure, and we've divided them into three teams. The first is developing a less potent version made by weakening the infectious agent. This can be used to strengthen a patient's resistance to the disease, similar to the medicine we use to combat rabies.

"The second team labors to develop an anti-mittsual drug using lichens and other substances that suppress the disease agent's effectiveness. And the third team is trying to manufacture a serum from components produced by the bodies of infected patients to fight the disease. We can only make a small amount of this serum, so we won't have enough if many people contract black wolf fever. However, by combining all three approaches, we hope to achieve significant results.

"Already, we have procured some substances that look promising, but drug development is a painstaking and time-consuming process, and even the most promising have so far only been used on rats. They have never been tested on a human patient."

The room fell silent. For some time, no one spoke. Utalu maintained a stoic front, but Yotalu, who stood to the right of the governor, paled visibly. He slowly wiped a hand across his face. "So...that means...there is nothing we can do..."

Hohsalle looked at him and quietly replied, "Disease is a strange thing. Two people can be infected by the same illness, yet one will die while the other lives. In the case of black wolf fever, many Otawalle who were bitten by infected black wolves developed symptoms and died, yet it is said that the peoples who inhabited the remote regions of Aquafa, Oki, and Toga survived without manifesting any symptoms. The period between infection and developing symptoms is extremely short. Thus, I think it would be best to inject a solution containing the weakened disease agent immediately. If we do, we may be able to prevent the symptoms from appearing. Even if the dogs were diseased, the injection could help the patients resist it, just as the people of Aquafa did in the past."

Something hopeful shone in Yotalu's eyes. "That may be true. The sole survivor in the salt mine was Lone Antler Van, and he belonged to the Toga Ofal Oma, the People of the Toga Mountains."

Utalu laughed derisively. "So the poison of those filthy beasts isn't even toxic to those who live with them. Lucky you, Yotalu. You don't need to worry about your wife."

Yotalu clenched his jaw but said nothing and refused to look at his brother. The governor, however, fixed his eldest son with a stern gaze. Utalu looked surprised. He took a deep breath, coughed several times, and then fell silent.

"I beg your pardon," Hohsalle said. "But I notice that you have been coughing. Would you allow me to examine your throat?"

Utalu responded with a look of distaste and waved him away. "It's just a cold. There's no need to make a fuss."

Hohsalle stared him in the eye. "The first symptoms of both rabies and black wolf fever are very similar to those of a cold. With rabies, unless the person is bitten in the throat or head, symptoms would not appear this fast, but as I mentioned earlier, the incubation period for black wolf fever is far shorter. Please. I implore you not to dismiss this as a cold. If you notice any sign of a rash, please inform me immediately."

Utalu snorted. "What for? There'd be nothing you could do."

The governor slapped his hand against his thigh so sharply that a loud *crack* reverberated through the room, making everyone jump. Glaring at his eldest son, he roared, "Utalu! Hold your tongue! I won't tell you again."

The arrogant sneer on Utalu's face vanished, and a hint of fear surfaced on his expression, then faded. "Yes, Father." He bowed his head, then turned and looked straight at Hohsalle. "Forgive me. I spoke without thinking."

Hohsalle shook his head. "I should have chosen my words more carefully. I beg your pardon." Facing the governor, he added, "It is my earnest prayer that Utalu remains healthy. However, black wolf fever is very contagious. Should anyone display symptoms, we must treat them and move swiftly to prevent any possible spread. I fear that I may need to be quite blunt at times, but given the situation, I hope you will excuse me."

The governor nodded. "Of course. The most important thing is to ensure that it doesn't spread. Feel free to speak plainly. I will listen to whatever advice you offer."

A look of relief crossed Hohsalle's face, and he bowed. "Thank you, sir."

"But we must also exercise caution," the governor added authoritatively. "You will consult me first before taking any action."

Hohsalle returned his gaze squarely and bobbed his head. "I understand, sir."

3
Two Different Approaches

Hohsalle and Makokan were already walking down the corridor when the massive door slid open behind them, and Yotalu came striding up.

"About that weakened potion for mad-dog disease," he said tentatively.

"Yes?"

"If it's used, is there any risk that it would behave like a poison if a person has contracted black wolf fever?"

Hohsalle shook his head. "No, I do not believe so. It just helps the soldiers fighting the disease in a patient's body to remember what the enemy looks like so that they only attack the disease."

Yotalu frowned. "Excuse me? There are soldiers inside us?"

Hohsalle smiled. "I meant that as a metaphor. They don't look like people. But they protect our bodies just like soldiers guard a fortress. Have you ever noticed that a dirty cut often becomes filled with pus?"

"Yes."

"Pus is actually the corpses of invisible soldiers killed when they consumed disease agents that entered a wound. There are many of these soldiers inside us, and if they are strong, the wound will eventually scab over. When the scab falls off, new skin appears beneath, and the wound is healed."

Yotalu's eyes grew round. "Ohhh... So when we say that someone is cured, it actually means that these soldiers, as you call them, have battled against the disease agents and won."

Hohsalle nodded emphatically. Then he added, "And there are many types of soldiers. Just as a regiment that protects a castle has lookouts, archers, and military engineers, our bodies have soldiers that are responsible for many different tasks. But it's hard to tell if someone's an enemy on a first encounter. In the same way, it is difficult for the soldiers inside us to identify just from their appearance which agents are toxic and which are not. We need to train them to recognize a specific disease when it first invades and give them the weapons with which to fight."

"I see," Yotalu said. "So the weakened version basically shows the body's soldiers what the enemy looks like by introducing them to ones that have been injured and lost the strength to fight. Is that it?"

Hohsalle's eyes lit up. "Yes, that's correct. People have known for a long time that there are certain diseases we only get once and never again. But it was my grandfather, Limuelle, who discovered the reason for this and thought of a way to introduce weakened disease agents into the body."

Yotalu raised his brows. "It was Limuelle?"

"Yes." Hohsalle grinned. "And it was I who built upon that and developed a medicine that could be injected." His grin twisted into a wry smile. "But what I was trying to explain is that the treatment works because the soldiers only attack enemies they recognize. Still, because we introduce a foreign substance, the treatment does tax the body to some extent."

Yotalu blinked. "Yet it still increases the chance that the person might survive, doesn't it? If so, then please give it to Sulumina and Olimu."

Hohsalle held his gaze for a moment without responding. Finally, he said, "The fact that it burdens the body makes it difficult to predict the outcome. In some cases, a patient may react violently and be left with severe mental impairment." Seeing Yotalu flinch, Hohsalle added, "It is not a high possibility. In the twelve patients I have tried it on, it never occurred. But we have not tried it on enough people to be certain there is no risk."

Yotalu stared at Hohsalle, his face tense. "But if you don't give it to them and they do develop mad-dog disease, there will be no way of saving them."

"I've made it a policy to avoid declaring anything impossible, but I'm afraid you are right in this case. For me, at this time, there would be no way of saving them."

Yotalu exhaled slowly and shook his head. Resolve filled his eyes. "In that case, please do it. The most important thing is that they live, even if the treatment disables them."

Hohsalle looked at him. "Then you consent? To injecting them with a drug made from the disease agent of a dog?"

"Yes." Yotalu's expression twisted.

Hohsalle frowned as he watched Yotalu waver. *Even someone as intelligent as this man fears defiling the body with a substance derived from a beast.* Inoculating other Zolians promised to be extremely difficult.

Yotalu heaved a sigh, and his lips made a bitter smile. "The god knows that I have chosen this, not my wife or son. I will bear the sin of defiling their bodies. Please give them the injection."

"I understand. I will have it ready by this afternoon and take it to your hall," Hohsalle said. His expression softened. "If I were in your place, I would have made the same choice."

Yotalu seemed to sense that Hohsalle understood his difficult position, and his face relaxed a little. "You mentioned earlier that this method could also be used for black wolf fever. Is that true?"

Hohsalle's eyes shone, and he nodded. "Undoubtedly. If we employ this same method, the chances of saving victims should increase markedly. Additionally, if we can develop a version that can be injected in advance, then the best way to prevent an epidemic would be to administer it to those likely to come in contact with ossam."

Yotalu reacted with surprise. "You mean inject people who haven't even been bitten?"

"Yes. In other words, we could make people from Zol resistant to the disease just like the people of Aquafa."

"Ohhh…" A light kindled in Yotalu's eyes. "I see. That would indeed be the ultimate solution. If you could do that, we'd no longer need to fear black wolf fever."

Hohsalle gave a lopsided grin. "We're doing our best, but it's extremely difficult to make a weakened version that can be injected into the human body. It certainly can't be done in a night and a day, and even if things move quickly, there is still a chance that it could cause a violent reaction. We must take our time and thoroughly test each prototype through trial and error."

Yotalu exhaled. "So it won't be easy… Yet we cannot simply stand by and do nothing."

"No."

"For now, we must focus on those who've been bitten. I'm counting on you."

Hohsalle nodded. "Of course. I will do everything in my power."

Yotalu bowed and, turning on his heel, headed back toward the inner chamber. At that moment, the door slid open, and Lona stepped into the corridor. Yotalu looked a bit uncomfortable as he passed him and disappeared through the door, but Lona's expression was unmoved. He bowed to Hohsalle and was about to pass when Hohsalle stopped him. "Doctor Lona," he said.

The man paused, waiting.

For a moment, Hohsalle regretted his impulsive action. If he asked too much, it could disrupt the delicate balance between them, but if he wished to ask, this might be his only chance. "Please pardon my ignorance, but I understood that the medicine of the Pure Heart Creed would only leave a patient to the will of the god when there was no other way of healing them."

Lona's eyes narrowed ever so slightly, but he listened without moving or speaking.

"There is a way to prevent rabies. Would you reject it and thereby refuse to save a person's life?"

Lona remained silent. Just as Hohsalle thought that the man didn't intend to answer, his lips moved. "Yes, I would refuse."

Hohsalle frowned, waiting for him to continue. After a long pause, Lona said, "The god shaped this world the way we see it. He made men as men, dogs as dogs, and insects as insects. There must be a reason why each was given a different form and a different way of life. To transgress that line would generate chaos that the god never intended. That is something humans should never attempt."

Hohsalle stood with his lips parted, staring at him. *I see... So that's how these priest-doctors think. But surely people's lives are more important.*

He asked, somewhat sharply, "And for that reason, you would ignore the life you could save? Are you, a physician, saying that we should not rescue all lives we can?"

Lona's expression did not waver. He answered quietly, "It is not lives that we wish to save."

"Excuse me?"

"We wish to save the human soul." His voice sounded flat and lifeless. "All living things someday perish. What matters is how you live the existence you've been given, not its length. As priest-doctors, we strive to the best of our limited capacity to live pure, with ease of mind, rather than to prolong our stays in defiled bodies."

Hohsalle stared at him blankly. He felt as if the ground beneath him was shaking. His grandfather had often complained, *"There's no talking with those priest-doctors."* For the first time, Hohsalle understood.

"It's like pushing against air." How could he ever find where to press without any common ground? Hohsalle had been working with priest-doctors for a long time, and it was never easy. But so far, all the issues with them had stemmed from political friction arising from their desire to protect their authority. There'd been no opportunity to discuss their approach to medical treatment before, so Hohsalle never realized the premise upon which Pure Heart Creed medicine was based.

Incredible. This was no political issue. *The medicine of the Otawalle and that of the Pure Heart Creed split at the very root.*

Hohsalle shivered. Fear crept up from the bottom of his stomach and gripped his chest. The priest-doctors would never consent to inoculating patients to prevent them from contracting a disease.

And if that option is rejected now, after mittsual has reemerged... The Zolians had no immunity. It could cause another epidemic, taking untold lives.

Forcing down his frustration and terror, Hohsalle said, "Then what do you intend to do for the victims of this incident? Will you leave them to the will of heaven and do nothing?"

Lona appeared a little taken aback, as though Hohsalle's words were unexpected. "I did not say that. It is the introduction of animal blood into the body to combat an illness that is against the will of heaven. If there is any other method you know of that could be effective, please use it. We are unaccustomed to this black wolf fever and have no way of treating it, but if there is anything we can do to assist, please inform and allow us to help."

With that, Lona bowed and strode away.

Hohsalle stared after the receding priest-doctor, his lips pressed together firmly.

"We're visiting the King of Aquafa next, right?" Makokan asked from behind.

Hohsalle blinked. "Huh? ...Oh." Then he shook his head. "No, the Zolian falconer comes first."

"Really? Shouldn't you see Sir Mazai first?"

Hohsalle started for the entrance. "When a dog bites someone, the first things we need to consider are rabies, blood poisoning, and tetanus. They're all hard to prevent, but we've done everything we can at this point. As I told Lord Yotalu, in the case of rabies, the symptoms don't appear immediately. It can take a whole month before any develop, sometimes several years. We can't predict when the disease will manifest. We do know, however, that the closer a bite is to the victim's head, the sooner symptoms occur."

"Oh. So that's why you want to visit the Zolian falconer first. The fangs grazed him under the chin."

Hohsalle nodded, but his mind seemed to be somewhere else, and he muttered, "The hall of the king after that, I guess."

Makokan frowned. "Is something bothering you, sir?"

Hohsalle cast him a quick sideways glance but said nothing. Walking beside his grim-faced mohalu, who for once seemed in no mood for banter, Makokan felt as though something heavy was stuck in his chest.

4
In the Hall of the King of Aquafa

The King of Aquafa dwelled on the outskirts of the old capital, Kazan. After relinquishing his palace to the Zolian governor, he'd moved to a manor surrounded by a lush wood. The chambers of other royal family members were also scattered about the spacious grounds.

The king welcomed Hohsalle into the sunlit parlor and treated him with a gracious hospitality that was quite a contrast to the governor's reception. "If you are just arriving now, you must have visited Governor Ohan first without having a proper breakfast. I expected as much and had some food prepared for you, so please eat first."

A delicious aroma had enveloped Hohsalle and Makokan from the moment they entered the room. The table was laden with a sumptuous breakfast, and the steam rising from the dishes caught the sunlight. There were thin leavened pancakes dripping with a fragrant butter known as laku and sprinkled with sugar and syrup, as well as several egg dishes and chopped fruit with lachu in a glass bowl.

"I appreciate your hospitality, but there is not much time. If possible, I would like to see Sir Mazai and Izam and examine their wounds."

The king waved his hand. "As soon as I received word of your arrival, I sent for them. They will arrive momentarily. Please eat while you wait."

The relationship between Hohsalle, a member of the Otawalle nobility, and the king was a delicate one, and they both spoke with polite ambiguity. As he listened to their conversation from a corner of the room, Makokan thought it mirrored the relationship between Otawalle and Aquafa perfectly.

Mmm… That smells good. His stomach rumbled.

Hohsalle cocked an eyebrow at him. "How can you let your stomach growl so eloquently at a time like this?"

The king laughed. "An empty belly will interfere with his work as your bodyguard. Let me have the servants bring something that can be eaten while standing."

The king rang a bell for his attendant and ordered him to bring more breakfast. Hohsalle watched him thoughtfully, but by the time he turned around, Hohsalle had wiped all expression from his face.

While urging Hohsalle toward a chair at the table, the king said, "Now then, how was Lord Utalu?"

Hohsalle's eyes narrowed. "As a physician, I am not at liberty to share the symptoms of any of my patients with a third party. However, the governor's decision was generally what I expected." He went on to share the explanation he'd given the governor concerning treatment.

So that's why he went there first, Makokan thought. *So that he could inform the king of the situation in the palace.* He wondered if Governor Ohan had discerned that.

What a pain. The thought that within this single kingdom, three political forces intermingled, constantly probing each other's intentions, was daunting. *Though I suppose that's the spice of life for those two old hounds.*

Once the king had heard Hohsalle's explanation, he readily agreed to Hohsalle observing those bitten and to administering the rabies vaccine if it was considered necessary. "In fact, I'd already decided to request that you do so. Please give it to all the Aquafaese." Then he sighed. "It's a terrible affliction. I saw someone with it once when I was a child. We all have to die, but I would choose any death over that one."

Scooping up some lachu, Hohsalle looked at the king. "It's true. Rabies is a fearsome disease. But we have found a possible way to suppress the development of its symptoms, and there is no fear of it spreading rapidly because it isn't transmitted to ticks or other insects. We believe that mittsual poses the greater threat."

"Yes. Exactly. That evil scourge has returned to haunt us." The king sighed and looked out the window. "I am sure the gods of Aquafa are trying to tell us something. We must strain our ears to hear them."

Hohsalle laid down his spoon. Peering at the king, he said quietly, "Diseases are caused by invisible agents. There are an incredible number and variety, and the human body responds to them in an astounding multitude of ways. There is still so much we do not understand, but someday it will become clear, down to the minutest detail."

The king shifted his gaze back to Hohsalle and smiled. "The nobles of Otawalle are fond of saying that disease has nothing to do with the gods or evil spirits."

Hohsalle nodded. "Yes. We believe that, at the very least, disease is something within reach of the human hand."

The king shook his head slowly. "I personally do not agree. No matter how far we may stretch, there will always be places that are beyond our grasp. These belong to the gods and evil spirits. I am reminded daily that we are held within something far, far greater than we can imagine."

Hohsalle gave a slight smile. "This may sound strange, but I believe that, too—that we are enveloped by something immensely great."

The king looked surprised. "Really?"

Hohsalle nodded. "But I have no intention of allowing it to bring me to a standstill. I do not desire to lump everything together and accept it as 'the realm of the gods,' to close my eyes and hold back from touching it. I will continue forward, to extend my hand and search until there is no life left in me."

Then his smile faded. "I think I'm simply a coward. I find that very greatness terrifying. The realm that lies beyond us is incredibly vast and ever-changing. If such piddling creatures as ourselves are to survive on the shore of that great, surging ocean without being swept into the surf ceaselessly pounding the sand, we must confront each wave that comes."

Hohsalle gazed at the king, a strong gleam in his eye. "Diseases are strange things. For ages, they may remain completely harmless. Then, suddenly, they will turn into an enemy one day. As such, we should never take them lightly. Or so I believe."

The king's eyes narrowed. He opened his mouth to speak, but a bell rang outside the door at that moment. He blinked, then turned and invited the person to enter.

The door opened, and Mazai walked in with his son, Izam. Izam was two years older than Olimu and already as tall as his father, but he was still slender, and Makokan felt sorry to see his bandaged ankle.

"I beg your pardon," Mazai said. "We are interrupting your meal." He turned to leave, but Hohsalle stopped him with a smile and bade him come to the window.

"It was a shame we couldn't witness your skill yesterday, especially as I put up with the boredom of waiting just to see it." Hohsalle spoke lightly as he sat Mazai in a chair and removed the bandage from his arm. Makokan opened the treatment box and passed it to Hohsalle. First, Hohsalle cleaned his hands; then, with a practiced touch, he disinfected Mazai's wound and examined it carefully.

"Considering that you were bitten by a dog, it is healing very cleanly, isn't it?" He applied an ointment and a new bandage, and then took out a flat metal tongue depressor. "Please open your mouth and let me look at your throat."

In the light from the window, Hohsalle looked down Mazai's throat and felt behind both ears, then he requested Mazai remove his shirt so that he could listen to his chest with a funnel-shaped wooden tube. Once the examination was complete, he nodded once and smiled. "For now, there are no concerning symptoms."

Mazai relaxed visibly, and a slow smile spread across the face of the king, who'd remained sitting at the table.

"You're next," Hohsalle said to Izam. "Please come and sit here." Looking a little nervous, Izam did as bade, taking the seat vacated by his father. While Makokan knelt before him and carefully unwound the bandage from his ankle, Hohsalle asked the boy, "Does the bite hurt?"

"Yes. A little." His voice sounded hoarse and faint.

Hohsalle's eyes narrowed as he examined the wound and gently probed the area around it. He pressed a spot in the boy's groin. "Does that hurt as well?"

Izam nodded. "A little."

Hohsalle angled the boy's face to the sunlight. He examined the child's eyes and throat without his earlier grin. Once he finished listening to Izam's chest, he said, "You can dress now."

Hohsalle's eyes remained on the boy as he pulled on his shirt, but his thoughts seemed distant. Finally, he stood to address the king and Mazai. "He has no critical symptoms, but I am just a little concerned. As a precaution, I would like to take him to the clinic for a while so that we can observe him closely."

Mazai and the king both tensed. "What is it that concerns you?" the king asked.

"The area around the wound is fairly swollen, and he also has a little swelling in the groin and under the ears, and his throat is inflamed. These are all signs that some kind of disease agent has entered the body."

The two men paled, but Hohsalle smiled reassuringly. "This is natural after being bitten by a dog," he explained. "Disease agents have entered your body, too, Lord Mazai, so if the swelling begins to spread or your throat turns raw, we will ask you to come to our clinic as well. As these symptoms are already evident in Izam, we'll want to keep a close eye on him, just to be on the safe side. It's always best to err on the side of caution."

The boy sat there looking stunned, and Hohsalle placed a hand on his shoulder. "Please tell your servant that you will be spending a few nights away from the manor and to pack your things accordingly. But be careful how you say it. If you exaggerate, his face might go pale, just like your father's and grandfather's."

The boy's expression relaxed a little, and he nodded. After he bowed and left the room, Hohsalle said to the king, "I have one request."

The king had been staring absently after the boy, but he blinked and turned his eyes to Hohsalle. "What is it?"

"There's a hunting manor in Jikalu Wood, isn't there?"

The king frowned. "Yes."

"Would you be willing to lend it to me for a little while? I wish to make a temporary treatment center there."

The understanding was evident in the king's expression. "An infirmary to isolate people with mittsual?"

Hohsalle nodded. "Jikalu Wood is just the right distance from this manor, as well as from Kazan and the governor's palace—not too close and not too far. I'd been thinking of asking you if we could use it. Should we wait until someone comes down with the disease, it will be too late."

The king sighed deeply. "Of course. Take it. I'll send workmen there to prepare it for you." Then he lowered his voice. "Do you suspect that Izam has rabies?"

Hohsalle met the king's gaze steadily. "At this stage, I can't be sure. He was bitten on the ankle, so it's very unlikely that he has developed it in such a short space of time. The symptoms he exhibits are common among dog bite victims and those who've suffered deep wounds. Still, I want to take every possible precaution. Because I'm a coward."

5
Outbreak

Milalle breathed a sigh of relief. "So we'll have a place to gather the patients, will we? Thank goodness. I was wondering what we'd do if other patients who need our care popped up."

Hohsalle gazed out the window and frowned. "But that means we're going to be even busier. We can't be in two places at once."

Right after the attack, Hohsalle had sent a message to the Sacred Territory by carrier pigeon. The head of the Academy of Deeper Learning had replied that he was dispatching doctors and nurses immediately. However, there was no remaining idle until they arrived. Hohsalle had issued detailed instructions to his apprentices that demanded the meticulous management of every aspect of care, from daily checkups to meals and the time patients were to be roused in the morning. However, not everything could be left to the apprentices, even though they were well versed in medicine. Hohsalle's and Milalle's workload needed to increase if they hoped to provide treatment to patients at the infirmary in the woods while continuing regular care at the clinic. Still, as Milalle had said, the isolated infirmary was a boon for which they must be thankful. Even if the likelihood of person-to-person transmission was low, mittsual was still contagious.

"Hohsalle," Milalle called hesitantly.

"Hmm?"

"Why don't we ask Lona to loan us an apprentice?"

Hohsalle's face darkened. Seeing his expression, Milalle explained, "I think that, in one sense, this might be a good chance. If they could see the methods we use…"

Bitterness crossed Hohsalle's face, and he shook his head. His eyes narrowed, and he was silent for a while. When he raised his head, he answered, "It's a gamble, but maybe we should try it."

Milalle's expression relaxed slightly, and she nodded.

Lona accepted Hohsalle's request without protest and dispatched a young apprentice named Mana to the clinic. He arrived bearing a cloth bag filled with priest-doctor instruments. Tall, thin, and slightly stooped, he did not inspire confidence at first glance, but he grasped the point so quickly when Hohsalle and Milalle explained medical procedures that they realized Sir Lona had sent them a particularly talented healer.

*

When the governor learned that Sir Lona had dispatched an apprentice to help, he was delighted and happily gave permission to move the wounded Zolians to the infirmary in the woods. In addition to covering various costs, he contributed a large sum toward their treatment. By the third day, nearly all those affected had been transferred. However, the governor's eldest son, Utalu, evidently convinced his father to let him remain at home and refused to budge.

Almost all the patients complained of fever and lethargy, but such things were common with infected dog bites. It was not until the morning of the sixth day after the royal hunt that the symptoms changed.

*

Mana rushed into the room with face pale. "Sir Hohsalle." It had been drizzling all night, and cutting through the inner garden to make haste left the apprentice with dripping hair he had to tame back. "The Zolian falconer has developed a rash," he said.

Hohsalle's face tensed. He glanced at Milalle and headed for the door. Without a word, she retrieved a wooden box from a shelf and followed after him.

"Here, let me carry that for you," Makokan said, reaching for the box, but Milalle shook her head.

"I'm fine. It's quite light. And it needs to be transported in a special way." Her voice was firm, but her face was pale. Her expression revealed to Makokan that she and Hohsalle had been expecting this and were already prepared.

"You can carry that cloth bag for me," Hohsalle said, and Makokan picked it up and strode after them.

That was the beginning of many sleepless days and nights.

Initially, the symptoms resembled those of a cold—things like a sore throat and fatigue. But once the rash appeared, the disease progressed rapidly. This was characteristic of black wolf fever.

The rash emerged early in the morning. By evening, the falconer had come down with a high fever. After complaining that his body felt as heavy as lead, he sank into a stupor. In the middle of the night, despite desperate attempts to treat him, his body arched in violent convulsions, and he breathed his last.

When Milalle covered the falconer's face with a white cloth, his wife and daughter, who'd been watching from a corner of the room, clung to each other in tears. It was a pitiful sight. Were his affliction not contagious, they could have at least sat beside him and held the poor man's hand to comfort him. But they could not even approach, let alone touch him.

With a sigh, Milalle closed her eyes and bowed her head. After a long moment, she opened her eyes and spoke softly to the falconer's wife and daughter, expressing her sympathy and urging them to move to another room to rest, saying that she would call them when the body had been washed. When she took them outside, Mana followed. He approached the bereaved in the corridor and said, "I am Mana, a priest-doctor."

The falconer's wife looked up at him with a startled expression and then stared at him imploringly. Regarding her with a compassionate look, Mana said gently, "It was a very painful end, but the god in heaven witnessed his suffering. He has surely taken your husband into his arms and embraced him, praising him for his efforts and telling him that he lived a good life. He will lead your husband to peace and ease in heaven."

There was no trace of doubt in his voice. His words brought tears to the eyes of the wife and daughter.

"Your hearts must be heavy with grief," Mana continued quietly. "But be strong and live nobly. The god is watching over you. If you live well the lives he has given, the time will come when you embrace your husband and father in heaven. Until then, you must be patient and strive your best to live praiseworthy existences."

The two women wept aloud. Yet their sobs sounded different, tinged with relief, as though they'd been set free.

Milalle gazed at the scene blankly.

Makokan watched Mana bend slightly over the women as he comforted them. *Those priest-doctors really are more servants of their god than physicians.* He mused that, when it came to things that transcended the power of man, perhaps the priest-doctors were better equipped to help.

Milalle watched Mana with a conflicted expression. Perhaps she felt the same way.

After taking care of the wife and daughter, Milalle returned with Mana and stood by Hohsalle, who peered down at the falconer's body.

"...Do you think there's any chance that it was tetanus?" Her voice sounded indistinct, muffled by her cloth mask.

Hohsalle shook his head wordlessly.

"I suppose not," Milalle murmured. "He showed no aversion to light or sound, and the convulsions progressed differently." Aware of Mana watching respectfully from behind, she gently touched a syringe that lay on the bedside table. "It didn't work, did it? I was hoping it might because it responded to the mittsual agent we cultivated."

"Mittsual agent?" Mana asked tentatively from where he stood in the corner of the room.

Milalle turned and beckoned the apprentice priest-doctor to come nearer. When the tall young man stood beside her, she explained quietly, "We believe disease is caused by tiny living organisms, which we call 'agents.'"

Mana raised his brows. "Living organisms cause disease?"

"I can show you later," Hohsalle said.

Mana's eyes grew round. "Really? You mean you can see them? They're that big?"

Hohsalle shook his head. "No, not at all. They're too small to be seen by the naked eye. There are some that are big enough to see by other means, although not the disease agents that cause black wolf fever. They're too small."

"How in the world—?"

"I'm sorry, but I don't have the energy to explain right now." After a deep breath, Hohsalle looked at Milalle. "It seems there's a high possibility that those beasts carried black wolf fever."

Milalle nodded. "Shall we give all the patients the new drugs before they develop a rash? I personally think we should do so as soon as possible. The symptoms turn acute very rapidly... To be honest, I'm worried that we may already be too late. Had we done so right after they were bitten, the results might have been different."

Hohsalle rested a hand on the syringe and was about to nod, when he paused. He pondered for a moment, then shook his head. "The weakened version and the anti-mittsual drug, yes, we can give them to everyone, but let's only use the serum on the Zolian patients."

Makokan, who'd been listening to their conversation, was puzzled. *Not the Aquafaese? Why?*

Mana appeared to have been thinking the same thing, because the question was already on his lips. Milalle explained carefully, and Mana appeared to understand, but Makokan remained completely in the dark.

I wish they'd speak in words I understand. But he knew that Hohsalle would only snap at him if he asked now, so he kept his mouth shut.

At dawn the next day, the other Zolian patients all broke out in a rash. The medicine, which had been injected before the rash appeared, must have had some effect, because they remained conscious until the next day. After that, however, they fell into comas one by one, were seized by convulsions, and died, despite every effort made to save them. At this point, the only surviving Zolians were Utalu and Olimu. Not one Aquafaese got a rash.

Hohsalle hardly slept. By the second day, his fatigue was evident to those around him. He was grabbing a stand-up lunch during a quick break when Mana approached him. "Sir Hohsalle," he said hesitantly. "Would you please drink this?"

Hohsalle examined the offered cup and frowned. "What is it?"

"A tonic made by brewing six types of herbs. It works very well to alleviate fatigue. Perhaps you already know of it, but if not, I recommend that you try it." He looked a little embarrassed. "Over the last few days, you have taught me many things I never knew before. Please accept this as a small token of my appreciation."

Still frowning, Hohsalle raised the cup and sniffed. "I'm not familiar with this smell." He downed it in one gulp and grimaced.

"Was it bitter?"

"Not really," Hohsalle said with a shake of his head. "It went down much easier than I expected."

Mana's face relaxed. "Good. In that case, it should be very effective. The fact that it was easy to drink is an indication that your body needs it."

Hohsalle thanked him and returned to his work. Toward the end of the day, he noticed a sensation of warmth inside. He was tired, but his body no longer felt shackled the way it had before lunch. That evening, he told Mana and thanked him. Mana's face lit up. "I am so glad to hear that. In the Pure Heart Creed, we priest-doctors believe that the greatest skill is the ability to brew medicines that help us lead healthy lives. It gladdens me to know that it helped with your exhaustion a little."

Hohsalle looked at him intently, then flicked his eyes to Milalle and back again. "I see." His voice was filled with emotion. "There are many differences in our medical practices, yet even so, we seek the same thing. I suppose that's only natural." Then he smiled. "I'd like you to teach me how to make that drink, if you're willing. I'd like to give some to Milalle."

Mana nodded happily. "Of course. I would be honored to. I shall write out the instructions. However, Milalle is a woman, and if my diagnosis is correct, the herbs that would suit her body are different. I will prepare a potion for her immediately."

Milalle smiled and thanked Mana sincerely. He blushed and bowed his head.

Makokan schooled his lips, struggling to disguise the unbidden smile that rose at this exchange. He recalled someone mentioning that priest-doctors of the Pure Heart Creed never married. Although he doubted this information was true, Mana's youth seemed so naive. He was ecstatic when Milalle spoke to him, yet became all tongue-tied when he tried to answer. Just watching these exchanges warmed Makokan's heart in a way he'd not experienced for some time.

6
Battling the Disease

On the afternoon of the ninth day after the falcon hunt, the bell at the entrance to the infirmary rang loudly, followed by a commotion. Hohsalle raised a wan face just as a messenger from the governor barged into the room and said, "Report to the palace immediately!"

He offered no more, but it was clear from his expression that there was no choice, and that alone was enough to make Hohsalle hurry.

Utalu must have developed a rash...

Leaving Milalle behind to continue treating the patients, Hohsalle handed Makokan his bag and climbed into the carriage.

By the time they reached the palace, Utalu had already fallen into a stupor. Lona and his disciples sat around the bedding on which he lay in the middle of a large room. The window shades had been lowered, and the faint scent of incense rose in the dim light. Hohsalle recognized the smell.

Meikonko... The priest-doctors used it when there was no hope of a cure. They put the patient to sleep with a painkiller and lit incense to help the doomed soul leave this world peacefully.

With Yotalu by his side, the governor watched over his eldest son from a short distance. He raised his eyes at Hohsalle's arrival.

"He hid the rash from us." His voice was husky, and the words came out slowly. "Last night, he looked pale, then at lunch, he collapsed. We undid his collar to help him breathe more easily... That's when we realized."

The governor's eyes were rimmed with red, and something glistened in the deep creases at the corners of them.

Hohsalle glanced away. *The face of a father. I wish I'd not seen that.*

He looked over at Utalu. His chest was rising and falling regularly. *The convulsions haven't started yet*, he realized. *Then perhaps...*

Yotalu seemed to read his mind. "Is there something you can do?"

Hohsalle raised his head and looked at Yotalu. "Maybe. If we inject some medicine. Yet up to this point, even when we have done so, the best we have managed is to prolong the patient's life for another day and night."

Yotalu's mouth twisted, and he looked at the governor. "Father," he said.

Governor Ohan clenched his jaw, and the muscles protruded. He looked at Lona, then at his son lying prone on the bed. Finally, he forced the words out. "When he collapsed, he begged me not to defile his body with Otawalle medicine. If you could guarantee that it would work, then I would ignore his wishes, but..."

Tears filled his eyes. "If it will only prolong his life for another day, then I cannot ignore his final wish. The god is watching."

He closed his eyes, and for a long time, his thick lips quivered. Suddenly, his eyes flew open, and he cried out, "Live, Utalu! Don't let this disease defeat you!"

Utalu, however, was beyond the reach of his father's voice. Following a pattern that was now all too familiar to Hohsalle, the man sank into a coma and went into convulsions. At midnight, he drew his last breath. Hohsalle watched with a sense of unreality as this man who'd shamelessly taunted his younger brother just a few days before, who'd stood at the vanguard and led his men fearlessly to battle, exited the world as easily as a withered leaf falling from the stem.

*

The loss of the firstborn son of the Ohan family was a bitter blow. Yotalu couldn't leave his father during this crisis. Looking worried and impatient, he beckoned Hohsalle into his office and asked hastily, "You said that Sulumina and Olimu haven't developed rashes yet. Is that right?"

"Yes. When I left the infirmary, neither of them had one."

Yotalu grasped his wrist. "What do you think that means? The fact that they have no rashes yet? Is there a good chance they'll survive?"

Hohsalle gazed back at Yotalu. "I don't know what will happen next, so I cannot say anything right now. But I believe the fact that they have stayed free of rashes longer than Utalu, who was a very healthy man, shows they have a strong resistance to the disease."

Hohsalle placed his hand over Yotalu's where it grasped his left wrist and brought his face slightly closer. "As yet, no Aquafaese has developed a rash."

A light gleamed in Yotalu's eyes. For a long moment, they gazed at each other silently. Then Hohsalle gently removed his hand and whispered, "You should prepare yourself for the worst, but there is reason to hope."

Yotalu moved away from Hohsalle and covered his face with both hands. "Olimu." It was a heartrending cry, filled with grief and worry for his son, who was only half Aquafaese.

But Olimu was not the next one to break out into a rash.

*

As soon as Hohsalle returned to the hall in Jikalu Wood, Mana called out to him. "Milalle wishes you to come immediately."

Hohsalle frowned. "Olimu?" he asked.

Mana shook his head. "No. It's Sir Izam."

Hohsalle grimaced. Pursing his lips, he hurried to the room where Izam lay. The morning light shone through a large window, gently illuminating the boy's body from the chest down.

As Hohsalle entered, Milalle turned. There were dark rings under her eyes, and her face was sickly pale. Hohsalle walked over to the bed and stood beside her. Although conscious, Izam appeared only vaguely aware. His eyes were vacant and unfocused, wandering from place to place. Small red spots showed here and there on his slender, sweat-drenched neck.

"...His temperature rose a little while ago," Milalle said quietly.

Hohsalle nodded, then gently touched her elbow. "I'll take over now. Go and get a little rest."

She opened her mouth to speak but then closed it and gave a brief nod. She seemed shrunken. Her shoulders drooped, and her feet dragged ever so slightly as she departed the room.

"Mana, I'm sorry but...," Hohsalle began, and Mana nodded immediately.

"I have already prepared a brew for Milalle. I will warm it and have her partake of it immediately. It includes herbs that relax a stressed mind. She will sleep soundly."

Hohsalle bowed deeply. Mana looked surprised but then quickly returned the gesture and followed after Milalle.

Once they'd gone, Hohsalle leaned over the boy lying on the bed and said into his ear, "Izam, can you hear me?" But there was no response. It was clear the path the disease would take from here.

Standing behind his master, Makokan turned his eyes away from Izam's boyish face—away from his vacant gaze that stared at a place not of this world.

That afternoon, Izam started shivering. His fever must have risen sharply. Bending over him, Hohsalle called out desperately. "Hang on, Izam! Don't give in! Stay awake! Stay awake!" Chanting this as if it were some incantation, Hohsalle beat his hand against his own forehead. His knees shook. He'd barely slept in three days.

He's reached his limit, Makokan thought. He went over and laid his hand on Hohsalle's shoulder, but his mohalu struck it away.

"Don't touch me!"

"But—"

"Shut up!"

Makokan looked at Mana, who sat beside Hohsalle. "What about that herbal potion?"

Mana shook his head with a look of regret. "He has already had some. Any more would—"

"I said leave me alone!" Hohsalle snapped. "This is no time to fret about me!"

The sound of the door opening overlapped his words. Hohsalle turned, and his eyes widened. With a stunned expression, he stared at the person who entered. "Grandfather," he whispered.

The elderly man, dressed in a light brown robe, quietly paced to Hohsalle and stood beside him. Milalle followed behind. She gave Hohsalle a slight nod and took position a few steps away. She had likely taken Mana's potion and slept deeply, because the color had returned to her cheeks.

Grandfather? So this must be Limuelle! Makokan thought. Limuelle Yuguraul—the celebrated physician who'd saved the Zolian emperor's wife. Grandfather of Hohsalle, and the man who'd raised him like a son. Makokan had difficulty believing the living legend was here in the flesh.

Limuelle was a tall man. Wavy gray hair framed his long face, gentle and calm, but a fierceness showed in his eyes. He glanced at Mana, and a look of keen interest flickered across his features, but he shifted his gaze back to Hohsalle and urged him to explain Izam's condition. When Hohsalle finished, Limuelle reached out a hand and gently raised Izam's eyelids. Moving the candle Hohsalle had handed him, Limuelle examined the boy's pupils. "No convulsions yet?" he asked in a low voice.

Hohsalle shook his head. "No."

"Then let's try injecting kokalu."

His words must have been unexpected. Hohsalle looked up at him with a startled expression. "Kokalu?"

"Oh!" Milalle exclaimed in a small voice.

Hohsalle turned to look at her. "What?" he asked.

Milalle came closer and gazed with deference at Limuelle. "Are you thinking of using the same treatment used during the time of the Mad Dog of Soola?"

Understanding entered Hohsalle's expression. He knit his brow and pressed his fingers against his forehead. "We didn't use kokalu then. We used bossa."

"Yes. But kokalu is more potent than bossa," Milalle replied.

"But..." Hohsalle was clearly torn.

Limuelle gripped his shoulder. "It must be administered before the convulsions begin. Otherwise, it will be meaningless."

Hohsalle took a deep breath and nodded at Milalle.

She turned on her heel and left the room. Assuming that she was going to prepare the kokalu, Makokan followed after her. "Please let me help," he said.

"Oh yes. Thank you."

Before Makokan closed the door, Mana placed a hand on it and stepped into the corridor. "May I also have permission to accompany you?"

"Yes, of course."

The sun had already begun its descent, casting long shadows on the hall. As the three hurried through strips of light and shadow toward the medicine storeroom, Mana asked, "Is kokalu dangerous?"

Milalle glanced at him. "It's rarely used on humans. Primarily, it's for sedating animals."

Mana's eyes widened. "To sedate animals?"

"Yes. It puts them to sleep quickly without interfering with respiration, which makes it a very useful medicine. However, it is extremely potent, and it's possible that the patient will never wake."

"Then why would you risk using it now?"

Milalle placed a hand on a post as she turned the corner. "A few years ago, Sir Limuelle saved a young girl who'd contracted rabies. The only successful case ever. At that time, he sedated her with bossa, which has the same effect as kokalu. I can fill you in on the details later if you wish, but basically, he suppressed the convulsions by rendering the patient unconscious and shutting out the brain's commands to the body."

She paused and then continued. "So far, all the patients here have died because the convulsions arrested their breathing. I think Limuelle intends to suppress the tremors by putting the brain to sleep, giving the body the necessary time to combat the disease agents."

Milalle pressed her lips together. Her face was pale, but there was strength in her eyes. Her silhouette radiated the determination of a mother protecting her child.

Once the kokalu was administered, Izam quickly fell into a coma. Although his breathing was shallow, it did continue. Limuelle waited until that was confirmed before turning to Hohsalle. "Have you injected him with all the new drugs?"

"Yes. But in all patients thus far, they only repressed the symptoms for about a day. Ultimately, we haven't saved any of them."

Limuelle's eyes narrowed. "How much stock do you have? Is there much left?"

"Milalle has worked steadily to prepare the anti-mittsual drug, so we have plenty of that."

Limuelle glanced at Milalle and smiled. Then he returned his attention to Hohsalle and said, "Then keep giving it to the boy."

Hohsalle's eyes wavered, but he nodded. "I understand."

Mana observed this conversation from behind with unconcealed excitement.

Milalle had patiently explained to Makokan what was transpiring, so he vaguely grasped what she and the others intended to do.

They're going to try and give him the strength to fight the disease by injecting the anti-mittsual drug while he's sedated.

Although it was a gamble as to whether or not the boy's slight body could win that cruel battle, the prospect of guiding him down a different path from the others reinvigorated Hohsalle and Milalle completely.

Izam did not succumb to convulsions, even in the middle of the night. By entrusting his treatment to Limuelle, Hohsalle and Milalle were at last able to return to their beds and rest.

7
The New Remedy

Izam was still alive the next day. When Hohsalle entered the room with Mana, Limuelle was sitting by the boy's bed, taking his pulse. The early-afternoon sunlight shone white on the side of Limuelle's face. He'd traveled far and stayed up all night yet showed no trace of fatigue.

Grandfather's so fit, he doesn't seem like he could possibly be over sixty, Hohsalle thought.

Words could never adequately express how much he cherished this man, who had initiated him into the art of medicine and taught him so much else, serving as a surrogate for his father, who died young. Yet whenever Hohsalle looked Limuelle in the eye, he felt his chest tighten.

He walked over and stood beside his grandfather, but Limuelle didn't look up until he'd finished his task. When he'd placed Izam's arm gently under the covers, he finally raised his head. "His blood pressure is a little low and his pulse is slow, but it's steady."

Hohsalle nodded. "Thank you. I'll take over now. Please go and get a little rest."

Limuelle stood and stretched. "Yes, I will, thank you. But if there is any change, let me know immediately. Spare no consideration for me."

"I understand."

Once he'd gone, a white stillness filled the room. Izam slept with his lips slightly parted.

What's going on behind that forehead? Hohsalle wondered as he watched the boy's face.

Skin, pale and smooth. A thin layer of fat beneath. Bone. Then brain. What motion within the brain caused people to think, to feel pain, to tremble?

As a child, his grandfather's explanations on the structure of the human body filled him with the strange illusion that his own form was transparent, exposing the interior workings. That image still came to him occasionally, despite the fact that he'd grown up.

The body, constantly working to support life, even when unconscious—a system perpetually in motion, even while at rest, as though a living entity separate from the thinking, feeling self.

Izam was sunk in a deep sleep, yet, regardless of his will, his body engaged in a desperate battle to survive.

The body… Life… What are these things? Whenever Hohsalle beheld the human form, he could not help but wonder.

Gently, he straightened the covers and sighed. Then he turned to where Makokan stood and said, "Would you bring some tea?"

"Yes, sir."

"Some for Mana, too."

Makokan nodded, but Mana looked flustered. "Oh no. Please do not trouble yourself," he protested.

"Don't worry. It's no trouble at all," Makokan replied with a smile. Just as he placed his hand on the door, however, a knock came from the other side. He opened the door to find Mazai standing there. His eyes were bloodshot, and he looked feverish.

"Sir Mazai!" Makokan exclaimed.

Mazai peered anxiously into the room. "How is Izam?" he asked.

Hohsalle rose and said, "Please come in."

Mazai walked over to his son's bed and looked down at the boy where he lay sleeping.

"We've sedated him, but his condition is stable," Hohsalle explained.

The tenseness in Mazai's face eased. "I see." Without another word, he rested his hand on the headboard and watched his son.

"You look like you have a fever," Hohsalle remarked.

Mazai's cheeks were flushed, and he turned and nodded. "My throat's been a bit sore since a little earlier." He eyed the syringe on the bedside table, then turned his gaze to Hohsalle. "I asked Doctor Milalle to inject me with the new remedy, but…"

"She refused, didn't she?"

"Yes." Mazai licked his parched lips. His shoulders heaved with each breath. "Why?"

Hohsalle sat him down in a chair. While taking his pulse, he said, "Because this medicine may cause a severe allergic reaction."

"Allergic reaction?"

"Yes. It could even stop your breathing and kill you."

Mazai frowned. "But you gave it to Izam."

Hohsalle blinked. "Yes, we did. Because it was clear that his body was already losing the battle with the disease."

Mazai remained silent for a while. Then, as though working to force out the words, he said, "I have a fever. My body aches all over. Isn't that a sign that I am also losing the battle?"

Hohsalle didn't answer but continued to look at him.

Mazai's breath was hot. "Does it always cause an allergic reaction?" he questioned.

"No, not always."

"If it does, will it kill me for certain?"

"No. There's a risk that you might die, but it could also help save you. However, there may be other adverse side effects."

"But it will not kill me for certain. Correct? Doesn't that mean there's a greater likelihood that I'll die of the disease?"

Hohsalle was silent. Mazai implored the man with his eyes. "Please," he rasped. "Give me the injection. I was bitten by a dog infected with mittsual, and my body is suffering. Whether you inject me or not, there's a high possibility that I'll die… I can't perish yet. I can't leave my wife and children behind. I'd rather gamble my life on a remedy that gives me a greater chance, no matter how small an increase."

Hohsalle pursed his lips, deep in thought. Eventually, he sighed and shifted his gaze to Makokan.

"Go tell Milalle to prepare what we need to respond to an allergic reaction and then return."

When Milalle arrived, Hohsalle explained the situation. Mana laid out the equipment, carefully following Milalle's instructions, while Hohsalle told Mazai what he needed to watch out for. "If you feel faint, weak, or a tightness in your throat, let me know immediately. An allergic reaction usually occurs within five to ten mul (minutes), but sometimes it can take only a few min (seconds). So if you start feeling ill, tell me immediately."

Mazai regarded Hohsalle anxiously. "My throat hurts, but that's not what you mean, right?"

"Correct. I want you to tell me if you feel like you can't breathe."

Mazai nodded. With deft movements, Hohsalle injected the medicine into the man's arm. "Please press the spot with this cotton cloth. How do you feel?"

Mazai swallowed. "I don't feel any difference, although my throat still hurts."

Time seemed to pass excruciatingly slowly. Hohsalle told Makokan and Mana to bring another bed into the room so that Mazai could be with his son. As he lay down, Mazai closed his eyes with relief. Doubtless, he was exhausted. Fever had his skin flushed.

Milalle attended to both patients carefully to ensure that neither became dehydrated, and someone—Hohsalle, Milalle, or one of their apprentices—was always in the room. After several hours, Mazai still showed no signs of an allergic reaction.

That night, Yotalu's son Olimu and his wife, Sulumina, came down with a fever.

8
Allergic Reaction

When Hohsalle and the others entered the room, Olimu was lying in bed. Sulumina sat beside him, stroking his hand. Olimu's face was flushed, but he had no rash, and his eyes were still alert.

"Does your throat hurt?" Hohsalle asked, and Olimu nodded. "All right. Open your mouth, then."

While Hohsalle looked down his throat, felt behind his ears, and checked his pulse, Milalle did the same for Sulumina. "Your symptoms haven't changed since this morning," she said, "although perhaps your throat is a little redder."

Sulumina's eyes were fixed anxiously on her son and Hohsalle while she listened to Milalle. "Will Olimu be all right?"

Hohsalle nodded. "There's no rash yet, and both of your symptoms appear quite mild compared to the other patients. We must still be careful, but I think there's much reason for hope."

Sulumina let out a held breath, relieved. "And what about Izam and my brother?"

From behind Hohsalle, Makokan listened to him explain their condition in simple terms. Although he was often moody and unpredictable, Hohsalle showed surprising sensitivity and compassion when speaking with patients and their anxious family members. *He's a doctor through and through.* Makokan always thought as much when he witnessed this side of his mohalu.

Sulumina appeared to be considering something as she listened to Hohsalle, but when she heard that Mazai had been injected with the new serum, her eyes lit up. "You gave it to him? That's wonderful! Milalle said we couldn't have it, so I thought there was no hope."

Milalle looked troubled and opened her mouth to speak, but Hohsalle stopped her and explained to Sulumina the risks involved, just as he had for Mazai. Sulumina nodded as he spoke, but it was clear from her expression that her heart was set on having the injection.

When he finished, she leaned forward. "I understand what you've told me, including the risks. But that doesn't matter. I beg you to give both of us that new medicine. I cannot bear to wait in fear, not knowing whether my son will be able to vanquish this disease." Her words came out in a rush. "Despite all my prayers, Olimu still came down with a fever. And so did I. I feel like I'm about to lose my mind. I'm just so afraid. So afraid."

Hohsalle laid his hand over hers and pressed it gently. "Please calm yourself. You are Olimu's mother. You must not let him see you like this."

Sulumina opened her eyes wide, as if coming to her senses.

"Olimu hasn't developed a rash yet," Hohsalle continued. "There is still a good possibility that he may survive without any intervention. We haven't been able to test whether the serum is truly safe for humans or not. I certainly don't recommend giving it to him and risking an allergic reaction just because you are afraid."

Sulumina stared at him. For a few moments, she struggled to control her ragged breathing. Finally, she closed her eyes and, after heaving a deep sigh, opened them again. "In that case, just give it to me. I am his mother. He was born from my body. I gave him my blood. If it works safely for me, then won't that mean it will be safe to use it on him as well?"

Hohsalle frowned. "We cannot say for certain. It is true that a child's sensitivity to medicine resembles the mother's, but—"

"My older brother didn't show any signs of a dangerous reaction, did he? We are siblings. Isn't it likely that our sensitivity to the drug is similar, too?" Her words tumbled over each other, betraying her desperation.

Makokan felt a twinge of concern upon seeing the obsession on her face—one that had nothing to do with medicine. *If he doesn't give her and Olimu the new remedy, it could create problems.*

Sulumina was the niece of the King of Aquafa, and Olimu was the king's blood kin. But he also happened to be the grandson of the governor. With such complex family ties, what would people think if they learned of the differing treatments? Mana, who was observing everything, would be able to accurately explain why, but officials and warriors without any medical knowledge would undoubtedly draw their own conclusions.

No matter what method we choose, this disease is lethal. It would be less trouble to give everyone the same treatment.

Hohsalle would certainly have thought of that already, but it was unlikely to make him change his approach. It was his creed that medical decisions should be made solely in consideration of the patient and their life. In this respect, he was incredibly stubborn.

"Makokan."

Hearing his name called, Makokan blinked. "Yes, sir?"

"Go and ask Sakkol how Mazai is doing. Be sure to inquire about other symptoms as well, not just signs of an allergic reaction."

"Yes, sir." Makokan left and headed for the room where Hohsalle's top apprentice, Sakkol, watched over Mazai. When Makokan knocked on the door and entered, he found Limuelle seated beside Mazai's bed, conversing with Sakkol.

"Excuse me for interrupting," he said quietly.

Limuelle looked up. "What is it?"

Makokan explained what Hohsalle wanted to know. When he finished, Limuelle, who'd appeared deep in thought, rose. "I will go with you. Show me to the room."

*

"Grandfather." Hohsalle stood from his chair when Limuelle entered. The older man nodded to his grandson and then smiled at Sulumina.

"How are you feeling?" he asked.

Sulumina described her symptoms, trembling slightly with nervousness over speaking with the illustrious Limuelle. Limuelle nodded as he listened and, when she finished, looked at Hohsalle. "I hear that Lady Sulumina wishes to try the new serum."

"Yes."

"I see. If she understands the risks involved and still wishes to do so, I believe we should try it. What do you think?"

Hohsalle frowned and gazed at Limuelle. For a few moments, they regarded each other silently. "Of course, there are many potential problems that we must consider first," Limuelle added. He turned to Sulumina. "My lady, you are the wife of Governor Ohan's younger son, and Olimu is his precious grandson. I would like to write a message to Lord Yotalu and obtain his permission before we start so that we may avoid any unnecessary problems arising later. Would that be acceptable?"

Sulumina nodded immediately. "Yes, of course. Please do."

Hohsalle followed Limuelle out of the sickroom into the corridor.

"Grandfather," he whispered fiercely. "Do you intend to use those two as lab rats?"

Limuelle turned to face his grandson. "The disease agents are multiplying rapidly in their bodies. The earlier the medicine is injected, the more effective it will be. They both appear to have some immunity, but their fevers are beginning to rise. It is possible that their symptoms will follow the same pattern as those of previous patients. I admit this is a gamble, but I think the odds are better if we cast our bet on suppressing an allergic reaction, which is something we know how to deal with."

Hohsalle's face twisted. "Stop trying to fob me off with an answer for an amateur." His eyes blazed. "Admit it. You want to see how their bodies will react."

Limuelle met his grandson's gaze steadily and said in a low voice, "If you knew that, then there was no need to ask."

Hohsalle pressed his lips together and glared at his grandfather. Then he let out a deep breath. "Damn!" He clucked his tongue. "You're as terrible as always. But I suppose I take after you."

Limuelle gave a faint smile and turned away.

*

As soon as word of approval from Yotalu arrived, Limuelle gathered the supplies he'd require if Sulumina had an allergic reaction and returned to the room where she and Olimu were staying. Even though she'd asked them to inject her first, her face tightened when she saw the syringe, and Olimu seemed as though he would burst into tears.

"Come now. Don't make such a face," Limuelle said brightly as he looked down at them. "I know it appears frightening," he said to Olimu, "but it won't hurt as much as you think. You know that, right? It will be over by the time you count 'one, two, three.' You have inherited the blood of a brave Zolian commander and the King of Aquafa. I'm sure you can bear the pain for such a short time. Don't you think so?"

When put like that, as the son of a warrior, Olimu could not very well show his fear. His boyish face tensed, and he nodded. "Just as I thought," Limuelle said. "A true warrior. You may be young, but your nature shows already."

After praising the boy with a smile, Limuelle shifted his attention to Sulumina. "I will give Olimu the injection first. His fever is higher than yours. If we are going to use it, the sooner the better. Once his condition has settled, I will inject you with the new serum, too. Do you understand?"

Sulumina's face paled at this. "If that al-, uhm, if that reaction occurs?"

Hohsalle raised his hand. "We are standing by, ready to help you. It's better not to fret. Now that you've come this far, just relax and take it as it comes."

Limuelle measured the serum carefully and sucked it into the syringe. After removing the air bubbles, he grasped Olimu's slender, trembling arm, wiped the skin with a cloth soaked in solution, and inserted the needle.

Olimu winced, but when Limuelle drew out the needle and said, "There. It's done. That wasn't so bad, was it?" he breathed a deep sigh and nodded, still trembling slightly.

Olimu showed no signs of an allergic reaction. The spot where the needle had been inserted swelled more than it had for Mazai, but there were no pronounced symptoms, even after some time had passed.

Sulumina, however, proved to be a different case.

Soon after the new medicine was injected, her face changed color.

"My mouth...," she said hoarsely. Then she turned white and grasped her throat. Sweat beaded on her forehead and trickled down her cheeks. She gulped for air, and her mouth moved like a fish's. She couldn't breathe.

This sudden and drastic reaction terrified Makokan, who watched from the sidelines, but Hohsalle and Milalle remained unflustered, responding with smooth and coordinated movements. Hohsalle held Sulumina's forehead with one hand, placed a finger under her chin, and raised it to secure her air passages. Milalle placed a sprayer nozzle into her mouth and squirted something into her throat. Meanwhile, Limuelle disinfected her arm and injected medicine with a syringe.

"Don't worry," Hohsalle said to Olimu, who observed his mother's sudden transformation in horror. "The medicine he injected is very effective. It's made from something secreted by one of the body's organs. See? She's already recovering. The medicine's working."

Mana's face froze when he heard what the medicine was made from. Noticing his expression, Hohsalle and Milalle glanced at each other but said nothing.

Hohsalle was right. Sulumina soon inhaled normally. Mana observed the medicine's dramatic and speedy effect with a frown.

Sulumina was pale and close to fainting, but Hohsalle continued to talk to her as he worked. "That's it. Everything's fine now. You'll be all right. It's not life-threatening, so there's no need to worry. Just breathe deeply."

Milalle, her hands flying busily, said, "That must have felt terrible. But it's over now. Your blood pressure dropped, so you may find your eyesight seems a bit dim and your chest feels tight, but it will soon pass."

Sulumina's condition stabilized gradually. She lay exhausted, eyes closed. Milalle took her slender wrist to check her pulse, when there was a knock on the door and an apprentice came in.

"I beg your pardon, but Sakkol is asking for you."

Hohsalle turned and nodded. "I'll be right there." He stood and followed him from the room, leaving the two patients in the care of Limuelle and Milalle.

"Has there been a change?" Hohsalle asked his apprentice. "In which patient?"

"Lord Mazai. He has a rash from his throat to his stomach."

Hohsalle frowned.

When they reached the room, Sakkol relinquished his spot to Hohsalle. "He broke out into a rash a moment ago. He's lost consciousness as well."

Hohsalle examined the rash, then felt behind Mazai's ears and raised his eyelids. "It seems like a different type of rash," Sakkol said, and Hohsalle nodded.

"It is. Probably a drug rash. He's likely suffering an allergic reaction to the new medicine." Hohsalle placed his fingers on Mazai's neck to feel for his pulse, his eyes narrowed slightly. "The loss of consciousness is the greater concern."

That night, Mazai went into convulsions. However, they weren't as bad as those of the other patients and ended quite quickly, never becoming life-threatening.

The next morning, Olimu and Sulumina also fell into a stupor, followed by convulsions, but again, these weren't critical. Once they subsided, the two slipped into a long, deep sleep. They awoke after about half a day looking disoriented, as though they'd returned from a journey to some distant land.

"Well done!" Milalle said brightly. "You'll be fine now." She patted Olimu's shoulder, unable to contain her joy.

He glanced back at her, looking slightly embarrassed. His eyes wavered as though he wanted to tell her something, but no words came.

"Did you have strange dreams?" she asked, and the boy nodded.

"Very strange dreams," he replied huskily.

"Tell me about them."

Olimu blinked and opened his mouth but then closed it again. Finally, he whispered, "...I forget."

*

Once the patients' conditions had stabilized, Mana returned to Lona. Although Hohsalle offered to show him the tiny organisms that caused disease, he declined the opportunity to see them with his own eyes.

Surprised, Hohsalle asked, "But why? I'm sure if you did, your understanding of illnesses would change remarkably."

Mana shook his head slowly. "I do not believe so. That is why I do not feel any need to look." He paused, searching for words. "The priest-doctors of the Pure Heart Creed do not believe that it is important to seek the cause of disease. Everything we need to understand is evident in our patients. If we look at the body, we can identify the problem from the body's perspective. You said that small organisms invade and cause disease, but that is simply another way of saying that some manner of defilement has entered the body. It is not necessary to identify the type of defilement, but rather to remove the obstacles that appear due to that defilement."

He smiled. "In which case, it is the human form that I should observe. I should inspect the ailing and help them to live good lives. I wish to devote myself to the pursuit of that path." So saying, Mana bowed deeply and left to return to his teacher's side.

Limuelle, who'd been watching this exchange silently while he sipped tea, gave a deep sigh when Mana departed. "...Such a pity," he remarked.

Hohsalle pulled up a chair in front of his grandfather and sat down. "It's as if those priest-doctors live inside a giant globe. No matter what the subject, they keep going round and round within the absolute logic formed by the teachings of their god."

Limuelle nodded. "They have the ultimate answer from the beginning."

"But…" Milalle hesitated and then continued. "I must confess that what they say is attractive."

Limuelle regarded her with a smile. "Really? I suppose I can understand." His expression hardened. "But don't forget. Even if a huge sphere surrounded our world, it would have chaos. Only by digging into each aspect of that chaos, by examining and considering what we find, can we take a new step forward.

"The priest-doctors have resigned themselves at the outset to the fact that people die from disease. The divine principles they preach were developed to be the final word to convince patients and their families to accept their fates, and to make the priest-doctors accept their own impotence."

Limuelle swept his arms wide and shook his fists defiantly. "We, however, will not give up. Not ever. And we will never force our patients to quit, either. A disease is not just the patient's problem. If the disease is contagious and a patient gives up hope, it could spread very quickly."

Hohsalle stared at his grandfather, somewhat taken aback. He'd heard him speak of this before, but never like this, with such impassioned gestures and the words pouring out of him.

Limuelle must have noticed Hohsalle's expression. He lowered his hands, but the stern light in his eyes did not fade. "It was a good idea to invite Mana to help with treatment. Find more opportunities for that in the future." His mouth twisted in a rueful smile. "I know there's no need to tell you, but Pure Heart Creed medicine is a chain that binds us hand and foot. Bringing the priest-doctors to our side would break the links. Once freed, Otawalle medicine could develop dramatically. We'd know ample funds and human resources. Spreading our knowledge to Zolians of every rank would change everything."

Hohsalle watched his grandfather with a slight frown. The thought that such hopeless frustration lay concealed inside the man made him feel sad. Limuelle had always appeared so cool and objective. His familiar face, illuminated by the clear autumn light that fell through the window, seemed like that of a stranger.

9
The Curse of Aquafa

Men robed in white bore a plain wooden coffin on their shoulders.

Zolian warriors were strict adherents of the Pure Heart Creed. To them, a funeral was a ceremony to elevate the deceased to the white heaven, and no weeping was allowed.

A white pavilion; white flags of mourning fluttering in the breeze; a straight path of white sand leading to the grave. The white-clad funeral procession passed through the blinding light of midday.

To the Aquafaese, Utalu's funeral was a very strange sight indeed.

After the funeral, the governor summoned Hohsalle, who'd come to pay his condolences. A servant led him to the audience chamber deep within the palace. Upon entering the room, Hohsalle stopped in surprise. The King of Aquafa sat facing the governor, who was seated at the head of the room before a large hanging scroll with the Divine Teachings of the Pure Heart Creed inked upon it in beautiful brushstrokes. To the governor's left sat Yotalu, while four senior statesmen sat silently on either side of the room. Behind the king were three attendants, one of whom was Tohlim.

Hohsalle had never seen such a tempestuous look on the governor's face. The king, however, appeared calm and composed, his gaze never wavering.

As Hohsalle took a seat beside Tohlim, the governor's attention shifted to him. "Lord Hohsalle, I thank you for saving my grandson."

Hohsalle bowed his head. "You honor me."

The governor stared at him intently without acknowledging the reply. "Let me speak plainly," he said in a flat voice. "Is it true that the Aquafaese do not die of black wolf fever?"

Makokan, who knelt on the floor in the west corner at the foot of the room, felt as though someone had seized him by the throat.

...Here it comes.

The rumor that the reemergence of mittsual was the Curse of Aquafa, divine retribution for those who'd violated this land, was spreading rapidly in Kazan. Makokan had known it was only a matter of time before it reached the governor's ears. Although rumors like this one were commonplace, the governor had just lost his eldest son, and it was not something he could ignore. The crafty old man's face was flushed with emotion, a fact which terrified Makokan.

"There are two things I can tell you," Hohsalle replied calmly, giving no indication that he felt any of the pressure directed at him. "First, we still do not know if it was black wolf fever."

The room buzzed excitedly, but Hohsalle ignored the commotion and plowed on. "Second, it would be false to claim that the Aquafaese will never die of it."

Silence fell.

"The last recorded outbreak of black wolf fever was nearly two hundred and fifty years ago. After that, it appears to have died out. The symptoms we have seen this time certainly resemble those in the historical records, but we can't be certain it's the same disease.

"In addition, concerning the baseless rumors being bandied about in the streets that only Aquafaese survive the sickness, there is no proof of this. Only Zolians died this time, but Izam's symptoms were far more serious than those of Olimu, who is half Zolian. If my grandfather, Limuelle, had not taken drastic measures, he would undoubtedly have perished. In other words, there is a possibility that the disease also kills Aquafaese."

The only sound in the room was the dull ticking of a lantern clock. The governor cleared his throat. "I see." His voice caught, and he cleared his throat again. "In other words, you do not think that this illness is the Curse of Aquafa."

Hohsalle's lips quirked up in a faint smile. "Not in the least." Wiping the grin from his face, he continued. "In fact, I actually fear that this absurd rumor that Aquafaese are immune could lower people's guard against the beasts that bear the disease, causing spread among the Aquafaese.

"The more people exposed to the illness, the greater the chance of its nature changing. Right now, only those bitten by dogs contract it, but if it has the same characteristics as black wolf fever, when the weather warms up and the numbers of fleas and ticks increase, there is a real possibility that the disease will proliferate by insects that drink the blood of infected humans and animals, resulting in an epidemic. I believe this issue is of far more concern."

The governor gazed steadily at Hohsalle as though considering. Then he nodded. "I understand. We need to act immediately. But there is one other measure that requires action." His eyes shifted and came to rest on the King of Aquafa. "Those dogs that rushed into the pavilion. They looked like hunting dogs to me. What do you think?"

All attention went to the king, who nodded after a moment. "That is how they appeared to me also. It was over so quickly, however, that I cannot be certain."

The governor's keen eyes never left the king. "If they were hunting dogs, then they must have a master. And if there is a master, then it was a premeditated attack."

The king remained silent.

"Naturally, I have already given orders to investigate who was behind the incident and increased the number of soldiers devoted to solving this case. Should there be a group of people plotting to disrupt Zolian rule by killing my son and spreading rumors that this is the Curse of Aquafa, anyone involved will be thoroughly questioned. I will not stop until every guilty party is dragged before me and beheaded."

The governor's eyes were bloodshot, and veins bulged in his forehead. "Know this, Former Lord of Aquafa."

The king's face remained unmoved. He regarded the governor silently for some time but then replied quietly, "I understand. I also will investigate, and if we find the perpetrators, I shall present them to you at dawn the next day. Considering what Lord Hohsalle has told us, I believe this isn't the time for political maneuvering. The lives of the Aquafaese also hang in the balance. And besides..." He stared straight at the governor as if to emphasize his point. "We have the movements of Mukonia on the western border to consider."

The governor's expression faltered ever so slightly.

The king continued. "We have been comrades of the Zolians for many years now. In contrast, Mukonia has threatened our territory for centuries and is our sworn enemy. We must prevent those barbarians from trampling over this land, no matter the cost. For that reason, too, we must do our utmost to prevent an epidemic."

The present ruler and the former one glared silently at each other.

Makokan had no way of knowing what thoughts slithered around the minds of the two cunning lords, but the atmosphere was so oppressive that he found it hard to breathe. The silence seemed to drag. Just when he thought he could bear the suspense no longer, Hohsalle spoke.

"About those measures to prevent an epidemic," he said. The senior statesmen turned to stare at him in astonishment. They appeared shocked by his impudence for speaking out without being called upon by the governor.

The governor scowled but took a deep breath and asked, "What about them?"

Looking perfectly composed, Hohsalle replied, "We must use the time from fall through winter to decide the best way to contain the disease in highly populated areas like Kazan."

"That's true." The governor nodded. "I want you and Doctor Lona to consult together. Report to me each time you come up with a proposal so that we may consider it." He frowned as if something had suddenly occurred to him. "But if ticks and fleas can spread the disease, it will be difficult to eradicate it completely. Can you improve the new drugs you've been developing?"

Hohsalle nodded. "Regardless of whether it's possible or not, that is something we'll have to keep trying. Judging from what we observed this time, the most effective approach seems to be repeatedly injecting patients with both a weakened version of the disease agents and the anti-mittsual drug as early as possible."

Hohsalle glanced briefly at Lona, then back at the governor. "But first, there is the issue of whether or not we can inject Zolians."

The governor's face tensed.

Hohsalle's gaze remained trained upon the man. "Aquafaese who lack resistance to the disease can die of it, too, but if we continue to develop and improve the medicine made from weakened disease agents, we will be able to save them. If, however, we cannot inoculate Zolians, then black wolf fever will only kill Zolians; in other words, it could indeed become a plague that only Zolians need fear."

This remark sent a stir through the room. If this treatment worked and those who refused it died, then it would become a Zolian-exclusive problem. The Zolians had come to this land, the disease's home, and they would die of it because they obeyed their god. Most would see it as divine will once they found out. It would become the Curse of Aquafa. Not only that, but the Zolians would have brought it upon themselves, and therefore they wouldn't be able to blame the Aquafaese.

The governor paled, and his brow furrowed. Lona, however, seemed unmoved, staring straight ahead with no change in expression.

Finally, the governor said hoarsely, "...This is not something that can be decided lightly. I must confer with Doctor Lona first."

Hohsalle nodded calmly, but he did not back down. "Of course, the decision of the people of Zol will depend on how they view this issue. However, disease waits for no one. To save those lives we can, I must develop effective remedies. Will you give me permission to continue making drugs to prevent the loss of any more lives to the disease that took your beloved son?"

The governor blinked. After thinking for a few moments, he said, "Yes, of course. Do your best to create and improve those remedies."

Hohsalle smiled with relief. "Thank you. The blood I extracted from patients with your permission was to improve the drugs we use. However, because we injected all the patients with the new medicine, we do not know if any of them would have survived without using it."

He forged on, giving no one a chance to interrupt. "The patient who was most dramatically affected by the disease and most quickly exhibited severe symptoms was the Zolian falconer bitten near the chin. The patient who showed the greatest resistance was Sulumina, followed by Mazai and Olimu.

"What is the cause of this discrepancy? If we could identify why some people are resistant to the disease while others are not, unrelated to such wild and politically motivated rumors as the Curse of Aquafa, we could formulate an effective strategy for prevention. It would be particularly helpful to understand why this sickness doesn't seem to have appeared in the remote mountain regions where black wolves once lived in abundance." His face clouded. "But that will be extremely difficult. There's no way we can possibly survey the whole of Aquafa, including the remote areas, to find anyone who has contracted and survived the illness. Nor is there any way to collect data that might have contributed to their survival. There is also no way of learning the present situation of the nomadic clans. It would all take too much time."

Hohsalle barely finished speaking when Yotalu opened his mouth. "Actually, it might be possible."

Hohsalle regarded him with surprise.

"We have a very thorough system of tax management. The collection officers gather information, even on the nomadic clans living in outlying areas like the Oki Valley and the Toga Mountains. Each group is categorized accurately, with records of how many people live in each place and their ages."

He smiled slightly. "Of course, a few people undoubtedly hide in the woods when the tax officers visit, explaining why we've had so much trouble finding Broken Antler Van. However, I believe the information we collect should still be quite accurate."

Hohsalle stared at Yotalu open-mouthed. Then he slapped his knee. "Wonderful! Trust the Zolians. When you do something, you do it right!"

Taken aback by his frankness, everyone smiled, even the governor.

"I particularly want data on the immigrants who live as nomads! Many reside in the frontier areas, don't they? They've intermarried with nomadic people. If we could determine the status of this disease among them, it could give us crucial information. In addition…"

Hohsalle looked from Yotalu to the governor, and then to the King of Aquafa. "…With information from that kind of survey, we'll definitely have a clearer picture. We'll know the sort of people with resistance to the sickness. Sir Olimu had greater resistance than Sir Izam, and we may find that there are those among the Zolian immigrants with similar qualities. Establishing that fact, will extinguish this absurd rumor as surely as a campfire dies in the rain."

If only that were true, Makokan thought. A campfire doused in water left a strong smell. He looked down, feeling as though that charred odor was pricking his nostrils.

Chapter 5:
Inside Out

1
Rumors

Winter came early that year, and just as Ohma had predicted, it was harder than the last. Snow fell heavily from late fall, and by early winter, blizzards blew frequently.

Kiya was not one to let her feelings show, and she worked as steadily as always. However, she occasionally gazed up at the dark sky with a distant look. Perhaps her thoughts reached Ohma and the others, because they managed to weave their way between blizzards to arrive home safely.

On the evening of their return, laughter filled the tent once again. The reindeer had sold for a fairly good price, and Ohma came back with necessary supplies and gifts like salted salmon and candied fruit. When roasted, the fat on the salty salmon skin tasted exquisite.

The reindeer market was held once in spring and again in late fall, and nomads gathered from all over at a large sorting station located beside the old capital of Kazan. Merchants also gathered there, and Ohma told of the huge banquet that was held once the reindeer had been auctioned off.

After dinner, Kiya and Manya went outside to store the remaining salmon in the shed. Ohma took Van by the elbow, as though he'd been waiting for this opportunity. In a low voice so as not to wake Yuna, who lay asleep on Van's lap, he said, "We heard an ugly rumor at the reindeer market."

"An ugly rumor?"

"Yeah. There's some kind of plague goin' around."

"It's not a plague," Tohma interrupted. "They said people don't spread it."

Ohma looked at his son. "Don't matter what it's called," he snapped. "Maybe people don't spread it, but dogs do, and the folks they bite all die. That makes it a plague, right?"

"I guess so."

As he listened to this exchange, Van felt a twinge of anxiety. "Mad-dog disease?" he asked.

Ohma frowned, and Van was surprised to see fear lurking in his eyes. "Naw…" Ohma rubbed his knees. "They say it's mittsual."

Van knit his brow. "Mittsual?"

Ohma looked at him closely. "Black wolf fever. You should know. It comes from your homeland."

Van laughed. "There's no sickness like that where I come from. Yes, black wolves from my homeland carried the disease that wiped out the Ancient Kingdom of Otawalle. However, the elders told us that no one from the Toga Mountains had ever died of such an illness.

"Besides, the soldiers of Aquafa supposedly hunted all the wolves down a long time ago. Hardly any remain where I'm from. You've got more of them here than we do."

Ohma scratched his cheek. "Yeah, you're right. There're a lot of 'em around these parts, and we still see 'em sometimes. And I never heard that anyone bitten by one got sick and died." He sighed. "That's what I don't like about this. It's bad enough when you've got a sickness goin' round, but even worse than that…"

Tohma had been watching his father the whole time, but now he turned to Van. "Everyone's sayin' it's no ordinary sickness," he said, his voice almost a whisper. "They're callin' it the Curse of Aquafa." His expression tensed. "Folks claim only Zolians die of it. People of Aquafa and Oki, they get bit, but they live. The disease only kills Zolians and immigrants."

"Ridiculous." Van practically spat the word. "They're just saying that because the Aquafaese didn't catch it in the past despite the downfall of the Otawalle."

Van looked to each of the men in turn. "People latch on to whatever they want to believe. This rumor stems from a hatred of Zol."

Ohma shook his head. "That's what I figured at first. Actually, I got into a big fight with one of the guys gabbin' on about it. If Tohma here hadn't stopped me, I woulda busted his head with the back of my hatchet."

Tohma grinned, but his lips were bloodless.

Ohma blinked, clearly troubled. "Turns out it's true, though. Even men I've known these thirty years told me a couple of stories. All of 'em sounded true enough."

Tohma looked at Van. "Seems a lot of people have died already. In the settlements on the Yukata Plains to the south, people bitten by dogs have been dyin' for a while now. On the south side of the Oki Valley, too. The same thing killed off some immigrants. Then, in the fall, the Hounds of the Gods closed in on Aquafa's old capital. Seems like somethin' terrible happened there."

He hurried to explain the tragedy that had befallen the royal falcon hunt. "Word is, even Sir Utalu got sick 'n' passed. Black dogs came outta nowhere and bit him. He got a rash all over and just up and died. Some Zolian ladies, too. But the king's kin, they were all just fine, even though the same dogs got 'em." With a gloomy expression, he concluded, "Hard to doubt it with so much evidence, y'know. The gods of Aquafa're gonna kill off all the Zolians for invadin' this kingdom. They'll return the land to its people."

"Don't be so stupid!" Ohma chided sharply. "It's just as Van said. People're twistin' the facts to suit themselves. I heard it paralyzed the leg or arm or somethin' of one of the king's own kin."

"Yeah, someone told me that. The son of the king's nephew. They say he can't walk."

"That's not all. Remember? The grandson of that Zolian governor survived, didn't he?"

Tohma smiled sadly. "You mean Sir Olimu? Don't you get it? Everyone's claimin' that's proof it's the will of the gods. They say he was saved 'cause he's half Aquafaese. The blood of Aquafa runs in his veins." Tohma sighed. "Lord Utalu always looked down his nose at us, and the disease took him, but Yotalu married the King of Aquafa's niece, and their eldest son survived. Ain't no one who can't guess what that means."

Tohma regarded Van as though he'd remembered something. "You remember when all the slaves in the salt mine died? It was right around the time we first met. Everyone says that's when all this began. The salt mine was a sacred place, a gift from the gods to the people of Aquafa, but the Zolians turned it into a hellhole manned by slaves. They defiled it, so that's why the Hounds of the Gods struck there first."

Tohma wrapped his arms around himself and whispered, "That pack o' dogs I saw in the forest that night... Maybe they weren't ossam but Hounds of the Gods. But then why did they let me live when I'm half—?"

Ohma reached out a hand and slapped his son on the back of his head. "Stop spoutin' nonsense! You're an Oki, idiot! The gods wouldn't go punishin' someone who lives an honest life."

His voice startled Yuna awake. She opened her eyes and looked around, then began to whimper. Van lifted her up and held her close. "Don't cry now. It's all right." She moaned a little more as he rocked her but quickly returned to sleep.

The little interruption seemed to have sapped the enthusiasm from Ohma and his son. Once Yuna had fallen back to sleep, Ohma breathed a little sigh. "Don't go tellin' Kiya now, alright?"

Van eyed him. "But she's bound to find out sooner or later."

Ohma nodded. "In the spring, yeah... I'd rather she didn't have to worry about such stupid talk, at least for the winter." At that moment, Kiya and Manya ducked through the entrance, cloaked in the scent of the cold night wind, and the evening returned to normal.

Despite the warmth of Yuna against his thighs, a chill ran up Van's spine. *Those beasts...*

Their eyes in the darkness of the salt mine had shone curiously, as though they'd known what they were doing—soldiers exacting orders. Van didn't believe they'd been sent by the gods, though. Men used the divine to explain what they already wanted to think. Every time sickness had run through his homeland, rumors abounded. If several villagers came down with a persistent cough, people whispered that someone spat on the root of a tree that housed a god. And if they suffered from loose bowels, people claimed that a person defiled the river, and a purification ritual was held soon after.

As a child, Van had believed what the villagers said, but now, such tales stirred up anger in his breast. He recalled the bright eyes of his son and heard his innocent laughter ringing in his ears.

My son...

What possible reason could there have been for his illness? If anyone deserved to be cursed, it was those who attributed whatever they liked to the will of the gods. Yet such people, and even the worst of sinners who committed the cruelest of deeds, often lived quite comfortably and happily to a ripe old age.

Life and death—such concepts could not be understood by the logic of men.

Van sat for a long time staring at the flickering flames with the warm weight of Yuna sleeping in his lap.

2
Change

The large tent contained a sleeping space, the walls and floors of which were draped in reindeer hides. Here they could sleep warmly without a fire and have no fear of freezing. However, on nights when a blizzard raged, Van's sleep was shallow, perhaps due to the noise of the tent shuddering in the wind, and he was haunted by many dreams.

One night, his rest was disturbed by a strangely vivid dream. He was crouched in the underbrush, listening to the wind. Gusts shook the treetops above so that they moved like waves against the night sky. Yet from within the underbrush, it was surprisingly quiet. Perhaps the thick tree trunks and the dense flora absorbed the wind.

Occasionally, a cold gust slid over him like ice, and flakes of snow buffeted his skin. Van remained crouched, waiting for the blizzard to pass.

Suddenly, he felt something, and his ears pricked up.

He sensed something jet-black on the move far away. Unsteady shadows came to him as sounds and scents… They were many, and they drew near. Stealthily. Moving closer. Slowly but surely.

Ossam.

The skin grew taut across Van's throat and stomach—goose bumps rose where they would bite if they found him.

Yet Van felt gripped by an odd excitement, and a shiver of anticipation rose within, the sort like when prey was nearly within range of his bow.

He felt a change coming over him, as though he was becoming something no longer himself. His flesh crawled. Terrified, Van rose to flee. At that moment, convulsive sobs rose from beneath his stomach, and he was catapulted out of his dream.

Yuna burrowed her way into Van's abdomen, clinging to him while trembling violently. She shook not with fear but a strange agitation.

"Ochan! Ochan!" she cried.

He held her small body close, whispering to soothe her without waking the others. "There now. It's all right."

Instead of quieting down, she flung back her head as though straining every nerve in her body. Before he could hush her, she began to growl like an animal.

Van sensed Ohma and the others sitting up. Someone asked groggily, "What's going on?" Yuna had woken up crying the night before, but the others were likely concerned by the unusual sound this time.

"A dream, I think." Van held Yuna and patted her back, but she gave no indication of calming down. Her wails ceased, yet she continued trembling.

Her small hands gripped Van's collar tightly, and she seemed to be saying something. It was as if she'd reverted to baby talk. She tried desperately to speak, but her tongue wouldn't cooperate.

"Ochan, Ochan…black…black…things…" Those were the only intelligible words she managed.

Van stared at her. The torch's light outside the sleeping area cast only the faintest illumination through a hole left for air circulation. Otherwise, it was almost pitch-dark. He should not have been able to see anything, but for some reason, her face was clear. Her eyes, in particular, seemed to glow.

Soaked with tears, they shone with excitement and looked straight at him.

Impossible...

Had she seen the same dream?

Had she also crouched in the brush and sensed the beasts approaching?

Van thought he heard something and listened intently. There was no mistake. He heard it again. A sharp *pyah* pierced his ears and vanished.

A warning.

The pyuika were sounding the alarm. The short, high-pitched, flute-like sound quickly became a low, menacing rumble, like something crawling up from the ground. It set Van's nerves on edge. Sharp pain pierced the spot between his eyes, and everything was transformed.

The scent of Yuna, of himself, of the others, flooded his nostrils, and every noise rang deafeningly, flowing together into a single mass and assaulting him.

A loud pounding, like the beat of a drum, shook the world. It took Van some time to realize that it was the beating of his heart.

Fear and excitement washed like waves through his whole body. He and the child in his arms were linked together, and he clearly felt the same waves breaking through her. He stood, still holding her.

The black beasts were coming.

Their feet were not yet turned toward this tent. They were bound for the pyuika enclosure. He felt the pyuika stomping around in a panic, sending tremors through the earth, as clear as if he were viewing it.

The hunting dogs, tied to stakes, were yelping—high-pitched, sharp, ceaseless.

After handing Yuna to Tohma, Van quickly donned his coat and gloves, then grabbed a hatchet. He looked back at Ohma, but for some reason, he couldn't speak. "Black...attacking," he croaked, barely managing to squeeze words from his throat. They sounded more like a growl.

"The Black Brothers?" Ohma asked.

Van couldn't answer.

The scene before him wavered, and language and thoughts grew distant. His sense of self reduced inside him. Van's arms and legs split from the person who observed them. Deep inside, he watched this other Van fling back the tent flap and dash outside.

The wind had dropped. The thick blizzard clouds had thinned. They raced across the sky, obscuring and revealing the half-moon in a cycle, sending countless shadows dancing across the snow-covered plain.

Everything appeared oddly bright.

Smells lanced through Van's nose into his head, the sounds of countless hooves crunching on snow, shadows that ran like black water from the edge of the forest—all these formed clear images in his brain. The place where the attackers would emerge became clear, revealed by a luminous path.

Van took off as though propelled.

His body felt incredibly light. The snowy plain seemed to fly beneath his feet, vanishing behind him.

Black beasts swarmed outside the enclosure, but they approached it in a roundabout way, as if to avoid something. Van knew why instantly.

Mohoki. The scent of it evidently confused their minds as well.

At some point, the scene he saw before him subtly melded into a space colored by various others. The black beasts ran through that landscape of smells. Several shapes skirted the enclosure with menacing growls, driving the frightened pyuika toward the opposite side. From that direction, another shadow crept silently toward them. The snarling beasts served as beaters, urging the game toward that far spot. The hunter was the one black creature approaching from behind. It had already crouched low, ready to spring.

It'll clear the fence.

Van saw the trajectory of that jump before the hunter even moved. The desperate heartbeats of the pyuika overlapped with his. Like a buck with his herd behind him confronting a pack of wolves, Van lowered his head and charged the beast from the side.

It turned.

When their eyes met, something strange occurred. Van split in two.

There was the Van who responded to the waves of fear emanating from the pyuika and knew he must protect the herd. But inside was another self, one that found the scent of the beasts achingly familiar and dear.

The beasts stopped as one and stared at him. The hot, pulsating thread of life that bound them together bound him, too, and he pulsed with them. The world around him had become rivers of light. Countless shining streams flowed incessantly in every direction, some intertwining and others pulsating. Everything in the heavens and on the earth became streams of shimmering light flowing at different speeds.

The forest, too, shifted, transforming into a luminous current of green that radiated into the sky. Superimposed on this glowing river were the thick, dark spruce trees.

Before Van stood a male beast as big as a boar. As he met its eyes, his vision wavered, and the next thing he knew, he was staring at a large man who towered over him, arms and legs spread wide. Startled, he looked up at the man and backed away.

Is that...me?

With that thought, his soul returned to his body, and once again, he saw a fierce-looking beast.

If Van wished, he knew he could slip inside any one of these wild dogs. Just by following these pulsating threads.

They are me.

Pulling on the threads would move them in congress...

The instant he felt this, something blew like a gust of wind from far way, jerking the threads of light, just as a rider pulls back on the reins.

The bundle of threads stretched toward a great spruce tree on the edge of the forest.

Something was there. It gathered and gripped those threads, snatching them out of Van's hand and severing his connection with the beasts. Everything grew quiet.

A fiendish radiance kindled in the eyes of the beasts that faced Van. Goose bumps rose on his skin as surely as if he'd been doused in cold water.

A male bared its fangs and leaped. Van lowered his head and brought the back of his hatchet down on its muzzle, like a stag striking with its antlers. He felt the dull shock of the blow in his hand as the animal shrieked loudly and hit the ground, bouncing like a ball.

As the beast somersaulted back to its feet, the rest of the pack attacked. Van cast aside his hatchet, clenched his fists, and punched each shape that flew at him from every side. When a blow connected, Van felt his arm being pulled, making it hard to punch. Yet with every strike, one of the animals went flying, landing with a *thud* on the ground and rolling away.

A high noise shrilled deep within Van's head.

The beasts stopped as one and looked toward the edge of the forest, as though listening. The next moment, they turned on their heels and began to run. Looking in the direction of their heading, Van started. They were making straight for the tent. Ohma and Tohma stood at the entrance, a torch held high, peering in this direction.

Van wanted to shout, "Look out!" but no words came.

A tiny shadow tumbled from the tent... *Yuna!* Kiya ran after her, bending down to catch her.

Van screamed. But the noise that issued from his throat was a howl.

*

Raising the torch, Tohma peered in the direction of the pyuika corral. He thought he spied moving shadows, but it was black as tar, and he couldn't tell where Van was.

"Can't see anything with the torch. Maybe we should go check on the pen."

Just as his father agreed, he heard his mother's voice from inside.

"Wait! No! You can't go outside!"

He turned to see Yuna raise the tent flap and run out. She was heading for the corral. Kiya rushed after her, barely managing to grab the girl, when a strange howling came from the distance.

Looking in the direction of the sound, Tohma saw black shapes speeding for them, and he heard paws scraping against the snow.

"Father!"

Before he could even point, the shapes were revealed by the torchlight. Tohma saw the sheen of black fur. Light gleamed in golden eyes and glanced off bared fangs. The leader launched itself into the air toward Tohma's father.

Ohma brandished his torch, but the animal turned its head in midair, dodging the blow, and sank its fangs into his arm.

Yelling, Tohma struck the beast with his torch. Sparks flew. With a yelp, the beast released Ohma and rolled across the ground.

Turning, Tohma saw his mother bend over Yuna, hugging the child against herself. Beasts were rushing at them. Shouting, he ran toward them, when something heavy collided with his ribs, taking his breath away. He collapsed on the ground, grasping his stomach and groaning. Upon opening his eyes, he saw the jaws of a beast, and its raw-smelling breath enveloped his face.

I'm done for!

Tohma squeezed his eyes shut and braced himself. Then came a dull *thud*, and his body felt light.

Surprised, he looked up and stared wide-eyed at Van. For a moment, he thought Van was glowing. The man's eyes flashed, and flames seemed to rise from his body. Punching aside another beast that flew at him, Van flipped nimbly through the air and grasped the animal climbing on Kiya by the neck. He ripped it away and sent it tumbling. Like a stag protecting its herd, Van lowered his head and kicked, punched, and flung the attackers. He moved so fast that the beasts seemed slow by comparison. Their fangs could not even graze him before his feet and fists sent them flying.

Tohma's eyes could no longer keep up with Van's movements. All he saw was one beast after another soar through the air.

Tohma sensed a noiseless sound resonate somewhere.

The beasts paused.

Van's face twisted at almost the same time. The pack swiveled as one toward the forest. They seemed to hesitate for a moment, then they laid their ears flat and raced toward the trees as though pulled by a string.

"Ah—!"

Tohma heard his mother's voice. Looking back, he saw Yuna wriggle from her grasp and set off at a run. She moved with a speed that seemed impossible for a child. The light of the torches that fell across the snow-covered field caught Yuna's figure as she raced after the beasts before she melted into the darkness. Tohma stood stunned, unable even to cry out, but Van took off after her. A moment later, he melted into the night, looking more beast than human.

*

A tiny light wavered ahead. Yuna, her small figure glowing faintly in the dark as she ran ahead of him. Her light was linked to that of the beasts. Van's was, too.

He forgot that he was breathing and merely ran single-mindedly.

The beasts' pace slackened ever so slightly, just as it would've if they were waiting for a pup to catch up. Yuna's form melted into the pack.

Van longed to merge with them, too. The warm, raw life breathing within his body ached to belong. It felt so good to run single-mindedly, drawn by the one who held the reins of light in his hand.

The wind rang in his ears. The scent of snow enveloped his body. Lights flickered.

Trees sped toward him. The forest smelled cool and clear—like underbrush buried beneath the snow.

Before he realized it, his heart had fused with Yuna's, and the earth loomed much closer.

Everything's so easy.

Grasses brushed aside by his muzzle slowly righted themselves, and snow hoppers roused from their dreams rose into the air, flapping their wings and drifting lazily down into different clumps of grass. He saw every vein in their wings and even the tips of their long thin legs.

When Van entered the forest, the scent of trees grew thick. An intense odor suddenly pierced his nostrils, and a white light shot through the back of his eyes to the crown of his head. It came from the mosses and lichens hanging from the branches and clinging to the roots of the trees. Each gave off its own scent, and these surged for him with a noise like a thousand tiny bells quivering. Ashimi was the most powerful. A beautiful green lichen that clung in abundance to the roots of a great tree, it exuded a complex and indescribable fragrance.

The moment Van took it in, a quiver ran through his body. Over and over again, like rolling waves, countless tiny creatures within him split into two groups, repulsing each other, swirling together, and then gently subsiding.

The pack slowed, and Yuna's pace dropped in kind. The beasts shook their heads, seemingly perplexed.

Van halted. The scent of ashimi seeped into him like surf lapping the shore, and the impulses that drove the myriad creatures inside him gradually stilled.

In a moment, all would be quiet...

At that thought, a pain shot between his eyes. Someone was pulling on the reins of light again.

The beasts raised their heads and shook themselves, then set off at a run. Yuna started after them. Just in time, Van reached out and swept her up in his arms. She squirmed and wriggled, growling like a little pup, shaking her head and flapping her arms and legs, but Van held her tight and did not let go.

The beasts ran. Watching them go placed a loneliness in Van's chest, the sort like a child left behind by its mother.

He wanted to go, too. He wanted to go with them, to the ends of the world.

Yuna, who was now pressed against his chest, was surely consumed with that same powerful urge. She cried like a baby. Still, Van did not slacken his grip. As the scent of ashimi gradually stilled the tiny creatures within him, Van felt his own familiar senses returning. Words popped into his mind.

You must not go. Don't let her go, either.

He buried his face in her hair, which smelled of sunlight, and hugged her little body close.

3
The Raven

The next day was clear without a cloud in the sky. Snow sparkled on the ground, dazzling the eyes.

Van, his expression dark, stood gazing down at a single black carcass that marred the pure white field. When he'd hurled this beast through the air, it must have hit a post and broken its back. It lay frozen solid; limbs splayed out on the snow. Van sensed no trace of the union he'd experienced last night, perhaps because the animal was dead.

Ohma stood nearby. He seemed so unlike himself. Van guessed that the recent events still clung to him like a bad dream. His face was wooden, and he couldn't look Van in the eyes. Van could guess all too well how Ohma felt. Even he found it hard to believe that the man he was last night was the same person standing here now. Van must have looked exceedingly strange, battling the ossam like a beast. Ohma had likely yet to shake off the trauma of that sudden attack as well. The thick sleeve of his coat had kept the beast's fangs from penetrating his skin, but the terror of being bitten undoubtedly shook him to the core.

"...This ain't one of the Black Brothers," Tohma's uncle Yoki muttered with his brow knit.

Ohma, who'd avoided so much as looking at the carcass, now stared at it. He grimaced initially but examined it carefully. Gradually, his rigid features relaxed, and a puzzled frown rose on his face. "You're right... This ain't one of the Black Brothers," he said.

The body on the ground resembled a wolf, but it wasn't. The height and shape of its haunches were similar, but its ears and jaw differed. Its pelt didn't match, either; a streak of light gold ran down its back.

It's got the blood of the wild mountain dogs in its veins, Van thought.

There were many ossam in the mountains of his homeland. Their coats were light gold, and people shunned them, claiming they bore the light of the next world on their backs. They bred prolifically, and after the black wolves had been culled, their numbers swelled dramatically. Van's people often hunted them in winter because they attacked pyuika.

The beast that lay prone before him was darker and larger than an ossam, but its face had the same sinister look. Van crouched beside it and examined the underside of its paws. *It's hard to tell*, he thought. They looked exactly like those of an ossam. Although the spread of the claws differed slightly, he would've believed them to belong to an ossam had he not examined them closely or instead found their tracks in the woods. A thought rose into his mind, and an icy chill spread across his chest.

Van had thought that the disappearance of young boar and deer in the forest was due to an increase of ossam. But maybe these were the creatures that had multiplied.

Ohma's voice interrupted his contemplation. "Is it a rochai?"

So Ohma's family also detest ossam, Van mused. *Just like my people.*

The word *rochai* was a derogatory term for ossam bred with wolves. The Aquafaese considered them intelligent and prized them as hunting dogs. While Van's people occasionally bred dogs with wolves, they'd never use any animal with ossam blood for hunting.

Ohma stood and straightened his back. Cocking his head, he said, "But if they were rochai, they must have a master. Or are they just naturally corrupt hybrids?"

With these words, an image flashed through Van's brain: a figure, standing at the edge of the forest, reins of light bunched in his hand...

The previous night's happenings seemed terribly distant, like the dregs of a nightmare he could barely recall. Yet certain moments in time were seared in his brain like scenes caught in a flash of lightning. The figure standing at the forest's precipice was one of them, but he couldn't tell Ohma or the others. Since last night, a certain possibility had plagued Van, and now, as he beheld the carcass here in the light of day, he was sure of it.

It's one of them.

One of those cunning beasts that had attacked the salt mine and slaughtered everyone inside. Those eyes that had gleamed with a strange light. The purposeful way they'd bitten each victim, one by one. Van had likened them to soldiers, and his intuition had proven mostly correct.

This creature was not a wild beast. It had moved as part of a pack, driven by the person who held the reins for some reason of his own.

Van clenched his fists inside his mitts. The sensation that lingered most vividly from last night was neither fear nor regret: It was the warm bond—a feeling almost of nostalgia—that had seized him the instant their eyes met in the darkness. What could that have been?

I was bitten by one of these creatures.

And after, he'd dreamed. In the time that followed, his body had changed. And he wasn't the only one who'd survived a bite.

Yuna.

Van saw her tiny figure glowing in the dark as she raced mindlessly like a pup after the pack. Had something invaded her body when she was bitten?

What will become of us?

Something icy unfurled in the bottom of Van's chest and crept across it like a vine while the skin from the back of his skull to his forehead went numb.

He took a deep breath. Fear would only paralyze his ability to think. His own life was one thing, but Yuna's was just beginning. Van had no time to waste being afraid.

Think.

He opened his eyes. *What I see now is just a fragment of the whole.*

But that shard was connected to an enormity. Something was about to happen. The incident in the salt mine—it was surely just the start.

Van opened his eyes and stared at the forest spreading darkly along the edge of the dazzling field of snow.

Whoever stood there saw us.

He'd undoubtedly realized that Van and Yuna were linked to him by threads of light.

But he couldn't have known we're survivors from the salt mine.

The logic did little to shake off the uneasiness, however. When Van was the leader of the Lone Antlers, this feeling had always spoken to the presence of enemies lurking nearby, waiting to ambush.

To ignore intuition was dangerous. The subconscious often knew something before it reached the upper levels of cognition. If Van sensed, as he did now, that he was being watched by some unknown entity, that he was being targeted, he should pay attention. A long-forgotten sensation woke deep inside him: the heightened awareness coupled with the cockiness that he'd experienced whenever he resolved to confront his attackers.

Van paced slowly toward the forest. If someone had been there, they must have left some trace.

"…Hey! Where you goin'?" Ohma asked.

Van turned. "I'm going to follow the tracks to see which way these beasts came from."

Ohma frowned, likely puzzled over why Van would bother, but he nodded vaguely and didn't press further.

Van continued on. The events from a short time ago were carved in the snow-covered ground. The signs of the beasts scattering the snow as they raced across its surface were plainly visible.

The man who'd held the glowing reins had stood under that tree, the one that towered above the rest. The tracks of the black beasts led toward it.

There's no mistake. Someone had stood beneath that timber and summoned the pack to him.

The snow thinned as Van continued into the forest, yet the beasts' tracks remained clear. Some paw prints had been trampled over, telling Van that many of the animals gathered in this one narrow spot before racing deeper into the woods.

However, there were no human footprints. Narrowing his eyes, Van examined the spot where he'd seen someone standing. He stepped back and surveyed the scene to confirm that this was the right place before studying the snow again. Still, there was no trace of a man. Instead, Van discovered something very odd—a ring of paw prints with all the claws pointing toward the foot of the tree, as if the black beasts had halted en masse.

An image floated across Van's vision like a mirage—the black creatures facing the great tree in a circle—hounds waiting for their master's signal. Yet there was nothing in the center, not even the tracks of a bird, just smooth white snow gleaming faintly.

...*Why?*

Had it been a dream? Had the glowing shadow never existed?

No. Something had definitely been there. Otherwise, why would those beasts have gathered in a ring?

Van's scalp prickled. He heard the slow beat of wings. Something crossed the sky, moving toward him. He knew it before he saw it—a raven. The large bird glided through the trees, then raised its broad wings and landed softly on a branch of the large tree. After folding its wings, it looked down at him. Van pressed his lips together and stared back.

There was no animosity in the raven's eyes. It gazed straight at him, making Van wonder what it was thinking. As they stared at each other, however, something odd occurred. Van could no longer see it clearly. Its black feathers dazzled, and its jet-black form swelled and radiated a majestic light that blinded him. A chill spread from his forehead across the crown of his head, and his skin stiffened. Whatever he beheld was not of this world. He had to stop looking. Now.

Finally wrenching his eyes away, he turned on his heel and ran from the forest.

"Ochan!"

Yuna was calling him. The sound of her bright, cheerful voice seemed to melt the cold that lay over him like a thin layer of ice, and warmth returned to his skin. She'd just emerged from the tent, dressed in furs and dragging Kiya by the hand. Kiya stood shielding her eyes with one hand while Yuna waved at Van.

"Look! Ochan! An ol' lady!" She pointed at the top of the tree where the raven perched. "Bwight and shiny!"

Van stared at her, speechless. Behind him, he felt the bird rise into the air and circle around, squinting as it vanished into the painfully bright sky.

4
A Messenger Bearing Wet Feathers

"Hey!"

Van turned to see Yoki waving to him. Tsupi butted Van and nuzzled him insistently. He patted her between her antlers, then bent over and placed a bundle of ashimi on the snow in front of her before walking over to Yoki. During mating season, pyuika ate a lot of this green lichen, and when they bore young, they seemed to crave it. Collecting ashimi from the woods, where it grew fresh even under the frost, and feeding it to the pyuika was an important job in winter. It was hard work slogging through the deep snow and digging up the lichen, but pyuika herders had no choice if they wanted their does to bear strong calves.

The fact that Van found the lichen just by smell made this task a little easier. He hadn't realized before that it possessed a scent, but now, just a whiff of it made him feel strangely agitated. Unlike mohoki, ashimi had a pleasant odor that attracted and repelled him, causing inner turmoil. Perhaps it also bothered him because it invariably sparked memories of the night the rochai came.

Van walked quickly and lightly over the snow to Yoki, whose face appeared stiff with worry.

"Van, you're in trouble," he said. "A messenger with the Wet Feathers is here."

"The Wet Feathers?"

Van was about to ask what he meant, but the wind changed, bringing with it an unfamiliar scent—a combination of grassy moss deep in the forest, food cooked with fragrant herbs, and a very faint whiff of rotten eggs. A visitor cloaked in this smell waited for him on the far side of the tent.

"The Wet Feathers. You mean you don't know?" Yoki asked, his voice impatient. "You ain't got no Echo Master in Toga?"

Van stared at him silently.

"The Echo Master can cross into the Twilight and send a messenger with a raven feather to summon people." Yoki must have been so flustered that explaining seemed too much trouble. He waved his hand irritably. "Just come, will you?"

He strode off, and Van fell into step beside him, recalling the morning he'd seen the raven. It had been so bright that he couldn't make it out. He'd been right to suspect that was no ordinary raven.

The Echo Master... One who could cross the border between here and Twilight. *Someone like the Master of the Dance?*

That was what his people called those who flew in spirit form between this world and the next. Perhaps there was someone like that here in Oki, too. Thinking of the Master of the Dance filled Van with a warm nostalgia. The one in his village had been good to him from the time he was a little boy. Her name was Yokkina. She had a cheerful nature and always laughed. She loved to tease, and the village children had heard so many tales of her from their elders that the sight of her sent them running.

Van had always liked her, though. Whenever she saw him, she'd call out, *"Hey there, you naughty little prancing deer, come here,"* and give him nuts or sweets made with honey. She'd saved his life once, too. During the period when Van and his friends were at their most mischievous, they'd gone into the forest at night to test their courage. Van had lost his footing and fallen from a cliff. He'd lain in the darkness, listening to the commotion of his panicked friends wondering what to do, but was too injured to make a sound. It was Yokkina who'd rescued him. Van never learned how she'd known his location. Yokkina had gone to Van's father and told him where he was.

Hers were the only words Van remembered from what had seemed an endless waking dream after the loss of his wife and child. She'd disappeared around the time the rumors of a Zolian invasion reached the settlement, passing the mantle of Master of the Dance to her daughter. Some people had claimed she was frightened by a terrible omen and fled, but Van thought she'd departed Toga for a reason.

He was sorry to have lost the one person he would have liked to consult in his time of greatest need, but he knew she would've likely told him, "My field is the flow of Twilight, not war." That would have been just like her.

If this Echo Master was the same kind of person, then perhaps their spirit had traveled with the raven. Van recalled what Yuna had said. *"Look! An ol' lady! Bwight and shiny!"* He frowned, feeling as though something cold had brushed his chest.

Van circled the tent toward the entrance and saw a small woman standing outside. There was nothing unusual about the reindeer hide she wore, but her thrown-back hood had many small blue beads sewn into it. They glittered brightly each time she moved. Ohma and the others wreathed her.

Catching sight of Van with her sharp eyes, Yuna dropped Kiya's hand and waved both arms at him. "Ochan! Ochan!" Everyone turned to look.

The small woman also turned and bowed. There were lines around her eyes, but she was not that old—perhaps in her mid-fifties.

Yuna ran to Van, and he took her in his arms before returning the woman's bow. In her hand were two glossy raven's feathers, one large and one small. She held them out quietly and then said in a clear, ringing tone, "I am the messenger of the Echo Master, who lives deep in the woods of Yomida Forest where the sighs of the fire-flows seep from the earth, and the boiling water gushes forth. My name is Assenomi. I have come to tell you that the master wishes to meet with you and your good daughter. I am sure this sudden request is confusing, but I must implore you to come with me now, while this break between blizzards holds."

Before Van could answer, Yuna reached out her hand and took the feathers. "Ochan, look! Pwetty." Smiling, she raised them to her nose.

"Hey," Van said, but before he could scold her, Assenomi smiled. "Tell me, little one," she said. "What color are those feathers?"

Yuna crossed one over the other and answered, "Shiny. Like shnow."

Ohma and the others looked puzzled, perhaps wondering what she could possibly mean, but the woman laughed merrily, clearly pleased with this answer. "Yes, yes. The color of snow." Her air of formality vanished. A rosy blush touched her cheeks, and her eyes narrowed kindly.

"What about you?" she asked Van. "What color do you see?"

Van examined the feathers. Until then, they had appeared to be black, but as soon as he focused squarely on them, their shapes blurred, and he could no longer see them clearly.

"I can't see them," he said.

Assenomi's eyes widened slightly. She peered at him for a moment as though in thought but soon nodded. "I see. Perhaps for some people, that is how they look." Then she asked him gently, "So what do you think? Will you come with me?"

Van did not answer immediately, looking down at Yuna instead. The Master of the Dance had spoken with the voice of the gods. If an Echo Master was the same, then Van couldn't refuse. He longed to know how the master had found out about them and why this summons had been sent, but he was uneasy, too.

Something strange was happening to him.

And probably to this child as well.

If the bite from those beasts was causing this change, then how would the gods view it? What if they decided that he and Yuna had been corrupted by those creatures and needed to be cleansed?

Kiya shifted and looked up anxiously at her elderly husband. Catching sight of her face, Van made up his mind. *Whether we go or run away, this is our problem alone. We can't bring trouble to Tohma's family*. Moreover, how would he find a way forward unless he knew what was happening to him? If it were just Van, it wouldn't matter, but the child cradled in his arms was just beginning her life. Van needed to find a path that would lead her to happiness.

He nodded at Assenomi. "We'll go."

She smiled with evident relief. "You will come with me, then? I am so glad. Please forgive me for not giving you any warning."

Ohma spoke up, perhaps encouraged by the visiting woman's friendly tone. "If you'll excuse me, ma'am."

Assenomi faced him. "Yes?"

Ohma cleared his throat. "Pardon me if I sound rude, but has this summons got anythin' to do with what happened the other night?"

Assenomi looked puzzled. "The other night? I'm not sure I understand."

Ohma cast a quick glance at his wife, then at Yoki, Tohma, and finally at Van. Apparently coming to a decision, he opened his mouth again. "It was about three days ago. A pack of rochai attacked our pyuika. Van here tried to save 'em, and... Well, he accidentally killed one."

Ohma cleared his throat again and plowed on. "It was wrong to kill instead of chasin' them away with fire, but he knows he made a mistake, and I'm sure he's very sorry. Besides, he was doin' it for us."

Assenomi appeared surprised as she listened. Her expression wavered slightly at the mention of the rochai, but she quickly composed herself. When Ohma finished, she cocked her head. "How terrible that must have been for all of you. Perhaps that's why the Echo Master sent me with this summons. But then again, it could have been for some other reason. I'm sorry, but I haven't been informed why."

Then, as if to allay their fears, she added, "But I really don't think there is anything to worry about. As I'm sure you know, the Echo Master serves merely to right the balance when something is out of alignment. If that's the case, you can be sure it will be fixed."

Ohma pressed his lips together and looked at Van. Assenomi had spoken gently yet with a certain firmness. Ohma stood silently for several moments, hesitating as though he wished to say something. Finally, he took a deep breath and blurted out, "If you wish to go, Van, go... We'll be here until the middle of spring. When it comes time to move on, we'll leave you a sign so you'll know where to find us."

Van gazed at him, then bowed deeply.

*

The journey to Yomida Forest, where the Echo Master resided, would take five days. Van spent the rest of the day preparing for the trip, and he left with Assenomi the next morning.

Were it any colder, the snow would've frozen, making it easier for the reindeer to walk and the sled to slide. Unfortunately, the snow under the trees remained soft, and the long journey was difficult for it. Van assumed that Assenomi, being a woman, must have felt anxious traveling on her own and sleeping in the snow, but she appeared unconcerned and perfectly at ease astride her reindeer. Perhaps she was well accustomed to it. The same could be said of her reindeer, which found narrow paths through the woods where none appeared obvious, forging ahead without losing the way.

Van expected Yuna to cry when they parted from Kiya, but she was in high spirits, looking very cheerful as she rocked on the reindeer's back in a little basket that the herders used to carry children on such trips.

The sky was covered in a thin layer of clouds, but occasionally, a ray of faint sunlight shone through, and the forest was peaceful. When the sun began to work toward the horizon, Van left Yuna in Assenomi's care and prepared camp. After locating a spot sheltered from the wind, he used a long-handled wooden paddle to raise walls of snow in a circle and then laid reindeer hides inside.

While he made a firepit in the center of the snow hut to keep sparks from singeing the hides, Yuna began somersaulting. "Look at me! Look at me!" she cried.

"Don't kick the walls," Van warned her, but she pretended not to hear and kept somersaulting her way around. She enjoyed it so much that she didn't stop until Assenomi finally picked her up with a laugh and tickled her cheeks.

Assenomi never asked Van about himself or told him anything about herself when they made camp in the evenings. She merely played with Yuna and hummed songs quietly. Likewise, Van didn't question her. Silence didn't bother him, and he was glad not to talk. Yuna was the only noisy one, chattering away in her childish lisp. But before each night grew too deep, she'd crawl into Van's arms, curl up against him, and fall fast asleep, leaving everything wrapped in the stillness of winter.

The popping of twigs in the fire that Van kept burning, the soft thud of snow falling from the tree branches where the smoke spiraled upward, the squeak of a mouse devoured by a fox in the brush—these sounds came to Van but seemed meaningless. Like the song of the wind, they wrapped themselves loosely around him and passed on.

He used to find the forest at night frightening, but now it didn't feel that way. Everything swirled around him and flowed, as though he were in the middle of a gentle stream. Van kept his hatchet close at hand in case of another attack by those beasts or by wolves, but he felt no sign of danger and drifted easily into a shallow slumber. Once, as he descended the slope toward oblivion, he briefly sensed countless eyes watching him from some distant place. He started awake, but the sensation passed swiftly, and he was sucked back into unconsciousness.

After four nights of camping outdoors, the morning of the fifth and final day broke. It was a cold dawn. Van had only slept lightly to keep the fire going all night so that Yuna wouldn't freeze, but by the time the first rays of the sun appeared, he awoke clearheaded.

Assenomi, who'd risen earlier in the faint predawn glow, had put a pot of water on the fire to boil and now added tea leaves. Van didn't recognize them, but they carried a refreshing smell. Assenomi poured some tea into a cup, stirred in a lump of cloudy white honey, and passed it to him. Van sipped it slowly as it cooled, and the warm, sweet liquid seeped into his chilled body, bringing it back to life.

Yuna, who'd woken up grumpy, either from sleepiness or the cold, became cheerful again as soon as she partook.

"Do we still have a long way to go?" Van asked as he chewed on a piece of jerky toasted in the fire.

Assenomi smiled and shook her head. "We should arrive by early afternoon. Evening at the very latest."

Shortly after they set out, the forest ended, and a smooth snowy field spread before them, the snow was so bright that it hurt the eyes. On the far side, many strangely shaped dark rocks reared their heads, leading toward a dense wood. Beyond stood a tall mountain. When Van saw the shape of that peak, he halted his reindeer.

During the journey, he'd sensed they were traveling toward his homeland, and now he knew that feeling was correct. He was gazing upon none other than Mount Otogaya, located on the northeastern edge of the Toga Mountains. The angle he viewed it from made it look a little different, but there was no mistaking it. Beholding the familiar shape sent a pang through his heart.

"Ochan! What's dat? Onbah?" Catching the note of fear in her voice, Van plucked Yuna from the basket and sat her between his knees.

"No. Not monsters. They're just rocks."

"Wocks?"

"Yes. Rocks."

He understood why she was afraid. Lumpy and grotesque, like writhing creatures frozen in place, these stones differed from anything she'd seen before.

"Kachi stones," Van murmured.

Assenomi turned and nodded. "That's right. Fireblood stones. You know of them?"

Van squinted his eyes against the glare from the snow and answered slowly, "Yes. This resembles a place near my homeland."

It reminded him of Fireblood Field on the other side of Mount Otogaya, a fire-breathing mountain that occasionally belched smoke. The elders had often said, "The skin of the earth is thin near the fire mountain." It was true that the pulsing of the earth felt much closer there. In some spots, hot water boiled up in the shadows of the rocks along the rushing mountain stream. Pools had been made in places where the hot and cold water mixed, and the villagers often bathed in them. Washing and soaking in these baths was one of Van's earliest memories. He'd missed them when the war took him far from home, and, of course, there had been no such thing as a hot bath in the salt mine, let alone while living with the reindeer herders. Recalling the pools alongside the river in his homeland made him long for a good soak.

If the earth's crust is thin here, too, maybe there are hot springs. He laughed inwardly at himself for the notion, but there was a chance.

As they drew closer to the copse of stones, the odd shapes became clearer. Although smaller in scale than Fireblood Field in Toga, it looked very similar to Van. According to legend, Fireblood Field had formed long, long ago when Otogaya spewed fire high into the heavens, and its burning blood flowed down the slope and hardened. It was so eerie looking that it would have been the perfect place for young boys to prove their courage, but the elders had warned against it. Demons lurking among the stones breathed poison on any who came too near, and children were forbidden to set foot there. Someone had actually seen a bird flying overhead drop dead from the sky, and the stench that sometimes wafted from the field was so overpowering that no one had dared to disobey.

As they crossed the snow-covered clearing, the wind's heading switched, bringing the smell of rotten eggs. Van swiftly put his hand over Yuna's nose, but Assenomi smiled. "It's all right," she said. "It does smell like a demon's breath, but it's not enough to harm anyone. It's the north side of the mountain that spews poison. The fumes never reach this side or the caves in Yomida Forest where the Echo Master lives."

She pulled ahead to guide Van, assuring him that they were close to their destination, and she deftly steered her mount through the black stones. As they came abreast of the first rock, Yuna stiffened, but once they were weaving among them, she leaned forward, her eyes sparkling as she examined each one.

"Look! A weindeer! And dere's an ol' lady! Oh! An' a mouse!" Yuna cried, announcing what each one looked like.

The stench intensified or weakened depending on the direction of the wind, but once Van got used to it, it no longer bothered him. Passing out of the field of stones, they entered a gloomy forest. The blood of the fire mountain surely flowed here as well, because when Van looked closely, the stones that played host to the trees' roots were the same color as those in the field.

The words of a song the elders used to chant came back to Van.

Even on land where fire once flowed, soil gathers, and trees and plants grow...

As he suspected, the earth here must have been thin. This forest was slightly warmer than the other. Perhaps that's why moss grew on the trees and ivy hung from branches. Through the vines, a towering cliff covered in green and white moss came into view.

Assenomi turned and smiled. "We're here." A dark hole stood gaping in the face of the cliff, and it promised to lead to the bottom of the world.

5
The Woman in the Bath

Assenomi pulled a whistle from her cloak and blew. The piercing note, which seemed too loud and clear to come from such a small thing, rang in the air and was sucked deep into the opening. She blew it three times, and as the last reverberations died away, a woman dressed very much like Assenomi appeared at the mouth of the cave.

Van bowed. Reaching into his cloak, he took out a small pouch of copper coins, which Ohma had given him with instructions to present it when he reached Yomida Forest. The woman, however, refused to accept it.

"Thank you for your thoughtfulness," she said with a smile. "But the Echo Master instructed me not to take anything, because you are our guests." She bowed deeply. "We are honored to welcome you. Traveling through the snow must have been exhausting. Please come in. If you give me the reins, I will take care of your reindeer for you."

Van returned her bow and handed her the reins. Holding Yuna in one arm, he followed Assenomi inside.

It was much larger than Van had expected. He stood at the edge of a huge cavern that extended far into the darkness, with tunnels and chambers branching off. Unlike the salt mine, a product of human hands, this enormous cave had been crafted by nature itself. Even before entering, Van had detected the presence of people within, and now, he could hear many voices echoing hollowly from different tunnels. Shafts of light poured through small holes that penetrated the cave walls in many places, making the interior much brighter than he had expected.

"It's quite dry, isn't it?" Assenomi said with a smile.

"Yes it is." In Van's experience, caves were damp, dark places that instilled a blind fear, enveloping intruders with the cold breath exhaled from the depths. But this cavern, although certainly grand, did not feel overwhelming.

"Long ago, our ancestors spent many years making this a comfortable place to live. It must have been very hard work to accomplish by hand." There was a note of admiration in Assenomi's voice.

Footsteps sounded to the right. A few moments later, a middle-aged man emerged from one of the tunnels. He was short, and his left shoulder sagged slightly when he walked, perhaps a remnant of an old leg or hip injury. He bowed slightly to Van and then turned and welcomed Assenomi.

"Is the master here?" Assenomi asked.

The man scratched his chin and replied, "I'm afraid he just crossed over. We'll have to ask the guests to rest a spell." Unlike Assenomi, he spoke with a southern accent.

"Oh dear. Someone needed treatment?"

"The Tonami clan brought a child in this morning."

Assenomi nodded and turned to Van. "I'm terribly sorry to have to make you wait after you have come all this way, but it appears that someone has suddenly taken ill."

Van shook his head. "Please don't worry about us. We don't mind waiting."

Assenomi smiled. "Thank you. In that case, Nakka here will guide you to the baths so that you can warm yourselves. We'll prepare some food for you in the meantime."

"You have baths?" Van asked. His voice must have betrayed his joy, because Assenomi's smile deepened.

"Yes. The waters here are excellent. Take your time and have a good soak."

The man she'd called Nakka nodded. "If you'd come with me, please, I'll show you the place."

Taking a lantern from a small hook that had been driven into the rock wall, he led the way into one of the branches. Van followed, carrying Yuna with his left arm. The entrance was narrow but not so low that he had to duck, and the tunnel gently twisted and turned as it stretched deeper. The lantern swayed with Nakka's rolling gait, sending large shadows dancing across the walls.

The first chamber they came to was about the size of a tent. There was a small hearth in the center, and Van spied the red of the banked fire in the ashes. Sunlight entered through two smoke holes in the rock, making it brighter than Van expected. Reindeer hides were spread thickly across the floor; Van assumed they were for sleeping. And there were more hides stacked along the wall. There was also a basin filled with water.

"The toilet's through here. Do you wish to use it?"

Van looked at Yuna. "Do you need to pee?" he asked, but she shook her head vigorously. He raised an eyebrow and looked at her intently. Not long ago, she would've shaken her head like this even when she needed to go, and she'd frequently had little accidents. Recently, however, she seemed more aware of her actual needs, and Van decided she would probably be all right. "Just show me where it is," he said.

Nakka nodded. "Leave your luggage here, and I'll take you to the baths. The toilet's on the way." Van placed his things on top of a reindeer hide as Nakka had indicated but felt a twinge of anxiety. There was no door to this cave, and anyone could walk in and out as they pleased.

Nakka smiled as though reading Van's mind. "There're no thieves here. Those who come are all desperate for healin', beggin' the gods for help." He lowered the lantern and set off again.

So, Van thought, *the Echo Master is like the Master of the Dance.* Someone who cured the ailing and aided those in the grips of evil spirits. People undoubtedly brought their afflicted loved ones here for treatment.

Nakka showed Van and Yuna the toilet and continued on toward the baths. The tunnel gradually brightened, and the smell of steam wafted. At the end of the corridor, the entrance to another cave came into view.

"The baths're through that door there," Nakka said as he turned around to look at Van. "You ever used a hot spring bath before?"

Van nodded. "There are hot springs in my homeland, too."

Nakka looked relieved. "That's good. If you'd never tried 'em, I'd have to teach you step-by-step. The hot water flows from the back of that cave. You can undress near the entrance and wash yourself with a dipper before gettin' in. I'll let you know when your meal's ready. Take your time till then." With that, he left.

Van placed Yuna on the floor. She grabbed his sleeve as if she was a little uncertain. "Ochan? What's in deah?"

"Hot water for soaking in. It'll warm us up." Van took Yuna's small hand in his and ducked through the entrance. The chamber was so large that it almost made him gasp. Several baskets were placed near the entrance to hold people's clothing, and one of them had been placed against the far wall with a cloth spread over top. Someone had entered the bath before them. A screen stood between the changing area and the baths, so Van couldn't see beyond, but from the faint scent flowing, he deduced that the bather was a woman. The scent seemed slightly familiar, but he couldn't remember why.

For a moment, Van wondered if it would be rude to enter a bath occupied by a woman he did not know, but Nakka had not seemed concerned, and Yuna was chattering away as usual. Whoever it was had surely heard them by now. Her silence signaled she didn't care who entered the bath. Van assumed it was likely an elderly woman no longer concerned with gender.

Van stripped off his clothes quickly, then helped Yuna, still talking away merrily, to remove hers, and placed them all in a basket. The floors of baths could get very slippery, so Van picked Yuna up to keep her from falling. She squealed with laughter, seemingly delighted by the feel of skin against skin.

Steam rose thickly on the other side of the screen. Thin threads of evening light fell through vents that pierced the walls near the ceiling. In the loose net woven by the fading rays of sunlight and wisps of steam, a woman sat alone in the bath. She looked to be around thirty. Her skin was smooth, and she still retained a youthful look.

Their eyes met. Startled, Van hastily lowered Yuna to conceal his lower body. The woman looked down and bent her face over the water, but her pale shoulders were shaking—with laughter. Realizing how ridiculous he must have appeared, Van burst out laughing, too.

"I'm so sorry," he said. "I didn't realize there was a young woman in the bath." He turned to leave, but she called after him.

"Wait…" She paused, overtaken by a fit of coughing. Van waited silently. She raised her head and took a deep breath. "Please don't worry. Go ahead and bathe. Once you're in, you can't see anything." Tears pooled at the corners of her eyes.

"Why she laughin'?" Yuna asked, looking puzzled.

Van looked at the woman and smiled. "Because I acted silly." Then, with a nod to the woman, he lowered Yuna. Crouching, Van laid the girl across his knee, scooped up a dipperful of hot water, and poured it gently over her body. It was the perfect temperature.

"Hot!" Yuna shrieked.

"No it's not." Van laughed and poured another dipperful over her.

"Is too! Weally hot!" She pursed her lips.

"All right, then. You stay here. I'm getting in," Van said.

Yuna grabbed him, puffing up her cheeks. "No! Me too!"

Van picked her up and sank slowly into the hot water. At first, Yuna clung to him stiffly, but once she was in as far as her shoulders, her face lit up. "It's wahm."

The woman laughed. Yuna frowned and looked at her. "You laughin' again. What's so funny?"

"Sorry," the woman said, still grinning. "You're just so cute, that's all." Then she asked gently, "What's your name?"

Yuna regarded her warily for a moment and then finally replied, "Yunacha."

"How old are you, Yunacha?"

Yuna peered up at Van questioningly. "She's almost four," he answered. "Although she still speaks with a bit of a lisp."

The woman blinked. "Four years old. I see." Sadness cast a shadow over her eyes. They softened as they took in Yuna, though.

Yuna gazed back at her with interest. "What's yoah name?" she inquired.

The woman's eyes widened, but she smiled kindly. "Sae. My name is Sae."

"Hmm." Yuna glanced up at Van, then, as if to conceal her embarrassment, began kicking at his knees, splashing hot water everywhere.

"Hey, cut that out." He raised her up and set her back on his lap, then looked at the woman called Sae.

"Were you injured?" he asked. A long scar stretched from her shoulder to her elbow. The wound had to be quite old, because it was already white.

Sae looked down at her left arm and nodded. "I fell into a river and was cut by a stone on the bottom." She explained that winter had already settled in, and the icy water prevented her from losing too much blood. Still, she'd nearly frozen to death. Sae looked at Van's arm. "Did you come here to heal your wound, too?"

Van frowned. "Wound?" he asked.

"Yes. The one on your arm."

Van followed her gaze and started in surprise. The scar on his left arm where the beast had bitten him had turned a purplish green. Purple lines stretched along the veins like a web of grassroots. For the last few months, Van had worn thick furs and hadn't seen his arm, but it certainly hadn't appeared this way in the summer.

Heaving Yuna out of the water, he examined her ankle and found that her scar had also changed color, although more faintly than his own. Van's expression must have been grim, because Sae inquired if something was wrong.

Van exhaled. "No. I just hadn't realized it turned this color."

"Does it hurt?"

Van shook his head. "No. It's an old scar."

Sae's face clouded, and she said quietly, "It should be all right if it doesn't hurt, but it might be good to have the Echo Master examine it for you."

Van nodded, still gazing at his arm.

6
The Echo Master

It was not until the evening of the next day that Van was able to see the Echo Master. It had taken the Echo Master until dawn to follow the child's spirit, and he'd slept until the afternoon.

Assenomi apologized profusely for the wait, but Van was glad to have a whole extra day. He slept very well, perhaps because the caves were cradled in the bosom of the mountain. The food, though simple, was familiar and delicious, helping him shake off the fatigue of the journey. It was Van's habit, developed over many years of experience, to assess a new place for defensibility and escapability in the event of an attack, and while Yuna slept, he wandered through the different tunnels, imprinting the layout on his mind.

The sick liked to talk about their ailments, and Van was frequently stopped by patients who wished to chat. He was grateful for this opportunity to learn more about the Echo Master. Some described him as kind to the core, others as hard to fathom; all of them seemed to have difficulty pinning him down in words, yet none doubted his powers.

There were plenty of charlatans around who bragged to convince people of their ability, but the Echo Master didn't appear to be one of them. Even those who told funny stories about him still spoke of him with awe. The discovery that several patients were Zolian immigrants came as a surprise. According to Assenomi, although they had their own healers, Zolians often came here for help once they learned of the Echo Master's skill.

Van thought he might meet Sae again, but he did not.

By the time Assenomi arrived to lead him to the Echo Master's chamber deep inside the cave, the afternoon light had faded and was turning the color of sunset. Van took Yuna by the hand, but she protested grumpily, perhaps made sleepy by their early supper. He was wondering what to do when Nakka, who'd come to take their dishes, said, "Let her sleep. I'll keep an eye on her."

Van felt bad, as he was sure the man had work to do, but at Assenomi's urging, he thanked Nakka, put Yuna down to sleep, and left.

They traveled for quite a distance along the winding passages, with the light of the lantern swaying in front, until Assenomi finally came to a halt before a large opening covered by an unbleached cloth. "This is as far as I'll take you. Please enter."

Van nodded and thanked her. Smiling, she said, "Not at all," and departed.

Finally, the time has come.

After uttering a word of greeting, Van lifted the cloth and ducked beneath it. When he raised his head, he drew in a sharp breath, stunned by the sight that met his eyes. The chamber was enormous: both wide and strangely shaped. A huge cavern opened before him, and countless gigantic apertures pierced the rock wall beyond, slanting upward through the stone. It was impossible to see how high these holes ran, but Van was sure they must have been linked to the outside, because sunset rays cascaded down like a magnificent golden waterfall.

"Beautiful, ain't it?" someone remarked cheerfully. "You're standin' in the belly o' the forest, watchin' Sunset Falls. It can only be seen at this time o' day, durin' this particular season."

Startled, Van looked in the direction of the voice and spied a plump old man sitting cross-legged in the shadow of the rock wall. A gentle light haloed his form, cast by a hearth on the stone dais where he rested, one step above the floor.

"The belly of the forest?" Van asked.

The man smiled. It was a guileless expression resembling that of a child delighted by the question. He spread his arms wide. "Look closely and imagine. A thick wave of smolderin' earth plows down a slope forested with many great timbers. With a loud roar, the network of roots is ripped from the ground, and the trees, engulfed in flames, begin to fall, only to be trapped by the hard stone surface behind, and so they remain stuck, half-fallen, wrapped in burnin' mud. The fire consumes the trees, while the mud cools and hardens..." He looked up and pointed to the large cylindrical shafts that stretched diagonally above him. "...Leavin' behind those holes to mark where the trees had once been, y'see."

Now that he knew their story, Van recognized that the shafts resembled holes left by trees mowed down in a landslide. It was as though he was looking up at them from their roots. As he examined each trace engraved on the rock's surface, the horrific event took shape before his eyes like a vision from the past, and goose bumps rose on his skin.

A forest had once stood here. Engulfed by the earth's fiery blood and the burning mud that had gushed from the fire mountain, its giant trees were incinerated, leaving only these cavities.

"This here is Yomida Forest," the old man said, his voice echoing hollowly in the great cavern. "You must be cold down there. Come on up." He beckoned Van with a wave of his hand, speaking to him as he might an old friend.

Van walked cautiously toward him. When he reached the hearth, the man made a sweeping gesture with his hand. "Welcome to my home."

Van bowed and said quietly, "Please tell me why you summoned me."

The old man grinned. "You don't waste time on idle talk, do you? Let's get down to business, then." He glanced up at the ceiling. "Hey! You old crone! Get on down here!"

Van heard the flap of wings from the cavern's roof. A large raven glided slowly down, as if sliding on oil, and landed on the old man's shoulder. Even with its wings folded, it was bigger than his head. He raised his arm slightly so that it could perch with one foot on his shoulder and the other on his arm.

The Echo Master grimaced. "Ouch! I told you not to dig your claws in like that!" The raven began to play with his ear, giving it a little nip. The man hunched his shoulder as though it tickled and gave Van a crooked smile. "This bird here was my wife's pet and likes to chew my ear just like she used to." He looked sheepish. "They worship me as the Echo Master, but I'm no master. I'm just a geezer who knows a bit about sicknesses."

He cupped his hands over the raven's back and stroked it gently. "Still, I can hear this bird's voice pretty well. She sees spirits much better than I do. I just repeat what she says, like an echo."

Suddenly the Echo Master stopped, and his eyes went blank. His expression changed, and for a moment, Van thought he glimpsed the raven peering out at him through the elderly man's eyes. He stepped back, feeling as though he'd been doused in ice water. The Echo Master's head slumped forward, and his body swayed as though his knees had given out. Rushing forward, Van grabbed him before he struck the floor. His skin felt cold and clammy, and he was soaked with sweat.

Van gently lowered him to the ground beside the hearth, where he lay for a long time, unable to move. His eyes were closed, and his breath came in ragged gasps. The raven hopped anxiously around the hearth and circled the Echo Master's head, cawing occasionally, but the old man just waved his hand weakly, seemingly irritated by the noise. In a listless voice, he muttered, "I'm all right. Don't worry. I'd be fine if you'd just leave me be for a minute."

Noticing a cup by the hearth, Van asked if he would like some tea, but again, the old man waved his hand. It seemed better to do nothing, so Van sat cross-legged by the fire, watching him.

Finally, the man opened his eyes and cleared his throat. "Oooh, that was exhausting." He groaned. Then he glared at the raven. "Honestly! You stupid crow! Why'd you have to jump inside me like that? You almost killed me."

The raven cawed again, as if mocking him. The old man took a swipe at her head, but the bird jumped nimbly aside. Grunting, the Echo Master raised himself up and sat cross-legged.

"Are you all right?" Van asked.

The man nodded slowly. Wiping a hand over his face, he sighed. "Sorry 'bout that. Must've looked pretty strange, huh? That old crow, she never possesses me when people are around. Must've wanted to see you through human eyes pretty badly."

He looked at the raven and grimaced. "Yeah, I can see he's your type, but honestly!" The raven thrust her beak into the air and cawed raucously as though laughing at him. "Don't be ridiculous! If I were a little younger myself—" He looked at Van and stopped with an embarrassed smile. "Sorry."

He cleared his throat and adopted a serious expression. "So let's start again. I hadn't introduced myself yet, had I? I'm Suohl."

"I'm Van."

"All right then, Van. I asked you to come 'cause I saw you when I rode on Granny Crow here the other night."

Van frowned. "You flew on the raven?"

"Yeah. I can ride her, just like she rode me. I don't sit on her back or anythin' like that. She carries my spirit."

Suohl grinned. "Perhaps you already know this, but when I saw you the other night, you were completely otsufah, inside out."

"Inside out?" Van repeated blankly.

"Yup." Suohl coughed and then said, "You were runnin' with those rochai, black wolves crossed with ossam, right?"

Van's eyes narrowed. "So they *were* a mix of ossam and black wolves."

"Yeah. And there's somethin' important I need to tell you 'bout them, too, but we can talk about that later. First, this otsufah thing. I saw it clear as day. You and your daughter were runnin' with the rochai, completely inside out."

Van knitted his brow. "What do you mean?"

Suohl made a gesture as if pulling off a glove so that it was inside out. "You as a soul and you as a body switched places. Assenomi said that Granny Crow's feathers didn't look black to you and the girl, so there's no mistake. That means you're already a bit inside out, even when things are normal. When your body switches places with your soul, it affects your sight and smell, you see."

Van stared at him dumbly, and Suohl grinned. "I guess it's hard to follow. Look. It's like this. Living creatures are pretty strange. We haven't a clue what's goin' on inside our own bodies. For example, if we see meat roastin' on a fire when we're hungry, our mouths water. We don't tell our mouths to water; they just start droolin' of their own accord. Right?"

"Yes."

"Y'know, we assume it's the part of us that feels anger, that thinks and talks, that's really us. But actually, it's the body that lives and moves, that likes eatin' and lyin' with a woman. It's not the soul. Though I s'pose the soul can tell when somethin' tastes or feels good." Suohl cocked an eyebrow at Van, then his face grew serious.

"Have you ever wondered what happens to your body when you get sick? What's occurrin' inside it? We can't see or hear what's goin' on inside us. Even though they're ours, we know our bodies less than we know other people's."

Van nodded, feeling like he was on the verge of comprehension.

"I've been treatin' sick people a long time, and I'm beginnin' to think the human body resembles a forest."

Van frowned, feeling his dawning understanding slip from his grasp.

Suohl grinned. "You don't get it, huh? S'pose that's only natural. But think about what it was like when you were inside out. When you were runnin' with the rochai, you saw lights, didn't you? Countless little lights?"

A scene from that night leaped vividly into Van's mind. Infinite lights, gathering and scattering in waves, like the radiance that danced across the northern sky at night. They'd shimmered in the beasts and in Yuna's little body, too.

Van opened his mouth. "Yes I did. What are they?"

"I'm not sure." Suohl shook his head. "But I see 'em when I ride Granny Crow. I'm guessin' everything alive glows like that."

Van's eyes narrowed. "Each one?"

Suohl nodded. "We keep a lot of livin' creatures inside our bodies. Well, maybe *keep* ain't the right word. It's more like there's countless little lives inside us, and all together, they form a person.

"Remember how I said the human body's like a forest? Well, that's what I meant. Beasts live in the forest, and so do bugs. Grasses grow there, and mosses, too. Birds roost among the trees. Sometimes, they might cause some mischief. Like the way bugs chewin' on leaves can make trees wither. But at the same time, birds in the forest eat the bugs, and their droppings make rich soil…" Suohl gestured busily with his hands as he spoke. "Together, all these many lives that are livin' there make the forest, you see?"

Van drew a quiet breath. He felt as if he was being shown something quite extraordinary. Suohl watched him closely. "The human body's the same," he said. "Normally, we can't see 'em, but our bodies're inhabited by tiny little lives. I don't know if they're there from the time we're born, but some enter our bodies later. And I think we get sick when a few of these creatures get up to mischief, just like when bugs eat trees."

He raised a finger. "If a muddy thorn pricked your finger, you'd pull it out and suck on the wound, wouldn't you? If you cut your finger with a dirty blade, you'd let it bleed a little to wash out anything bad, right?"

Van nodded. As he rubbed the scar from the rochai, he felt the skin on his scalp tighten. Quietly, he asked, "Are you saying that something bad entered my body when the rochai bit me, like how the saliva of a sick dog can infect a person they attack?"

Suohl's eyes narrowed. "So one did bite you… That explains it, then."

At that moment, urgent voices sounded in the distance, and hurried footsteps approached the entrance. The curtain was flung aside, and Assenomi rushed into the room, followed by a group of men bearing someone on a wooden door. Assenomi looked up at the dais and cried out, "Echo Master, this man's been bitten by a rochai!"

7
Behind Me, My Child

The victim was a young immigrant. He'd wounded a hibernating bear and, while tracking it down, had run into a pack of beasts that resembled wolves. One of them had bitten him.

"He seemed fine until yesterday. He just had a sore throat. But today, he's been dead tired and—"

The men who appeared to be the afflicted's kin rushed to explain what had happened, but Suohl hushed them, his face grim. He told the men to strip the young man. The patient lay there and let them do as they wished without protest. Although conscious, he looked terrified and deathly pale.

The bite must have been on his arm, because when they tried to pull off his sleeve, he groaned in pain. Revealed beneath was a dirty, infested wound. Suohl looked up, and Assenomi handed him a knife that she'd heated in the hearth. Then she placed a cloth in the young man's mouth.

Turning to the men who stood helplessly, Suohl said, "Hold him down so he doesn't move." They pinned the young man's limbs while Suohl took a bottle from Assenomi's hands and tilted it to pour a liquid over the wound. After confirming the spot, Suohl placed the blade against it. "This'll hurt. Try and bear it," he said. He sliced the wound open. The youth groaned and twisted, but Suohl pressed the blade against the wound for some time, squeezing out blood and pus before pouring more liquid from the bottle over the cut and binding it with a clean white cloth.

The youth spit the gag from his mouth, his chest heaving, and collapsed limply.

"Were we in time?" Assenomi whispered.

Suohl groaned. "I don't know." He was about to continue when the young man's expression changed. His body bent backward, turning rigid, and his jaw muscles clenched so powerfully that they bulged and quivered. His throat constricted, the muscles moving in spasms.

"Watch out! He's gonna choke!" Suohl grabbed the poor young man's jaw and tried to shove it upward to clear his air passage, but the youth's teeth were clamped so tightly that his jaw wouldn't budge.

"Here. Let me." Suohl was surprised by Van's remark. He was about to say something, but Van stopped him and, moving around to the young man's head, pushed his forehead down with his left hand while pulling his jaw forward with his right. The young man's mouth, which hadn't budged for Suohl, shifted easily. The convulsions eased, and the young man's muscles relaxed. He inhaled noisily, and Suohl's shoulders dropped in relief.

"You did that like a pro," he muttered.

Van didn't answer. During the long war, he'd done this many times. Some of his friends had lived. Others had not.

"The convulsions are over. What should we do next?" Van asked.

Suohl's face darkened. One look told Van there was nothing the Echo Master could do. Although he said nothing, his eyes spoke eloquently. He must have treated people bitten by those creatures before. He stared at Van for a few moments, then turned his eyes to the patient's kin, who waited anxiously.

"I've squeezed out as much of the bad blood as possible. But it's way too late. It should've been done as soon as he was bitten. Not much point otherwise. The poison's already spread through his body. Whether he makes it or not'll depend on whether he's strong enough to fight the disease. All we can do is wait and see."

The men gazed at the youth silently. Eventually, the eldest said, "If his spirit leaves, will you follow it for us?"

Suohl sighed. "'Course I will. But even if I bring his spirit back, if his body ain't strong enough to hold it, there's nothin' we can do."

Van peered down at the youth. When things got this bad, everything depended on the strength of the patient's body. Regardless of his longing to live and how much his loved ones wished to keep him alive, if his body could no longer support life, he was finished.

Suohl's right, Van thought. *We can't see inside our own bodies. When we're healthy, we think we control our bodies with our minds, but when we're sick, our bodies ignore us and act of their own accord. It's only then that we realize our minds and bodies are separate things.*

Van felt a tickle at the back of his skull, and a strange aching sensation stirred deep in his nose.

Again...

The smells around him sharpened acutely, and his vision began to alter. Even the sounds and the feeling of his skin changed.

Something brushed against the tip of his heightened awareness. He raised his head, and the raven that had sat motionless on the rock shelf, melting into the darkness, launched herself into the air.

"*Caw! Caw! Caw!*" Screeching, she swooped across the cavern and shot up one of the shafts left by the ancient trees.

"...What's that?" Suohl stood, his face waxen. "The rochai have entered the cave?"

Before he'd finished uttering the words, Van took a hatchet in his right hand. "Assenomi," he said. She turned to him, her face tight. "I'll stop the beasts. In the meantime, gather everyone in here."

Van worried for Yuna, but his awareness told him that the rochai approached from the opposite end, far from the chamber where she slept. If Van could stop them in one of the narrow passages, he'd have enough time for someone to bring her here.

"Yuna... Please..." Van's face twisted. It was so hard to speak.

Damn! He ground his teeth. *So that's what he means by "inside out."*

When Van was inside out, words disappeared. Human thought vanished. He couldn't relinquish his body to those sensations.

"Yu... Yuna...bring...her...here," Van said, clinging desperately to his self-awareness. After a deep breath, he shook his head and faced the men who'd brought the youth. Pointing to the south corner of the cave, he shoved the words out. "Over there. Make a barricade. If the beasts come, hit them with hatchets and swords. Don't use arrows. They move very fast. If you miss, they'll attack before you can shoot again."

The men appeared to be having difficulty grasping what was going on. They looked at each other, perplexed. However, the elder who'd asked Suohl to follow the youth's spirit looked in the direction Van was pointing. Understanding dawned on his face when he realized Van was indicating a hollow, one surrounded on three sides by rock walls with a low overhanging ceiling. Seeing the man nod, Van set off at a run.

His head tingled. The colors around him changed.

Not yet... Not yet...

Van raced through the dark tunnels, struggling to retain a grasp on his consciousness, which was on the verge of turning.

The beasts were padding steadily closer.

He ran toward them, away from the sounds of Assenomi shouting and the footsteps of the patients hurrying for the rock chamber.

This part of the cave had not been modified by human hands. It was probably too damp to be habitable. Water dripped from the rock ceiling, turning the floor slick and making it hard to run.

Something niggled at the back of Van's mind, but it was too hard to think, and he couldn't pin it down. He chased the thought round and round his mind, feeling like he was grabbing after a slippery fish, until finally the source of his unease became clear.

Why are they coming in this way?

If the rochai wished to attack the people in this cave, coming from the other direction would've been faster.

Maybe this is just a feint, and they're actually planning to attack from the other side. However, Van felt the beasts' presence with his entire body, and they were only encroaching from the front.

Van stopped thinking after confirming this. If there were no beasts behind him, then instead of fretting over the why, his first priority ought to be intercepting those before him.

While candles and torches lit the tunnels that ran among the living quarters, here there were none, and it was almost pitch-dark. Yet he saw the rock surface of the walls. The beasts surely saw just as well. Van heard them clearly now. Their claws clicked against stone as they glided across the floor.

Van came to a halt and looked around. Although the tunnel was narrow, there was still a fair bit of space above his head and on either side. He might not be able to stop them by himself. There was no one to ask for help, though. The rochai's fangs were poisoned. Even a slight graze would doom a victim to wander the border between life and death. Like that youth.

Van dropped into a fighting stance, a hatchet in his right hand and a hunting knife in his left. From the murky depths of some other place, he heard singing.

"My spear, these shining antlers…"

Faint voices reached him—those of the Lone Antlers, his comrades who were no longer in this world.

"Behind me, my fawn. Bend low, Antlers, to shield this young life…"

The song of men who had no children and no parents of their own, who'd lost everything, yet who still sang, their hearts focused on those who depended on them for protection.

In his mind, Van saw Yuna, her cheeks shining as she lay sleeping, sucking her thumb.

Behind me, my fawn...

Though not born of Van's own blood, she was his child, more precious even than life.

His right palm was sweaty, and he readjusted his grip on the handle of the hatchet. At that moment, he caught the gleam of a beast's eyes like a golden trail in the darkness ahead. More shadows slunk up behind it.

8
A Burning Arrow Piercing the Darkness

The beasts didn't attack. Instead, they approached slowly, seemingly gauging the distance. One, then another, and another, lined up before Van and stopped, heads lowered, fangs bared, snarling all the while. Yet despite their growls, they didn't move.

Why?

Van crouched low and waited, keeping his hips loose.

Still the beasts didn't budge.

One circled around from behind the leader to creep nearer, and Van lunged forward, thrusting his knife for its muzzle in a feint. Immediately, the beasts recoiled, and their growling rose in pitch.

When Van stepped forward, they stepped back, keeping just out of range of his knife. They didn't attempt to encroach upon the space between them and Van, but neither did they flee. If Van stepped back, they instantly jumped forward.

Watching them brought an image to Van's mind. Hunting dogs. This was how hounds contained their prey in one spot until their master arrived.

Are they holding me at bay?

A chill numbness spread across Van's forehead. He focused his attention on the rear while keeping the beasts in sight. He heard the *twang* of a bow deep in the darkness, and an arrow lanced through the air toward him. Van twisted aside instinctively, but a searing pain shot through his left shoulder. The arrow had grazed him. His thick clothing kept it from being a deep cut, but it was enough to stagger him.

The beasts pounced upon this chance. They surged for Van en masse, and the smell of their bodies and their breath assaulted him. The smell erased something in his brain, something that had kept him in check. Everything around Van changed. The sensations within him, too. His body moved while his mind vanished, leaving only his body.

He smashed the leader's nose with his hatchet, rolled forward with the momentum of the blow, and stood, crushing another beast between the wall and his body while kicking away yet another.

A whistle blew. Instantly, the beasts froze. They retreated as though pulled by threads. Van barely managed to suppress the urge to race into the darkness after them. As they receded into the distance, he gradually felt himself return. Shoulders heaving, he stared down at his body and at the beasts fallen on the floor. His clothes reeked of blood. He shook his head.

What was that all about?

If they'd intended to attack the people inside the cave, they should have come in from the big entrance on the other side.

If the goal was to kill me... Just two or three more arrows would have done it. One of them would certainly have found its mark.

Did they refrain from shooting because I was tackling the beasts?

But if the master controlled them so completely, they could have called the creatures off to get a good shot. Something about this made Van very uneasy. Some other purpose guided these events; Van just wasn't certain of what.

He needed to return to the inner chamber. Although he could no longer feel the presence of any beasts or enemies, he didn't drop his guard. There'd be no relief until he confirmed with his own eyes that Yuna was all right.

*

Many people had gathered in the inner chamber, crowding into the hollow in the corner, just as Van had told them to, and they anxiously muttered to one another. After catching sight of Van when he entered, Suohl hurried over to him. He stopped once he was close, and his lips parted.

"You been hurt?" he asked.

Van shook his head. "It's the blood of the beasts. I was just grazed. Is everyone here?"

Suohl's face clouded. "Almost. There's still a few missin'. Assenomi's taken some men to go and look for 'em—"

Before Suohl had finished speaking, Van turned and ran from the room.

Yuna wasn't there. She must have been among those who didn't make it. As Van dashed through the door, he noticed people hurrying over, with Assenomi at their head.

"Assenomi!" he called.

She looked up, her relief plain in her expression. "Van! You're all right? Thank goodness!"

Checking the faces of those who followed behind her, Van frowned. "Where's Yuna?"

"She's fine. She's right behind us. With Nakka."

But Nakka was not among the others. Assenomi spun around. Noticing Nakka's absence, she blinked. "That's odd. He was here until just a moment ago..."

Van brushed past her and hurried into the stone tunnel. "Yuna!" he shouted, and his voice echoed hollowly down the passages. There was no answer.

He called again and again, expecting to hear her call out, "Ochan!" at any moment, but there was no response from that sweet little voice. Van ran through the dark, empty tunnels and out into the night. A cold, icy wind struck his face. Snow swirled in the jet-black darkness, buffeting his cheeks.

Van's head throbbed. The pain made him feel ill. His throat was dry, and his vision blurred...

Had there been something smeared on that arrow?

Van gritted his teeth and stared at the snow that lay between the entrance to the cave and the forest. It was littered with footsteps, most of which were already partly buried in new, falling snow. The tracks likely belonged to the men who'd borne the youth to the cave, because they all moved from the forest to the cavern mouth. Among these, one set of prints led in the opposite direction, however. Van stared at them, gasping for breath. They were still fresh. Their outlines were more prevalent than the rest, and they were deeper. Van bit his lip. Nakka must have carried Yuna away.

He set off at a run, following the tracks, but as soon as he entered the forest, the darkness deepened, and he could no longer see the footprints. The injury must have dulled his senses, because he only picked up vague scents and sounds.

Should I go back for a lantern?

With a light, Van would be able to follow the tracks. However, if he went back to get one, Nakka would have put considerable distance between them by the time he returned. Yet without a light, he couldn't follow.

The distance between him and Yuna increased with each moment. Fighting his impatience, Van stepped back out of the forest. The *twang* of a bowstring sounded from high above, and a sphere of flame soared through the air. It split the night sky, tracing a wide arc, and plunged into the forest. Moments later, a light spread, illuminating Van's surroundings. A tree was burning. The flaming arrow had found purchase in a branch, which now crackled with flame. Van's eyes widened at the sound.

Hokuso… Oil-rich hokuso trees burned easily. Van had used the same trick many times when ambushing Zolian warriors.

The light shed by the flames illuminated the footprints clearly.

But who in the world?

He turned in the direction of the bowstring noise and spied a figure standing partway up the cliff, above the entrance to the cavern. They were silhouetted by the light of a flaming arrow.

Van couldn't believe his eyes. The shape appeared to be a woman. Perhaps she noticed him looking her way, for she waved her bow, as if to say not to worry for her. Van bowed and turned around to resume his chase. The tracks moved southwest.

Wind whistled through the trees, striking Van's face. The snow came down thicker.

I have to find them before the prints are buried...

Van clung to that thought while dragging his heavy body through the drifts. But even as he pushed ahead, Nakka's footsteps grew ever fainter beneath the falling snow.

Each time the flames of the burning tree wavered in the wind, shadows danced. They writhed and flitted across the white snow, wavering over the tracks and blurring their outlines. Even without that, Van would've had trouble seeing. He couldn't tell how much time passed, but after a while, he caught the gentle sound of approaching footfalls. He halted and turned, twisting his hatchet in his grip.

A figure with a bow slung across its back emerged from the darkness.

"Van."

As he'd suspected, it was the woman he'd met in the bath. She smelled faintly of pine resin. The scent merged the image of the shadowed figure on the cliff with Sae, who stood before him now.

"Were you the one who loosed the burning arrow?"

She nodded. "I'll explain later. Right now, we must follow Yuna," she said quietly.

A hammering pain spread from Van's head to the rest of his body. He felt confused, and the strange movements of the beasts flowed through his mind repeatedly.

If they were trying to keep me in that part of the cave...

Then Yuna's abduction at the same time was no coincidence.

I must go.

Van had to move his feet, yet his body refused to budge.

For a moment, everything grew dark, and the next thing he knew, his forehead was resting on the cold snow.

"Van, are you all right?"

There came a worried voice, and a slender hand slipped inside his hood, searching for his pulse. "I'm all right. Leave me. Find Yuna…," he replied.

At least, Van believed he did. But he didn't know if he spoke the words aloud.

Somewhere, Van caught the anxious cawing of a crow. That was the last thing he remembered before the darkness took him.

Chapter 6:
In Pursuit of Black Wolf Fever

1
Stepmother, Stepsister

Snow pattered against the glass each time the wind brushed the windows lining both sides of the corridor. Through them, Hohsalle saw the blue darkness left by the setting sun, along with a cluster of buildings. Their vague outlines were buried in the dancing snow. Each building was devoted to the patient study and exploration of a specific field, such as medicine, mathematics, metalworking, or architecture. Each had been studied by one clan for the last thousand years. The Academy of Deeper Learning, nestled in the bosom of the mountains, had scarcely changed in appearance for a millennium. However, within its halls and towers, research and technology were developing at breathtaking speed.

A large door stood at the end of the corridor, and Hohsalle slowed his pace. He cherished the person who lived on the other side, yet he hesitated to open this door every time. After a short sigh, he pulled the bell rope. There came a chime, and the way opened.

An elderly woman with shining cheeks peered out. Her eyes lit up at the sight of Hohsalle. "Young Master!" she exclaimed.

Hohsalle smiled. "I'm back, Moiya."

She's aged, he thought as he looked into her face. She'd served for many years as his stepmother's maid and was surely in her midseventies by now. Every time they met, Hohsalle recalled how much taller she'd seemed while acting as his nurse. Of course, he knew this was primarily because he had grown so much since then, but it was clear each time he saw her that she was also shrinking.

"Are you taking the medicine I gave you?" he asked.

She looked amused. "Of course I am."

"Every night before bed?"

"Yes, yes, Young Master. The medicine you give this old hag is so bitter that it's hard to swallow, but I drink it faithfully, I promise you." Moiya placed a plump hand on Hohsalle's back and pushed him forward gently. Hohsalle stepped inside, grinning.

The room was large and sported a high ceiling, yet it didn't feel cold at all. A fire blazed in the stove at the center, and ceramic ducts in each corner conveyed the hot air throughout the building to heat it. Hot water circulated through pipes under the floor as well.

Every time Hohsalle felt this room's warm embrace, he remembered how his father used to spread his arms wide to envelop his stepmother. He'd built this cocoon especially for her.

The rocking chair by the window bobbed gently. Hohsalle's stepmother was so small and slight that the chair appeared to be empty and rocking of its own accord. A tall woman stood beside it. As Hohsalle approached, she smiled softly.

"Hohsalle."

He smiled back and nodded. "Sister."

At the sound of Hohsalle's voice, his stepmother appeared to notice him for the first time and gazed at him vacantly. She regarded him suspiciously at first, then a light kindled in her eyes, and she beamed with her whole face. "Ahnolle!" Calling Hohsalle by his father's name, she stretched out her arms. He embraced her tenderly. The scent of the medicinal bath pricked his nose. Even her favorite perfume did little to mask that smell, which seemed to permeate her body.

"I. Was," she began, voice faint. She paused to take several breaths, then continued. "Waiting for you. I know you must be terribly busy, but still."

At that moment, a particularly strong gust of wind rattled the windowpanes. Hohsalle's stepmother started and clung to him. "I don't like that wind. Why does it blow so much? It will wither the utsuge buds, and that would be a shame, especially when they're set to bloom any day now."

She seemed so frail that her body would break if he applied any pressure. Closing his eyes, Hohsalle held her gently and listened to her fret about early summer flowers at the sound of the winter wind driving snow against the window.

"You should. Really. Come more often," she said softly into his ear. "The nurse you hired is much kinder than the other one. But I still miss you."

Hohsalle pressed his lips together and took a shallow inhale. By the time he removed his stepmother's arms, her eyes were half-closed. It was always like this. She dozed off in the middle of talking.

Hohsalle looked at his stepsister, Luliya, who smiled and shook her head as if to tell him there was no cause for worry. She never became irritated, even though her mother had long forgotten her and believed her to be a nurse.

Hohsalle was born of his father's previous marriage, yet his stepmother was convinced that he was her husband. It seemed that no trace of her first husband, Luliya's father, survived in her memory. They'd lived together for fifteen years, yet she never mentioned his name. However, she frequently spoke of Hohsalle's father, Ahnolle, who'd quietly entered her heart after her first husband died. They had only lived together for about eight years before Ahnolle fell ill, yet somehow, he was fixed in her mind.

Both husbands had belonged to families descended from the ancient ruler of the Sacred Territory of Otawalle, but there was a great difference in their ranks. Both Hohsalle's stepmother and her first husband had belonged to the Three Sacrosanct Houses, often referred to as more sacred than the Sacred, direct descendants of the divine ruler. In contrast, Hohsalle's father had come from the Eight Hallowed Houses, which were merely indirect descendants. For many, this disparity in standing meant a great deal, but for Hohsalle's stepmother, it no longer held any significance whatsoever.

Luliya gently laid a blanket over her mother and then, gesturing with her head, invited Hohsalle to sit by the stove. "I'll pour some tea," she said.

At this, Moiya hurried over, but Luliya waved her off. "Don't worry. I'll do it, Moiya. You should get some rest. You hardly slept at all last night."

"Well," Moiya said, "if you're sure that's all right, I will accept your kind offer and lie down for a little bit."

"Yes, please do. I don't know what we'd do if you collapsed."

Moiya gave a tired smile. "Thank you, my lady. Good night, then, Young Master." The old woman bowed deeply and, after donning the overcoat that hung on the wall, walked to the door.

Hohsalle called after her, "I'll bring you a present the next time you get a break, and when I do, bake me some of those yam sweets of yours."

She turned back and nodded with a smile, then she bowed again and left. When the door closed, the room became noticeably quiet. Hohsalle watched Luliya, listening to the sound of the wood crackling in the stove and the *clink* of the teapot against the cups as she poured the tea.

"Mother's not sleeping?"

"No. She's awake most of the night."

"I changed her medicine, but I guess it isn't working."

Luliya cocked her head. "I can't be certain yet, but I think what you were giving her before was a little more effective."

A pleasant aroma wafted from the tea Luliya placed before Hohsalle. "It's so strange, isn't it?" he muttered. "She's awake at night but sleeps all day. It's the middle of winter, yet she lives in early summer." While watching gentle ripples play on the surface of his tea, he continued. "If illness can change time and even our memories, then what is reality?"

Luliya laughed. "Are you planning to switch fields to philosophy?"

Hohsalle grinned. "No. I'll leave that to the experts." He took a sip of his tea. "Is Tomasolle back?"

"Yes, he's back. He arrived yesterday. Or was it the day before that? At any rate, he's home."

"You should take better care of him," Hohsalle remarked with a crooked smile. "Let someone else care for Mother. Otherwise, he might find himself a lover."

Luliya laughed again. "He already has. And it's not a temporary fling. He's dead serious, making it impossible to do anything about it. Of course, the worst part is that the object of his affection is not even a woman."

Hohsalle's brows rose. "Oh, you're mean. If he heard you, he'd deny it in no uncertain terms. 'I don't sleep with horses!' he'd say."

Luliya shook her head. "Horses were one thing. But now, thanks to you, he's hooked on mice. As well as—"

"Wolves, I bet." Hohsalle's smile faded. "I suppose that's why I was summoned."

Luliya's expression grew serious. "So it's true? Mittsual is spreading?"

"Well, it's not actually spreading." Hohsalle paused, remembering those who'd been bitten and died. Then he recounted to Luliya the sudden emergence of this strange disease. Soon, however, he noticed the exhaustion in her eyes and stopped. "My dear sister, you should get a little rest. You haven't slept, have you?"

She brushed back a stray lock of hair from her forehead and nodded. "I suppose you're right. I'll rest a bit. But be sure to tell me later. About the Curse of Aquafa."

Hohsalle's eyebrows shot up. "The Curse of Aquafa? Are people calling it that here, too?"

"Yes. They're saying that those who defiled Aquafa have been cursed. Moiya mentioned it, and so did my dear husband."

"Tomasolle, too?"

"Yes."

This came as a surprise. Moiya was one thing, but his brother-in-law was the type of person who dismissed curses as nonsense.

"I was surprised as well. But he told me quite seriously that we should not take this Curse of Aquafa lightly."

"Hmm."

Seeing the fatigue in Luliya's face, Hohsalle insisted that he would stay until the next maid came on duty and ushered her to her room. Once she'd gone, the silence grew so deep that he heard his stepmother breathing. Curling up in the chair as he'd done as a boy, knees drawn to his chest and a hand placed against his mouth, Hohsalle listened to her inhale and exhale.

2
Tomasolle

After he opened the door, the rank smell of beast hit him in the face. Numerous cages and baskets lined the walls of the large room, and the noises of scurrying mice and fidgeting birds sounded constantly. Hohsalle walked among the cages under the steady scrutiny of their inmates. When he approached one large cage, the wolf inside raised its head and gave a low growl, but perhaps because it was ill, or perhaps because Hohsalle's scent was familiar, it did not rise to its feet.

The School of Living Creatures, which was devoted to the study of all facets of this subject, had the most extensive grounds at the Academy of Deeper Learning, including three ponds, wetlands, a riding track, a beast stable, and a tower that housed the scholars. In return for all that space, many of the animal experiments required for admission to the School of Medicine were conducted here. As medicine was the most respected field at the academy, some students of the School of Living Creatures referred to it sarcastically as the Other School of Medicine, but its director, Tomasolle, had no interest in such foolish comparisons.

This room was his stronghold, a perfect reflection of his personality. Here, comfort for the creatures housed within took priority over that for humans. Most of the room was only dimly lit so that sick beasts could rest, and Hohsalle had to navigate carefully to keep from bumping into things. One area in the very back was lit with an incandescent gas lantern. There, it was as bright as day. A tall, lanky man crouched over a large basin, staring at something. When Hohsalle approached, the man raised his head.

"Hohsalle!" His unshaven face lit up with a smile. Although over forty, his eyes carried the naivete of a young student.

Smiling, Hohsalle bowed slightly. "How did the survey go, Brother?"

Tomasolle shook his head and took Hohsalle's arm, pulling him close. "That can wait till later. First, take a look at this! You're amazing. That medicine you brought last time is clearly working."

The water in the basin was cloudy. A single mouse, its nose just poking above the surface, swam around this pond of diluted milk. Tomasolle released Hohsalle's arm to reach for a piece of paper that lay on the table.

"I asked Shikan to continue the experiment while I was gone, and the results were so astounding that I just had to see them with my own eyes. So you see—"

At that moment, the door opened, and footsteps approached. The wolf, which had been lying in the cage, began to snarl savagely. Rather a threatening growl, it sounded like fear and rage. There was a loud *crash* when the young man who'd entered passed the beast. The wolf was throwing itself against the bars. The young man's eyes flicked to the animal, but his expression stayed unchanged, and he strolled right past without pause.

Tomasolle grinned at the sight of this arrival. "What did you do? Embrace a dog while you were out?"

The young man looked puzzled and raised his thick eyebrows. Though small, he was fit and of sturdy build.

"You really have no sense of humor, do you? I'm asking you where you picked up the scent that got that wolf so excited," Tomasolle said, pointing at the cage.

"Oh," the young man muttered. "The kennel master asked me to check one of the hounds." He returned to silence after the reply.

Tomasolle and Hohsalle smiled wryly as their eyes met. Although easily misunderstood, Shikan's expressionless face hid a surprisingly sharp intellect. He was a reliable and very capable assistant who excelled particularly at training hounds and horses, and his services were highly valued in both the kennels and the stables. Although barely twenty, he was a sober sort with not a breath of scandal attached to his name.

"How about paying your respects to Sir Hohsalle Yuguraul here?"

At Tomasolle's urging, Shikan muttered something that sounded like a greeting and bowed his head perfunctorily. Hohsalle accepted his aloofness with a faint smile. Shikan's attitude never changed, no matter whom he was with. Any normal person who wished to serve the Sacred Territory of Otawalle would have been overcome with nervousness while in the presence of someone from the Yuguraul family. Although Hohsalle had known Shikan long enough that there was no need for deference, he still possessed the power to significantly impact Shikan's advancement. Yet the young man still showed no trace of respect or nervousness in front of him.

"'The stubbornness of the Ahfal Oma is charming in its own way.' Whenever I see you, Shikan, I can't help thinking of those words," Hohsalle murmured. A fierce light flared in Shikan's eyes for a moment, and he looked like he was about to speak, but in the end, he said nothing.

Shikan was from the Yukata Plains in southern Aquafa, making him a member of the Ahfal Oma, breeders of the fire horses that were the pride of Aquafa. Tomasolle was fascinated by every living creature, but his love for the fire horses was exceptional. During his younger days, he'd headed for the Yukata Plains to live among the Ahfal Oma and study their horses whenever he had time.

The typically good-natured Tomasolle had been furious when the Zolians conquered Aquafa and banned the Ahfal Oma from raising their steeds, transforming the plains into pastureland for their sheep. He'd taken Shikan under his wing and paid a large sum of money to the Ahfal Oma to purchase twenty of the best stud horses before the Zolian army could get their hands on them. He would have probably bought them all if he could, but it was both financially and politically impossible. According to Luliya, the head of the Academy of Deeper Learning had severely reprimanded Tomasolle for his obsession.

Tomasolle scratched his jaw and smiled at Hohsalle's teasing remark. "It's true. You are rude and unsociable, you know, Shikan. It would help me if you could learn to be a bit friendlier."

Without acknowledging this remark, Shikan turned to Hohsalle as soon as Tomasolle had finished speaking. "Sir Hohsalle," he said. "Makokan was searching for you. He said it was urgent."

Tomasolle clapped a hand to his forehead. "Oh! I was the one who told him to find you. I completely forgot because I was so excited by the results of this experiment."

Hohsalle burst out laughing. "Poor Makokan. That's the role he always ends up playing. He works so hard to find me, only for all his efforts to be wasted."

"I just passed him in the corridor," Shikan said. "I will fetch him." Giving Tomasolle no time to stop him, he strode from the room. As he passed by, the wolf lunged at the side of its cage again.

"We'll talk about the reason I sent Makokan to find you after they return. In the meantime, look at this mouse."

The little thing had stopped swimming and now rested with its face sticking out of the water. There was only one spot where it could touch bottom like this, and it was hidden beneath the cloudy liquid.

"It's a fattened mouse."

Hohsalle's eyes widened. "How many days ago did you start administering the drug?"

"About fifty. It now remembers where the ledge is roughly as swiftly as a healthy mouse."

Excitement welled inside Hohsalle's chest as he stared at the mouse's nose quivering just above the liquid. Fifty days ago, it had begun suffering from forgetfulness. Even when taught where the ledge was, it could not find it again and would end up swimming around until it became so exhausted that it almost drowned. Mice that were continuously fed a high-fat diet soon after birth tended to exhibit senility typically only present in older mice. Hohsalle had noticed this and managed to develop fattened mice with memory defects. For many years, he'd been conducting repeated experiments in an effort to develop a medicine that could revive memory. Some medicines that supposedly affected memory already existed, but as of yet, no one had managed to develop one with clear results.

"You really are the Devil's Spawn, aren't you?" Tomasolle laughed, shaking his head. "I was surprised when you came up with the idea of developing fattened mice, but this is really one step toward a miracle!"

Hohsalle narrowed his eyes. "It's only one step, though," he said.

"That's still tremendous progress." Tomasolle had been smiling, and now that expression faded. "If this works on humans, the Most Sacred of the Sacred will kneel at your feet, weeping with joy."

Hohsalle stared silently at the mouse. Descendants of the divine founder of the Ancient Kingdom of Otawalle shared a peculiar characteristic: They had a higher incidence of memory loss than could be considered coincidence. Moreover, many developed this condition while still in their prime. Privately referred to as the Divine Ruler's Curse, it was particularly prevalent among those born into the Three Sacrosanct Houses, who were revered as the Most Sacred of the Sacred.

For this reason, all those born of the sacred line lived in fear of this scourge that threatened to erase everything they'd achieved in their lives. Some people claimed it was divine punishment for the greedy pursuit of knowledge that brought men closer to gods. However, Hohsalle was of a different opinion. If all those who sinned were afflicted with disease, then the world would have become a paradise long ago. Illness had no feelings, and it cared not for good and evil. That was precisely what made it so terrifying.

To prevent knowledge of this affliction from spreading, it was forbidden to speak of the "curse" beyond the halls of the Academy of Deeper Learning. Behind the pursuit of medicine and other fields in the Sacred Territory lay a yearning desire, one akin to a prayer, to be liberated from this disease, passed on in an unbroken line by the descendants of the divine ruler. The fate of a thousand years' worth of victims now rested on this little mouse, with its tiny pink nose and shiny black eyes, resting in the milky pond.

"Even if it works for mice, there's no guarantee that it will for humans," Hohsalle said. "We still have a long way to go."

At that moment, the wolf, which had been crouched in its cage, stood. Its low growl overlapped with the noise of the door swinging open, and Shikan and Makokan entered. Tomasolle regarded them as one might after waking from a dream and then returned his attention to Hohsalle.

"They're here… We can speak in more depth about this later. It's time to switch our brains to the other curse."

Hohsalle cocked an eyebrow, and Tomasolle gave a wry smile. "The Curse of Aquafa. We've got the results of our survey. That's why I called you here." After acknowledging Shikan's and Makokan's bows, he said, "Wash your hands and comb your hair. And Shikan, change those clothes that reek of dog."

Smiling at Makokan's puzzled frown, he added, "We're going to meet the head of the academy."

3
The Head of the Inner Circle

A chill wind stung their cheeks when they stepped outside the tower. The snow was lighter than when Hohsalle had visited his stepmother the previous evening, but the sky was covered in dull gray clouds, and the dim light made it difficult to believe it was noon.

The large umbrella that Makokan held over Hohsalle's head smelled faintly of mildew. "Next time there's a sunny day," Hohsalle began, and Makokan bent down to hear, "hang this umbrella out to dry properly, would you?"

Makokan gave his mohalu a look of disbelief. "You're worried about an umbrella at a time like this?"

"What's wrong with that? If I don't mention these little details when I think of them, I might forget."

They argued as they walked, and eventually, black flagstones came into view. Although damp with snow, these stones that marked the entrance to the House of the Inner Circle never became slippery, even when wet. Makokan folded the umbrella and gave it to the doorman. In exchange, he received several pairs of indoor slippers and distributed them to everyone. After removing their boots, they stepped into them.

The sturdy building was almost a hundred years old, but the interior was not at all dark thanks to strategically placed lanterns with reflectors. The high-ceilinged entranceway was cold, though. The doorman had warmed the slippers, and the heat felt wonderful on feet chilled by the snow. A wide hallway stretched straight ahead from the entrance, flanked on either side by a staircase that rose with a gentle curve. Hohsalle was used to climbing these steps, but Makokan, who'd never been to the second floor, appeared a little nervous.

The decor at the top was completely different. A long carpet embroidered with spring flowers ran straight down the middle of the hall, shimmering with the soft colors of a meadow in the light from the ceiling lamps. The plush weave seemed to swallow their footsteps as they made their way for a room at the far end of the corridor. Tomasolle must have informed the director of their visit in advance, because as soon as he announced their arrival, the doorman bowed and immediately pushed down the heavy handle to open the door.

A delicate fragrance greeted the guests as they entered. Aromatic wood burned in the fireplace. Beside it, at the far end of the spacious chamber, was a stout man sitting at a large table. An elderly woman, plump and petite, sat in an armchair beside it. Both looked up when the visitors walked in, and they stood slowly. The woman only came up to the man's chest. He smiled and called out to the guests in a lilting voice. "Hohsalle Yuguraul. Tomasolle Nahahl."

Hohsalle and Tomasolle bowed deeply. "Director Rotoman Okiraul," they greeted in unison. Then they turned to the elderly woman beside him and bowed again. "Lady Cheehana Okiraul." She inclined her head graciously.

Hohsalle felt Makokan tense behind him and guessed that he'd been startled by the sight of the one who commanded the Servants of the Inner Circle. People of lower rank weren't permitted an audience, and most had no idea that she was a woman. Lady Cheehana ran the academy from behind the scenes.

"Enough of the formalities. Come sit by the fire," the director said, waving them toward the fireplace with a pudgy hand. "You've done well. You must both be tired after traveling through this winter weather." Servants stationed in a corner of the room glided forth bearing chairs, which they placed for Hohsalle and Tomasolle. Another servant brought a tray with cups of fragrant tea and a plate of thin, delicious-smelling cookies and set it on a small table.

"There now, have some tea. You can talk while you warm up." The director had already taken a teacup in his hand. From the smell, Hohsalle judged that the brew contained a high ratio of spirits.

The director noticed Hohsalle's gaze and raised his cup. "Would you care for some?"

Hohsalle smiled and shook his head. "No thank you. This is fine. If I drank spirits while sharing my tale, it might make me woozy."

The director nodded. "I can understand that. Who will speak first?"

Tomasolle glanced at Hohsalle, indicating that he should start, and Hohsalle gave a succinct but detailed account of the manifestation and course of the disease among those who'd been bitten at the falcon hunt.

After listening, the director said, "Hmm. Exceedingly strange. The conditions under which people contract that disease, as well as the speed and the mortality rate, are highly unusual. I suspected this when I read Limuelle's message, but having heard you describe the particulars in person, I find the abnormality quite pronounced. However, some who were bitten survived, correct?"

"Yes. Of those I treated, Sulumina, who is Aquafaese, might even have survived without any medicine."

A thin smile appeared on the director's face. "It's too bad that you didn't have the chance to test that theory, although it wouldn't do to experiment in such a way."

The corners of Hohsalle's mouth twitched. "That is a terrible thing to suggest. You must be of the same breed as my grandfather."

The director's grin deepened. "I will accept that description without protest. But I would say the same is true for you. Am I right?"

Hohsalle shrugged. "I suppose so."

"How did the anti-mittsual drug work?"

"I think it was partially effective. We haven't narrowed down exactly what that effect is, but it seems to have potential."

"That's a relief. It's made from an ashimi extract, isn't it?"

Hohsalle smiled slightly. "Yes. That was Milalle's achievement. She's been studying lichens for many years."

The director nodded. "Yes, I remember. It sounds as though we should pay attention to those regions with lichens that possess beneficial effects. We might discover a relationship between them and those who are immune to the illness."

"Ashimi is very widespread," Tomasolle interjected. "And because lichens and mosses are symbiotic, there are numerous similar species. The disease-resistant properties of ashimi and others like it are quite similar. It's possible that people who regularly consume reindeer or any other animals that feed on such lichens are resistant to the disease."

"That's what Milalle suspects, too," Hohsalle agreed. "She said if we're considering diet as a contributing factor, the quickest way to know would be to look for foods that the Aquafaese like and Zolians avoid."

Tomasolle laughed. "That lover of yours is very perceptive. With someone as intelligent as that, you'd better watch out if you cavort with anyone else."

Hohsalle grinned wryly. "I don't think I need to worry. Right now, my perceptive lady is completely obsessed with what Sulumina and Mazai like to eat that Izam doesn't."

The director stroked his chin absently. "Wasn't there someone who survived without any medicine?" he inquired.

Hohsalle's face grew sober. "There was one man who survived the tragedy at the salt mine of Aquafa. Van, from the Toga Mountains. It would be wonderful if we could find him."

"Yes, if you could extract some of his blood, you'd have a chance at producing a highly effective serum."

"Makokan followed his trail to Oki with a Molfah tracker after the attack on the mine. They never found him, but you know that story already."

Cheehana had been listening silently, and only now did she raise her head to look at Makokan. "We're fortunate to have the man himself with us today. Would you describe the situation for us once more?"

Hohsalle gestured for Makokan to speak. He started nervously, and while he wandered a little, he left nothing out, perhaps because he'd recounted these events to Hohsalle before. When he described what befell Sae, Cheehana's expression grew pensive. A faint smile formed on her lips, yet her eyes appeared deep and contemplative.

When Makokan finished his tale, the director let out a long breath. "The beasts attacked from a cliff, didn't they? I noticed that in your report. It seems very unnatural, don't you think?"

Hohsalle nodded. "Yes, it does seem suspicious."

The director rested his chin in his hand. "If the attack was intentional," he mused, "it means someone's trying to prevent us from catching the escaped slave from Gansa, the one man who survived the disease. Which means that, just as Governor Ohan feared, the assault on the falcon hunt and the massacre in the salt mine were not random attacks by beasts but part of a premeditated scheme. Perhaps the Gansa clan is deeply involved."

Cheehana shook her head. "The Gansa are a hard bunch." Then she turned her attention to Hohsalle. "After we received your first report, we immediately sent someone to the Toga Mountains to investigate, but the Gansa and their neighboring clans are very shrewd. They kept their guard up."

Her large brown eyes were trained on Hohsalle's face. "Whether they were dogs or wolves, training them to attack like that would have taken a considerable amount of time. Perhaps we missed signs of such instruction. We can't cover every inch of the mountains and forests, after all, but I'm sure we would've noticed if there was any change in a group's behavior. To implement such a long-term strategy requires organization, and if this were introduced at the clan level, we'd have uncovered something by now."

The director knit his brow. "Even so, if the Gansa are involved, it will be very troublesome. The Toga Mountains are the last barrier against an invasion from Mukonia. Many Zolian troops are stationed there. From the governor's perspective, there is no worse place for the flames of rebellion to arise. That's why he warned the King of Aquafa outright."

"He did, yet he's not totally convinced the king is behind this," Hohsalle replied.

"Regardless, Aquafa's destabilization is undesirable. There's nothing more dangerous than jumping at shadows. The attack certainly appears to have been premeditated, but is there any chance these incidents were the result of a combination of coincidences?" the director asked.

Hohsalle shook his head. "Unfortunately, after seeing the conditions at the salt mine and the attack on the falcon hunt, I believe there is definitely a human hand guiding things. Someone planned and executed those attacks in service of some goal."

The director's expression betrayed his surprise. "If that's your impression, then the likelihood is extremely high. But it's still too soon to dismiss other possibilities. Even though it looks intentional, we can't rule out coincidence yet."

"Yes, that's true. If we stick to one hypothesis at this stage, we risk missing the truth." Stroking his chin, Hohsalle continued. "I'd actually been wondering about that possibility because so few cases of people experiencing mittsual-like symptoms have been reported. There's been no major outbreak since the falcon hunt." He smiled and glanced at Cheehana. "Mind you, were the King of Aquafa pulling the strings, that would make sense. Not only did the governor explicitly threaten him, but it's now apparent that the Aquafaese can die from the disease like anyone else. He might have elected to abandon the whole thing."

Cheehana smiled but said nothing.

"Well then, let's try looking at it from the other angle," the director said. "What were the results of your investigation into the possibility that the process of contagion is unrelated to human intention?"

Tomasolle took the initiative, replying, "Concerning that point, let's first consider whether it's possible." He turned and motioned to Shikan, who stepped forward and handed him a large tube. Tomasolle pulled out a scroll of paper and asked Shikan to hold it up for all to see.

"I requested that Cheehana help us gather data on any incidences of people infected with similar maladies. We've summarized the results on this map."

Hohsalle's eyes widened as he scanned the chart. Red dots were scattered here and there across the entire territory that had once been the Kingdom of Aquafa. "There were that many cases before the incident at the salt mine?"

Tomasolle nodded. "We found people with mittsual-like symptoms in the Yukata Plains to the south all the way to the Oki forests in the north where Makokan pursued that fugitive."

Cheehana took that moment to speak up. "In addition to the breadth of distribution, there is another crucial factor. Servants of the Inner Circle reported that the oldest case occurred as far back as eight years ago." She grimaced as she brushed a stray lock from her face. "I suppose it was careless of me to have overlooked that, but at the same time, we would never have found these stories if we hadn't suspected the possibility of a mittsual outbreak."

"You're right about that," the director agreed. "If a farmer or nomad came down with a high fever and died after being bitten by a wolf or ossam, no one would bother mentioning it unless a series of such events occurred back-to-back."

Hohsalle looked at Tomasolle and Cheehana. "So they didn't happen in succession?"

They both shook their heads. "No," Tomasolle responded. "The anecdotes collected were all individual instances of wolf or ossam attacks. In each, only one or two people at most contracted the illness. There were no reports of it spreading." His mouth twisted. "Odd, isn't it?"

Hohsalle nodded. "Yes, because even if we assume the disease is not communicable from human to human, wolves live in packs. If a wolf bite is infectious, then after the first case developed, subsequent cases of the disease should have emerged more frequently within the territory of any pack with a contaminated wolf. Several years have passed since the first case, meaning ticks and mosquitos have had a few summers to breed and multiply. If this truly was mittsual, it ought to have spread more widely."

Hohsalle examined the map as he spoke. "The distribution of cases over such a wide area with only one or two victims in each spot seems highly unnatural. We need to determine what is preventing its spread."

The director narrowed his eyes. "But what if the victims were all Zolian immigrants...? And they were, weren't they? They were all Zolians, right?"

Cheehana nodded.

"If the Aquafaese are immune, wouldn't that explain why there are so few cases?"

Hohsalle cocked his head. "Pardon me, but I think that logic is faulty. Remember, this is the disease that brought down Otawalle. It was precisely because it proliferated through carriers like ticks that it was so disastrous. Any wolves or ossam with the disease inhabiting the forests near Zolian settlements would spread the sickness to creatures like ticks and field mice. There should be a much higher infection rate among people in such regions."

Tomasolle nodded emphatically. "Exactly. And from my perspective, there is yet another puzzling aspect."

He pointed to the map. "Ossam and wolves are quite widespread. They're found in the plains of the south as well as in the forests of the far north. There are many different species, too, and their shapes and sizes differ depending on where they live. In general, the farther north the beasts reside, the bigger they are. When you compare wolves from the far north with those in the south, the former are obviously larger."

He cleared his throat and continued. "What I'm trying to say is that if cases with mittsual-like symptoms are this far-reaching, then any wolves or dogs could be carriers, regardless of where they live. However, if that's true—"

"Then the number of human cases is still too small," Hohsalle finished.

Tomasolle nodded. "Right. If the disease was as lethal as the one Aquafa fears, a sickness that killed off almost everyone who developed symptoms, then as Hohsalle remarked, there should be more cases in the last eight years. Secondary infection from ticks and other creatures ought to run rampant. Everyone would be talking about it by now."

Hohsalle frowned. "What could be the reason for the lack of secondary transmission?"

Cheehana said in a low voice, "It seems likely that the beasts that are hosts have not stayed in one place long enough to transmit the disease to ticks."

The room grew silent for a moment.

Tomasolle cleared his throat. "Indeed. However, as we are currently considering the possibility that the process is unrelated to human intention, we must consider whether it occurs naturally. In that regard, there is yet another mystery. How did the disease spread to dogs and wolves over such a wide area? Look at how widespread the attacks are. There's no possibility whatsoever that wolves from the north mingled with those in the south."

"Could it have transmitted from one neighboring pack to another?" Hohsalle asked.

"That's the only method for a natural spread. But if so, there's another factor that seems even stranger."

Tomasolle motioned to the map. "The numbers beside the red dots start with the oldest cases. Follow the order, and the abnormality becomes apparent."

Hohsalle examined the chart closely. The oldest infection occurred in a settlement of Zolian immigrants at the edge of the Yukata Plains in the south. However, the next one was in the mountains of the northwest. "How?" he breathed.

Tomasolle's lips crooked into a smile. "It's bizarre, isn't it? Were the disease moving across neighboring packs, we wouldn't have this pattern."

Hohsalle's eyes narrowed. "Not necessarily…"

"What?" Tomasolle asked.

Hohsalle looked up at him. "You'd be correct if wolves and ossam were the only carriers. However, this type of distribution might be the result of a different animal's involvement, a migratory bird, for example."

Tomasolle's eyes widened. "I see. I'm ashamed to say I hadn't thought of that. But if so, then the possibilities are unbelievably complex and diverse."

Makokan jerked. Hohsalle turned to look at him. "Come on. Out with it. If you have something to say, don't hesitate."

Makokan coughed and licked his lips. "I may be completely off the mark, but when I look over the order of these events, it seems to me that they're gradually moving closer to the center of the country."

Hohsalle's eyebrows shot up. After examining the map again, he let out a slow breath. "You're right," he said. "That's a surprisingly keen observation." He smiled ruefully. Hohsalle had been so distracted by the relationship between the beasts and the disease that he'd failed to recognize that simple fact.

"Actually, I noticed that, too," Cheehana said. One of the servants standing off to the side glided forward, bearing a different chart. He spread it open for all to see beside Shikan, who still held the first map. It showed the entire Zolian Empire with certain sections colored in, and it was covered in arrows and numbers.

"I'm sure you can guess the purpose of this map without me telling you. The colored sections indicate where immigrants from the Zolian frontiers have settled. The arrows trace their movements, and the numbers indicate the order of formation."

Hohsalle stared at the new chart with eyes narrowed. It pinpointed an intriguing trend that had escaped his notice. While Zol had seized control of every part of the region from east to west and north to south, the ratio of immigrants was overwhelmingly higher in the western part of the empire. The colored sections and arrows were particularly dense in Ohan Province, the region that was previously the Kingdom of Aquafa.

"The Ohan Province is quite amazing," Hohsalle muttered, and Cheehana smiled.

"Isn't it? When looked at like this, you can really see how much effort the empire has devoted to colonizing Aquafa. I suppose that's only natural considering that the powerful Kingdom of Mukonia borders it on the west."

Hohsalle nodded. "And people settled in the plains and forest regions, areas that had low populations to begin with, which would have made it seem like they had more room for Zolians."

Tomasolle snorted. "A common mistake of the ignorant. Those areas have their own peculiar florae that support specific fauna. While the Yukata Plains, where the fire horses roamed, resemble Zol's fields, the region is suited to completely different vegetation. Converting it to sheep pastures and rye fields was bound to upset the balance."

"Come now, Tomasolle," the director said soothingly. "While I agree that it may have been foolish in some regards, it's interesting that the areas they colonized were ones that could actually support an increase in population. The black rye the immigrants brought seems well-suited to the poor soil of the plains and is actually hardier than the wheat the Ahfal Oma grew. These qualities may bring about major changes. The Yukata Plains could become more prosperous than before."

Out of the corner of his eye, Hohsalle saw Shikan flinch. Although his expression remained stony, his jaw tensed, and Hohsalle wondered if he was silently cursing the director.

By contrast, the anger on Tomasolle's face was plain to see. "Forgive me, Director, but—"

Cheehana interrupted. "Save it for later. We're getting off topic." Her voice was sharp, like the crack of a whip. Tomasolle drew his lips together tightly, but a blue vein throbbed on his forehead.

Cheehana pointed to the maps. "Compare the two. Do you notice anything else?"

After examining them once more, Hohsalle's eyes widened immediately. "Ohhh." He pointed to the location of the first infection. "The oldest case occurred in the first colonized area."

Cheehana nodded and glanced at Tomasolle. "This spot is closest to the settlement beset upon by the Ahfal Oma in their quest for revenge. Surely you must have realized this, yet you never mentioned it."

Tomasolle stared at her for a moment with a rigid expression, then he shook his head slightly. "My intention wasn't to withhold information. I was waiting for the right opportunity."

Cheehana sat back in her chair. "Well, now is the time. Tell us."

Tomasolle kept his eyes trained on the old woman's face as he replied, "I was cautious about sharing this information because it could lead to certain people being falsely accused."

Cheehana arched an eyebrow. "By that I assume you mean the Ahfal Oma, yes?"

Tomasolle bit his lip and exhaled. "Yes. Do you know of the god called Kinma?"

Hohsalle had never heard of him, but Cheehana and the director appeared familiar. "A small deity that takes the form of a fly, right?" Cheehana said. "One the Ahfal Oma fear."

At this, Shikan raised his head and stated vehemently, "We do not fear him. We revere him. Kinma, the god who resides in a fly, knows many things and shows us many paths. We will never give in, even if those who are ignorant of Kinma should be so foolish as to hold him in contempt and revile us."

For a moment, no one spoke. Then Tomasolle coughed and said, "As Shikan explained, Kinma is a very important deity to the Ahfal Oma. Please keep that in mind as you listen. It is a long tale.

"The incident you mentioned changed many things. The Ahfal Oma were chased from their homeland. While they took up other occupations elsewhere, many found it hard to adjust to new ways of life and turned to drink, destroying their health.

"However, those who became nomadic herders and hunters in the Oki Valley in the north and on the Toga Mountains in the west acclimated better. Can you guess why?"

The director frowned. "Because their new ways resembled their previous lives."

"That is certainly part of it. However, reindeer and pyuika are not at all like horses, and in that sense, I'm sure they had greater difficulty than you'd imagine. Shikan told me that those Ahfal Oma who live in the north are more renowned as hunters than as herders."

"Is that so?" the director asked.

"Yes, and the reason is…" Tomasolle paused and then concluded quietly, "They have extremely good hunting dogs."

A spark of understanding lit the director's eyes, but Cheehana must have known this already, for her expression didn't change. Hohsalle remembered the well-trained dogs in the Molfah village he'd visited with Tohlim.

"Their hunting dogs," Cheehana said, and all eyes fell on her. "They're rochai, a cross between black wolves and ossam, are they not? The Ahfal Oma call them a gift from Kinma."

Tomasolle frowned. "If you already knew that—"

She waved her hand. "I am only aware of an old story." Her voice took on a low, melodic quality as she recited, "'If your horse dies, do not bury him in the earth, but burn him,' the god Kinma proclaimed. 'So that the wolves will not dig him up and learn the taste of horse flesh. But if your horse should die of sickness, bury him,' the god Kinma proclaimed. 'So that the wolf will suffer and never wish to eat horse again—'"

Here, Shikan took up the chant, his sonorous voice drowning out Cheehana's. "One harsh, cold winter, when both horses and men starved, the god Kinma came to a bitch in whelp, her pups sired by a wolf. 'You, dog,' he said. 'Do you wish to bear your pups despite the pain it will bring you?'

"The bitch replied, 'Hear my answer, O great god Kinma. I wish to bear my pups despite the pain.' Then the god Kinma led her to a mound. The mound where sick horses were buried. Oh, the luminous blue mound of Kinma. Oh, the shrine of the god, bathed in light. The bitch ate the dead flesh and fell sick. She bore her pups and died. Those pups grew and flourished, becoming the best hounds in the village."

When he finished, Shikan stared Cheehana straight in the eyes. "When there were many fire horses, we buried those that perished of illness in the mound and then later dug the carcasses up and fed them to bitches in whelp. Unlike the ancient song, they did not die, but their pups did indeed grow loyal and strong, never succumbing to sickness."

Shikan stopped there. Tomasolle sighed and picked up the tale. "When the horses died from eating poisoned rye, the Ahfal Oma also buried them in a mound and fed them to bitches in whelp."

The director leaned forward. "So then…"

Tomasolle gave a wry smile. "Exactly. It would explain a great deal if the pups became carriers of the disease." Then he shook his head slowly. "However, that wasn't the case. The bitches bore no pups. I confirmed this with my own eyes. They suffered and died."

A hush fell over the room. It was Cheehana who finally broke the silence. "But the first case of mittsual occurred near there."

Tomasolle nodded. "Yes. That's right. I cannot say for certain that it has no relation to the poisonous rye incident." He gave Cheehana a steady look. "For that reason, I ask your permission to investigate so that I can uncover the truth."

Cheehana remained silent, lost in thought. Eventually, she glanced at the director. He met her eyes, and she nodded, then returned her gaze to Tomasolle. "I agree that this demands further probing," she said. "However, I cannot agree to you being the one to do so. You are too close to the Ahfal Oma."

Tomasolle frowned. "But—"

"Hohsalle Yuguraul," Cheehana cut in, facing the young man. "How about you? Why don't you investigate this case for us? Both to find the truth and a cure."

Hohsalle gave a bark of laughter. "You make it sound so simple. But it's an enormous task. And I have so much other work that needs to be done."

Cheehana shrugged. "What could be more urgent than stopping an outbreak of this plague? Something about this whole thing is very disturbing. It seems unwise to ignore it. We will help you with whatever you need, so please see what you can do."

She turned her attention to Makokan. "Your servant is but half a man who abandoned his training in the middle, but he's from the Yukata Mountains, correct? He should possess some knowledge of the region. Perhaps he can be of use to you for once."

Hohsalle couldn't help but smile as he glanced back at Makokan, who looked like he'd bit into a bitter bug.

4
A Bleak Winter Village

Barren fields ran below the dull gray sky. It was a desolate landscape, yet the air buzzed with short bursts of life as white birds glided down to land on the marshes dotting the empty fields. Flame-red streaks on the undersides of their wings flashed with each measured stroke, like sparks flying on the wind.

"Those birds are quite striking," Hohsalle remarked.

"They're matsukala, spark ducks—migratory birds common around here in winter," Makokan said. His mount shook its head and snorted, as if annoyed with him for turning in his saddle to speak with Hohsalle. Frosty white breaths puffed from its nostrils.

There was little snow, but the wind was freezing, and Hohsalle had wrapped a cloth around his face to shut it out, leaving only his eyes exposed. "It's such an empty place," he grumbled. "Nakohli was at least a fairly lively town, but here the roads aren't even properly maintained."

Makokan shook his head. "This is the true landscape of the Yukata Plains. Nakohli's just a scab on its skin."

Hohsalle cocked an eyebrow. "Well, that's certainly an interesting description. A scab? What do you mean by that?"

Makokan kept his eyes on the birds wheeling above the reeds. "Nakohli looks good to you because you don't know what it used to be like. When I was a boy, my father often took me to Yukkalumu. That's what it was called back then—Fire Horse Town. I was shocked to see what had become of it yesterday."

"Has it changed that much?"

"Changed?" Makokan practically spat out the words. "That doesn't even begin to describe it. It's a totally new place. It's like they ripped the old one up by the roots, smashed it to pieces, leveled the ground, and built something entirely different on top."

Makokan's anger at the sight of the Zolian black-tiled roofs poking up endlessly through the town still smoldered in his breast. In his eyes, something precious had been ruthlessly trampled into the ground. He bit his lip. "Yukkalumu was a good town with its own distinctive character. It wasn't large, but it flourished as a trading center for fire horses. Although it did get pretty quiet when there was no market."

Hohsalle grinned. "Is that why you were in such a foul mood?"

Makokan glared down at him. "You were the one in a bad mood. You ignored me when I talked to you."

Hohsalle snorted. "Well, of course I'm cross. We've been sent here on a pointless mission."

Makokan knit his brow. "How is it 'pointless' when the lives of people depend on it?"

Hohsalle gave a bark of derisive laughter. "Are you dense? Think of all the lives I could be saving if I had even one more day at the clinic."

"I suppose that's true," Makokan conceded.

Hohsalle ignored him. Gazing at the flock of ducks in the marsh, he snapped, "I've been sent to the middle of nowhere to investigate and expose the secrets of my own kin. You could at least let me grumble."

Makokan's face froze. He felt as if something cold had touched his chest. *So he knows.*

Hohsalle gazed searchingly up at Makokan, then looked away. "You've realized it, too, right?"

Makokan remained silent. Hohsalle returned his gaze to the desolate fields. "Cheehana is pretty underhanded, don't you think? I suppose it's only natural that she's so nasty given that she runs the Inner

Circle, but she didn't have to send me to indict my own brother-in-law for whatever he's hiding. She could have done it herself."

"That's because she—," Makokan began, but Hohsalle cut him off with a wave of his hand.

"I know. It's her way of being considerate. Because if I happen to discover the truth, I can search for a loophole before I report his crime."

Hohsalle's face was expressionless, but there was a dark shadow in his eyes.

He really does care about Tomasolle, Makokan thought. *Or maybe it's Luliya he's worried about.* "But we don't know yet whether your brother-in-law really was involved," he said.

Hohsalle shrugged. "No, he is undoubtedly connected. At the very least, he's protecting the real culprits. I just hope he's not the ringleader."

Cheehana's map, which traced the movement of Zolian settlers, and Tomasolle's map, which showed the disease incidents—Tomasolle had kept silent about what they added up to when juxtaposed. He'd used the tale of the god's gift to explain that the Ahfal Oma weren't really involved, even though they looked suspect. But he'd omitted a crucial fact. Not only had the first case of mittsual occurred in a Zolian settlement here on the Yukata Plains, but the following one in the northwest also occurred where many of the exiled Ahfal Oma settled.

If pressed on that, Tomasolle probably would've replied, "So what?" He'd surely assert that the Ahfal Oma couldn't be responsible, because they wouldn't knowingly stir up trouble somewhere that would place suspicion squarely upon them. However, that only made plain that the incidents were intentional to start with.

The Ahfal Oma raised exceptionally intelligent hounds that were both fierce and obedient. They also nursed a powerful hatred for the Zolians. Plus, the first and second occurrences of the disease were near Ahfal Oma settlements. With so many related factors, it would be foolish not to consider their involvement.

Tomasolle had probably hoped to steer the discussion toward his being appointed official investigator. In that role, he could have informed the Ahfal Oma of how much Otawalle and Zol knew, then taken other measures. However, Cheehana was the leader of the Inner Circle and thus too shrewd to go along with his scheme. Hohsalle had sensed some subtle negotiation taking place in that room, but he was disgusted to have been played as Cheehana's trump card.

"I also thought it was kind of strange that Tomasolle would talk about the Kinma dogs without mentioning their handlers," Makokan said.

Hohsalle turned to stare at him, a piercing gleam in his eyes. "Handlers? What do you mean?"

Makokan regarded his mohalu with surprise. "You mean you don't know?"

"No I don't."

Ah. Now I see... Makokan recalled the meaningful look Cheehana had cast his way. *So that's what she meant about me being of use.* Having grown up in the Yukata Mountains along the edge of these plains, Makokan's knowledge of the Ahfal Oma, a natural consequence of his upbringing, would be useful to his mohalu during this investigation. Makokan was just about to explain what handlers were when he heard the sound of dogs barking behind them. He placed a hand on his sword hilt and turned.

"Tota! Roh! Haiee!" A middle-aged man strode toward them, calling back the hounds in Zolian. He wore the uniform of a low-ranking officer but looked almost too good-natured to be a government official. Upon seeing Hohsalle, his face relaxed as though with relief. "I beg your pardon, but I believe you must be Sir Hohsalle. When I failed to find you at your lodgings, I was worried I might have missed you. I am very pleased to have found you."

Hohsalle waved his hand lightly in greeting and nodded. Before leaving the academy, he'd sent a letter to Yotalu, the governor's son, asking him to notify someone who knew this area well of his visit. It appeared that Yotalu had acted upon that request quickly, and Makokan noted yet again that Yotalu was a useful man.

The official dismounted and watched Hohsalle with unconcealed curiosity. "I am Taya," he said. "The chief of this settlement."

Hohsalle smiled. "Pleased to meet you," he said, bowing slightly. The gloom that had darkened his face a moment before vanished.

*

Taya led them to a house surrounded by farm fields and sheep pastures. The rye that had been planted in late fall was already sprouting in the bitter cold. When the wind changed direction, it carried with it the odor of sheep, and Makokan grimaced.

The Aquafaese ridiculed the homes of Zolian farmers as "mud huts," and the dwelling before them fit that description perfectly. Its heavy walls of mud and straw were crowned with a thatched roof. Taya opened the wooden gate to the yard, and they rode through. A flock of hens clucked noisily and hurried behind the house, flapping their wings. Taya called out, but there was no answer from inside.

"That's odd. There should be someone here." He dismounted and tied the reins to a tree. An uneasy Makokan slid from his horse and helped Hohsalle down. No one had replied to Taya, but Makokan sensed there was someone inside.

"Mohalu," he said, and Hohsalle looked at him and nodded, as though to convey that he understood.

"Hello there! Makan, Tomeh, are you home?" Taya said as he opened the door, then he gasped and began asking what had happened.

Hohsalle moved to enter, but Makokan stopped him and stepped into the dirt-floored entrance first. The interior was dark, and the rank smell of smoke and manure caught in his throat. As his eyes grew accustomed to the dim light, he spied someone lying on a straw mattress near the hearth. It looked like a young boy. A woman who appeared to be his mother knelt by his pillow with a hand on his forehead. The worry was plain on her face.

"Did he catch a cold?" Taya asked as he stepped up into the room.

The woman finally pulled her exhausted eyes from her son. "He's had a fever since yesterday."

Makokan heard a noise and peered deeper inside. An old woman sat in the shadows. Head down, she muttered under her breath as she turned something round and round in her hands. He guessed it to be some kind of charm.

Having grasped the situation, Hohsalle said to Taya, "Let me have a look."

"Oh yes, please do," Taya replied. "We would be ever so grateful." He explained to the mother, who eyed Hohsalle suspiciously, that he was a famous doctor who'd come specifically to ask her something. Meanwhile, Hohsalle stepped into the room and knelt by the boy. After asking for permission, he looked into the child's face, took his pulse, raised his eyelids, and examined his eyes. He checked his tongue and throat, raised the boy's shirt, and listened to his chest for some time. The patient lay listlessly throughout.

Touching a spot behind the boy's ears, Hohsalle said, "A bit swollen." He turned to the mother. "He doesn't appear to have a cough or runny nose. Did you notice anything different before he came down with a fever? Did he have a cut or scrape, for example?"

His mother frowned. "Can't say he did. But he got real cranky yesterday afternoon and bawled his head off till he fell asleep. I thought maybe he'd got a cold 'cause he was kind of wheezin' like, and his face looked flushed." The mother seemed to be the type who went nonstop once she got started. She told Hohsalle that her husband was in town picking up some things, but that when he came back, she'd get him to dig up a frog, and they'd boil it up and give the boy the broth to drink.

While listening and offering sympathetic noises, Hohsalle removed the boy's clothes and examined his body thoroughly. His eyes fastened on the boy's right calf, and he probed it gently. The boy jerked away and began to cry. After checking the groin, Hohsalle said, "It appears to be cellulitis." He looked up and added, "Get me the medicine bag."

Makokan had already brought it in expectation of this, along with a box of supplies. He placed both on the floor.

"Some tokusalol?" Makokan asked, opening the bag of medicines. Hohsalle looked surprised. "Hmm. You've learned a lot, haven't you?" Makokan shrugged. "I've seen you treat cellulitis many times."

Hohsalle took the medicine and exhaled quietly. "I guess that's to be expected. Cellulitis is quite common." He removed the moisture-proof wrapper and took out a small pill, then looked at the mother. "He probably got a scrape or cut while playing outside, and something bad entered his body through it. Have him drink this pill with plenty of water. There're seven days' worth of pills in this little pouch. Make sure he takes one every day."

As Hohsalle wound a clean bandage that Makokan had handed him around the boy's calf, he continued. "This illness can go on for a long time if you aren't careful. Place something under his leg and keep it raised, and make sure he gets lots of rest."

The boy's mother made no move to take the medicine. Instead, she looked at Taya with a troubled expression. "Y'know, we ain't got much. No way we can pay yer for it."

"There's no need to pay," Hohsalle said. "Please. Give him the medicine right away."

Still, she hesitated, gazing at Hohsalle's face. Finally, she took the pills from him and helped the boy to swallow one.

5
Toxic Grain

Once her son had fallen asleep, the mother gently pulled the thin quilt up to his chin. "He's usually real healthy," she said, "but the winters here, they're cold as death. I keep tellin' him not to play outside, but y'know how it is."

The old woman in the back of the room snorted. "Nothin' good comes of this land. It's cursed." She gripped the charm in her hand tightly and heaved a long sigh. "How I wish we could go back to Nakoshino. I can't bear the thought of dyin' in this forsaken place."

The boy's mother cast a dismayed look at Taya. Turning to her mother-in-law, she reminded her that there were guests present and that she shouldn't say such things in front of company.

Taya said gently, "Don't worry, Tomeh. It's normal that she misses her homeland. You know I would never blame her for that."

Tomeh thanked him, but her expression remained troubled. "Yer a kind man, Sir Taya. You wouldn't ever yell at us, but if any of the other village chiefs heard, we'd be in big trouble."

Taya glanced at Hohsalle with a wry smile. "My apologies. I'm sorry you had to hear that. Please don't report it to your superiors."

Hohsalle smiled. Although it seemed such a trifling matter, he supposed that it wouldn't do for outsiders to know that Zolian immigrants were discontent with their government's policies. "Of course. I won't say a thing," he assured him. "In fact, I was just thinking how fortunate it is that you are our guide. Were it someone who was a stickler for rules, it'd be hard to ask certain questions."

Taya blinked. "Really?"

Hohsalle nodded. "Perhaps you've already heard, but I'm here to investigate previous occurrences of a particular disease. Illnesses have many causes, some of which seem so insignificant that we'd never suspect any correlation. If that woman feels that nothing good comes of this land, perhaps the disease or it's cause is to blame in some way."

Understanding surfaced in Taya's eyes. "I see... Which means complaints about livin' here may prove important," he said with a crooked smile.

"Exactly."

Tomeh, who'd been listening to this exchange, looked flustered. "Oh my! Here we've got important guests and I go and forget to serve tea." She half rose to her feet, but Hohsalle stopped her.

"Please don't worry about us. What I'd really like is for you to answer a few inquiries."

Tomeh looked uneasy. "What about? What would I know that could be of any use?"

The elderly woman behind her stood. With a sour look, she retrieved the tea things down from a shelf and put them by the hearth. After stirring the embers, she began to prepare the tea. Despite her disgruntled expression, she poured carefully.

Tomeh looked from the old woman to Taya and back again, clearly uncomfortable.

"It's all right. I'm not going to ask anything difficult," Hohsalle said gently. "Someone I know mentioned a story that your father once told him..."

"Ah." Tomeh's face clouded. "Pa passed away two months ago."

"Yes, I've heard. That's why we've come to see you."

"Oh."

"I'd like to hear about how your grandfather died. According to what your father said, you were there when a wolf bit your grandfather."

"Yeah…" Tomeh's anxious frown eased a little. "So you wanna know 'bout that, do ya? It was real scary. Sheep were bein' taken every night, and Grandpa got very cross. Said he was gonna kill those brutes and laid some traps. But they were cunning beasts, all right. Didn' catch nary a one." Once Tomeh fell into the story, the words flowed uninterrupted. "The sheep were upset even durin' the day. So Pa and Grandpa took their bows and went to see. There was such a fuss that I went, too, followin' along behind. I thought there must be a pack of them wolves, but would ya believe it? There was just one. And a little runt at that."

"Little? You mean it wasn't full-grown?" Hohsalle asked.

Tomeh shook her head. Her expression darkened, perhaps because she was recalling the scene. "Nah. It was full-grown, all right. Clever and quick. It was alone and real nasty. Greedy, too. It just kept bitin' the sheep, one after the other, on the leg. Had it attacked outta hunger, I would've understood, but that weren't it. It just liked to bite, and it bit every sheep it could."

Hohsalle leaned forward. "Was it drooling?"

"Droolin'? Dunno. Couldn't see that clearly, but it bared its fangs, kind of like dogs do when their gums're itchy. Grandpa was chasing after it when it bit him on the leg." She grimaced.

"Did he collapse on the spot?"

"No. It weren't a bad injury. He spit at the wolf and cursed. Pa managed to graze it with an arrow, and it ran. Everyone came home grumblin'. Grandpa was fine that day, but the one after, or maybe the next after that, he said his throat hurt and lay down…" Tomeh's voice trailed off, and she rubbed her arm.

"It was awful. He twisted and turned and went so stiff. Like there were a board inside him, and his face got bright red… He suffered all night. Next mornin'… Guess his body was just too old to fight it."

Silence fell over the room when she finished speaking, broken only by the sound of the lid rattling on the iron kettle.

"Was anyone else attacked by wolves after that?" Hohsalle asked.

The old woman by the hearth grunted. "That weren't no wolf."

"What?" Hohsalle turned to look at her.

She took the kettle handle with a cloth and removed it from the hearth. "It were a dog. That little runt that gave us such a hard time. I saw it, too. Maybe it had wolf blood in it. I dunno. But it wasn't no wolf. It was a dog."

Tomeh nodded. "Maybe she's right. Its muzzle was like a dog's."

"But your father said they were attacked by a wolf," Hohsalle said.

Tomeh looked a little embarrassed. "That was Pa, all right. He liked to talk big, y'know. It wouldna sounded good if they were attacked by some dog. So he told everyone it was a wolf."

Hohsalle felt Makokan fidgeting behind him. Turning, he said, "If you have a question, ask."

Makokan nodded and looked at the two women. "If it was a dog, did you see its master? Or do you think it was an ossam?"

Tomeh cocked her head, but the old woman glared at him fiercely. "Why're ya asking?"

Makokan frowned at the animosity in her voice. "Well, I, um," he stammered.

Hohsalle came to his rescue. "Is there something about this man that troubles you?" he inquired. "I noticed that you've been watching him."

The old woman wrinkled her nose. "Not 'specially. It's not that I don' like him… But he's a native, ain't he?"

Makokan's eyes widened. *She recognizes my tattoos.*

The People of the Yukata Mountains tattooed their foreheads to protect their souls. If the old woman had lived here for more than ten years already, she would have had many opportunities to see people bearing such marks.

Understanding dawned on Hohsalle's face. "I see. I must apologize. I should have explained this to you at the beginning." He smiled. "You have nothing to fear. This man is my servant. He's an outsider, exiled from his clan in the Yukata Mountains. No matter what you tell us today, we won't use it to cause you trouble. We're only interested in investigating a certain disease. Did you hear what happened in the salt mine of Aquafa?"

The old woman's gaze hardened. Beside her, Tomeh nodded and said,

"Y'mean the Curse of Aquafa? We heard a lot of slaves died. And didn't somethin' terrible happen in Kazan, too?"

Hohsalle sighed. After glancing at Makokan, he returned his eyes to the old woman. "That wasn't a curse. They all died after being bitten by dogs."

The elderly woman's cheeks stiffened, and Tomeh cried out and put a hand to her chest. "Like Grandpa? Oh, so that's why…"

As though to reassure them, Hohsalle shook his head. "It's only one possibility we're considering. That's why we came here, to learn more from you. We don't know anything for sure yet. The illness carried by the dog that bit your grandfather resembles the one that killed the slaves, but we don't know if it's the same or not. No one else here came down with it, correct? It was just your grandfather?"

Tomeh looked at the old woman, who nodded and said, "That's right."

Tomeh furrowed her brow. "But a lot of sheep died."

"Yeah, we lost a lot," the old woman agreed sharply. "They just kept dyin' off. A lot dropped after gettin' bitten by that brute, but even before that, we'd lost a lot to ticks and toxic grain. Everyone said we should never have come to this cursed land."

Hohsalle bent forward. "The sheep died after eating toxic grain?"

"Darn right they did! The natives here, they were a real twisted bunch. Their dogs were worse than wolves. And the grain they raised was a horrible red color—"

Tomeh broke in, as though trying to keep the old woman from saying too much. "Y'know there was that big uproar 'bout their horses dyin'? They burned one of the villages to the ground. Not ours, though. It was terrible."

"You're talking about the Ahfal Oma's revenge."

"That's right. It was the grain that killed 'em."

Hohsalle nodded. "I'd heard that. Their horses ate the rye brought by your people—"

"That's a lie!" the old woman cut in. "It wasn't our grain they died from. That ornery lot chose to believe so, but that ain't true. They hate us so much, they blame us fer everythin'."

"But—"

Glaring, the old woman shook a finger at Hohsalle. "It wasn't our grain they ate! It was the red wheat those pig heads grew themselves that killed their horses!"

"Now, now, Nohmeh," Taya soothed. He cast Hohsalle an apologetic look. "I'm so sorry. Nohmeh's older brother was killed at that time, and she gets like this whenever she remembers. Please forgive her."

Hohsalle nodded. "No, I should apologize for making her recall such a painful thing. But that's the first I've heard of this. Red wheat is native to Aquafa, isn't it? If so, then the fire horses must have been fed that grain for generations."

"It's more complicated than that," Taya said quietly. "The fire horses indeed fed upon Aquafa wheat farmed by the Ahfal Oma, but it seems it was crossbred with some of the rye we brought with us."

Hohsalle's eyes grew round. "A hybrid strain?"

"Yes. We didn't deliberately create it, though. Some rye pollen was probably carried into their fields on the wind. It gave us no end of trouble. Hybrid grain is more likely to be toxic, and the poison is very strong, too. I'm sure the fact that it killed their fire horses was a disaster for the natives, but many of our sheep perished from eating the toxic grain, too. It made them jump and leap about like they were dancing before they went into convulsions. We called it the sheep-dancing sickness."

Taya rubbed a hand along his arm. "After the Ahfal Oma were exiled, we spent a long time burning off the Aquafa wheat until we were finally able to grow rye safely."

For some time after Taya finished, Hohsalle stared at him blankly.

"Sir Hohsalle," Makokan finally said.

Hohsalle started and heaved a sigh. "I see. So that's what happened. Thank you. Now I understand." Then, as if to himself, he added, "So the grain killed both horses and sheep. But not dogs?"

The old woman gave a snort of laughter. "'Course not. Dogs don't eat grain. They dug up dead sheep and ate 'em. That's how they got a taste for sheep."

Hohsalle's head jerked up, and he stared at her. "They ate them? The dogs ate sheep poisoned by the grain?"

The old woman grimaced in disgust. "Darn right. Their masters actually forced 'em to. Just shows you how perverse they are. I can tell ya I was pretty pleased when those greedy dogs died a horrible death after. Served 'em right."

"They died from it, did they?"

"Yeah. And they deserved it, too. But then that lot went and blamed it on us, even though they were the ones who fed their dogs the dead sheep. Said we'd defiled the earth. What a rotten lot. We were only too glad to see the last of 'em, I can tell ya."

Hohsalle asked quietly, "And you're talking about the People of the Fire Horse?"

Nohmeh shrugged and was silent for a bit. Then she shot a look at Makokan. "Dunno. Why don't ya ask him?"

6
Makokan's Home

Hohsalle glanced back at Makokan as their horses scaled the mountain path, which was lined with soft, green-gray thatch grass. "Knock it off, will you?" he asked. "If you keep on dragging your feet like that, we'll end up camping outdoors."

Makokan scowled at him. "Camping's fine with me. In fact, I'd be happy to just go on camping forever."

Hohsalle's expression relaxed. "Quit acting like a spoiled brat. You're a grown man. Do you really mind going home that much?"

Makokan sighed and looked at the mountain path stretching before them. "Yes I do."

Yet despite his words, the sight of this route was so familiar that it made him want to weep.

Makokan would rather die than come back—that's what he thought of his homeland. In the spring of his fifteenth year, he'd run down this road in the opposite direction, yet here he was, back again at almost thirty… And this time, he was the servant of a young heir to a distinguished family of the Otawalle. The god of fate certainly had a warped sense of humor.

Little birds chirped as they flitted from branch to branch. The twigs bent under their weight, and the brightness of their light green breast feathers was jarring. On reflection, Makokan realized that his future, which had seemed ash gray at the time, had probably been vibrant with the colors of life. There had been so much that he simply couldn't see with his inexperienced eyes. He recalled his father's stern gaze, tinged with sorrow and resignation, and sighed inwardly.

The Shinock family had been Servants of the Inner Circle for centuries. As the eldest son, Makokan's father had accepted his fate without question and served the Inner Circle from his youth. Within his own clan, he was revered as a nobleman well versed in the workings of the outside world. From childhood, Makokan's older brother and sister had been trained in this trade and entered service to the Inner Circle from a young age, traveling extensively as secret agents. To Makokan, who was ten years younger than his brother and eight years younger than his sister, his siblings were mysterious guests who visited only once or twice a year and were warmly received each time. He looked forward to their visits. Perhaps because of the disparity in their ages, or because they met so seldomly, they were always kind and treated Makokan with great affection. Makokan adored his elder siblings. They seemed so sophisticated and worldly-wise compared to the brothers and sisters of his clan mates.

As the second son of the Shinock family, Makokan was trained by his grandfather and uncle, who'd already retired from their work for the Inner Circle. If nothing had happened, he would've set out for the Sacred Territory of Otawalle at the age of fifteen, declared his allegiance to the sacred houses, and served the Inner Circle. But in his thirteenth winter, tidings came that drastically altered his life. His brother had caused a scandal and had been executed for it by his sister.

When Makokan's family received this news, his mother had wept so uncontrollably that he feared she would break, but his father and grandfather showed no sorrow. His brother had fallen in love with someone he should not have and betrayed the sacred houses of Otawalle. To demonstrate the loyalty of the Shinock family and their clan, his sister had killed him with her own hands.

Makokan's father had called the thirteen-year-old Makokan to his room and explained everything. No matter how justified the decision might have been, the fact that the Inner Circle had forced his sister to execute her brother kindled rage and deep distrust in Makokan, and time did little to extinguish it. Everything he'd believed in growing up was turned upside down. All he learned thereafter about the workings and structure of the Inner Circle seemed tainted.

Now that he was a man, Makokan understood things better. In this cruel world, where so many countries sought to devour one another, the role of the Sacred Territory and the rules the Inner Circle had established to protect it made more sense. But at that time, everything related to the Inner Circle had seemed like a dark and heavy chain. In the spring of his fifteenth year, when he should have left on his journey to serve the Inner Circle, Makokan had turned his back on a life bound by those hated rules. However, refusing the fate he'd been born to was akin to not being born at all. When Makokan refused to take his vows, he was disowned by the Shinock family and expelled from the clan.

The winter sunlight fell softly on the mountain path leading to his home. Makokan's grandfather and father had passed. His cousin, eldest son of his uncle, was now head of the Shinock family. Makokan had heard that his mother still resided in the family manor with his aunts, though. She had to be quite old by now.

Hohsalle, who rode beside Makokan, muttered, "Some people long to return to their homeland, while others balk at the very idea."

Makokan didn't respond, so Hohsalle continued. "Like that old lady back there."

Makokan frowned, remembering the way she'd glared at him. "She was a mean old thing, wasn't she?"

Hohsalle chuckled. "She has to be that tough to survive. She was forced to leave her homeland and spend the rest of her life in a place she had no desire to be. It wasn't her choice, but the natives still hated her and her people. Nothing went right. Who wouldn't turn mean in those circumstances?"

The immigrants were all poor farmers or herders who'd lived on the edges of the Zolian realm. When the emperor conquered new territory, and the borders expanded, they were the ones ordered to settle the frontiers and construct Zolian-style communities. They served as an unarmed vanguard deployed to raise the crops and livestock preferred by the Zolians, to build towns in the Zolian method, and to mingle with the conquered natives, transforming the new territory into a truly Zolian land before anyone realized what was happening.

Taxes were lower for these settlers than if they'd remained at home, and the land they cleared for farming was wholly theirs. The policy certainly had advantages for tenant farmers who were bound by landlords, but the grief of never being able to return to their native land ate at the hearts of many. That old woman surely bore that sorrow.

Remembering her fierce eyes and scowl, Makokan said, "I guess you're right."

Hohsalle looked up at him and grinned. "There's no nodding meekly for you, I suppose. You're a native of this land, after all."

Makokan frowned. "Stop that. Don't lump me in with the rest."

"But it's true, isn't it? Who knows? You might even be involved in this conspiracy yourself." There was mirth in Hohsalle's eyes, but there also shone a glint of sincerity that surprised Makokan.

"You've got to be joking."

"You think so?"

"Yes. And if you aren't, I'll knock you down."

Hohsalle looked Makokan hard in the face, then burst out laughing. It became such an uproar that he startled his horse. Makokan glowered at him.

"You really are totally unsuited to the role of a servant, you know," Hohsalle said as he wiped the tears from his eyes and took deep breaths. When his fit of amusement was under control, he added, "I wouldn't stand a chance if you were to knock me down with those great big hands of yours. Honestly, it's perfectly natural for me to doubt you. You're from here, yet when we investigated the massacre at the salt mine, you never once mentioned the possibility of dog handlers, even though you knew about them."

Makokan looked down at Hohsalle with a shocked expression. "But you said they were wolves."

"Well, yeah. But surely anyone would consider the idea that someone commanded the wolves."

"You're the only one who'd consider that. It certainly never occurred to me."

Hohsalle burst out laughing again. "Oh, that's good. I just love your stubborn streak."

Makokan waited somberly, not seeing the joke. Hohsalle shook his head and sighed. "Never mind. Just tell me everything you know about the handlers before we reach your clan's city."

Makokan furrowed his brow. "I know very little. Just what I saw and heard as a child, and that was before the immigrants came from Zol. Surely you'd prefer to wait until we reach the town, where you can ask someone more knowledgeable."

Hohsalle grinned. "Stop sulking. I want to hear it from you first. Just tell me whatever it is you remember."

A wind rustled the treetops. Listening to the sound of the leaves, Makokan recalled the elderly man he'd once encountered as a child while walking down this same path with his father. Slowly, he began to talk.

"There is a band of men among the Ahfal Oma who specialize in hunting wolves. I think they're called the Kinma Handlers. They dress rather oddly, wearing a horsehide outfit that can be slipped over the head and that covers them from head to toe. They travel with a pack of dogs between the mountains and the plains, stalking wolves."

The handler had looked like some kind of apparition, and a terrified young Makokan had clung to his father. He still remembered the fear that had gripped his stomach.

"When I lived here, they resided on the plains, so I rarely met them, but I think they must have had some interactions with the people of my clan, because I met one of them around here."

"Hmm," Hohsalle hummed. "So the People of the Fire Horse couldn't hunt freely in this area?"

"Of course not. This is the Ofal Hazak, the territory of the mountain clans. Anyone who didn't belong to the mountain peoples would have been punished if they hunted here without permission." Makokan reeled in distant memories as he spoke. "But I think they must have had opportunities to hunt together. I have vague memories of the mountain hunters and the Kinma Handlers dressing and dividing up the game they'd caught in the yard behind the clan chief's hall."

Hohsalle nodded. "That kind of connection makes sense."

Makokan continued thoughtfully. "Yes, I suppose it does. My father told me that long ago, the three clans of the Yukata region—the Ahfal Oma; the Ofal Oma; and the Yusula Oma, the People of the Marsh— were one people."

Hohsalle raised an eyebrow. "I'd heard that the People of the Fire Horse and the People of the Mountains shared the same roots, but I didn't know there was any such thing as the People of the Marsh."

"Really? Well, I suppose that's not so strange. The Yusula Oma is a very small clan, and its members serve the Ahfal Oma, the People of the Fire Horse. You wouldn't be able to tell them apart unless you knew two groups existed. The Ahfal Oma would be pretty mad if you confused them with the Yusula Oma, though."

Hohsalle snorted. "Really? Well, at any rate, their relationship was close enough that they shared the same roots. When the People of the Fire Horse were chased off the plains, the Kinma Handlers must have hidden themselves among your clan."

Makokan kept his eyes on the road ahead without responding. Again, he felt the cold uneasiness he'd experienced in the settlers' house when the old woman had glared at him as though she believed he was acting ignorant.

The Ahfal Oma had been driven from the Yukata Plains after Makokan abandoned his homeland. Taya, the chief of the settlement, had asked Makokan later if he really knew nothing about it, and he truly didn't. He had no idea whether Kinma Handlers sought refuge among his clan after their exile. If they had, however, then there were undoubtedly Kinma Handlers living with his clan when the first case of the disease occurred.

"Makokan," Hohsalle called. Makokan started and looked at his mohalu. Hohsalle's expression was far more serious than usual. "Before we reach your home, let me tell you this: We are not here to convict people of any crimes. Remember that."

Makokan frowned and gazed back at Hohsalle, puzzled.

"For example," Hohsalle said, "even if it turns out that one of the Kinma Handlers has been spreading this disease, the Sacred Territory of Otawalle will not judge this as a crime. That is not our position. Someone using mittsual as a weapon of revenge on Zol is not cause for us to intervene."

As Hohsalle's words gradually penetrated his brain, Makokan's eyes widened. *I see.*

Now that he thought about it, he supposed it made sense. Having witnessed the horrific scene at the Aquafa salt mine, Makokan had assumed that if people were behind the attack, they should be caught as soon as possible to prevent further harm. But that harm was only befalling Zolians. The rumor whispered in every corner of the land claimed this was a curse on the rapacious Zolians who'd defiled the land of Aquafa. Almost all who'd died from the disease were slaves brought from the east or Zolian immigrants.

A disease that occurs naturally is terrifying, but if it's controlled by humans, perhaps it doesn't seem so frightening. Makokan's eyes narrowed. *If the Ahfal Oma are responsible and seeking vengeance on Zol, then the people of Aquafa and Otawalle have nothing to lose. In fact, they may stand to benefit.*

The Sacred Territory of Otawalle and the Kingdom of Aquafa were both under the rule of the Zolian Empire, but they had no obligation to capture and hand over those who were exacting vengeance. This thought brought Makokan a sense of relief.

"However...," Hohsalle added. Makokan turned to look at his young master, who continued in a low voice. "Disease is simply too unpredictable a weapon."

Recognizing the deep apprehension in Hohsalle's thin face, Makokan forgot to nod and simply waited to hear what he'd say next. Staring straight ahead, Hohsalle whispered, "Even those of us who've spent many years studying them have no idea what diseases really are. They're constantly shifting and changing. We don't know the true nature of any sickness. There are so many complex facets, and they're so connected with living things that it's hard to get the whole picture."

Anger blazed in his eyes. "If those Kinma Handlers are plotting to use this illness as a weapon, then they are beyond arrogant. They may be able to control dogs, but no one can control disease."

The two men crested the mountain path while absorbed in their conversation, and now they gazed out over a majestic landscape. A gently rolling valley lay as though cradled in the bosom of a vast mountain range that stretched into the distance. Patches of green showed through a light mantle of snow—tufts of Aquafa wheat planted in the late fall that awaited the coming of spring. Several rivers meandered through the fields, and flat discs, most likely ponds, shone like silver pieces on the plain. Houses dotted this peaceful scene.

Partway up a peak on the right was a cluster of sizable manors surrounded by a sturdy rampart. Even from this distance, it was clear that the town was surprisingly large, matching the proportions of a small caravan city at least. To have built a walled city of this scale in the mountains was an impressive feat.

Hohsalle remarked, "So that's…"

Makokan nodded. "Yes, that's the clan city. Can you see the bell tower on the west side?"

"The green one?"

"Yes." Makokan squinted. "The black-roofed manor beside it on the right is where I was born."

Just as Hohsalle nodded, Makokan felt a prickling at the back of his scalp. He turned and froze. Eyes gleamed beneath the trees on both sides of the path. A whole pack of dogs crouched in the underbrush, watching the two.

"What's wrong?" Hohsalle asked.

Cold beads of sweat trickled down Makokan's face. "Don't move. We're surrounded by dogs."

The beasts emerged from the trees as though Makokan's words were a signal. They bared their fangs and snarled but didn't attack. Moving slowly, so as not to alarm them, Makokan reached for his sword hilt. Unfortunately, Hohsalle jerked and fell like a ripe persimmon from his horse at the same time.

"Sir Hohsalle!" Makokan shouted. A sharp pain blossomed in his neck. He clapped a hand to the spot and felt a small needle.

Blow darts...

His head lolled forward, and he fell into oblivion.

*

Makokan stared blankly at several rosy lines. Gradually, it dawned on him that they were rays of sunset falling through the bars on the window. With that realization, the dull pounding in his head became sharp and fierce. Groaning, he spat out the saliva pooled in his mouth and tried to wipe his face, only to find his hands tied behind his back.

The room smelled of wood. He twisted his head and saw firewood stacked against the wall.

A woodshed?

That's what it appeared to be. By moving his hands, he felt something pull against them. His wrists were bound together and tied to a post. He was the only person in the little hut.

Sir Hohsalle... Where could he be? And what was going on?

Makokan tried to think through the splitting pain in his head, but all the possibilities he conjured up were grim.

Did the Kinma Handlers sedate us with blow darts and lock us up?

That seemed the only plausible explanation, yet he couldn't understand why. If they didn't want people prying into the truth, they could've killed Makokan and Hohsalle on the spot.

A dog barked outside, as though fawning upon its master. The door opened with a *creak*, and light flooded the room. A figure stood in the doorway, silhouetted by the setting sun. Makokan's eyes narrowed. It was a woman.

She closed the door behind her, shutting out most of the light. However, now that she was no longer backlit, Makokan could see her face. She was middle-aged, large in build, and well-featured.

As he gazed at her, Makokan felt his pulse quicken.

It can't be…

He stared at her, taking shallow breaths. Makokan knew those eyes and pursed lips.

His voice came out a croak when he uttered his sister's name. "Il…ia?"

End of Part II

THE JOURNEY CONTINUES IN THE MANGA ADAPTATION OF THE HIT NOVEL SERIES

AVAILABLE NOW

SPICE & WOLF

Spice and Wolf © Isuna Hasekura/Keito Koume/ASCII MEDIA WORKS